THE FOURTH
WHORE

Published by Raw Dog Screaming Press
Bowie, MD

First Edition

Cover Image: Daniele Serra
Book Design: Jennifer Barnes

Printed in the United States of America

ISBN: 978-1-947879-16-4

Library of Congress Control Number: 2019957022

RawDogScreaming.com

Acknowledgements

A few years ago, I decided it was time to take my passion for writing seriously. I stumbled across a little black book called *Instigation: Creative Prompts on the Dark Side* by Michael Arnzen. It was exactly what I needed. I told myself that if I could write something every day for a year, then I would know that I cared enough to dedicate the sort of time it took to write a novel. So, using his chapter titled "Prompts: 365 Sick Scenarios," I reached my goal with 365 short fiction pieces to show for it. More importantly, Mike got in touch with me after seeing my blog of short stories inspired by his prompts and cheered me on. He became my unofficial mentor and then, after I applied and began matriculation at Seton Hill's MFA in Popular Fiction program, he became my official mentor. Mike, this novel wouldn't exist without your influence and for that, I am forever grateful.

Seton Hill's MFA program was the structure I needed to brush up my grammar and creative writing skills and allowed me to meet and interact with so many talented people. Victor, Gwen, Shawn, Chad, Kristin, Virginia, and Vanessa—thank you so much for shaping this novel, for suffering through all the changes I made and the rewrites. Your input was, and still is, invaluable to me. Paul Goat Allen and Scott Johnson—my "unofficial mentors"—your guidance and encouragement kept me going through a tumultuous time in the middle of the residency. Scott, your hugs, your emails, your presence, and your RIGs were my lifeline.

Katherine Miller Haines, my first mentor at SHU, may have suffered the most for this final tale of Lilith and her whores. I wrote an entirely different novel for a semester. But, in November of 2016, the political climate changed drastically and suddenly, I had something more to say than what my little story at the time could have handled. Kathy, you didn't have to let me pitch a whole semester's worth of work and start over from scratch at the last minute, but you did. Lilith's badassery in this novel is all on you for allowing me to follow my heart. Thank you for that.

And to those who marched beside me in Washington D.C. on that chilly January 21, 2017. I have never felt such strength or experienced the rush of so many standing together peacefully telling the world, that we would not back down or accept anything less than equality for all human beings. Thank you to every single man, woman, nonbinary, and child who marched either physically beside us or in spirit. You inspired this work, you inspired its message and while Lilith was born in November, Kenzi rose from the ashes in January.

I cannot forget the the Horror Writer's Association, and specifically Lee Murray, Stephanie Wytovich, Jodi Lester, Raw Dog Screaming Press (Jennifer Barnes and John Lawson). Before I'd even started the novel, about three quarters of the way through my first year of short story writing to Mike Arnzen's prompts, I joined and attended my first

StokerCon. For some reason, I thought reading one of my shorts alongside the talented Jodi Lester would be a good idea. By the last day, when we were slated to read, I was terrified. Completely over my head. But Jodi, Lee and Jennifer came to hear me—a little nobody—read. They applauded my efforts, encouraged me to keep writing, and have become peers as well as friends. Stephanie, an SHU alum, welcomed me to her Stoker Awards table with open arms. Truly, everyone at the HWA made (and still makes) me feel like family. Thank you, thank you, thank you.

My friends, my family, my husband, my kids—you know I cherish you and your support means the world. Raw Dog Screaming Press—thanks for giving this book a chance, thanks for believing in me, and for being probably the coolest publisher in the world.

For Kim, who walked beside me and sometimes carried me through the darkness and for Matt, my light at the end of the tunnel. I owe this book and my life to you both.

THE FOURTH WHORE

EV KNIGHT

RAW DOG
SCREAMING
PRESS

Genesis 1

The bird carried a bolus of half-digested grub in its gullet. Her babies were most certainly waiting. Soon, they would be ready to fly, and she would begin the cycle again, but for now, they relied entirely on her to feed them, protect them, and teach them. The dry desert air offered little resistance to her massive black wings. As she neared the nest, she heard no hungered chirps.

Swooping downward to gain the momentum needed to reach the steep incline where she'd carefully built the nest, she saw them. Three broken, fuzzy bodies lying dead on the ground below. Dead. Her babies. Without further thought, she swallowed the grub and flew away. Far from the nest, never to return.

Prologue: Book of Conquest 1

She was dying. The man had no doubt. Her screams overpowered the water gushing from the gutters while the midnight storm raged outside. Thunder rocked the house and he imagined it was his wife's tremors shaking the foundation. When she moaned and whimpered he relaxed, hopeful the noise had ceased for a while. Then another contraction struck, and her volume rose like a wave smashing against his eardrums. Labor was not as the videos suggested. There was no calm breathing and soft groans while he caressed her hair. The tub they'd bought sat filled with water gone cold. His wife never used it. Her howls of pain left him feeling helpless and stupid. But, at least in this state, she probably hadn't realized he'd left her side to go downstairs.

His emotions swung from pity to anger. Why hadn't she just seen a doctor like every other pregnant woman they knew? What was so great about a home birth anyway? He certainly couldn't help her if anything went wrong. He picked up the phone, determined to call an ambulance, because she was no longer in any shape to decide what was best for her or their baby. It was his baby too, wasn't it? He should have a say.

A loud knocking startled him, and he dropped the cell. His heart skipped a beat. *Suddenly, there came a tapping as of someone gently rapping, rapping at my chamber door—Good Lord, I've gone 'stark raven mad'.* He giggled nervously and sighed. Help. No matter who it was, they were here and had to help him. Someone needed to talk some sense into his wife. This had gone too far. She wasn't Ricky Lake, and this wasn't some celebrity reality show. So what if a B-list has-been had a home birth? She probably had a team of private physicians on the side just in case. His wife couldn't see that. But now, there was someone else—an unbiased voice of reason.

The man opened the door enough for the wind to shove it through his sweaty palms and whip it against the wall. The knob left an exclamatory "O" in the drywall. A hooded figure stood motionless on the porch. Black fabric shaded the face and the cape kept the shape of the body androgynous. *Just some kid playing a prank in the storm.* His heart sank back into a mired beat.

"I am the midwife. May I come in?" a decidedly female voice asked.

Did his wife have a midwife? He'd never seen one, but what did he know? Had he paid any attention to what she'd been doing these last nine months? Truth be told, he hadn't done any research on the risky decisions she was making. No. If this was indeed her midwife, he wouldn't look a gift-horse in the mouth. He stood aside offering entrance.

"She's upstairs. Follow me," he said.

The woman accompanied him silently to the laboring mother-to-be. The man knocked at the door gently. It swung open revealing his wife, naked and sweaty, bent over the bed. What once would have been a sexually suggestive pose now disgusted him, although he was embarrassed to admit it even to himself.

The midwife breezed into the room that smelled vaguely like sweet bleach mixed with copper. The man hesitated at the threshold. He had nothing to offer and found that he felt no guilt for it either. Meanwhile, his guest guided her patient into bed. The crinkling of the plastic liner beneath the sheets protested the weight. His wife, recognizing that help had arrived, assumed a frog-legged position, giving the cloaked stranger access to her nethers.

"This will help."

From beneath her cape, the midwife pulled a golden metal device and held it out for his wife to see. The scene reminded the man of the evil queen offering Snow White a poisoned apple. He feared the function of the fruit-shaped thing, but morbid curiosity kept his attention.

"It was the apple, after all, that got us into this mess, was it not?" the midwife asked.

His wife whimpered, and the man thought he heard her whisper something like *please help.*

The still-hooded figure worked the rounded contraption into her patient's vagina. Blood seeped out, staining the sheet. He grimaced. How would that help anything? When she was done, only the tip of the apple's stem protruded from the swollen, purple hole. His wife moaned. Her eyes rolled back in her head, and her chest rose off the bed as if possessed.

The midwife began to manipulate the stem, turning it like a wind-up toy. Perhaps it was a sort of vacuum she was attaching to the baby's head. The man leaned forward anxiously awaiting the appearance of his son or daughter. He wondered how exactly she could see to work properly with her cloak on.

His wife screamed, and the midwife looked directly at the man. Her green eyes glowed from the darkness of the cape. They were mesmerizing. His instinct to run to his wife faded, and the door slammed in his face. The spell broke as his wife's cries escalated in volume and intensity.

"Hey." He pounded on the door. "Hey!"

Shrieks turned to gurgling sounds. Wet splashes punctuated cries of pain. The man hurtled against the door again and again. His wife's protests weakened. A loud crack that the man mistook for thick wood splintering gave him hope. He rammed his shoulder against it as hard as he could expecting it to give. Instead he bounced off it and onto the floor. Guttural mewing came from the other side. It frightened him. He knew the mother of his child made that sound, yet it was like nothing a human could vocalize. A soft, squelchy thud followed this then the room fell silent.

The lock clicked, and the door swung open. A god-awful smell hit him before his eyes focused on the scene. Shit and piss mingled with vomit, blood, and a hint of ozone. He recoiled and brought his arm up over his nose. There was blood, so much blood everywhere. His wife lay on the bed, her legs dropped off the side at odd angles. A purple cord hung from the cavernous maw between her legs. It looked like a bomb had gone off inside her. He followed the rope of tissue to the other end, which was attached to an equally dusky baby boy, eyes swollen and closed. There was no doubt they were both dead—mother and child, wife and son. Beside the baby—*Jacob, we were going to name him Jacob*—lay a golden, segmented bowl much larger than the form it took when closed. It wasn't some internal explosion that killed his wife, it was the apple that had been maliciously cranked open by the woman he'd let in to help her.

Amidst the deluge, stood the midwife. Her cape gone, she was completely naked. Long, black hair hung to the small of her back, its waves accentuating the curves of her olive-toned body. The only thing marring the perfection of her skin was a snake tattoo that wound its way around her left leg, her torso, and finally ended with the head of the thing lying on her right shoulder, nuzzled against her neck. She stared at the man and lifted the first two fingers of her right hand. They dripped blood. He couldn't move. She rubbed her fingers over her lips, leaving them a glistening crimson.

The man had an unrelenting urge to kiss those lips. He wanted to taste her mouth, her breasts. His eyes dropped to the small but perfectly shaped tuft of pubic hair. He wanted to part it with his tongue and lose himself within her musky chasm.

He stepped into the room. The floor was sticky, so he kicked off his shoes. Socks went next. They dropped on top of his son's outstretched hand. He didn't notice. His dick was rock hard, and he could think of nothing else than this goddess standing in front of him, waiting for him to take her. She held out her arms and he stepped into them.

The kiss was metallic and cold. She tore at his clothes until he was as naked as she. Instinctually, he nudged her, assuming she would ease herself back into the standard missionary position. His cock throbbed—he couldn't wait any longer. She didn't take the gentle hint, however. Instead, she shoved him hard, catching him off balance. He tumbled onto his ass, slipped in a pool of bodily fluids, and landed flat on his back.

In an instant, she was on top of him, lowering herself onto his member. She rode him in that position for some time, her head thrown back in ecstasy. Her breasts, perky and full pushed out as her back extended. He moaned. It had been so long what with his wife being pregnant and uncomfortable.

Something was knocking again, but this time on the window glass. Gently, as if maybe a light hail. The man's mind swam in a sea that smelled mostly of death and sewage, but also vaguely like his wife. The sound came again, this time almost frenzied, an S.O.S from a sinking ship. *Surely, said I, surely that is something at my window lattice*—his wife! His wife was in labor and he had let this woman in to help.

With that thought, a pang of guilt rolled through him and he softened. His partner, as if in response, dropped forward onto him. Her left hand wrapped around his throat. The inherent danger in this woman compressing his windpipe as they fucked in a pool of his wife's blood hardened him again, and he bucked his hips up to meet hers.

The man didn't feel the subtle change in pressure or the caresses around his torso as he neared orgasm. With his eyes closed tight he didn't see the snake was no longer tattooed to her body, but instead wrapped around his own. His shallow panting seemed physiologic until he lurched into her. Her muscles squeezed in response until he no longer knew if he was spurting into her or she was somehow pulling it out of him. He had little time to ponder the question as the snake began to compress him. Its own undulations allowed for movement in only one direction. It coiled tighter, and he could no longer breathe. The man felt as if she drew his entire essence into her womb while his body withered away within the deadly embrace of the serpent.

The Raven watched through the window, its white, infinite eyes unbothered by the heavy rain and steam on the inside of the glass. It watched as the human man died just two feet from his late wife and newborn son—his dried and shriveled corpse a direct opposite of the swollen, bloated bodies beside him. Not a soul was left in the room. The immortal bird saw the demoness, cloaked in black—snake tattoo in its proper place once more—let herself out. She stopped, arms outstretched, letting the rain wash away her sins. Water caressed her belly as if it knew the secret. The raven knew—mothers could always spot other mothers—that within the demoness's womb, she carried three mortal souls. For what purpose, the bird did not know…yet. Perhaps the demon Lucifer, who also watched her, knew.

With one last look at the carnage, the raven flew away. Back to its master, back to their punishment.

Chapter 1: Book of Kenzi 1

24 hours previous

Kenzi lay naked on the filthy mattress counting water stains on the ceiling. *Yep, still twenty-four, nothing new since last month.* Duke's doughy white ass faced her as he chugged a beer in front of a single, grimy window. Sweat worked its way down his hairy back like a plinko disc from *The Price is Right*. At least he wasn't smoking. The air in his apartment already hung heavy with the smell of cigarettes and old grease. If he lit one up now, she might puke.

"Are you finished?" she asked.

His scent clung to her like a swamp leech. She wanted to take a hot shower, so hot it would burn off his stench. He swallowed his beer, belched, but couldn't be bothered to face her.

"Yeah, I'm done." He took another swig of PBR. "So, get the fuck out. I gotta get the shop opened back up."

"OK, then," she said, gathering her clothes. "March rent is paid, so don't come hassling me until next month."

Her thighs were slippery. At least it was condom lube and not Duke's jizz. The deflated prophylactic hung precariously from the edge of the sofa bed. She shivered.

"You ain't worth thirty days of rent, ya know."

"Yeah, yeah," she said. "And that dump ain't worth fucking you for either, but here we are."

Shoes were a must before venturing far from the bare mattress. She would shower back home, where she could be sure not to step on any cockroaches in her bare feet. His apartment wasn't much bigger than the four-room hovel she shared with her mom, but at least at her place the surface of everything wasn't sticky from a three-and-a-half-pack-a-day habit. God only knew what else added to the layer of dirty yellow gunk clinging to everything. She felt it sucking at her fingers when she grabbed the door knob.

"Silvio's lookin' for you, by the way. You owe him too." He farted. "And he ain't as nice as me. He don't want no pale-ass, skinny, scarred up, freaky-eyed, drug-whore like you. So, you better have his money if you know what's good for ya."

An almost imperceptible tilt of her head allowed her hair to fall over her bright white left eye leaving only the deep blue one exposed.

"I'm no druggie. I've never touched the stuff, and you know it." Her arms itched beneath the long sleeves of her hoodie. "I'll find him," she said and slammed the door.

It was a warm day for late March, warm enough that the stink of the stairwell rose from its winter tomb. A rotting bouquet of piss, puke and cheap beer formed a nauseating stew of odors as if an entire fraternity joined the Heaven's Gate cult and committed mass suicide months before being discovered. Kenzi held her breath until she reached the alley between The Duke of Pawn shop and his fenced in yard of shit that didn't fit in the store. It was all a big ruse anyway— the pawn shop. Everyone knew it was a front for Silvio Ruiz and his heroin cartel.

Silvio's boys wouldn't be around for a few more hours at least. They usually did deliveries until dusk and then could be found hanging around the shop. Duke would piss around for at least another twenty minutes before he rambled back down to open up. She had time.

Heading behind the shop, she let herself in the loading doors with the key she'd pilfered from him six years ago. He was such a stooge—rather than changing the lock when he found it missing, he simply decided to bring everything in through the front glass doors. It wouldn't take long to grab a few things for Gloria and Al.

Kenzi worked her way through the shop like a tweaker who'd left their baby in the car so they could load up on cheap booze and cigs. On the way in, she spotted a couple new Koontz paperbacks. While they weren't Gloria's favorites—she had a thing for Tess Garritsen—her honorary god-mother wouldn't refuse. Two books fit in the waistband of her jeans perfectly.

Duke had some army surplus ponchos on sale for ten bucks a piece.

"As if, asshole," she said shoving them in the front pocket of her sweatshirt. Thuds of a heavy, flat footed lardo echoed from the ceiling. Scurrying around the counter, she grabbed a handful of Twizzlers and a bottle of Mello Yello from his personal stash. She spied an old Gameboy and grabbed it, too. The bell above the front door rang just as she locked the back door. The pawn shop was back in business.

Being a scrawny girl in thrift store hoodies had its advantages—lots of room for stolen goods. Thank god it was March and not July, when she had to start carrying the big macramé tote bag everywhere.

She managed to squeeze through a small hole rusted in the fence and slalomed between the old cars and broken appliances. Cutting through shaved ten minutes off the walk home and avoided the sidewalks where deals were currently going down.

The junkyard faced the backyards of houses nobody ever dreamed of living in. Most were vacant or condemned by the city. Squatters like Gloria and Al needed these homes right where they were, but Detroit was bound and determined to demolish them in some half-assed beautification attempt. The thing was, life here just wasn't beautiful, and the buildings had little to do with it.

"Ooh, that's good. 'it's life here that isn't beautiful.' I gotta remember that." The book, her memoir, was her ticket out of this hellhole, the only reason to keep plugging away at survival. She had to get it finished. But first, a delivery to her homeless friends.

Three houses down and almost directly behind the northernmost corner of the junkyard, she would find them. A home they used to rent before Al lost his job and the landlord went bankrupt. Still, Gloria and Al could always be found squatting in the abandoned house that even the bank couldn't sell. Amongst the spray-painted dicks and the wildly artistic gang tags was a childish scrawl of three words stacked on top of each other— **vag** on top of **cunt** on top of **gangster**. Gloria always laughed sitting there, calling herself "The Original VCG" which made Kenzi laugh, too. Laughter in their neighborhood was as rare as a college degree.

Al was dozing, the ratty sleeping bag crumpled up at his feet. His salt and pepper beard showed signs of breakfast—although not necessarily today's breakfast. He was undoubtedly a handsome man in his prime. He looked a little like an old version of Denzel Washington. Gloria waved wildly and shouted an entire conversation at Kenzi who couldn't hear a thing except the occasional inflection and profanity. From this angle, the sag in the porch appeared substantial, as if it would fold in half and sink into the earth at any moment. The house itself looked like a locust shell—hollow, broken, and barely there. Human beings deserved better than this. If her book ever made her a millionaire, Gloria and Al would never have to step foot in a place like this again.

The open space of the backyard, filled with city weeds and broken bottles, offered no place to hide should any of Silvio's lackeys drive by. She hurried, head hung so that her mess of copper curls hid her face.

"Come here right now and give your mama a kiss, girl." Gloria held her arms out wide. Gloria was Kenzi's version of Mammy from *Gone with the Wind*, only she wasn't sure if Mammy wore tight corn rows under her handkerchief. Kenzi fell into the meaty embrace feeling all her ill-gotten goods smash in the front pocket. She didn't care, Gloria's love was all she had, and nothing mattered more than that.

"You been at Duke's today." It wasn't a question. Kenzi nodded like a toddler caught stealing a cookie.

"But look what I got you," she said, pulling out her gifts and brushing pocket lint off the Twizzlers.

"Hey, I ain't your mom. You're not gonna buy my distraction. How bad is it?" Gloria took the stash and set it beside her.

"I owe Silvio five hundred. I got three at home, and I guess he wants it now." The truth—that it was due two days ago—could be left out. No need to worry Gloria more than necessary. "I got a gram back at the house cut into ten bags. Might be able to double it if I get crafty. That'd make up for what I had to spend springing Marilyn out last Saturday." She grinned sheepishly.

"Baby, that man will break your leg for twenty dollars. You gotta stop messing with that shit."

"Oh yeah? Huh, never thought of that. I'll just quit selling dope, and see what I can get for all this," Kenzi gestured at her body. Gloria rolled her eyes and made a tsk sound.

"What about your book? That's good stuff. You should be home working on that, not out here selling that death powder."

"Well, if Marilyn could stay sober for an hour or two, and I wasn't running after her, maybe I could. But we gotta live, we gotta eat. She sure as hell can't keep a job and look at me! No one wants to give me a chance."

"You know you the only one that thinks that. People with tattoos and piercings and horns growing out of their heads get jobs around here. You think they even gonna notice your scars? And that eye of yours, that could just be some sty or conjunctivitis or glaucoma or something."

Kenzi laughed. "OK, OK, you got me there. I'll look into it. But first I gotta get home and get that junk cut before they find me." She pulled her TracFone out of her jeans pocket to see if she'd missed any calls. Word on the street was one thing, but when Silvio went out of his way to contact you, you were in a lot of trouble. "Shit."

"Dead?" Gloria asked.

"Out of minutes. Fuck. I'm so screwed."

"You get out of here. Get home, get your shit sold. I'll keep an eye out and see if I can't hold them boys up for ya. But you think about what I said, girl. You don't need to live like this. End up like me and Al, here." Al stirred, grunted, scratched himself, but never opened his eyes. "Go on, get." She shooed Kenzi off the porch.

I'm dead. I'm dead. I'm dead. The mantra repeated in her head the whole way home.

The door was locked—Marilyn was getting high again. *Damn it.* She pulled her key out. The red stained claws of the now hairless rabbit's foot keychain called out to her. *You'd feel so much better if you just took a minute and made a small scratch, just a little one. Enough to let all this stress out. Feel it physically and then let it go. One tiny cut…*

Kenzi's skin itched. She shoved the door open. Sure as shit, there was her mother, sprawled out on the faded blue Goodwill couch, high as fuck. A shriveled tit hung free of the robe she wore. Her legs spread just enough that if Kenzi cared to look she'd easily see all her mother's secrets. She tried hard to remember how those pock-marked arms once comforted her in her own times of weakness. That was a long time ago. Since then, those same arms had become an anchor, pulling her down. There was no sympathy left. Her give-a-fuck basket was empty. On the three-legged orange chair, kept balanced by an old can of peaches, some shirtless, greasy asshole spread out dead to the world. A black leather belt still clung tight around his upper arm. Syringes, spoons, lighters, and small plastic baggies littered the glass coffee table in front of them.

Marilyn had a pulse. Kenzi didn't give a shit about the asshole in the chair. She knew her mother didn't have the money for all of this, so whoever the guy was, he must have brought the stuff…Money. *Oh, no. Shit. No, please, Marilyn. Not now, not today.*

She checked the big ceramic mushroom cookie jar where she kept the stash to sell. Empty. All ten bags, gone. Her heart pounded like native drums warning of something terrible to come. She pulled out a thin plastic lawn chair that served as part of their dining set and climbed up. Her dad's coffee mug, the one Kenzi had made for him at school—a cheap plastic thing with a colored picture inserted between two layers of clear acrylic—was not on the top shelf where it should be. She looked down. It was in the sink and there was certainly not three hundred dollars in it.

"You fucking bitch, Marilyn!" she yelled. "Are you fucking stupid?" She smacked her mother upside the head.

A line of drool worked its way out of the corner of Marilyn's lips, but otherwise there was no sign of life. Marilyn was three sheets to the wind and probably wouldn't come around until tomorrow some time.

"What the fuck am I going to do?" She ran her hands through her crop of rat's nest hair. She was the stupid one. She should have hid it all better before bringing Marilyn home. It was just that, damn it, Marilyn knew if she stole that money or the drugs, they were both fucked.

There would be more than a broken arm to pay for this. She rubbed her forearm where the satiny raised scar of her own name, printed in a hesitant child's scrawl, faced her. The first cut she'd ever made, the first of many more to come. She remembered being ashamed of it as it healed in violaceous pinks. At least then there'd been a real purpose. Her way of reaching the strange friend she'd made when Robbie died. Now it just reminded her of her fragile mental stability. *Be careful* it warned, *or you'll be talking to imaginary men again.*

The rabbit's foot keychain—her cutting implement of choice—dangled from her pocket like a fishing lure. It was at least seventeen years old. As a child, she'd sworn the Scribble Man gave it to her. Most likely, she'd picked it up in the aftermath of the crash. Something strange had happened that day, and her child-mind made up a story to make it all reasonable and easy to deal with. That was the sticking point in the book. How to write the events of that day. What actually happened?

She wandered into her bedroom. Bright yellow curtains mocked the starkness of the rest of the room. A bare bulb hung from exposed wires above a twin box spring and mattress plopped on the floor. A single thrift-shop-purchased nightstand held all her cherished belongings. She fell onto the bed and unlatched the keychain from her belt.

The last bit of hair had rubbed off the foot leaving nothing but a mummified claw. The tips of its nails were stained a rust color from the years of clawing away at Kenzi's flesh. She found a bare spot above her collar bone and began to scrape. It burned, but only for a short time. The repetitive cuts brought on a sweet numbness warmed by blood. A small rivulet worked its way down her breast and around her nipple. She exhaled. Her mind cleared; she could think again. She was all right. She could deal with this situation. Five hundred dollars was a lot of money to come up with out of thin air, true, but she would figure this out. She just needed a little time.

Chapter 2: Parable 1

The tension flowed out with her blood, and she was suddenly exhausted. Twenty or thirty minutes lost to a nap wouldn't change the situation. Plus, the answer to the lost money would come easier to a refreshed mind. Her eyes made the decision for her, and she drifted off into a dream of Robbie and the Scribble Man.

Robbie died on a Sunday. Seven-year-old Kenzi was sitting on Daddy's lap watching "the damn Lions handing the game away" when Robbie leaped into the living room from the kitchen, carefully avoiding the burnt-orange colored carpet. The lightweight hops of his slender frame onto the furniture never bothered Daddy as much as Kenzi's baby-fatted thuds.

"Kenzi, I am the Ice Lord, and I have come to your Lava Kingdom to make peace with you," Robbie said smiling.

Robbie never asked if you wanted to play, he just sort of started the game. Kenzi, always one for pretend, slithered off Daddy's lap onto the carpet. She tried not to get too close to it with her nose though, because no matter what Mommy did to try to make it smell better, it still stunk like pee and cigarettes. Mommy said they'd never get a new carpet without paying more rent so they should just "try not to sniff at it."

"Ice Lord," she declared in her best British accent—which was awful, "you will not last long this far into my fiery kingdom. Let us travel back to the borderlands where we can make a deal."

"It's not *make a deal*, Kenzi, it's negotiate. That's what a queen would say." Robbie corrected.

"I'm the Lava Lord, and I can say it however I want!" she yelled.

She did not like to be corrected.

"You're a girl. You can't be a lord, freakazoid."

"Don't call me that!"

It wasn't her fault she had two different colored eyes. She stomped her feet and put her hands to her hips, so Robbie could see how serious she was.

"OK, you two. Dad's trying to watch the game and Mom's sleeping. Let's keep it down, all right?" Daddy said, not too angry yet.

"I can be a lord if I want to be, Robbie," Kenzi reiterated.

"Kenzi-girl, come here," Daddy said, grabbing her arm and pulling her to him.

He leaned up off the chair. She thought he might be taking off his belt to give her a spanking, but he pulled his wallet out instead.

"If I give you two some money, can I trust you to stay with your brother and off the street all the way down to The Honey Bear? You can get yourselves a couple cokes and some chips?"

This was unprecedented. Pop was a huge treat, not to mention that she never got to pick out her own chips. She always got stuck with the barbeque ones that everyone else liked, when she wanted cheese puffs. She hopped up and down, nodding her head.

"Yeah, yeah, yeah!"

She grabbed the dollar bills out of Daddy's hands without even counting them. There was a lot, that's all she knew.

"Rob, this is a big deal. Can I trust you?" Daddy asked.

Her brother nodded and ran to get his shoes.

"Rob!" Daddy called. He stopped and turned. "To the Honey Bear and back. That's it. No short cuts, no messing around."

"Yep, to the store and back," Robbie said.

"You prove to me you can be a grown-up, and maybe this can be a regular thing now that I'm back on short hauls, OK?" Robbie nodded as Kenzi pulled him through the door.

She took off down the block when Robbie called out, "Hey. C'mere."

Kenzi stopped.

"It's this way," she said impatiently, marching back to her brother.

"Listen, you wanna go to the pawn shop instead? Jake said they got Pogs. Rare ones!" He said it as if it were something that would interest Kenzi. She didn't collect those dumb things. He did.

"But I want my pop and chips," she whined.

"Look, what if I promise that next weekend, if you don't tell and Dad gives us money again, I'll give it all to you. Then you can have two pops and two bags of chips or maybe a bag of chips and a candy bar! Just do this with me, please, Lava Lord? Can we negotiate?"

He held her hand and pulled her toward the street where they could cross into the backyard of the neighbors' house and cut through the lot filled with car motors and appliances behind the Duke of Pawn shop. Kenzi caved—she always did when it came to her big brother, who, as far as she was concerned, was better than all four of the ninja turtles combined.

Before she could mourn the loss of her Cherry Coke and cheese puffs, they were sneaking through the hole in the fence beside Duke of Pawn where their parents never let them go.

"Too dangerous, Kenzi-girl. Bad people hang out there," her dad had told her once when they passed it and she had seen an American Girl doll in the window. He was right, of course. It was a deadly place; something Kenzi would find out in another twenty minutes. The day she saw the doll, she'd figured he'd only said that because they were poor and couldn't afford the toy.

They weaved their way through the mechanical dinosaurs in the fenced-in yard of The Duke of Pawn. Kenzi had never understood the point of the fence. Kids played in here all the time. Even grown-ups could fit through some of the holes in it. They couldn't stop to play though. If they weren't quick, Dad would suspect and come looking. Just before they squeezed back through the fence on the other side, Robbie stopped and grabbed Kenzi by the shoulders.

"Listen, if Dad asks us where our pops are, we're gonna tell him that we bought ice creams instead and ate them on the way home."

Robbie had the 'I'm very serious' look in his eyes.

She agreed. *Yes, of course. That made sense.*

Robbie looked both ways and grabbed Kenzi's hand. The street was clear. Just as they started to run across, a bird cawed. A high-pitched and scratchy sound. Kenzi stopped to find the source and saw him. The Scribble Man. Only he didn't have a name then, he was just a strange looking man with a big black bird on his shoulder standing on other side of the street. The bird lifted off and flew toward her. She tried to squeeze Robbie's hand, but it was gone. Robbie had kept going, and she was alone.

Even in her dream, Kenzi saw the man as clearly as she had that day seventeen years ago. He slowly stepped onto the street, following his bird. He was white, whiter than any person she had ever seen before. The hood of his sleeveless black hoodie covered most of his head. His arms were lumpy-bumpy, covered in what looked like a bunch of scribbly lines to Kenzi. The hoodie hung open showing a bare chest beneath. The skin there was also scarred. A black strap crisscrossed his white skin and an hourglass hung from the belt it all connected to. His bird was weird too. It'd flown close enough that she could see its eyes. Milky-white—both of them—just like her one ugly eye.

Robbie was almost to the other side of the road, so intent on his Pogs that he hadn't noticed the bird or the strange man. And Kenzi was so transfixed on the two newcomers that she didn't see the car come flying around the corner. Adult, dreaming Kenzi heard the screeching tires that little Kenzi thought was the bird again. In the slow-motion dream replay, she had time to smell the acrid stink of burnt rubber on asphalt before hearing the thud of Robbie's body rolling beneath the front tire and that sickening pop of his skull giving way to the pressure of the rear one. Dreaming Kenzi's heart pounded as her child-self finally tore her attention away from the man advancing toward her brother.

Robbie's crushed and bloodied face stared blindly at the scribble-covered man who bent over him. This close, Kenzi could see that the scribbly lines were actually that fancy writing that grown-ups used mixed in with the kind of writing Robbie did. The bird landed at her feet, as if it too were just a passer-by witnessing the tragedy unfold.

"Is Robbie gonna be OK? Can you help him?" Kenzi asked the man.

He looked up at her and opened his mouth like he was going to answer but then closed it again. The bird hopped over and peered down at Robbie's smashed face as if trying to figure out what the boy once looked like.

"Did you come to take us away?" Kenzi asked. It was the sort of thing kids in her neighborhood were taught to expect.

He didn't answer her. The bird pecked at Robbie's face, near where his forehead should have been. She watched, fascinated, as it pulled a silvery web like a gypsy moth's nest out of

Robbie. It was a neat magic trick. The Scribble Man opened the top of the hourglass that hung from his belt and dropped the cotton candy swirl into it. It slipped through the top glass and lay coiled up in a shimmery pile on the bottom.

"What about me?" Kenzi asked.

"I don't know," he said. His voice was rough and scratchy.

"Are you gonna put me in that glass, too?"

"I don't think so…guess you outsmarted your fate." He smiled. It looked strange on his face, but it made Kenzi smile too. "No one has ever seen me coming before."

"Well, you're kind of dressed funny if you don't want people to notice you," Kenzi said. Then she remembered her brother. "Is Robbie dead?"

She had a fish once that died, so she knew it meant going away and never coming back. That made her sad. Maybe it wasn't the same with people though.

"Yes, I'm afraid so," the man said. "But you need to go home, quick. I don't know what is going to happen now."

"But what should I tell Daddy?" she asked.

Seven-year-old Kenzi was too mesmerized by the conversation to notice what dreaming Kenzi had all the time to see. The world around them had frozen. Time stood still. Where there should have been a crowd gathering around the dead child, no one moved.

A fuzzy grey rabbit's foot dangled from around the Scribble Man's neck. It looked so soft and comforting. Kenzi reached for it but jumped when the giant bird squawked and took off into the air. She followed its course as it swooped behind her and around so that she had to scramble backward to keep it from knocking her over. The bird grabbed the foot in its sharp claws and broke it free from The Scribble Man's neck. Another loop brought the bird once more behind and then in front of Kenzi. It dropped the foot onto the pavement beside her before perching again on its master's shoulder.

"Do you think it will protect her, Enoch?" the man asked his bird.

Kenzi surreptitiously stroked the fur with one finger.

"I suppose that's yours now," he said to the little girl. "It is your talisman. It once belonged to a very strong woman just like you."

Kenzi hugged the foot tightly to her chest before looking down at what was once her brother.

The sight of it was so upsetting that it brought Kenzi out of the dream. She never saw exactly how her child-self made it home that day. Her conscious adult brain refused to remember it. Even the days that followed the funeral—when Dad left for good and Mom OD'd on her pills—were nothing more than a haze of pain. After that, eleven years of memories worth keeping filled only the small knapsack Kenzi carried between her mom's and foster homes. Now, she was back with her mother out of necessity, and she feared it would be the death of her.

Chapter 3: Book of Sariel 1

The overcast skies of St. John's Wood threatened early afternoon rain, which suited Sariel perfectly. He didn't need to walk anywhere; as the angel of death, he had the ability to appear wherever he was needed. *Angel of Death—as if that's some sort of honor.* But the grey atmosphere matched his mood. If he could pick anywhere in the world to live as a mortal, it would be London.

Enoch flew ahead as it was wont to do. Always on the alert for trouble. The bird was like some willful child. Another part of his punishment—having to drag that feathered nuisance around for eternity. To make matters worse, this particular avian could sense a demon from a mile or more away, while Sariel could not. If he ever wanted to regain his rightful place in the Hereafter, he needed Enoch.

The bird alighted on the front porch of a duplex and, to further exasperate the day, decided to allow himself to be seen.

"Oh my goodness, what a big boy you are."

Enoch turned its head back to Sariel with a knowing look. Sariel did not quicken his pace.

"I wonder if you'll stay there long enough for me to bring you out some crumbs, love?" A woman in a well-worn house dress got up and shuffled to the door. Enoch flew after her before the screen had a chance to swing back shut.

"Damn it, Enoch," Sariel sighed.

The cacophony in the house forced him to make the switch into the living room rather than continue the mortal way. The bird had knocked over a dozen framed pictures. Glass littered the floor and every flat surface in the place. The woman's fists clenched handfuls of salt and pepper curls, a silver tray at her feet, and scones—*blueberry, I remember blueberries*—were strewn about the floor like discarded hockey pucks. The screaming was enough to drive him right back to the sidewalk, but Enoch wouldn't act out this badly without a reason.

All the photographs lying among the broken shards were of the same boy at various ages. In each, he'd gotten heavier until the most recent where he spread out on a day-bed as if permanently attached. As realization settled in, the familiar sulfur scent wafted on the whirlwind created by Enoch's incessant flapping.

"Come on, leave this poor woman be. She'll have enough to deal with when we're through," Sariel said and followed the stink downstairs.

The smell of sweat and spoiled food almost overwhelmed the demonic reek. Disguised as the son of the woman upstairs, the demon sat propped up by a myriad of pillows and folded comforters. He filled the space of the twin bed. On a large screen television, a medieval role-playing game currently held the creature's attention. Large headphones pushed his already protuberant cheeks into a comical toddler-like pout. On the floor beside the bed, sat a half-empty two liter of Mountain Dew with its cap off and a half-full gallon milk jug of a similar colored yellow non-carbonated substance with the cap on. Sariel shuddered. There wasn't much a mortal could do anymore to surprise him, but they never ceased to disgust him.

"Come on, ya stupid fucks," the creature said into the microphone, spittle flying. "Mum! Where's my—" His words stopped abruptly. "Sariel, I presume? Figured you'd find me sooner or later."

Enoch lit on Sariel's shoulder.

"And ya brought your bird, I see." He sighed. "Well, can't exactly run from ya, now can I? So, how'll it be then?"

This one made it far too easy. Sloth or not, no demon had ever just given in. He would need to tread very carefully—it could be a trap. Enoch ruffled its feathers and stepped back and forth, settling itself better onto its master's shoulder.

"You know how this goes, Belphegor." Sariel stepped toward the mortal-suited demon.

"Gotta go, lads. Something's just come up." The demon pulled off the headset, and his jowls slid back into place. Like a walrus, he worked to adjust himself enough to see Sariel without straining his neck. Sariel waited motionless, making him work for every centimeter.

"Look, if you're gonna do something, do it. Spare the old lady. She's a good mum. Let's not make this any more traumatic, shall we?" He grinned. His yellowed teeth seemed to glow in the dim light of the room. The interior gloom continued to brighten beyond the ability of unbrushed teeth, as if the sun had decided to take the stairs of this house down tonight.

"Oh, but have ya met my dad?"

Suddenly the sun was indeed in the basement with them, and all became a brilliant white light. Sariel, unnerved, waited for the visual fanfare to recede. When it did, a man—too beautiful to be mortal—stood between the slob on the mattress and Death himself.

"Tell me, brother, what do you think is really going to happen when you have us all in your jewelry box?" the radiant one said.

Sariel sighed. This whole thing had gone on for far too long. He could be out enjoying the shitty London weather, but instead he was in this pit, cavorting with demons.

"Lucifer, you know it is my duty. You know what I must do. I have, in my generous way, allowed you to have the same time on this Earth as me. Why must you constantly interfere with collections?"

"Well, seeing as the 'collections' you speak of all happen to answer to me, work for me—do all of my evil bidding as it were—I guess I'm not quite ready to hang up the 'going out of business' sign just yet."

"Let me take Belphegor, and we'll be on our way. I have a mission to complete. Nearing the end of my time with these," he gestured to the ample-bodied mortal on the bed and sneered, "creatures brings me as much satisfaction as I can find in this hollow shell."

"Yes. Your little 'punishment'," Lucifer used air quotes to punctuate his sarcasm. "You're getting pretty close to finishing now, eh? What do I got left? Six, seven, if you leave me this one?"

Sariel said nothing.

"Gotta get back to the big ole Garden of Eden in the sky. I wonder though, is it going to be that easy? I mean, a millennium later, and the Big Guy's just going to smile before throwing open those pearly gates to welcome the prodigal son back home? Or..." He held out a forearm to Enoch, offering a perch. The bird did not move. "And hear me out, what with no opposition left on Earth of any kind, will he simply forget about you and end the season on a cliff-hanger? You know this is his version of a reality show. He doesn't want you to complete your punishment. Not really."

Sariel snorted. He often wondered the same thing. Perhaps The Creator had meant for his to be an eternal sentence. After all, He had only ever spoken once to Sariel, and that was to put the mortal girl under his guardianship as another punishment for disobedience.

Lucifer sat on the bed beside the obese demon. His legs crossed in a relaxed and confident manner, as if he knew what Sariel was thinking.

"Life would be so empty without us, eh Belf?"

He pulled a snack size bag of cheddar and sour cream flavored chips from his white outback style trench coat and handed it to the slob. *Oh wonderful--orange, greasy fingerprints all over everything. How long will I have to suffer this fool and his piggery?*

Sariel stepped forward, deciding to end the whole thing. It no longer mattered if he re-entered the Hereafter or if the world ended, as long as mortal-coated demons like this were out of his sight.

"Whoa!" Lucifer put out a hand to stop him. "Watch out for that jug of piss, there. Anyway, what do you say, you give me a couple weeks, let this guy go? Look at him, he ain't running anywhere. You think about it, brother, really think about it. If you decide to end it all, great! Come on back and take it. Hell, I'll pull the token out for ya," He grabbed Belphegor in a head lock and gave him a good hard noogie. "But if your creator gets bored and wipes everything out, what happens to you?"

"Enoch," Sariel said, making a shooing motion toward the demons. "If you would be so kind."

Enoch cawed and dug its feet into Sariel's shoulder. Using its master's sturdy body, it pushed off and flew up the stairs. All three creatures watched the bird go.

"I guess he's with me on this one. I always said that was one smart bird of yours." Lucifer laughed more than the statement warranted. Belphegor snorted in amusement. Sariel contemplated the situation he was in thanks to that damned bird.

"Shit," he said and vanished.

Chapter 4: Book of Kenzi 2

Before the dream faded, Kenzi grabbed her journal off the nightstand and quickly jotted notes. *Where did the rabbit's foot come from? Who was the Scribble Man? Was he someone I saw that day? Was there a bird? Talk to Gloria about school pictures, letters to the Scribble Man.*

The blood was dry and itchy on her chest. She wiped the sleep (not that restful after all) out of her eyes and got up to start the shower. The steam from the hot water gave the room a fantasy-like quality but the rust stains in the tub kept her anchored in the reality of her shitty life. She could still smell Duke's stink between her legs. The reminder of the things she did to survive made her shudder. Saliva flooded her mouth and she had to spit. It mixed with the brick colored water before circling the drain and disappearing. She closed her eyes, refusing to see the discolored tub and slimy shower curtain. These things were the parts that made up the sum of her worth. She sold her soul every day for a four-room dump with fake wood paneling and avocado green appliances in both kitchen and bathroom. She fucked a disgusting pig of a man for the god-awful orange carpet that had been fun when she was seven and pretending it was lava to avoid. Now it was just worn and dirty quicksand from which she could not escape.

The water washed away the dried blood, semen, and tears. She imagined this wasn't her bathroom at all, just some truck-stop quick clean up until she and her dad headed back out on the road. Someday she would find him and they'd get away from all of this together. She would write and he would drive. It was her mother's fault he'd left, not hers. If she could find her dad, she knew he'd let her come with him.

She ran her hands down her too-thin body. Hip bones jutted out like those of an awkward thirteen-year-old, and her skin was covered in speed bumps. She touched the newest one beside her shoulder. It hurt but in a good way. If she didn't get Silvio his money, that hurt would not be good.

She turned off the water and heard the knock.

"Shit."

She grabbed a towel and dried off. "Shit, shit, shit."

Glancing in the mirror, she pulled her wet matted hair back and twisted it into a loose bun. She'd pay for it later, when she had to try to brush out the knots in her natural curls, but there was no time to worry about that. She needed a story and fast. Where was the money? The knocking, light and staccato, continued. This was not the heavy-handed pounding of one of Silvio's men but more like that of a man who wears a big clunky gold ring on his right middle finger. A ring with that stupid Superman symbol because S stands for Slivio, using it to tap, tap, tap on her door.

OK, calm down. If it is Silvio, he is just here to warn you, give you more time maybe. Silvio never does his own dirty work.

Tap, tap-tap, tap, tap. It was getting more impatient, more frenzied. She grabbed her sweats and a t-shirt but left her post-coital panties on the floor. No bra needed. She'd never been blessed with large breasts.

There was no one at the door. She looked out both ways. *Tap, tap, tap.* There it was again; this time followed by a soft thudding. She turned around. No one else in the house except the two junkies. One on the couch, the other on the crooked chair. Neither of them stirred. No one was choking on their own vomit or seizing.

The tapping was coming from the kitchen.

"Please don't let it be a rat." Kenzi muttered.

She padded barefoot into the kitchen which was really just an extension of the living room—a false border made up of the end of the nappy rug and the beginning of curled-up vinyl flooring. No less hideous than the orange carpet, the kitchen floor was white with glittery gold specs that reminded her of the church basement she used to go to when vacation bible school rolled around and her mother used it as free babysitting.

She began opening the cupboards beneath the sink when the thud came just above her head. She jumped. There was a huge black bird at the window. She leaned over the sink for a closer look. Could birds get rabies? This one had crazy white eyes, like maybe it was blind. It threw itself into the window with the full weight of its body. The glass cracked.

"Hey!" she yelled. "Great."

The fissure spider-webbed outward. If it did it again, the bird would break through the window. It flew back and started to work on the center of the web, with its beak tap, tap, tapping. The damn thing seemed hell-bent to get inside her house.

"That's it you psycho bird!" She slipped on her Chucks and shoved the door open. She could hear it still working on the glass as she rounded the corner. "Shoo! Get out of here!" She waved her hands and ran at it. The bird was huge. Some kind of vulture maybe? Hard to say. It sounded like a helicopter when it took off.

She was surveying the damage when the screaming started, followed by a string of profanity-laden outbursts that clearly came from Gloria.

"Fuck," Kenzi whispered and made her way around the corner to peek down the street. There was Gloria, going toe-to-toe with two of Silvio's behemoths. She was distracting them and being loud enough to warn Kenzi. But these guys were nothing to mess with. If she didn't back off, they'd kill her and Al both. Kenzi couldn't have that.

"Hey. Assholes!" Her heart pounded. This was the dumbest thing she'd ever done. And that was saying a lot. The biggest one turned around, saw it was her, and headed toward her. The smaller one gave Gloria a shove before he, too, headed her way.

"You better run, honey," Gloria yelled, hands still propped on her hips.

Kenzi didn't need the advice, as she'd already stumbled backwards a few feet. The men slowly picked up their pace until they were jogging. The flight part of her central nervous system won and fight took a backseat. She ran.

Kenzi made it three blocks from the house before she slowed. Where was she going? Where could she go? It was getting dark and she had no friends, no family—no one who would take her in. Sure, she could probably go to Duke's, but besides the possibility of being seen by more of Silvio's goons, she would have to "put out" for the privilege of safety. Right now, the idea of submitting to that man, even if it meant life or death, was unimaginable.

"Hey!"

She knew the voice, but couldn't place the name. It was the big brute with the gold tooth and knuckles the size of golf balls. She refused to turn around and look. Instead, she took a hard left. Brick buildings flitted by in a strobe effect; graffiti colors then light, dirty white-walled cement then colors again.

Dodging water-logged diapers and soggy bags of McDonald's trash, she ducked into the space behind an abandoned nail salon and the fence that separated businesses from the housing projects.

"You better stop bitch, or you're fuckin' dead."

That was the smaller one, still way bigger than her, but smaller than the other guy.

If she continued down this make-shift alley, she could take a left just before it opened to the highway and loop around all the way back to Duke's junk-yard. It still held the same rusty shit it offered her as a child playing hide-and-seek. For someone who needed to escape, that kind of knowledge was life-saving.

Kenzi could navigate the skeletal remnants of vehicles, the old coke machines, and pinball games long since passed from rigor mortis to fossilization. She knew if she could make it there with even as little as a minute head start, she could find a way to disappear.

More than one set of feet chased after her, the thuds working together in a rhythm that mimicked her heartbeat until the harmony fell apart and she could count two, maybe three separate runners. She pulled the ninety-degree left and then another after passing the first building, to run back the way she'd come. She couldn't waste time worrying about the perpendicular alleys between the two parallel ones that might give away her plan. She just kept going.

The chain-link fence glinted in the fading daylight like a military formation of fireflies. She picked up her pace. A child-sized hole in the far corner offered sanctuary. If she was going to get through it unseen, she would need to cut right and meander around the cars parked on the street, ducking down as if she was on the SWAT team.

She eyed a front loader washing machine that Duke had picked up when the local laundry closed up shop. Years ago, it was a perfect place for a quiet little girl to find peace away from her mother on a drug binge or one of the men of the week who weren't picky when it came to the age of the pussy they tried to stick their dicks into.

Kenzi bet her life on her ability to still fit inside with the door closed. Without the rubber seal, the door gaped enough to keep a kid or young adult from suffocating. Her hand grazed the brick of the pawn shop when she made the turn, rubbing skin off her knuckles. Her sharp intake of air came at the same time that she heard two gunshots. She pitched forward and made a split-second decision. She let her body fall flat on to the pavement and army crawled under a car.

The slush of a late March thaw soaked into her sweats and long-sleeved tee, but there was no time to worry about skinned joints or wet bellies. She held her breath and stayed motionless, trying to keep her head down below the curb.

She focused her senses, listening for the footfalls that should be rounding the corner any minute but her nose demanded an audience in her brain. The smell of liquefied rot with its thick, throat-squeezing fumes writhed up out of the sewer grate beside her. The need to peek through the bars and assure herself there wasn't some zombie or other such monster waiting for her overcame her.

She knew it was stupid, but one of her foster mothers (an elderly woman who insisted Kenzi call her "Nana" for the three mercifully short months she'd lived there) once told her the devil's creatures lived beneath grates like these, waiting to devour bad little children. Nana insisted they could smell a bad child and would pull a lever which opened the bars, dropping the unsuspecting naughty bugger into their jaws.

On particularly bad sewage days, Nana would say "can you smell the fumes of Hell down there? I hope you've been a good girl this week." From that day on, Kenzi never again stepped onto a sewer grate.

There was so little light beneath the car that she had no hope of seeing anything in the dark abyss but still she inched herself forward to where her eyes could peer over the edge. A small, white, oblong shape glistened in the gloom. Black orbs hovered side by side against a yellow-white beak. Kenzi shivered, unable to stay in this spot. The peeled-back piece of fencing was in a direct diagonal to the left of her head. It would take little maneuvering to wriggle her way over to it and through the small hole. Once she got that far, it would be easy to roll from one obstacle to another until she reached the washer.

Maybe she lost them. The usual sounds of music blasting from cheap speakers and screaming mothers threatening physical abuse continued without the interruption of footfalls or heavy breathing. Now was the time to break from the death car. She shimmied across the semi-frozen ground and pushed herself through the rusty-edged fence, tearing her shirt and the skin of her back in the process. The washing machine was further away than she recalled. Still, the road and alleys were deserted as far as she could see, so she risked a beeline run to it and climbed in, curling herself into a breech fetal position before pulling the door gently shut.

The smell of damp mold tickled her nose, coaxing a sneeze, but she willed it away. The dirty glass window beaded with condensation as the air warmed and then grew stifling. Kenzi's hip ached. She straightened her leg a bit to adjust herself and felt the rusted wall of the tumbler give. She pulled her foot back before it broke through. Her hip screamed in protest at being put back into the same position and the dirty cuts in her back called out in response. *Relax. Just relax and think* she told herself. *Relax, relax, relax.*

Live bird, dead bird, live bird, dead bird. It felt like a sign. The Scribble Man had a bird like that black one she'd just seen. Those milky eyes peered into her soul. The bird, not the man, had given her the rabbit's foot. Had she really dreamed it all up? So what if the bird pecking at her window had been her imagination too? "Stress-induced hallucinations" was the term the doctors had used when foster parents showed them her drawings of the Scribble Man with Robbie's ghost inside his glass timer. *Words, too. There had been messages to and from the Scribble Man.* She remembered. Had she, as a child written notes to herself? Her skin itched. She wanted the foot, the claws that saved her, that had saved her so many times before. Where was it? She couldn't get to it in this cramped space.

She needed to check on Gloria and Al, go home, and call an ambulance for Marilyn and get her admitted for the umpteenth time. Maybe even get to see that cute Indian doc—and hunker down in the hospital for a few days to buy some more time.

The door swung open easily but the pins and needles working their way up her feet and legs did not allow her to move. She tried once but fell. Slowly, she rose, adding her weight a pound of pressure at a time, letting her nerves come back to life. When she could trust her limbs again, she took a few hesitant steps. She worked her way through the labyrinth of junk to the far side of the fence where a bigger hole waited to let her escape.

The house closest to the junk yard and directly across the street from Gloria's porch was boarded up, scrawled with spray paint, and filled with junkies and horny teens. The next house over used to be occupied by a mom with her six kids. Kenzi babysat them— most of the time unasked—while the mom was off getting high or sucking cock for crack. Then one day there were the sirens—police and an ambulance without its lights. After that, the house stood empty. *Just another day in the hood. Hmm, might make a good book title.*

This time, crossing through the backyard, it felt all too quiet. The air was thick and Gloria wasn't there waving her in. Kenzi stopped at the top of the steps. The bloodied bodies of her friends lay slumped against each other. Al was dead. His left eye was nothing more than red stew in a black bowl and his forehead bore a red angry volcano spilling forth a dark ooze of lava. Gloria was swollen and mangled. Both eyes bulged closed like a newborn robin's. Her arm draped seemingly boneless over Al's legs, certainly broken. Her ample cleavage had caught and still held one of her teeth. She was breathing.

"Mama? Gloria? Hey, wake up." Kenzi held the woman's face in her hands and shook her ever so gently. Nothing. She pulled the woman's heavy head to her chest and cradled it. Her hand was warm and sticky against Gloria. She held her tighter and as she increased the pressure, the woman's skull crunched like eggshell.

"Oh god."

She had no choice but to leave them there and get home to call 911. She crossed the yard without concern for the men who had been after her and leaped over the three steps to the door and shoved it open.

It took what seemed like hours to comprehend the scene. Every cupboard door was open. Broken dishes were everywhere. The chair that sat on a peach can was overturned and her mind noted in the chaos that another leg had broken off. *We can't afford two cans of peaches.* The junkie who had so recently occupied it was sprawled on the floor. His forehead bore the same "we were here" hole as Al's had. That wasn't really a surprise to Kenzi, given both killers standing amongst the mess. Her mother, now very much awake and sober, was being held up in a headlock by the smaller one—a squirrely little white boy wearing a black skull cap. The bigger one—*Marco. I think it's Marco*— held the gun pointed at her. Snot mixed with tears covered her mother's bruised and bloodied face.

"Where's the money, bitch?" Marco punctuated the question with a jab of his gun.

"Kenzi," her mother whimpered.

"Shut the fuck up," White Boy said and punched Marilyn in the head.

"I said where is the money?"

"Hold on a sec," Kenzi said.

She leaped at Marco. The gun went off just as she slammed into him. She heard her mother scream, but it faded into a wet gargle followed by the thud of her body hitting the floor. The gun skittered across the linoleum. Suddenly, Kenzi was on the biggest thug like a monkey grabbing at his face and poking his eyes.

The next thud came from behind her and it brought her to her knees. White Boy had taken a bat or maybe a metal pole to her lower back. She tried to curl herself up, tucking her arms and legs in like a pill bug. The attack felt like it came from every angle. The bat and a knife took turns pummeling her. Her kidneys throbbed. She didn't even know she could feel her internal organs until now. She'd have to thank Silvio for the medical lesson.

Marco kicked her in the ribs. At least one broke. It was hard to breathe. Each intake of breath caused a stabbing pain to rake through her. She got herself up onto her knees and he kicked her again, rolling her over onto her belly. White Boy had a knife—a big one, a jungle knife—pointed at her.

"Bitch, Silvio says you're late with his money. Way we figure, you owe him an even K. You got two minutes to hand it over or you're dead. You got it?"

She coughed. *A thousand? No fucking way.* It hurt so bad to breathe, but she took in what she could.

"Five hundred." She coughed and spit a dollop of blood onto the floor.

She tried to get up, to face them. White Boy put his foot on her belly and pressed his weight into it. The sharp edge of a broken rib pierced something inside her and a deep cramp seized her belly.

"Uuughh," she huffed. It came out involuntarily.

"The extra pays our collection fees." He leaned closer into her face, the knife was now poking into her throat. "Damn, girl. Why your eyes all fucked up like that? You got cataracts or something?" He pulled back as if she was contagious. His foot came off her belly too and instinctively she took a deep breath. Something popped inside her and black edged into her eyes. If she didn't do something soon, she was going to die. She slowed her breathing. She tried to take short quick sips of air. The rabbit's foot was in her pocket—if she could get to it.

"They're two different colors, asswipe." She probably shouldn't have said it to the guy with the knife but she needed the distraction and making them angry was all she could do. "It's genetics. Science. You know, the reason your face is as ugly as your mother's."

"Listen here, freak, you go get that money, right now, and Imma let you live, I ain't even gonna fuck ya ugly ass." White Boy was down so close to her face she could smell the burnt plastic stink of meth on his breath.

She used the opportunity to wriggle her hand into her pocket. The foot almost jumped into her palm. She'd lost track of Marco, but there was little time to worry about it. She slashed out at White Boy with it and used the momentum to roll herself away from him. He screeched a high-pitched old lady squeal.

"ook ut at itch id oo ee."

Kenzi hazarded a look back and saw him holding a flap of cheek up. She must have caught the corner of his mouth with the claws and literally ripped his face off—at least half of it anyway. Blood plopped on the floor from above her like rain.

"You fucking cunt!" Marco had the gun but White Boy got one good kick at the side of her head before falling down. A drop of his blood hit her face, or maybe it was her own running in her eyes. Her world turned red. Pain seemed to come from everywhere. She was going to die. The gun went off and she was shoved sideways. It stunned her diaphragm and when she was able to take a breath again it whistled. There was something hot inside her chest and it was squeezing her heart.

"Help me," she whispered.

Somewhere in the distance the tapping started again. She heard glass breaking. There were muffled frantic voices in the background. Blackness swam into her peripheral vision as her brain began shutting down nonessential functions. She was going to die. Her life, filled with misery and pain would soon be over. She relaxed and quit fighting. This was the solution to everything.

The shadows in her vision began to move, coalescing into a vaguely female shape. She was probably hallucinating. *This must be a stage in the dying process.* Most people see a lighted tunnel, but she saw the form of a woman with a perfect body that she'd never had. It darted between her and her attackers.

Suddenly oxygen flooded through her like a tsunami washing the room in color. Once again, she saw a woman with black hair and tan skin standing over her. The crazy, white-eyed bird had tucked itself into Kenzi's armpit and buried its beak into the whistling hole left in her lung by the bullet. Something cool brushed against her leg. She looked down to see a large snake wrapped around White Boy, squeezing the life out of him.

But none of this was real, was it? Surely, she was near death and just seeing things—bits of memories sewn together like a drunken dream. The dark-haired woman had Marco by the throat. He wasn't even fighting. Suddenly, her mouth opened unnaturally wide.

A universe swirled inside. That was the tunnel. Somehow, Kenzi needed to go there. She wanted to. But Marco was going there. As his body shriveled up like a skin wrapper, the rest of him was sort of sucked into that darkness inside the woman.

When Marco was discarded, the woman bent down to Kenzi. "Hello sister, and thank you."

Before Kenzi could answer, the bird pulled itself out of her with a squelchy pop. The whistling began again. The sensation made her cough and she spat blood. Heat radiated off of her, she could almost see it, like a hot road in the middle of August, yet she shivered. She smelled the coppery scent of blood which over years of cutting had become aromatherapy. But this blood smell was all wrong. It was sour and metallic and much too raw.

Numbness blanketed her. Sounds were muffled against the roar of a sanguine ocean in her ears and the cacophony of a frantic bird cawing at the woman and snake. Some internal alarm was going off in time with her breathing: screaming siren, stop, siren, stop. Maybe the cops were coming.

"We'll meet again soon, sister," the woman said, her face just inches from Kenzi's.

She tried to see her savior but everything was a crimson haze. A swooping sound like a fist or maybe a giant black bird came from just above her head, and then Kenzi's world went black and there were no more thoughts.

Chapter 5: Book of Conquest 2

Burnt lamb offerings scented the air which drew Lilith to the village. The sign said Monroe St., which meant little to her. So many mortals—more than she'd ever known could exist—wandered amongst structures so tall they must touch the moon at night. The ground was firm, similar to the packed earth of the desert. The strange coverings on her feet kept her off balance. It was dangerous not to feel each step, yet all around her, the humans wore them. It was imperative to blend in. If they knew, they would try to destroy her. She needed to gather strength, just as she had so long ago.

She was aware of the changes she'd undergone during her imprisonment by Sariel. At least the demons gave her a chance. Trapped in the talisman, she could do nothing but evolve into the creature man and myth had made her. An example, a warning to women. Now she was a baby killer, a seductress, a demoness. And Sariel, the one she'd trusted, the one she'd come to love, allowed it. He did nothing to stop her vilification. He kept her to himself until finally abandoning her—to a child no less.

So many voices, languages surrounded her. She recognized some of it. It was hard to assimilate the emotions inside. It was difficult to know what to do. She was mostly angry. Angry at The Creator, at Sariel, at every demon who tried to destroy her, and at man himself. Men who believed as Adam, who told her tale to their daughters and women—as well as women like Eve who would lie down and submit.

The cloth she'd covered herself in rubbed at her skin. It reached into the crevice of her womanhood and irritated it. This was Eve's doing as well. All these women wearing strange garments proudly, as if hiding away the very essence of femininity was a virtue. She hated them. Never again would she give away her power.

"…of the Lord. I say repent. For the end times are coming, folks. The apocalypse is upon us." The voice interrupted her thoughts.

It came from a man standing farther down the street. His head was well above the crowd and he had a device up to his face that made him sound much like The Creator. Ignoring the flashing lights and ringing sounds coming from inside the buildings, she made her way to the small group that had gathered to listen.

"Is this place, this Greektown, any different from the marketplace Jesus shunned?" Spittle filled the space between his mouth and the trumpet he spoke into. "This is a center of sin. Gambling is a sin. Prostitution is a sin. The Lord has given us this book, has entrusted us to read and study his word so that we might enter the kingdom of Heaven and what do we do instead? We drape ourselves in gold, we worship our material wealth, we engage in gluttony, lust, sloth, and pride."

"Maybe that's your problem. You need a little lust in your life, preacher man," a woman in the crowd yelled out. Her arms were crossed, covering her ample breasts which were barely covered in a strip of black fabric. Another strip of the same material covered her buttocks and triangle of hair in the front. Her face was painted to accentuate her lips and eyes. Lilith touched her own bare lips and wondered why a woman might choose to do such a thing.

"Oh, the harlot speaks," the preacher man said. "A daughter of Lilith who goes against her own creator. A succubus who sells her body for pleasure. Go back to hell with your mother demon. The Lord has no use for women like you—whores, witches, and baby killers!"

Thunder rolled through Lilith's chest. Heat rose to her cheeks.

"Fuck you! You cling to that book 'cause it's the only way you could even hope to have any power over a real woman." The whore walked away.

"I watched as the Lamb opened the first of the seven seals. Then I heard one of the four living creatures say in a voice like thunder, 'Come and see!' I looked, and there before me was a white horse! Its rider held a bow, and he was given a crown, and he rode out as a conqueror bent on conquest," the preacher man read from the book he held.

Conquest for a crown, a kingdom.

"When the Lamb opened the second seal, I heard the second living creature say, 'Come and see!' Then another horse came out, a fiery red one. Its rider was given power to take peace from the earth and to make men slay each other. To him was given a large sword."

War. Make men slay each other. Baby killers. Take peace away from this earth, this creation.

"When the Lamb opened the third seal, I heard the third living creature say, 'Come and see!' I looked, and there before me was a black horse! Its rider was holding a pair of scales in his hand. Then I heard what sounded like a voice among the four living creatures, saying, "A quart of wheat for a day's wages, and three quarts of barley for a day's wages, and do not damage the oil and the wine!"

Ergot, famine, disease, mass hysteria. I'll need a witch.

"When the Lamb opened the fourth seal, I heard the voice of the fourth living creature say, 'Come and see!' I looked and there before me was a pale horse! Its rider was named Death, and Hades was following close behind him. They were given power over a fourth of the earth to kill by sword, famine, and plague, and by the wild beasts of the earth."

Sariel. No. No. His little love. He's had his chance. She will help me, she will take his place. Death will ride with me. When we—all four whores of the apocalypse—have destroyed this world, I will give birth to a new creation. I will take back everything that was taken from me. Conquest is mine. In the end. I will wear the crown.

The preacher man faded into the background as Lilith walked through the crowd. Behind the crate he was standing on, the preacher had left his black hooded cloak neatly folded on the ground. A golden apple sat on it, keeping it from blowing away. She retrieved both without pause and continued past the casinos, shops, and restaurants back into the night. She put the cloak on and gradually shed her mortal garments. There was work to be done and no time to spare. Sariel would find out soon enough. She'd need to get to the girl before he did. The Apocalypse was coming.

Lucifer watched Lilith take the cloak he'd left behind the milkcrate. He wasn't really reading from the Bible anyway. That was a book he knew from heart. After all, he'd helped write so much of it as it was. More than choirs and souls and church picnics, The Creator loved his drama and that just happened to be Lucifer's specialty. As long as he kept The Creator entertained, he had access to all the sin he wanted.

But had he just stirred the pot a little too much with this one? No one noticed her in her hood. No one tripped over the discarded clothing. How much trouble could she be, really? More importantly, how could he take advantage of this new turn of events?

"Welcome back, sweetheart," he muttered before bringing the megaphone back to his lips and opening to the Old Testament.

Chapter 6: Book of Sariel 2

It was a nice day to die and the kid picked a peaceful enough spot. Sariel sat on the park bench watching the young man trudge onto the scene. He was right on time. The name, Ryan Trudeau had only just appeared on Sariel's arm, burning slightly. It was a warm enough day, yet the boy wore a heavy letterman's jacket. Twenty-three, living in the past.

"Fucking idiot," Sariel said. "Hope he's not dumb enough to be a jumper."

The park was designed around this elevated bridge that swung high over the river. This was not the first time he'd been to this park and certainly wouldn't be the first time he'd had to go in after a body—but a break would be nice. Maybe the kid would employ a quick shot to the head, maybe a drug overdose?

Ryan walked past Sariel, past the trees with their rings of pinks and purple petunias landscaped in circles and bee-lined for the bridge.

"Damn it," Sariel muttered. "Would've been nice to not have to get wet for once."

The kid had made it to the bridge and was still on the incline to the middle of it where it was highest off the water. Sariel walked to the river bank and stood among the wildflowers to get a closer look. A gull cried out in pre-mourning. *Where was that fucking Enoch anyway?*

Ryan took his jacket off and laid it over the railing of the bridge. He pulled a long chain up over his head and placed it neatly on top of the coat. Then he climbed over the rail and stared down into the water.

"Just fucking jump already," Sariel said. His mood had been shitty since the London incident. "Let's get this over with."

"You're starting to sound like me," Lucifer said, from behind him.

"You know, this day seemed not quite fucked enough, but now that you're here, I'm feeling more optimistic."

"Aww, hey now. That's not nice, Sariel." Today Lucifer was dressed like the star quarterback of the town's good old, all-American football team. His outfit was similar to what Ryan Trudeau likely wore every day of his life when he was in high school. Jeans, a natural cotton undershirt, and a green and gold jersey tucked in like a proper young gentleman would.

The gull cried out again, reminding Sariel of his duty.

"Where's your fine feathered friend today? Off searching for more of my good men?"

"I don't know. I don't share a mind with that bird." The splash behind him heralded an increased burning on his arm. Ryan's name was glowing red, searing as if branded. "I have a job to do."

"Oh, yeah, you got a job all right, you got a big job ahead of you and it's got nothing to do with that floater out there." Lucifer warned, while some of the joviality drained from his voice.

"Whatever it is you have to say, say it. I don't have time, nor do I wish to stand here listening to you any further. If Enoch were here, I think today would be your last day as well. I'm done giving you berth."

"What happened to that necklace you used to wear? That old hare's foot?"

Sariel touched his chest. The long absence of the foot had not made the flesh beneath it any less sensitive. Within his chest, a heart like that of a mortal's had been cut in two. One half belonged to the original holder of the hare's foot, the other belonged to the current one. "It's safe," he mumbled, lost in the past.

"Is it, really? Tell me, Sariel, if one of my demons looked like a beautiful, fragile young woman who was more than willing to suck your scarred-up cock, would you free them? Is that what I gotta do for you?"

Sariel stepped forward. Within an inch of Lucifer's perfect face. "What the fuck are you getting at, demon?"

"If we've stooped to name-calling, then I'll put it this way: your whore of a girlfriend is back from the uh…*foot* of the grave. Forgive me for assuming anything, but she seems a little pissed."

"What are you talking about?"

"I said Lilith is back. Lilith has already killed a number of mortals. She's got something up her sleeve if you ask me. If I were you, I might consider laying off the demon hunting and clean up your spill."

"Impossible." It was all he could think of to say. *Where was that goddamned bird?*

"What about your other girl? The little one you got saddled with when you let her live?"

Sariel twitched at the swelling burn of Kenzi's name, the only one that never healed, never scarred on his body. *She was in trouble if what Lucifer said was true. But then, it couldn't be true. Fucking Enoch. Better get his ass here asap.*

"Listen, I have a job to do. Which I intend to see to right now. Whatever tale you're trying to spin for whatever reason is lost on me. The Deadly Seven are on my list. All of them. Including Pride. Do you understand?"

Lucifer grinned. His white teeth sparkled. He put his hands up.

"OK. OK. I'm done here. Don't want to end up trapped in a gold medallion. Let me say what I came here to say and I'll be on my way."

Sariel snorted. "You mean you haven't yet?"

He couldn't hear anymore. His head was spinning with thoughts of Lilith and Kenzi. *How did Lilith get released from the talisman? Impossible.* He needed to finish his job and focus.

Lucifer ignored him. "I never trusted that woman—Lilith. She's always had a mind of her own. I'd be open to helping you take her back, put her in her proper place that is, in exchange for a favor or two."

"Uh huh. I'll be sure to keep that in mind. Now, if you'll excuse me." Sariel turned and waded into the river. A new name began to bite into his arm and that name worried him all the more. That name gave credence to everything Lucifer had said.

Chapter 7: Book of Sariel 3

The bird returned just as he arrived to collect the soul of Albert Roland. The homeless man was a friend of Kenzi's and a companion of the woman Kenzi called Mama. The woman, although in bad shape, was not dead. He gently rolled her body aside to attend to Al's.

"About time you showed up," he grumbled to the bird. Sariel wasn't in the mood for this. He needed to find Kenzi.

Enoch's head was clotted with blood.

"What's happened to you? Where have you been?" he asked impatiently. The bird couldn't answer, he knew that, but it could lead him to the answer. The bird delivered the old man's soul and landed hard on Sariel's shoulder, digging his talons in.

"What is it?" Sariel asked the raven.

There was no response.

"Enoch!" he shouted when the claws dug deeper. It burned like the names carved into his flesh. Like the one that seared into him continuously.

"What's happened to Kenzi?"

He knew it was her. All of this screamed trouble. He used to be able to see her whereabouts, sometimes even hear her thoughts. They would leave each other messages on her pictures. But that faded as she grew. Now, their bond hadn't completely disappeared but since she'd taken to writing her own history, the connection had dulled to nothing more than a mortal-like bond.

The bird released its grip and flew into the air. Sariel ran his hand over the swollen wound. A sorrowful cry from the bird left a hollow ache in his middle.

In one step, they stood in the sunny yellow bedroom. Kenzi wasn't there, but her journal lay on the nightstand, open to the most recent work. He pocketed it. There was nothing in the room to suggest a problem. Enoch shifted its weight back and forth, one foot to the other, as if anxious to move on, but in no hurry to do so.

The living room was a different story all together. Furniture was overturned, broken glass and papers were scattered and wet with blood. It seemed as if it had rained blood in the house. A fine spray of it covered surfaces everywhere he looked.

Blood was concerning, but a lot was contributable to the bodies on the floor. Marilyn Brooks's name grew hot on his skin as he came upon her body first. This was a long time coming. He stepped over her and the next body—a Gerald Ruiz—no one of significance. He'd tend to them both in a moment.

Beyond them, where the kitchen met the living room, lay three more bodies. Two males, one female. The female was obscured from the chest up by the husk of a man—

made of flesh, but otherwise shriveled and empty. No names had come yet for these three who were undoubtedly dead.

The body beside the heap was also malformed and lying in a blackened, sticky pool that must have originated from the jagged tear across his cheek, exposing a half grin of yellowed teeth. There was no blood seeping from the corpse now. It was mummified. Thick ligature-type gouges spiraled around his body ending at the neck.

It might have been rope—although one that thick wrapped around the body in this way would be a new one on him. The serpiginous smear that drew the blood across the linoleum to the door told him that if a rope was used, it was alive. A shapely curved calf, olive skinned, flashed in his mind. It had a thick-bodied serpent tattooed around it in a lover's embrace. In his mind's perfect memory, he could have followed it the whole way up and around a body that he knew well.

But no, his mind was playing tricks on him. He shook it out of his head and pointed to the mummified man lying on the floor. Enoch hopped down and stood on the head, but made no effort to remove the soul.

"What is going on here?" he asked.

No name had appeared on his skin. In all the millennia he spent as Death, he'd never *not* been notified by pain. That was his punishment after all. He shooed Enoch away and shoved his hand into the small center just above and between the eyes. Empty. The corpse felt like dried corn leaves—and it was just as hollow. He let the body slide off his empty fist and settle onto the floor. It made a scuttling sound, like a scarab beetle rolling the shit of this day somewhere to bury it.

Enoch hopped to the pile and picked at the flattened flesh of the first man.

"Enoch, stop."

Enoch did not stop. Instead he bobbed his head again and again until he had a large purchase of flesh in his beak. As if he was trying to tear a piece off to eat, he pulled, jerking back and back until the body began to slide.

A faint whistling sound penetrated the dead silence of the room. Enoch flapped his wings and croaked noisily. He galumphed triumphantly over to the bubbling hole in the side of the female body and shoved his beak directly into it.

"Kenzi!"

She was hurt badly. Shot at least once, but alive and breathing. Sariel rolled her onto her back and shoved the man-husk off of her. She'd taken quite the beating but the girl was tough. *Tough like Lilith.*

He patted her down. The hare's foot was gone. He straightened up and looked around. *Nowhere.* He kicked the dried mummy over. *Not there.*

"Enoch, listen to me. Kenzi's fate has been left to me. I'm going to summon help. We will gather the souls as called for and leave. I fear Lilith has been freed. We must find her. We must protect Kenzi. Lilith may see Kenzi as a threat, or even as her keeper. Either way, we must right this wrong."

He left much unsaid, but Enoch knew that, of course. Enoch had surely thought of the consequences of a demoness set on revenge being freed. The commotion she could cause would rouse The Creator's attention. What that meant for the two of them was frightening enough. Then there was Kenzi, his child, his love, his precious gift. Sariel dialed 911 on the telephone and dropped the receiver.

"Come, let's finish here and we'll find her in the hospital."

Chapter 8: Book of Sariel 4

Sariel watched the ventilator rise and fall in synchrony with Kenzi's chest. Gasps of the machine ticked off the seconds of a life he was entirely responsible for. He'd intervened many times over the last twenty years, choosing her fate for her, allowing her no free will to make a fatal mistake.

He leafed through her journal. She was writing a book—her autobiography. Perhaps she was also rewriting her own past and a new destiny. It would explain the recent disconnect; his inability to tap into her emotions and determine her whereabouts. Admittedly, it was for the best. As his punishment neared the end, he, too, had let their bond weaken in the hopes he could let her go. He pretended he couldn't feel the familiar ache in his chest that had no business being there. *Not again.*

"Is Lilith back, Enoch?"

The bird raised its head and cawed in response.

As the days passed, the fear that Lilith had indeed returned solidified. If she had something to do with what happened in Kenzi's home, which seemed likely, why had she let Kenzi live? Would she have felt his connection to the girl? Would Lilith, having remembered his feelings for her when she was mortal, decide the only way to find him was to use the girl as bait? His gut told him that if Lilith had returned, she would be looking for him. After all, she was either alone and afraid, searching for her lost love or—and this was far more likely—furious and vengeful, seeking not love but retribution for what he'd done to her.

"We must protect Kenzi. If what Lucifer said was true, and it certainly appears to be—"

Enoch shivered and ruffled its feathers.

"Yes, you're right, there is no doubt. Maybe we should go after Lilith, rather than wait for her to come to us."

Would Kenzi have written anything about Lilith in her journal? The book thrummed in his hands. He wanted to read it and explore the girl's inner thoughts. If he was being honest with himself, he'd like to see if she had written about him.

"There may be something in here." He thumbed the pages.

Enoch shook off the tremor and shifted its weight back and forth from one foot to another. Once satisfied, the bird snugged down into its body and closed its eyes. Sariel opened the journal and read. Full chapters written in longhand filled most of the book followed by a section of notes and cryptic phrases. He skimmed through her childhood until he got to the day her brother died and he became her guardian. It was the most recent entry.

"She questions our existence," he reported to the sleeping bird. "Ha, here she refers to me as The Scribble Man. Remember Enoch, how she drew pictures for us." He laughed and shrugged his left shoulder up and down rousing the bird. "She insisted you were a girl! She drew that picture of you in a dress wearing a fancy little hat." The bird cooed, Sariel chuckled. "She wrote 'Do you like to wear dresses like me?' That's when we began leaving notes for her as she slept."

Enoch flew to Kenzi's bed and lit on the side rail.

"Our sweet little girl. Remember the first year after her brother's death?" We never left her side. We couldn't have. Her father abandoned the family and her mother's drug use was completely out of hand, and The Creator turned his back on her. We had to stay."

The Creator. He dared not think poorly of Him, but it was hard not to question the motives. Lilith was nothing more than a product of her creation, and for His mistake, she'd suffered. Sariel had been chosen to do His bidding and when the angel hesitated, questioned, the punishment was swift and harsh. Now what might happen? Would he never learn?

"Kenzi almost released Lilith before. Perhaps we should have taken the talisman away that day." He looked at Enoch who sat as a statue watching over the girl. "Sometimes you are a great pain in the ass, you know that? But you do make me laugh and you did manage to rescue the hare's foot." He stood and threw his hands up in the air mimicking Gloria in a falsetto voice. "Oh, that nasty-ass bird grabbed that foot right off me! You either wash it or Imma throw it right in the trash!"

Sariel bent over laughing. It was a good time in Kenzi's life. A time when she had allies.

Chapter 9: Parable 2

After the funeral, Kenzi's father had taken her rabbit's foot off the long cord and attached it to a keychain. No one could get a straight answer from Kenzi about where it had come from. They had finally decided she'd picked it up amongst the litter of the crash. While the thing was old and practically hairless, she clung to it as if it was a piece of Robbie. Mac refused to let his wife take it from her.

She carried it everywhere, hooking it on the belt loop of her pants. She'd worry at it when teachers lost their temper with her constant doodling of birds and hourglasses, or when the other girls would laugh at her two different colored eyes and frizzy hair. When the foot could not soothe her, Sariel was there.

His presence calmed her and soon the keychain would be once again, hanging at her side. Her warm little hand grasping his as she walked the gauntlet of perplexed teachers and snickering kids.

"Hey, Frankenstein, nice rat you got tied to your pants," RJ Donalds said.

RJ had been Robbie's friend before the accident but in the two years since, he'd grown into quite the sixth-grade bully. He grabbed the keychain in his hand and tugged at it, pulling her at the same time. Kenzi spun away from him trying to pull it out of his grip but she heard the rip of her jeans too late to stop and the chain slid off, fully into RJ's possession.

"Look at this nasty thing." He shook it so the gathering crowd could see. "Only a freak like Frankenstein would need to carry around spare body parts in case she loses another one. Was that ugly eye of yours on a keychain too or did you steal it from your brother before they buried him?"

RJ laughed and turned his attention to the onlookers, checking to see that his humor was being properly appreciated. In the instant he let his guard down, Kenzi snatched the foot back. Sariel smiled. That was the spark he'd seen in her eyes the day he spared her. The spark that brought another beloved to mind—one from a long time ago.

"Ow! Hey!"

The boy looked down at his hand. Four red lines ran across his palm, two of which were welling with blood. One rivulet was already tracking down his lifeline. Murmurs pin-balled through the crowd.

"Did she cut him?"

"She clawed him with that disgusting foot."

"Oh my god, she is a freak! Watch out, she's going crazy now."

RJ bawled like a baby, holding his hand to his chest as if it was about to fall off. Sariel wanted to rip the soul out of his overly large melon and stick it like chewed up gum on the side of a locker but he didn't need any more problems with The Creator. Kenzi's eyes were the size of plums. Her heart fluttered like a that of a rabbit about to skitter away through the brush. Her mother constantly warned her that if she acted up at school or even behaved strangely, the cops would take her away and they'd never see each other again.

Sariel took Kenzi's hand and tugged. They should go back to class, let the situation fizzle out on its own. But Kenzi seemed mesmerized by the crimson stream coursing down RJ's wrist. She squeezed the rabbit's foot in her own hand. Sariel ached as if it was his heart she held.

"What is going on here?" A tall, thin, bird-like woman burst through the crowd of children. Her wrinkled fists pushed against the vinyl belt of her teal polyester dress.

The last layer of children parted for the teacher, revealing a bloodied RJ standing opposite Kenzi.

Sariel sighed. *Well, I guess we're going home again.*

"Don't say a word," he whispered to her while the rest of the children told Mrs. Mitchell the tale of crazy Kenzi and the attack.

He stayed by her side in the principal's office while they tried to get ahold of her mother. After some time with no answer, the exasperated principal said, "Where's your father?"

Kenzi shrugged.

"Well someone needs to come and get you immediately or we'll have to call Child Protective Services."

"Give them Gloria's number," Sariel whispered to her.

Gloria was at the school in minutes in her Sunday best—complete with yellow hat and large carpet bag.

"She's being expelled, Ms. Paulson," Mr. Bruno, ever the professional, said. "She attacked another student. We simply don't have the staff or programs available for students with Kenzi's special needs."

"You're kidding me, right? There are gang shootings across the street from this very school at least once a week. I bet half your students are selling drugs on the goddamned playground and you're going to tell me that Kenzi scratching a boy with an old rabbit's foot gets her kicked out? Horse shit."

"The foot has sharp claws and I've been told the boy she *scratched*," he put his fingers in the air and made quotation marks, "may need stitches."

Gloria made a chuffing sound. Sariel choked back a laugh. He'd seen the scratches and that's all they were. The kid deserved it. He patted Kenzi's leg. Enoch squawked in solidarity.

"Kenzi, let me see that keychain," Gloria said.

Mrs. Mitchell had taken it from her in the hallway, promising that Kenzi was never getting that "nasty, germ ridden piece of filth" back ever again. Kenzi opened her empty palms, miming her loss, and let the hot tears slip out of her eyes.

Gloria pivoted back to face Mr. Bruno.

"Where is her keychain?"

"It has been confiscated. She can't have it back."

"Where is it?" Gloria repeated.

"Mrs. Mitchell, who found the two just after Kenzi attacked the boy in question, took it away from her before she could hurt anyone else or herself. I've asked her to hold onto it in case the boy's family chooses to press charges."

"Press charges? Are you fucking kidding me?" Gloria stood up and looked as if she was about to beat him with her bag.

Kenzi's own mother had never used this tone of voice in defense of Kenzi. It was a parental voice that said 'just you try to do something to my child'. This was good. Perhaps Gloria was the chance for the girl to be loved and looked after properly without being bounced around in the foster care system. Beside him, Kenzi sat up straighter, as if thinking the same thing.

"You pick up that phone and you call that holier-than-thou bitch and tell her she has exactly sixty seconds to bring that keychain back down to this office before I go find it myself, and I'll start with a cavity search. Do you understand?" She leaned on Mr. Bruno's desk, her face just a few inches away from his. "That keychain has not been out of her possession since the day she watched her brother die. It's all she has left of him and she needs it. Do you understand what it means to her? I want it back now or I will be the one pressing charges."

Spittle flew from Gloria's mouth and landed in Bruno's coffee. Sariel laughed. Kenzi suppressed a little grin too.

Mr. Bruno's eyes worked as if watching a volley of thoughts in his mind, likely determining the validity of the woman's threats. The red-faced man didn't say a thing. He picked up his phone and instructed his secretary, Ms. Fisher, to find Mrs. Mitchell and tell her to bring Kenzi's keychain to his office. Gloria sat back down beside Kenzi and put her hand on her honorary daughter's other leg.

"Ms. Paulson," Mr. Bruno began, sighing. "I don't know how aware you are of the problems we've had with Kenzi. While we understand her grief, she is still expected to participate in class. She is disruptive, she talks to herself—"

"Not to myself. I talk to The Scribble Man and Queenie bird," the child interrupted. She pointed to Sariel as she talked, even taking a moment to look at him and smile. Mr. Bruno ignored her.

"She draws pictures on all of her school work and frequently fiddles with that foot. It is distracting to her fellow students and now she has managed to hurt someone with it."

Just then, Mrs. Mitchell came sweeping through the door. She had a smile on her face until she saw Kenzi and Gloria sitting there contentedly. She looked around at everyone in the room.

"What is this?" she asked.

"Can you please return the keychain to Ms. Paulson?" Mr. Bruno said.

"What? No. It was used a weapon, Paul. What if the police—?"

"Just give it to her, Liz," he interrupted.

Mrs. Mitchell didn't say another thing. Instead she slammed the foot down on the edge of the desk, glared at Mr. Bruno, and walked out of the office.

Kenzi reached out to grab it, but Gloria beat her to it. She looked at it, turning it so she could see the nails. Sariel stiffened. The thing could only ever be in either his or Kenzi's possession.

"I don't see any blood on it," Gloria announced and Sariel relaxed. "I'm taking Kenzi home. She won't be coming back to this shit hole. I'll make sure of it. We'll stop by tomorrow for her belongings, and I will be checking to make sure that all her stuff's there."

Gloria gestured at Kenzi to get up and swept her forward toward the door. The principal's face was so purple and sweaty that Sariel took a moment to check for the man's name carved into his flesh somewhere, but it appeared Bruno's cardiac arteries would soon snap out of it and he'd live another day.

Kenzi left the school building holding onto Gloria who continued to carry the foot by the chain. She had it pinched between her thumb and first finger as if it was a dead mouse. Enoch did not like that at all. It appeared to the woman, plucked it from her and gave it back to Kenzi.

"Oh, that nasty-ass bird! You wash that thing and your hands as soon as we get home!" Gloria yelled.

Sariel walked over to Kenzi's bed. He gave Enoch a scratch on the head and then placed his hand on Kenzi's.

"I was with you that day, Kenzi—and Enoch too. We are real. As real as you. You're safe now with us."

Enoch turned its head almost all the way around to glare at its master. Its white, milky eyes glared in disagreement.

"She is safe now, though. We'll tell Kenzi the truth, the whole story of Lilith and their connection."

Enoch cawed.

"She'll understand. She hasn't been through the same things Lilith has. Her heart hasn't hardened. She'll forgive me for the choices I made."

Chapter 10: Book of Kenzi 3

"Calm down, Ms. Brooks," a muffled but distinctly male voice echoed from the darkness in her periphery.

Someone was trying to smother her. They'd put a gag far back into her throat and she couldn't breathe. Her hands had been tied down and she fought weakly to release them.

"Ms. Brooks, Kenzi, you're OK." She felt a hand on her forehead, soft and kind. "There is a tube down your throat to help you breathe. We're going to take it out if you can try to remain calm. Otherwise we'll have to give you medicine to put you back to sleep. Can you be calm?"

Kenzi opened her eyes. It was so bright. Her body ached and burned. She bit down on the hard, plastic tube that filled her throat and tried to swallow against it. Something was shoved into her mouth and suctioned at her tongue and the sparse saliva she'd just tried to swallow. She winced. Her cheek and upper lip were being pulled. It stung.

"Settle down, honey. Can you hear what Dr. Patel is saying to you?" A female voice this time. The man's voice had the musical lilt of a familiar accent to it. She wanted him to do the talking. It made her feel more at ease.

Her watery eyes began to dry and focus. Besides the giant spaceship-sized light hovering above her, there was a lot of white and blue. A soft beeping kept time in the background like a metronome. Had it always been there? She shivered.

"Let's get this tube out of you and then I'll get you a nice warm blanket, ok?" the female voice asked.

She was aware of the hand still rubbing its thumb across her forehead and now a smaller one mimicking the movement over her forearm. It was both soothing and irritating to her. She tried to speak around the tube.

"No, no. Don't try to speak, Ms. Brooks." The man's voice said from her left.

A face peered down at her. Exotic but not unpleasant spice notes floated on his breath. Her vision had cleared enough to see a young man with a dark complexion and black curls that snuck out below a surgical cap standing over her. His eyes were kind. He was the doctor. She knew him somehow. How did she know him?

"Maybe you should wait for Dr. Childs before you extubate her," the female on the right said.

"She's been fighting the vent all day. She's breathing on her own and I honestly think if we can get her extubated without having to sedate her again, she'll be more likely to stay off it."

The conversation went on over top of her while Kenzi tried to focus on her breathing, her hearing, her vision, and every other sense that she could awaken. Her neck felt stiff, her shoulders ached. If she could stay calm, the nice doctor would take this thing out of her throat. Right now, that was the only thing she could think about.

"Well, it's your butt, not mine. If you extubate her and she fails, you can explain to Childs why she had to be reintubated." The soft female voice was harder now, angry.

Kenzi felt bad for the doctor. Why was the nurse trying to bully him? The beeping in the background picked up its pace. Maybe the woman knew what she was talking about. Maybe it would hurt to have this thing pulled out of her. How far in did it go? They never showed it coming out on the TV shows. She tried to cough but her chest felt tight. She hated how she couldn't seem to just grab a breath, rather she had to pull it into her through that tube.

The beeping became frenzied and the sound of it made her panic more. She wriggled and pulled at her arm restraints. Tears rolled down her cheeks and an alarm went off.

"Goddamn it, Patel!" a booming voice shouted from the direction of her feet. "I told you to keep her sedated. You think that crisp long coat gives you magical powers?"

The yelling sent Kenzi into a full-blown panic attack. Air would not come readily through the damn tube and her heart was clawing its way out of her ribcage. The restraints wrapped around her wrists strained against her adrenaline-fueled anxiety and suddenly the light was blotted out by a head, and then many heads and hands reaching for her.

Stomping, beeping, a bell dinging, and the voices all speaking at once swirled together like soapy water going down the drain.

"Re-bolus the Propofol and start a drip," the mean doctor yelled.

"It's here doctor. I brought it in when Dr. Patel arrived."

"You see, the nurses here know more than you. That degree your daddy bought don't mean shit to me."

"I apologize, Dr. Childs. She was responding and following commands. I thought perhaps with the tube out, she would remain calm and avoid more sedation."

"Patel, a sedated patient is the best kind of patient. You'll figure that out real quick on this rotation."

Ice prickled under her skin and began to swim upstream toward her heart like horny salmon. The lights dimmed and she blinked. Her eyelids pulled cotton across her corneas. Someone slowed the speed of the spinning room down to 33rpms and she was sinking, sinking deep into the earth beneath her.

"Can you squeeze my hand?" a voice asked.

Someone was shaking their fingers against her palm. She caught them and made it stop. It was annoying.

"Good. Can you hear me, Ms. Brooks?"

Kenzi knew the voice but she couldn't think of a name or face to go with it. He wasn't grabbing at her tits or pussy, so that ruled out most of the men she knew. She tried to lick her lips to talk, but her mouth was too dry. Her cracked tongue and lips offered no moisture either. Resigned to not speaking, she nodded.

He pulled his hand free of her grip. She thought she'd been holding it tightly, but he slid his fingers out effortlessly. Her eyes were closed but she was too tired to open them just yet. Something cold and scratchy touched her lips and she flinched. Water dribbled down her chin.

"This is just a wet sponge for your mouth."

The moisture was heaven and she opened her mouth like a baby bird. The small barrel-shaped thing on a lollipop stick was mercifully cool and wet. He swizzled it around her tongue, gums, and cheeks. She snapped her lips down on it and sucked greedily. He pulled it back out.

"Easy. Too much and you'll make yourself sick. You haven't had anything in your stomach for a week."

Sweet water again on her lips. This time she opened her mouth without being asked and let him paint it with delicious water.

"Can you open your eyes?"

She probably could with a lot of effort, but she wasn't ready yet. She needed to allow her body to reach a higher level of consciousness, and that meant easing it into wakefulness one sense at a time. The beeping metronome was still there but the sound of Darth Vader breathing down her neck was gone. She vaguely remembered being tied to the bed and a long thick tube scraping against her throat as it slithered out of her mouth. She could swallow now—but damn, it hurt. Lifting her left hand and discovering it to be free, she had a sudden urge to scratch her nose. There was something there poking at her nostrils, she ran her fingertips over it.

"Leave that there. It's extra oxygen for you." He took her hand away from the tubing and held on for what seemed to be much too long. She wondered how awake he thought she was. Then, she wondered why she continued to let him do it. But his hand was warm and soft. She'd never been touched so gently before.

A high-pitched alarm echoed in the room. Kenzi jumped.

"Shit. sorry." The beeping stopped as quickly as it began. "That was just my pager. I need to go, but I'll stop back after my shift ends. Maybe you'll be more awake then."

He squeezed her hand.

"Get some rest, Ms. Brooks."

Kenzi peeked out through squinted lids. Black curls tickled the collar of a white coat. The familiar doctor—Paul? Was that his name? Peter? No. She couldn't even remember when he'd told her, or if he even had. Maybe she'd dreamt it.

The steady rhythm of her pulse lulled her back to sleep.

Chapter 11: Book of Conquest 3

Steve stacked three chips on the green-felted table. The color was so vibrant. Maybe it was the booze doing the thinking, but it had to be tough to keep the felt this bright and fresh on a blackjack table in Vegas. He looked up to ask the dealer how often they changed those covers, but he'd just waved out last hand.

New dealer, new deck, new shuffle. Thoughts of perpetually grass-hued tables were pushed away by a rush of possibility and a different kind of green. He put one more chip on the stack and took a gander at the incoming dealer. Steve fancied himself an amateur Sherlock—believing he could read people well. If he got a good read on the card jockey, he could usually charm them. Whether this led to good hands, Steve didn't know, but why take chances?

Jackpot. For the first time today, it was a smoking hot chick. He and Bill, the guy beside him had endured a couple of old women with croaking voices from years of cigarettes, a fat chick who looked barely old enough to gamble let alone run the table (and she was so nervous, her sweaty palms made the cards sticky. It was all he could do to keep playing), and a black guy that reminded Steve of Isaac Washington from *The Love Boat*. Once the game started though, that big toothy smile put their four other table mates out of commission, leaving Steve and Bill alone to take on several average-looking nobody dealers including the guy who'd just finished. That guy, Chip, wasn't much of a talker, but he played a tight game.

Now, though, for this little Mediterranean number, he'd risk losing a round or two. Steve dropped his hands under the table and shimmied off his wedding band, surreptitiously pocketing it. Bill smirked at him and signaled a waitress for two more whiskeys. A pack of college boys wearing designer jeans and polo shirts filled the table. Bachelor party maybe, or spring break. Didn't matter, this bitch looked too feisty for babies like them. What she needed was an experienced man to show her a good time.

Bill added two chips to his stack and Steve realized he was thinking the same thing. Bill was probably mid-to-late forties, the grey salting his hair made him look that way anyhow. Otherwise, he was just average—a small but noticeable middle-aged paunch, crow's feet when he laughed. He had a good smile though, and white teeth even if they weren't all straight. The addition of one more chip than Steve placed was an unspoken challenge; whoever had the most at the end of this curvy little olive-picker's deal, got to make the first move.

She smirked knowingly at the men ogling her—eyes a deeper green than the table in front of them. She began to deal.

"OK, boys," she said with a smooth, alto voice that reminded Steve of the phone sex operators he used to call on Fridays when Danielle went to book club. "This is my last table of the night. Don't disappoint me."

The drunken idiots made a lot of stupid moves that cost both Steve and Bill a pretty penny. Even so, between them both, they broke even by the end of her run.

"Thanks guys, that was fun." The dealer purred, breasts practically tumbling out of the black corset she was wearing.

Isaac Washington returned to take over and Steve jumped up from the table.

"Hey, uh, Lily!" he called after her, hoping he remembered the name on her badge correctly. She stopped and turned.

"Yes?"

"Can we buy you a drink?" Bill interrupted. Steve rolled his eyes, irritated. Now it was on.

She walked directly toward them narrowing the space to an intimate closeness.

"Let's cut the bullshit. You don't want to buy me a drink, you want to fuck me; both of you." She grabbed their collars, one in each hand. "Don't you?"

Steve's cock was immediately hard and throbbing against his tight denim. Bill's heavy breathing said he, too, felt the same.

Steve had never been in a threesome before, and he sure as shit never imagined he would be in one with two men and one woman instead of the other way around. But here he was, stroking himself as he watched the naked woman with a badass snake tattoo riding Bill's cock. It was pretty hot to watch although he would have loved to be more involved. Just as he decided to walk around and stick his dick in her face—no reason she couldn't blow him while fucking the old man—she called out to him.

"Fuck me in the ass. I want to feel you both at the same time."

This was also something Steve had never done. Danielle would have kicked him out for even bringing it up. He almost came just from hearing the words. He hawked up a mouthful of spit and used it to lube himself up. He bent his knees, awkwardly at first, trying to find his spot amongst the tangled limbs on the floor. He slid himself into her without trouble. Her ass was nice and tight and he could feel Bill's dick rubbing against his own with just a thin layer of Lily's cunt between them. He found a rhythm that matched theirs and closed his eyes in an ecstasy he'd never known before.

Steve lost himself among the grunts and growls of pleasure and the sloppy wet sucking sounds of pure sexual abandon. As he neared climax, he became aware that Bill had slipped out of her and now Steve was doing all the moving. He opened his eyes and looked down to watch himself, alone, sliding into this gorgeous little whore.

But it wasn't Lily's ass that he saw when he looked down. It was Bill's wide-eyed, terror-filled face staring up at him as his own dick slid in and out of the bloody hole torn into Bill's throat. It was too late to stop the orgasm that had just begun when he opened his eyes. Cum spurted out, falling into Bill's open throat. It appeared before him almost in slow motion. Steve's mind tried to wrap itself around all that was happening amongst the sea of hormones released at once into his system.

The blood and semen swirled together but didn't mix. In that frozen moment, Steve saw the jagged edges of his new friend's throat, the bubbles of blood that circled the bright white tube jutting out of the wound, and the claw marks that had shredded the lower border of his cheeks.

He fell backwards. Time was moving faster now. His cock was flaccid and sticky with Bill's blood. He turned on his hands and knees and puked. Whiskey burned his throat until there was nothing left. Feet, with perfect skin unmarred by a tattoo, appeared on the floor in front of him.

A hand grabbed a fistful of hair at the back of his head and pulled, forcing him to look upward. The green-eyed bitch smiled at him, teeth jagged, mouth covered in blood.

"How does it feel to be a whore?" she asked.

The snake, that was no longer wrapped around her body, forced its head into Steve's ass. Its undulating muscles pulled it deeper into him, breaking through intestines too small to hold its girth, until it was completely inside. Steve couldn't get enough air in his lungs to scream, the pressure was so intense. A burning pain in his neck took precedence as the room spun rapidly around. His eyes and brain, however, had enough oxygen to see the snake slithering out of his headless body before everything went black.

Chapter 12: Book of Plague 1

It was the third time the Mercedes rolled by. Daisy knew he was going to stop and she sure as hell was going to be the girl he picked up. She hadn't killed a man in three months and that was back in Miami. This was Las Vegas and so many exciting opportunities awaited.

There were men who paid for sex because they were lonely. Their wives had passed, or they were just socially awkward and it was the only chance they had. She'd never hurt these men. They were good-hearted, well-meaning gentlemen who always gave her more than she asked and never lasted long.

Then there were the men who drove Mercedes-Benzes, like the midnight metallic blue one that was currently window shopping for a date. Men like him bought sex for the same reason they did Rolexes—because they could. Afterward, they discarded the hooker where they found her, went home to their white-collar jobs and their trophy wives, and threw five bucks in the offering plate at church.

Men like Mr. Mercedes married nice girls like Daisy's sister and made them mothers. Then, after a while, when they got tired of the responsibility, they'd shoot and kill their wife and son. Men like Mr. Mercedes would find a way to blame the victim. The cops would look the other way when a rich white man says his wife (who was just poor trailer park trash) went nuts and he had no choice. She'd seen it happen, she'd felt the pain.

Those men deserved to die, and Daisy found enjoyment in putting a stiletto through their skulls. The metal, pointed heels looked hot and went just fine with her dominatrix persona. Johns never questioned her outfit and by the time the spike was parting their grey matter, they didn't care.

She smiled and walked up to the curb, maneuvering herself just in front of the other girls. They all looked like shit in their Goodwill furs and spandex skirts. Daisy kept herself clean, off drugs, and she was proud to say that her teeth were her own. Men who drove high end sports cars liked these traits in their whores.

The Mercedes rounded the block for a fourth and final time. Daisy stepped out and waved him over like a taxi. It was all he needed. Pulling up to the curb, the automatic window slid down as smooth as the smile on his face.

"Hi honey," she said. Daisy never leaned into the window—she'd learned that the hard way. Putting her hand on her hip instead, she said, "You've driven around this block at least three times. Are you lost? Need some help?"

She found with this type of guy, she had to let him take the lead. He laughed.

"Not lost, just checking out the merchandise."

They always thought they were so clever. She smiled innocently.

"See anything worth buying? Looks like you could have pretty much anything you want."

Compliment them, give them all the power.

"I might. You got plans tonight?"

"I guess that's up to you, sweets." She winked.

He leaned over and opened the door for her. She sashayed around the front of the car and got in.

"I'm Jon," he said checking the rearview mirror before pulling out.

"Pandora."

She had a thing for mythology and liked to think of herself as a living Pandora's box. Men filled her with the evils hiding inside her, evils she would release on the world. Men like her drunken father who pushed her sister Rosy to marry Darren for the money. Men like Darren who took away the two people Daisy had ever truly loved and every man like them since, who thought they had a right to do as they pleased with a woman's body. Men who bought women for sex and called them whores. It was only fair that they reap what they sowed. Pandora was simply going to help them harvest.

"Pandora, huh? That's a new one," he said. It was obvious he knew she was lying but he didn't give a shit. She could have told him her name—Daisy Fields, child of drugged out hippies, if she wanted. He'd never live to tell anyone.

"So whatcha lookin' for tonight, sweetie?" she asked.

"Drop the sweetie shit. This is a business transaction. I don't need your flirting," he said, his tone changing once he'd accelerated away from the curb.

Daisy sighed. This one was going to be a pleasure.

"So, what do you want? Anal's extra," she said, dropping the fake hooker-talk.

"How much for anal and then you suck me off?"

"You're a sick fuck. It's gonna cost you big time," she said.

"I got the money—"

"Five hundred cash and I want to see it before anything happens."

"Oh of course. I know how this works, whore."

"And we go where I say. I'm not doing it in some penthouse fucking Armani suite. The color schemes make me nauseous."

He laughed. "Whatever you say, Magellan. Point me in the direction of your finest brothel."

There was a place in the desert she'd scouted for men like Jon. Sand absorbed blood well enough and there were plenty of rock formations with crevices she could roll even the heaviest of bodies into. The desert's night crew of scavengers worked as evidence disposal for her.

She took her boots off for the anal, telling him it was too hard to bend over and balance with heels that high. Getting fucked in the ass was not her favorite but she'd taken worse when she was not in control. Now she had the upper hand and she could pretty much take anything. She kept the boot within reaching distance and tried to block out the sound of his piggish breathing as he unbuckled his jeans. It helped to think about burying her heel into his left eye.

The spitting sound heralded the oncoming discomfort and she tried to relax. His hand snaked around to grab her tit in a firm and dispassionate way. She closed her eyes tight and reached for the boot. Like a cat, she remained motionless waiting for the perfect moment to pounce. His mouth-breathing turned to grunts as he thrust into her. He wasn't very big—thank God— and she wondered why his stupid wife couldn't just suck it up once a month and save girls like Daisy the hassle. *But then I'd have no fun either.*

He neared climax and she began moaning to move the excitement along. Without warning, he suddenly pulled out—no, he jerked out of her. A high-pitched whistle-like sound accompanied the movement. She brought the heel of the boot up defensively, spinning around to face whatever was about to happen.

In the car's headlights, the outline of a woman—taller and wider-hipped than Daisy— approached her. Jon, was on his back with his knees still bent and his legs and feet tucked beneath him. His cock stood at attention, rock hard as if no one had told it plans had changed. A thick, smooth rope of some sort was wrapped around his neck. Daisy let out a peep of surprise when the rope moved, and she realized it was a large snake. What were they called? An anaconda? No, not that big, a boa constrictor—yes, that was it. A big boa. They'd show up in people's toilets sometimes in Florida—discarded pets. The woman must have brought it with her, because she showed no fear of the thing which was squeezing the literal life out of Jon.

"Put the boot down, Daisy," the woman said. Her voice deep and husky like Jessica Rabbit's. "You won't need it ever again."

"Who are you?"

"I am your goddess, and you belong to me now. I have chosen you to stand beside me as we take the earth back."

"What the fuck? You got some problems, girl. I mean, mad props for this kind of shit." Daisy gestured to the snake, which was finishing with Jon the john. "But, uh, I got me, OK? I mean I don't need no goddess or some mythical shit."

The woman approached Daisy, stepping effortlessly over the snake and its victim. Daisy threatened with the boot, but the woman knocked it to the ground. The goddess pushed Daisy backwards and straddled her. Daisy had never been raped by a woman before, but she guessed the crazy bitch would need a strap on or something. She felt nothing between them. Suddenly a tingling sensation that seemed to drop out of the woman on top of her crawled like a centipede around Daisy's vulva and into her vagina.

"I heard the living creature saying, 'Come.' I looked, and behold, a black vine; and she who grew it had a pair of scales in her hand. And I heard the goddess's voice in the center of the living creatures saying, 'A fuck for a denarius, and pestilence for a denarius; but do not damage the public reputation.'" The goddess laughed.

Icy jolts of frozen lightening shot into her core. With it came a universal knowledge and a vision of the world to come. Daisy Fields stood with the three other women who would bring about the apocalypse. In that moment, she saw the end of this world and the beginning of a new kingdom where Lilith would reign as the Holy Goddess. If she agreed to give herself, body and soul, to the goddess, Daisy would hold court beside her. Yes, of course she would—in fact, she already had. For this, the goddess provided her with a new weapon, far better than a cheap boot. A living tattoo of deadly vines that beckoned from her sex and drew victims to her would spread like kudzu across the flesh of the earth. Her victims would suffocate and waste away.

"When you share this with others, you worship me," the dark woman said.

Daisy watched as the snake's shadow merged with the goddess and the darkness swallowed them.

"Yes," she said.

She drove Jon's Mercedes back to town and left it in a parking garage five blocks from her apartment. The two girls she shared the place with were still working. Daisy would go back out tonight too. First though, she'd need to hide the money she'd taken from Jon, whose real name was Phillip Simon Price, and ditch the wallet. She passed the filthy full-length mirror hanging on the door to the only closet in the entire place and stopped. Black lines peeked out from the top of her skirt. She pulled the skirt down, she had no underwear on, and laughed. Coming out of her cunt were at least a dozen black branches that ended just below her hip bones. They looked like trails the goddess's cold lightening had left behind, as if someone had tattooed them onto her. She touched her skin and the lines rippled and inched up onto the tip of her finger. She pulled her hand back and shook it. Looking at her finger, she saw tiny tips of black that had managed to settle into her flesh in that split second of connection.

What would those things do to a dick? She smiled at herself in the mirror. Oh, but she knew. She knew so much now.

The widower—Guy, his name was—the one who only ever asked for a blow job and always ran his fingers through her hair gently while she did him, was waiting for her. She saw the headlights of his pick-up come on as she stepped back out onto "her" corner.

Tonight, he wouldn't be getting a BJ. Nope. Guy was going to be honored as the first man to truly open Pandora's box.

"You won't be lonely anymore, Guy," she promised as she walked up to his Chevy S-10.

Chapter 13: Book of Kenzi 4

Kenzi woke when the nagging pain in her shoulder became too much to bear. A beam of sunlight fell over her ankles. She tried to move her legs to kick the covers off but found them both immobile. The room was large and private and familiar. This was the ICU. She'd been in these rooms many times over the years when her mother OD'd or got a bad batch of some street drug. She may have even been in this very room before. She couldn't be sure—they all looked the same after a while.

She remembered a little. She was going to bring her mom in again, maybe try to see the cute doctor, too. So, where was her mother and what was she doing here as a patient?

She tried to lift her right hand, but her shoulder screamed in protest. Lifting her left, she touched her head. Her hair was a matted, greasy mess. Patting herself down from there, she assessed her situation. A bandage covered the front of her right shoulder which was probably why it hurt to move it. There was a big IV line that went into her upper arm on the left and it was secured there with a piece of clear plastic tape. It was her belly that alarmed her the most. Fresh scars crisscrossed in a crooked T shape. Snuggled in to the small square of uncut flesh to the left of the T was a plastic bag. It was taped to her stomach and a fleshy pink ring could be seen just inside it. In the bottom of the bag, there was a brown fluid. No. This was not what she thought it was. No. She'd rather be dead than to have to shit through her stomach into a bag for the rest of her life. Gang Bangers who got shot or stabbed ended up like this. Not her. An image flashed in her mind. Gang bangers— one with a knife and one with a gun.

"Hey," she tried to scream but her dry throat refused to let out anything more than a squeak. "Help."

Nothing. She looked around the bed, her lower half forgotten. There had to be a call button somewhere. The rails were up and she couldn't reach the tray table. Her left hand patted the bed on her right side. It came upon a firm plastic tube. She followed its course into the side of her chest.

"Oh my god, they tried to kill me. Why didn't they?"

She was so weak that there was no way she could even pull herself up. There was no call button anywhere. She was alone.

The sunlight that had warmed her feet was now just a tiny sliver on the floor by the far wall. It was dark in the room otherwise and, with no one there to witness it, Kenzi broke down. Tears spilled from her eyes, ignoring the drought warning from her dry mouth, and soon turned into sobs which turned into chokes. Every hiccough hurt her throat, her ribs, her stomach, but fresh, raw pain felt good and so she let her cries release her.

"Ms. Brooks, you're awake," a soft, feminine voice said from behind the curtain pulled halfway around her bed.

A nurse, dark hair, about Kenzi's height but with a much better body—even underneath the scrub top and pants—came into view.

"They tried to kill me," Kenzi croaked.

The nurse navigated around the mechanical obstacles without turning on the lights and Kenzi appreciated that. No need for anyone to see her puffy, red eyes. She sat down beside Kenzi, her arm propped on the other side of the bed, thus pinning her patient in place. With her free hand, the nurse pushed Kenzi's hair away from her forehead in a motherly gesture.

"Yes, they did. Men did this to you. Men abandon you, they use you, they sell you like property and they hurt you. They always hurt you. Then when you are at your lowest, another comes along to *save* you and manages to make everything even worse."

This was not what she expected from her nurse.

"You have beautiful eyes. Has anyone ever told you that?" the woman asked.

Kenzi squirmed and cocked her head, a habitual move that caused her hair to fall back down, covering her "ugly eye."

"No," she answered honestly.

The nurse leaned into Kenzi's face. "There are more men waiting for you. Police want to talk to you, doctors want to poke at you, and there is still drug money to be paid, isn't there?"

The heart rate monitor picked up its pace as memories came back in clips.

"My mom! I need to check on her." Kenzi sat up, ignoring the burning protest from her gut.

"Your mother is dead. Your friend Gloria is here, two doors down, brain dead."

"No. That's a lie."

"The men know what's best for you. They will tell you when they decide you are strong enough. They will want you to make the call—pull the plug. She has no one else. Oh Kenzi, so much pain is still ahead for you."

"Why are you saying these things to me? Why aren't you helping me?"

Her throat ached from talking. Her tongue was sticky, and she was so very tired.

"I *am* helping you, Kenzi. But you have to help me, too. I need you."

"What?" Nothing was making sense and Kenzi could not keep her eyes open any longer. The lights in the room flickered to life behind her eyelids.

"Is that you I hear, Ms. Brooks?" This was not the same woman she'd just been talking to. The voice was deeper, and gravely—that of a life-long smoker.

Kenzi opened her eyes. There was a new nurse standing at the curtain, her hands in the pockets of a scrub jacket. This one was older with her grey hair cut short and wire-rimmed glasses high up on her nose. Had she dozed off and they changed shifts already?

"I thought so. You must have been talking in your sleep but that's a good sign." She checked the printed EKG strip. "And it must have been a doozy of a dream too." She jotted some notes on the strip where the spikes were close together.

Kenzi watched in silence.

"You need your whistle wet?" She picked up a cup, dipped a pink sponge-tipped stick into it, and ran it over Kenzi's lips.

"More," she asked. There was strength to her voice now.

"Here, take it."

She put the cup in Kenzi's right hand and the stick in her better working left.

"I'm going to call Dr. Patel to come see you. He'll be happy to hear you're awake," she said, reaching for the call box that sat on the mobile tray stand on the far side of the bed. "Meanwhile, if you need anything, push this red button. My name is Jane. I'll be taking care of you tonight."

"What was the other nurse's name? The one that was here before you came in?"

"You mean the day nurse from this afternoon?"

"No, it was night, the other nurse here with you. She was in here right before you came in."

"Honey, there was no other nurse in here before me. You were dreaming."

"No, I wasn't. She was here. We talked, and she said my mother is dead and my friend Gloria is a few doors down, but she isn't going to survive, and the police want to talk to me." Kenzi said after sucking all the room temperature water from the sponge.

The nurse stopped arranging the tray, and looked at Kenzi, her face confused.

"Where did you hear that? How long have you been awake?"

"So, it's true? My mom is dead? And Gloria? Please tell me she'll be OK. Why do the police want to talk to me? I don't know anything." But she thought she did. Maybe she remembered everything all of a sudden, even the bird and the snake.

The monitor alarm interrupted, warning Kenzi to calm down. Jane took the cup of water back and put a warm but wrinkled hand to her cheek. She leaned down so that her face was looming over Kenzi's. Yes, she was a smoker and a coffee drinker. Kenzi suppressed the urge to crinkle her nose.

"Now, I need you to calm down before we have to give you some medicine. I don't want to do that." She rubbed her thumb soothingly across Kenzi's cheek.

The sensation of a loving gesture coupled with the menacing stance and awful breath almost sent Kenzi over the edge. She inhaled as deep as she could. She had to get control of herself if she was going to get any answers. Otherwise these people would just keep giving her medications to make her sleep and she would never get out of here. The alarm stopped. The beeping returned— still rapid but obviously not too fast.

"Good girl. Now, I am going to go call Dr. Patel to come see you. He is a nice young doctor, probably around your age. I think you'll like him. He is working with Dr. Childs who might come in tonight as well or may wait and see you tomorrow morning." She adjusted Kenzi's blankets, tucking her in.

"But the other nurse that was here. She said my mom…"

"Listen, I think maybe you overheard people talking while you were still sedated.

Your brain made it into a dream that a nurse was here telling you these things. I'm sure no nurse would ever tell you that. Dr. Patel will explain everything to you when he gets here. Nothing for you to worry about right now, OK?" She headed toward the door, effectively cutting off the conversation.

"There was someone in here—you had to have passed her when you came in. She sat on my bed, right here." Kenzi patted the bed on her left.

Jane turned at the door. "There was no one in here. I promise you. I know this because there are guards standing at your door. No one gets past them unless cleared by the nurse on duty and that's me. Now just try to get some rest."

Before Kenzi could respond Jane turned out the light, leaving her in darkness yet again. If anyone else visited her that night, she wasn't aware.

Chapter 14: Book of Kenzi 5

Dr. Patel—Kenzi remembered his name—came around the curtain without waiting for her reply to his knock. Oh god, it was the cute doc who always seemed to be stuck taking care of her mom. She wondered if he remembered her, or worse, the time Marilyn tried to set the two of them up. *Please don't remember that.*

"Good day, Miss Brooks. It's lovely to see you up and alert. You're looking more like your old sassy self." *Shit, he remembers.* He smiled. Kenzi couldn't help but notice how every part of his face participated in the smile. It sparkled like fireworks in his midnight colored eyes. "How are you feeling?"

Her mouth was still dry. She swallowed.

"OK, I guess."

Her throat tried to catch the words as they came out and it hurt. She had so many questions to ask, but she didn't know where to start. The thing was, she didn't know how many of her own thoughts and memories were real and how many were fragments of drug induced dreams. The last thing she needed was to say something that made him question her sanity. She decided to let him do the talking and ask questions from there.

He walked to the bedside stand and picked up the cup and sponge.

"No," she croaked. "Water please."

"That's not up to me, Miss Brooks. I'm sorry. This is all I can offer you right now."

He pushed the cup at her again, and she took it. She swabbed her mouth.

"Then what *can* you do for me?" she asked. "I mean, why are you here?"

The smile fell off his face, his shoulders slumped, and he hung his head for a moment before straightening up and facing her once more. The subconscious movement that lasted only seconds, may have been missed by any other patient but Kenzi knew the look of self-defeat well and saw it for what it was. She knew he was a doctor in training from their visits before, so she did understand that he had to get permission from other doctors to make certain decisions.

"I'm sorry," she said. *Good job, Kenzi. He'll remember you now that you're acting just like your mother. Demanding he do something.*

"I'm a resident physician, Miss Brooks. I can see to your medical problems and write some basic orders, but any major decision about your health has to go through both my attending and the other specialists involved in your care." He touched the bag attached to her belly. "The general surgeon gets to decide when you can eat."

She nodded. "I understand, I do. I'm just still a little confused. I don't remember exactly what happened to me." *Lies.*

"That's not unusual. There's plenty of time to consider it. We don't know exactly either. There are many questions." He paused. "We were hoping you'd be able to tell us."

She shrugged.

"The police have been waiting to speak with you. So far, we've been able to keep them away because of your medical condition, but you're doing so much better. We won't be able to for much longer."

It was as if he could read her thoughts. He knew she remembered more than she was telling, and he was warning her.

"I don't remember anything," she said, trying to sound nonchalant. "So just tell them I have amnesia and I don't want to press charges."

"You really don't remember, do you?" He sat on the side of her bed and took her hand. "When they looked in your house, they found three dead men and your mother—"

She sat up, her stomach and shoulder screaming in protest. "My mother is dead. I know." Dr. Patel squeezed her hand.

"Your mother was shot in the head, Miss Brooks. She was dead when they arrived at the scene. You were the only one found alive. I'm so sorry. Your mother was always a challenge, but I enjoyed caring for her and visiting with you."

"No. I'm dreaming. This is a dream." And then, "Gloria Paulson—is she here?"

"So, you do know her? Yes, she is. We've been trying to find the next of kin."

Kenzi shook her head interrupting him, "She has no family."

"Your name was on some things that were found in her bags."

"She's like my mom, more so than Marilyn really."

Tears pushed themselves past the emotional dam she'd built against her mother and ran down her cheeks. Perhaps she loved her mother more than she'd thought or maybe she was finally mourning the loss of the mother she never really had.

"Mrs. Paulson. She was beaten very badly, very, very badly." He pronounced his v's like w's. "She suffered significant brain damage. She was alive when they found her, but I'm afraid the EEG results are not very optimistic."

"EEG?"

"Oh, I'm sorry. An EEG measures brain activity."

"Gloria would agree with that," Kenzi said half-joking. She did not want to face any of what he'd just told her. Three dead men in her house. One was surely her mother's newest drug buddy, the other two would have been the men who attacked her. She remembered a lot but didn't necessarily trust her own memories. Had she actually killed the guy with her rabbit's foot, or were the other things—the bird, the woman and that giant snake—real too?

She reached around to the tube in her chest. The hole there was quite tender. The bird had stuck his head into it.

"Don't pull on that, OK? It's a chest tube. You were shot and there was some lung damage. It won't be there forever though, I promise." He paused. The pause brought her back from her thoughts of beaks plugging bullet holes and snakes killing bullies.

"Miss Brooks, are you all right? Do you understand what I said? I'm so sorry about your mother. I really am, but right now, you must focus on getting better so you can remember what happened. The police only want to help you." He picked up the journal laying on her bedside table. Kenzi's heart skipped a beat. How had that gotten there? Had he read it? Who brought it here? "Maybe try to write some things you do remember in here. It might help jog your memory." He plucked a pen from the pocket of his white coat. "Now, I don't give my pens to just anyone, Miss Brooks—"

She snatched the journal from him and grabbed the pen, too. "Would you please call me Kenzi? That Miss Brooks crap is irritating. My mother caused a drug war inside my house. You already know all about my mother. I'm sure you've heard about my house and what it looked like. I don't know why the cops care about any of that. They don't seem to care when people shoot each other on the streets." She fought back angry tears and cursed her weakness.

"OK, Kenzi, I'm sorry to upset you. Once again, I am truly sorry about your mum. I'll let the police fill you in on everything else. We don't need to talk about it anymore." He stood up and walked out.

What the fuck is wrong with you, Kenzi? Be nice. He's sure trying.

Kenzi watched him, her throat on fire and eyes watering. Why did she care what he thought anyway? He'd never considered her as anything more than ghetto trash, because that's all she was. Patel was just another doctor who didn't give a shit about her beyond her blood pressure and heart rate. *You know that's not true. He does care. He's a good person.* She didn't need him. She wondered if he knew the whole truth of what they must have found in her house. She closed her eyes, let the tears slip down her cheeks. Gloria always said to never show your weakness. 'Be strong, show them what you got, and later, in private, you can cry all you want.' It was OK now though, OK to cry.

Footsteps approaching her bed and the noise of the curtain brought her out of her slumber. That exotic scent wafted in on the breeze. Dr. Patel. She kept her eyes closed pretending to be asleep. He sat down on the bed again. *Do all doctors do that?*

"Open your eyes, Kenzi," he said gently as if he knew she was faking. She obeyed. He held a glass of ice chips and a spoon in his hand. "Ice chips?"

She sat up and opened her mouth like a child. He spooned some in. There was nothing in this world better than those small bits of ice. She took spoonful after spoonful in silence. Dr. Patel was smiling. *No way do doctors do this kind of stuff. This is for nurses. Why is he being so nice?* The moment was strangely intimate, but it was also comforting.

"Now, this is just between you and me, OK? I didn't ask the surgeon, so none of this happened." He winked.

"You have heterochromia." He blushed. "I'm sure you know that of course. I just wasn't sure if you knew the medical term."

"I don't know what you're talking about," she said, her mouth full of ice. A piece fell out and landed on her lap. He picked it up and threw it across the room. They laughed. This was nice.

"Your eyes. Heterochromia—different colors."

Kenzi stiffened. The temperature in the room dropped ten degrees and her stomach decided that the ice chips did not taste so great from its vantage. She dropped her head, letting her hair fall over the colorless one as she'd done so many times before. He pushed it back behind her ear with a slow sweep of his hand.

"It's actually quite rare." He stumbled over words. "And very becoming, if I might be so bold. And, uh, fascinating from a mythology standpoint. I've always been interested in things like that. Ancient Greek and Roman mythology, polytheism, and such. I've done a lot of research on Ambrosia, you know, the 'nectar of the gods' and some experts believe it was honey based, like a mead. That's how I got into bee keeping. I want to develop my own Ambrosia."

He rattled on, far off the subject of her eyes. It didn't matter what it was he talked about. She wanted to hear more. The way he talked—so easy and down to earth and just so nice—made her forget who she was. She let him continue, patiently, waiting for him to get back to the point. He paused. Her stomach decided it would give the ice another try. Kenzi used the opportunity to pick up the spoon and take another scoop of ice.

"Careful not to get sick. We'll both be in trouble," he said but never lost his pace. "Some cultures believe that a person with heterochromia can see into heaven and earth at the same time. They are sensitive to beings from both the here and the hereafter." He smiled at her. "What do you think of that? Have you ever seen an angel?"

Had she? The Scribble Man, the giant black bird, and the shadow woman with her snake— were they angels sent to rescue her? Why, though? There was nothing special about her.

"Patel!" a deep male voice yelled from the doorway.

He jumped up, knocking the cup of ice off the table. Kenzi watched, devastated as her precious ice and the promise of an actual drink from the small amount of melted water at the bottom of the cup spilled out across the floor. The man standing in the doorway was much older and certainly not as pleasant.

Dr. Patel stood silently, hands at his sides, head dropped.

"Yes sir," he said. He stepped toward the door and slipped on some ice.

Regaining his balance, he walked out of the room without looking back at Kenzi. She heard the other doctor ask if he had spoken to a Dr. Altrey about the ice chips but did not hear Patel's answer.

With Dr. Patel's diversion gone, all her anxieties came rushing back as if they lived in the fire kingdom and the ice had frightened them away. Her mother was dead. Forever. For good. And Gloria was probably not coming out of this alive either. The police wanted answers she couldn't give them. Whatever happened in her house was bad. There was no way, she decided, that she could have taken on two men and killed them with just a small rabbit's foot. Therefore, someone else *must* have been there.

She had to get out of the hospital as soon as possible.

Chapter 15: Book of War 1

"Wow, coming in with twenty minutes to spare! And on a Monday, no less," Doug sang. "You must have had a boring weekend, doc."

Dr. Cynthia Parris shot her nurse the stink-eye before dumping her tote beneath the desk and setting down the Starbucks carrier.

"You should be thankful for boring weekends," she said, handing him the chilled soy caramel macchiato and the bag with his lightly buttered croissant.

He could be such a diva. She smiled cheerfully at her private joke. Doug was a godsend, really. Since leaving the hospital practice behind and opening the Women's Acute Care Clinic, good help proved hard to find. She'd been hesitant to hire a male nurse initially, since the women coming to her were often self-conscious about the type of help they needed. But Doug had a way of making them feel at ease and immediately welcomed, without judgement.

"Packed full today. I guess some people live exciting lives on their weekends off anyway. I'm so jelly," Doug said.

The comment earned him a warning look from Cynthia. No woman coming in for an STD check or an unwanted pregnancy felt lucky about their lives. Doug put his hands up in surrender.

"My bad, my bad. You know I'm only joking, Cyn. It's stressful enough being a gay man in this world. I can't even imagine having a uterus with white-haired politicians crawling all over it like flies on shit. Women are lucky to have you at least." He sipped his coffee.

The first three patients were straightforward. A forty-two-year-old with chlamydia— an anniversary gift from her philandering husband of twenty-two years—followed by two patients with sore but otherwise intact vaginas after weekends of rough sex. She was just finishing their charts when Doug knocked gently on the open office door.

"The next patient is here. She's ready when you are."

Cynthia nodded, "OK."

Doug stayed in the doorway.

"Look, I…you know I am not one to question a woman's motives for the choices she makes or the story she tells us. Lord knows, we've heard some tales. But there's something really off about this one." He fiddled with the corner of a manila folder.

Dr. Parris had two separate record keeping systems—the electronic records she kept for billing purposes and the paper charts for the special "under the table" consults.

"What makes her different than anyone else?" Cynthia asked, shoving a chunk of cold bagel in her mouth.

"Well, for one, she looks about twenty-eight weeks along. It's going to be tricky. She is just off, I don't trust her. Be careful, and if you need me, buzz me." Doug dropped the chart on Cynthia's desk.

Cynthia opened it. Single, twenty-eight years old, unwanted pregnancy, unknown last menstrual period, no prenatal care to this point. The patient, Lily Adams, had no medical problems or prior surgeries. *Yes, because she never goes to the doctor.*

Twenty-eight weeks was further along than she was comfortable with, but at the same time, there must be a good reason for this woman to have waited. Maybe she was in an abusive relationship, maybe it was money. It didn't matter though, did it? If she started judging, she was no better than the people she fought against.

When Cynthia opened this clinic, it was for a reason. With the state of politics being what they were nowadays, women especially, deserved a safe place to go without Big Brother breathing down their necks. As far as she was concerned, there would be no more questionable looks or a line of hoops to jump though when a woman found herself in a delicate but undesired way. She would never forget that feeling of dirtiness, the way they tried to shame her. The things they shouted from the street outside. No woman under her care would ever feel that way. That was a promise.

She grabbed the recommended herbs from the large cabinet behind her desk. They'd need to be weighed, crushed, and distributed into four capsules. She would have the patient take two in the morning and two at bedtime the day before she wanted to abort. These herbs would stop the baby's heartbeat. The next morning, the patient would insert the evening primrose tablets into her vagina and labor would ensue. Then she would simply arrive at the hospital where they would discover the fetal death and allow labor to proceed.

She handed the bottles and the hand scrawled note with their correct ratios to Doug on her way to exam room one. He could prepare the tablets while she did the exam.

It was unnerving to walk into a room and find the patient on the table staring straight ahead. In fact, she couldn't recall ever having the patient not immediately turn to greet her. Now, all she could see was long straight black hair and a body swimming in the "one size fits all" sickly green exam gown.

"Hello, Ms. Adams. I'm Dr. Parris."

She walked around to face the woman. Immediately noticeable was her gravid abdomen pushing against the gown. This woman was further than twenty-eight weeks along. Dark eyes appraised the doctor at the same time she was evaluating her patient.

"Lily," she said in a husky yet sensual voice.

Kathleen Turner—Body Heat—*great movie.* The file said she wasn't a smoker, but her voice had that scratchy quality to it.

"Well, Lily, I'm pleased to meet you." She opened the chart and pretended to read it for the first time. "So, you think you are about seven months pregnant?"

It was best never to start with the abortion question, she usually kept the conversation open and nonjudgmental, letting the patient get to that on their own.

"Something like that. I need your assistance," she said.

She was going to get right to the point, then. That was fine too. The way the day was booked, Cynthia would be happy if they all were this straight-forward.

"You are a daughter of Tituba, the slave witch, are you not?" the woman continued.

The question took Cynthia off-guard. How would anyone know that? Parris was an old family name in New England, there had to be thousands of them. And most people, upon seeing that she was black, never connected her in any way to the incidents in Salem so long ago. She'd never told anyone about her heritage, not even Doug. But it was true. Tituba, the first woman accused of witchcraft in Salem, was her ancestor.

"I'm not sure what you mean. I am, however, a doctor. I can help you with your condition."

"You are the direct female descendant of Tituba, a slave owned by Samuel Parris, who confessed to witchcraft. She was a true witch. There is nothing wrong with that and you shouldn't hide it. That is why I sought you out," the woman said.

Cynthia sat down on her wheeled stool in front of the bed. Lily Adams had done some significant research on her. While a little disturbing, it was also flattering and almost freeing. The woman's olive-skinned legs hung bare. She hadn't used the paper sheet to cover her lap. A tattoo of a snake wound its way up her left leg with the tail beginning on the top of her foot. It was a beautifully detailed piece. Cynthia admired the work of a skilled tattoo artist. She was warming up to this exotic young woman.

"Yes, Tituba is my ancestor and the only confessed witch to be released. I am proud of that heritage," she folded up the band on her wrist covering a pentagram tattoo. "I just have to be careful here. Many in the community would never approve of who I am and what I do."

Cynthia smiled reassuringly. The woman smiled back, a small twist of her lips that did not reach past the corners of her mouth to show in her eyes, but it was a welcome change from the otherwise flat affect.

"Now," Cynthia continued, "how can I help you, Lily?"

"Something is wrong with this pregnancy. It's gone bad, everything inside me is bad. I need you to look; I need your help with it."

This wasn't the first time Cynthia had seen a woman convince herself there was something wrong with the baby to ease the guilt of an abortion. She asked the basic health history questions, taking minimal notes, and then declared it time to do the exam.

Lily Adams placed her feet into the stirrups and slid her bottom toward the end of the bed without prompting. Cynthia didn't stop her although she was intending to first do an abdominal exam and listen for the baby's heartbeat. She could always do that afterwards. The patient was long overdue for a pap smear anyway.

She scooted her chair into the space between the woman's legs, noting that the snake wound further up the leg before wrapping itself around her torso. Cynthia didn't recall seeing a tattoo on Lily's neck; she wondered how far it went. She would look for it when she got to the abdominal exam.

Cynthia snapped the rechargeable light into the handle of the plastic speculum. It was such a great invention. This way, the light shone directly into the vagina rather than emanating from a lamp which sat either behind the shoulder or in front of it. Either way visualization was often limited by the shadow of the physician's head or the lamp itself.

She squeezed a dollop of lubricant onto the blades and smeared it with a gloved finger. Gently, she spread open the labia which surprisingly weren't shaved. These days all young women shaved themselves until they looked prepubescent. Cynthia hated it. No woman wanted to do that for herself, it was a lot of work. Men, sick perverts that they were, had encouraged this trend. But Lily's pubic hair was untrimmed but clean. This was the way nature had intended.

Sliding the speculum in, Cynthia opened it, first just a centimeter to see the tissue change from the wrinkled folds of the vagina to the smooth surface of the cervix. Only there was no cervix. Instead, the light disappeared into a swirling black vortex. Confused, Cynthia leaned in closer, losing sight of the snake's tail in her peripheral vision. The black hole at the end of the scarlet tunnel was hypnotic. A dark universe orbited in the infinite space. It was like watching the big bang as it began.

The obsidian vastness throbbed like a reverse strobe light. With each pulsation, it creeped closer to Cynthia. Pap smear forgotten, she reached up absent-mindedly to scratch at her throat where a hair or piece of lint tickled her. A reptilian tail suddenly thrust up beneath her chin tilting her head back. She opened her mouth to scream just as the nothingness had reached Lily's vaginal opening. It shot through the air like squid's ink and into Cynthia, forcing her jaws wide, filling the spaces inside her with its blackness.

The patient spoke, but the sound came from all around and within her. "And I heard a mass of living cells say 'come and see.' A rod, fiery red, was plunged inside. And it was granted to the one who sat before it to take peace from the earth, and that people should first judge and then kill one another; and there was given to her a voice to speak death to the masses."

Spreading like warm tea through her body, Lilith's hate-filled essence thinned into microscopic threads that slid easily between first cells and then molecules forming the cell walls. The sensation—as if an embroidery needle was working itself inside her—was not unpleasant, but foreign nonetheless. Filaments wove themselves around Cynthia's DNA like a caduceus, inserting bits of Lily's memories and awakening ancient occult knowledge within the doctor. The experience was profoundly erotic but not in a pornographic way. Instead the mixing of two bodies was more instinctual and ritualistic.

Cynthia walked out of the room, her mind filled with whispers of the past and instructions for the future.

"Did everything go OK?" Doug asked. "You were in there forever! I was just about ready to knock on the door."

"Everything is fine," Cynthia said.

It was fine. For the first time in a long time, Cynthia felt free. This job drained her of her inherited talents. She knew there was a higher purpose for her. Lily had made her see that there was nothing to be ashamed of. Her ancestry should not have to be hidden from anyone. Tituba was arrested and tortured, doctors like herself were shot, attacked, bombed as were the women they treated. Women were judged for the same things men were constantly being pardoned for, but women paid the ultimate price. Bitches, Whores, Demons, Sluts, Bimbos, Sinners, Baby killers, Black Widows, Homewreckers. She'd heard it all.

"Cancel the rest of my day," she said.

Doug stared at her, hands on his hips, brows furrowed.

"I'm fine, Doug, really," she smiled and touched his arm. "But I quit. I won't be back. Good luck to you. I'm sure there will be a place for good men like you when it's all over."

She took off her white jacket and handed it to her stunned nurse. The carefully measured herbs lay with her instructions on the counter beside him. There they would stay. That sort of medicine wasn't needed now; there was only one answer for the problems facing humanity. Lily knew, and now she did too.

Chapter 16: Book of War 2

The clinic opened at 9:00am but the church members arrived by 8:00, coolers in tow. Children ran around the legs of their mothers and fathers. Lawn chairs were set back from the sidewalk with umbrellas attached. If it weren't for the poster boards with hateful messages scrawled in blood-red and black, Cyn thought, it could all be easily mistaken for a fair or reunion in the making.

Across the street, in the parking lot of the facility, volunteers donned orange vests and stood waiting, kicking pebbles around nervously. They avoided eye contact with their adversaries across the way. The abortionist arrived at ten minutes to nine—an old man with a tuft of downy white hair that ruffled in the breeze of his forward momentum. The orange vests surrounded him. He too avoided a direct glance at the gathering crowd across the street. He carried a black leather bag reminiscent of doctors who once arrived in the middle of the night in a carriage to see to a laboring mother.

The signs across the street were hoisted. While the children chased each other gleefully, their parents hurled insults and hateful monikers at the old man.

"Murderer!"

"Baby Killer"

"Go to Hell!"

He never turned or acknowledged the haters, but his black, bullet-proof vest stood out amid the sea of orange. This uniform took the place of a white coat for any doctor who publicly provided abortions to women in need. Dr. Cynthia Parris was all too aware of that sad fact. The coolers, umbrellas, and the presence of children belonging to the protestors gave a false sense of security, but men and women were killed every day in scenes just like this. Clinics set on fire, chemical bombs and the like took multiple lives in the name of God. "Pro-life" meant different things to different people.

"Doc? Cyn? Is that you?" A man in an orange security vest called out from the parking lot of the clinic. It was Doug. Cynthia ignored him. Instead she set about distributing the contents of a red thermos into cups on the children's blanket.

"Is that man talking to you?" a tow-headed girl asked.

"I don't know. Maybe. He must think I'm someone else," she said, keeping her head down.

"He's a bad man anyhow, huh? He's helping those ladies kill babies in there." The child nodded as if needing no confirmation from anyone else.

"Here. Take your drink and run along," Cynthia handed her a cup.

Cynthia Parris, disciple of Lilith, who was known to her new friends as Melanie Pryor, had been a member of the church for a week now. This was her first protest. Melanie volunteered to oversee the snacks and water. She made sure the kids all had a drink before things got crazy. Initially, for them, she'd considered grape Kool-Aid but thought it too cliché, so settled on tropical punch.

The children settled down after their refreshment and many napped on blankets in the shade. The cheap coolers wouldn't keep the contents ice-cold for long. This was good as the bombs inside were set to go off once the dry ice separating the reactants began to sublimate. It wouldn't be a large explosion, but a succession of smaller ones. The shrapnel spread would never reach the clinic across the street but should take care of the judgmental, God-worshipping hypocrites on this side.

Just as the dark thoughts inside her head had instructed.

When the job was done, Lilith would come to collect the souls and Cyn would stand by her side.

Nothing more than a spark to get the fire going but Cyn was still proud to be a part of it. She was War and her horse was the red blood of judgement. War took many lives and there were many more to take in the name of the Goddess. This small tragedy would be viewed as a counter attack by the pro-choice movement—a movement which, under the current presidential regime was struggling to keep its work legal and safe. As the lone survivor of the tragedy, Melanie Pryor would become an activist in the pro-life movement, a voice for a rally on Washington D.C. A call to action to rival that of the women who marched in Lilith's name the day after the president took office. That day would be her day to truly shine, to honor her ancestor, Tituba. No more petty battles, but a war for the after-life of earth.

Taking out those fools who had rewritten Lilith's history, who removed her from the story of creation, who vilified her and demonized her for her own rape and torture would be satisfying. But men, who thought they controlled women's bodies, who believed in their own sexual dominance, were also targets. There would be no place for souls like that in the Kingdom of Lilith. No, those who vilified the Goddess and women like her would suffer and suffer greatly until their souls disintegrated back to the dust from whence they came, never to know the God who created them in his own image or rewarded them for their evil misogynistic deeds.

Yes, there would be much to do once the war began, once The Apocalypse began. Cynthia had never imaged she would live to see it, but now, she was promised not only to see the end of the world but also the end of Heaven, the end of a timeless regime of hate and death in the name of scripture. She smiled. Soon, she would meet her ancestor again and share in the spoils of the power of womanhood.

Women who dared to patronize the clinic were rushed in by the volunteers. Some hung their heads in shame as the Christians spat at them, calling them killers and sluts and cursing them to Hell where murderers belong. They assured tearful girls that their God hated them. Cyn checked the temperature with an app on her iPhone. It was time—time to walk away.

She looked over at the children. Their pale bodies and blue lips had gone unnoticed in the frenzy of holy spite. God had taken many of Lilith's children, as had Death. She was warned not to let them suffer but their little minds had already been poisoned by their parents and were no longer salvageable. So, Cynthia had done as commanded. A bad seed would grow into a bad weed, and so it must be stopped. She was not sorry for it.

"I need to use a restroom," she said to the heavyset woman smoking in her lawn chair. "Can I leave my sign with you until I get back?"

"Yup," the woman murmured, cigarette moving with her lips as if conducting the chants of her cohorts.

The gas station was a block away. It would be a safe place to be when the bombs went off. She only wished she could watch, but she couldn't take the chance. Melanie Pryor had to be the victim too. There could be no question as to how she'd survived.

The bathroom was on the outside of the gas station and the key was attached to a paint roller minus the roll itself. It was a clumsy and awkward thing to carry, but at least it wasn't a hub cap. She'd seen movies where it was attached to a hub cap. Stupid. Who would want to keep a key to a nasty, filthy place like that anyway? It stunk and may as well have been an outhouse complete with a wide-open hole in the ground. Cynthia stood locked inside, holding onto the roller, and listening. She tried breathing through her mouth but could almost taste the sewage so switched back to nose breathing and tried to desensitize herself.

She checked her phone. *Any second now.* Waiting inside the concrete, malodorous bunker, she occupied herself with reading graffiti. *For a good time, call Mary. Life sucks, but death sucks more.* Her personal favorite: *There is no such thing as reality, so don't sweat it.* She laughed and wiped the sweat running down her own forehead. How true it all was. Several loud popping sounds like muffled gunshots came in quick succession rather than in unison as she had hoped.

Boom. Boom. Boom. Boom.

The ground beneath her shook and the air vibrated against her skin raising goosebumps. When it all stopped, silence reigned as if the popping sounds she'd just heard were that of her own eardrums leaving her deaf. She opened the door and the world outside greeted her with a splash of color and roar of chaos. A crowd was beginning to gather cautiously stepping away from their hiding places like the munchkins of Oz. Murmurs rose to shouts and screams. Everyone had their phones in hand, but no one was dialing 911. A thick plume of black smoke rose from the wreckage gradually displaying a bloody carnage.

Sirens wailed. Cyn ignored the onlookers as she walked through the smoke, allowing it to bring tears to her eyes. She pretended to be in shock. It was easy to see that among the former crowd—now just a myriad of charred limbs and broken bodies—none survived.

She had time for a surreptitious grin before an orange-vested volunteer grabbed and shook her shoulders.

"Are you OK?"

"I...I..." she stammered before buckling her knees and collapsing at the man's feet.

She was jostled to the lawn in front of the clinic and wrapped in a blanket. With knowing eyes above an expressionless mouth, Cynthia Parris, daughter of Tituba, watched the apocalypse begin.

Chapter 17: Book of Plague 2

The tattooed branches had spread. They covered her torso, buttocks, back, shoulders, arms and they'd begun inching up her neck. Daisy wasn't worried. The lines were beautiful, she looked like a goddess herself. The goddess of the winter woods, maybe. It never wintered here in the desert, but she'd seen pictures of leafless trees standing stark against the white landscape of snow. That was her body now. Only her branches were not in hibernation, they were very much alive and very deadly.

It was more interesting than worrisome the way this strange plague worked. It left a mark on its victims. Like hellbine on a tree, it grew around its host, gradually sapping the life out of it, leaving a dead husk behind to disintegrate into ash. But during its insidious attack, it would spread easily to anyone the host had relations with. Already, Daisy had shared it with at least thirty men. When they fucked, and the transfer took place, something pleasing must happen to their cocks, because word had gotten out about the hooker with the tree tattoo. She was more popular now than when she was fourteen. This kind of killing was so much easier.

Ami sat cross-legged in front of the grimy, nicotine smeared mirror. Her bag of cheap and stolen makeup emptied in a mishmash in front of her. No amount of cover up or concealer worked on the strange dark veiny things spreading out all around her mouth. Damned Daisy, it was all her fault, whatever fucking STD she picked up she'd spread to Ami on that last threesome call.

Of course, Daisy told them she'd let a client tattoo her like that. She prattled on about taking on a new character. No longer Pandora, she wanted to be a nature goddess, a Druid or something like that. Ami sighed and leaned in closer to the mirror. She traced the lines with her finger. A gentle, but not unpleasant vibration spread down her hand. Her skin was tacky and as she pulled her finger away it held fast to her like a lover saying goodbye.

Whatever that was all over Daisy, wasn't a tattoo. It was like no STD Ami had ever seen. And that was saying a lot because she had seen and been treated for pretty much all of them. Eyeshadow worked better than the cover up. She hoped she'd have enough to cover her entire face like foundation. Then she would just stay out of the street lights and insist on complete darkness with her clients.

She wondered if she offered a BJ special tonight could she give this shit to someone else and get it off her mouth? She knew STDs didn't really work that way, but this one might. It was so weirdly different. Fuckin' Daisy and her fucked up mythology shit. How did a girl like that always get the rich guys? After they had Daisy they either only ever wanted her, or they never came around again. What was her secret anyway? Even covered in those branches, they still wanted her.

Maybe she was just being jealous. Daisy looked out for her friends, she'd brought Ami in on that last call, hadn't she?

"Yeah and now look at me," Ami said to her reflection.

If she squinted, she could see those things beneath the make-up. *So what? How often do the men actually look at your face anyway?* Rent would be due soon. She stood up, legs stiff, shoved her scattered make-up into the fanny pack she used as a bag, and shimmied into her fake snakeskin skirt.

"Well…here I go again on my own," she laughed and headed out the door.

Mitch lay naked on his brown futon, each breath an exertion. Clothes hurt his skin and he'd had to line the futon with a tarp. The fabric dug into the deep crevices that crisscrossed his entire body like a child's version of a road map. It was painfully maddening. Air whistled as it was forced out of his lungs through a wind-pipe now shrunk to the diameter of a straw.

He should have gone to the clinic weeks ago, when those first black lightning bolts started climbing out of his pubic hair. That was the day after he had picked up that hooker. But he'd felt fine otherwise so he waited a few days, fucked a few more prostitutes and told himself she'd had some kind of henna tattoo that rubbed off on him (he knew better—the lines were too clearly demarcated and dark to be a transfer). In those ninety-six hours, the lines grew to cover his belly and thighs.

Searching online for the rash, he found nothing on any legitimate medical sites but found a couple mentions without answers in some patient chat rooms. The idea that at least he wasn't the only one allowed him to ignore it even longer. He wasn't married, didn't date, and worked in the dark of his living room on the computer that sat on an old card table. Mitch loved his job because when customers called with program issues, he could access their system remotely and fix it. And once he had access, he could snoop whenever they left their desk-top in sleep mode. It was a voyeur's dream job, not to mention the perfect hobby for a fat, geeky introvert too awkward to leave his house.

But then, in a porn watching frenzy, he'd overcome his hesitancy and called for an escort. The black-haired beauty with the tree tattoo showed up. She was gorgeous, way out of his league and she took his virginity with a number of creative moves. The next morning, he wouldn't have noticed the lines at all if he hadn't been treating a yeast infection in his belly fold. Pulling it up to dry it off before applying the medicated powder, he noticed his own set of branches.

Things went gradually downhill from there. It seemed as the lines spread, they cut deeper into his flesh and were almost eating away at his body to gain their momentum. Necrotic cracks and crevices completely covered him and his weight had gone from 340 to

125. His hair fell out followed by his teeth. By the time the couch fabric began to stick to his weepy skin, it was far too late to seek help.

One month later, he was dying. Twenty-three years old and the only sex he'd ever had was paid for. He wondered how all the girls he'd paid for after the first one were doing. Did they have this same wasting disease? How many others had they spread it to? Algorithms branched through his head like the dead rivers flowing over his body. *Should have gone to the clinic* was the last conscious thought he had.

Daisy hadn't slept in days. Her sexual prowess had gained a following that couldn't be satiated. It was fine, she couldn't go home right now. Ami, her roommate, was surely there. The girl had tried to go out once after contracting the vines all over her face, but Ami was never much of a looker even before the vines. The lines squeezed her lips into a permanent duck face. It was pitiful, and frankly, a boner killer. She didn't want to have to look at the pathetic thing and she certainly didn't want to deal with the girl's incessant questions and, god-forbid, tears. So, she'd insist on hotel rooms from her johns. Maybe she'd do a little hitch-hiking, get this virus spreading faster. The goddess was counting on her.

She pulled her hood up to cover the lines on her neck and stepped onto the curb. Facing the city, she put up a thumb and waited for her ride to Armageddon.

Chapter 18: Book of Kenzi 6

The second day of consciousness passed slowly for Kenzi. The handsome, but very agitated, Dr. Altrey turned out to be the surgeon responsible for both saving her life and rerouting her bowels into an external trash bag. He explained in no uncertain terms that only he could decide if she was ready to take anything orally. After a thorough exam and questions regarding her tolerance of ice chips, he declared she could have clear liquids and advance to a regular diet as tolerated. The nurse accompanying him nodded and took note. He left without another word to Kenzi and without giving her the opportunity to ask if the colostomy was permanent.

The orthopedic doctor was also a man of few words. He seemed pleased to find her awake but only because she could begin rehabilitation, which he assured her would only take a few months. The pins in her left leg, however, would come out soon. He approved a wheelchair ride to see Gloria if her primary doctor agreed.

"Can you call Dr. Patel and ask him?" she begged the middle-aged, heavy-set nurse when it was just the two of them left in her room.

"Dr. Patel is not in charge of your case. In fact, I'm not sure you'll be seeing him again, honey," she said, adjusting Kenzi's blankets. "We've been told to page Dr. Childs directly."

"Why?" Kenzi whined. "I don't even know that other guy. Dr. Patel was the only one who was nice to me."

This was no good. All these doctors were announcing what she could and couldn't do, and what she had to do. None asked her what she wanted or how she felt. Only Dr. Patel seemed to care. She wished she knew his first name. Right now, he was her only friend in the world.

"He's just a resident. They come and go. Best not to get too attached. I'll give the doctor a call but honey, I gotta tell you—there are a couple of detectives breathing down our necks to get at you. If Dr. Childs approves a visit to your friend's room, you better believe they'll be in here asking you all sorts of questions." She leaned over to Kenzi conspiratorially. "You know the answers yet?"

Kenzi shook her head. How was she going to get out of this? She wanted Dr. Patel. He could help her.

"Then just rest for now. I'll wake you up when your clear tray comes. We'll try some broth and Jell-O. It'll be lime if you're lucky." She winked and laid the large remote beside her. The thing was the size of a bicycle seat and had buttons to control the bed, call the nurse and turn on the TV.

Kenzi lay in the twilight listening to the cacophony of monitors from the rooms surrounding her own. She wondered which one Gloria's was. Her mind filled with all the possible stories she could tell the cops. It wasn't like she could sleep. She'd slept so much lately, she wasn't tired. What she needed to do was come up with a plan. Gloria would have to stay strong and hang in there until Kenzi could see her. She wanted to, of course, but not until she was also ready to answer some tough questions. What about Patel? Would she see him again? She hadn't had a friend like that since she was a kid. The Scribble Man had made her feel safe just like Dr. Patel did now. She needed to tell him she was sorry that he got in trouble for giving her ice chips. She'd tell him that Dr. Altrey agreed with him so he'd know he was not "just" a resident. He was a good doctor.

She hit the on button for the TV and let the noise fill the background space between the monitors and the telephone calls to the desk.

"…bombing that killed twenty-seven people, seven of which were young children. All were members of the Carmen Heights Baptist Church of Carmen Heights, Massachusetts. The victims were protesting across the street from the Women's Health Clinic. The protests were progressing peacefully when the coolers brought by the church members themselves blew up in succession. Police are still investigating when and how the explosive devices were placed.

"Violence is nothing new to the Women's Health Clinic. They've been the victims of shootings and arsons in their short five years of business. Protestors are required to remain fifty feet from the business as a result. A spokesperson from WHC stated she believes the bombing may have been perpetrated by another pro-life group in order to cast suspicion upon the clinic themselves. This, of course, is raising a lot of chatter among both pro-life and pro-choice groups.

"This bombing comes on the cusp of the pro-life movement's biggest annual event: The Right to Life Rally on Washington D.C. When asked how the movement plans to handle this tragedy, Kelly Ray Tarleton, chair of the rally, said they plan to use the tragedy as an example of the pro-choice movement's disregard for life."

The picture shifted from the pretty blonde with sparkling white teeth to a sour-looking, dowdy woman with a brown bob. She wore a big button that stated ALL LIVES MATTER with a curled-up fetus crushed beneath the weight of the statement. "It will be a good reminder of what we're fighting for. I think we'll have record numbers this year. This kind of disrespect for the sanctity of human life must be stopped…no matter the cost," she stated.

Kenzi wrinkled her nose in disgust. "She ought to come hang out in my neighborhood so she can see how all those babies they want to save have to live."

The station seemed to agree with Kenzi, as there was no further discussion about the bombing. The ever-optimistic blonde returned to the screen. "In local news, a family is found mysteriously murdered in their home. While the coroner determined the time of death to be similar, one body was strangely dried and mummified." The picture cut to paramedics wheeling tarp covered stretchers out of a lovely two-story home. The reporter held a microphone up to Clark Rennet, county coroner.

"It appears that the female body had just given birth quite traumatically. The newborn's umbilical cord was still attached to the placenta. The adult male, though, appears to have been sort of wrung out or squeezed to death in some odd way. I've never seen anything like it in my twenty-five years as coroner."

Kenzi's mind presented her with a slideshow: the image of a snake wrapped around a body, squeezing. A woman, dark, naked sucking the life away. Another body out there just like that. No wonder the cops were itching to talk to her. This was bad. Very bad.

"What is this world coming to?" a voice asked and chuckled.

Kenzi jumped.

The Mediterranean beauty no one acknowledged as her nurse was back for another night shift. How had Kenzi not noticed before that the she was pregnant?

"What? I'm sorry, I wasn't paying attention."

"Oh nothing," the nurse breezed.

The room darkened when she entered, as if her presence required all the energy in the small space—like a black hole, she'd pulled it into her.

"Sorry, I forgot your name," Kenzi said, sure that the woman had never offered it.

"Lily is fine for now."

The nurse wandered the room, inspecting it, picking items up, and dropping them again. She stopped in front of the monitor with the green blips indicating Kenzi's heartbeat and watched it dreamily.

Lily. Kenzi committed it to memory. She planned to confront the other night nurse who insisted Lily didn't even exist. Because if Jane was to be believed, this woman didn't belong here at all. And she might be right. After all, Lily certainly didn't act much like a nurse. But if not, what was she doing here? Goosebumps prickled her arms as she considered Jane's words about the cops outside. Maybe the woman was working undercover.

Kenzi wasn't about to let on that she was suspicious.

"Are you my nurse tonight?"

The woman approached the bed, leaned over, and tucked the blankets around Kenzi in a maternal gesture. Her ample breasts threatened to spill over the dam of her collared, old fashioned nurse's uniform. Sandwiched between her breasts and struggling to free itself was the tip of a familiar, hairless good luck charm. It hung from a black leather thong. Kenzi reached out for it without thinking, then snatched her hand back. What the hell was Lily doing with Kenzi's rabbit's foot? Her skin itched for the first time since awakening; she needed to cut.

"What makes you ask such a silly question?" Lily stood back up, her belly pushing tightly against the bleached white cotton top. "I'm taking care of you, aren't I?"

Kenzi's nails bit into her palms, scratching at the psychosomatic itch. She didn't care about the cops anymore, her addiction to cut took over and she wanted, no, she needed the claws of her proverbial safety blanket.

"The other nurse, Jane, said you weren't. She said you shouldn't even be here."

"Perhaps, she is jealous because I can offer you things she cannot. I can make you better."

"What does that mean?"

"It means I can fix all this," she swept her arm over Kenzi's body. Heat surged through her veins rolling from her ruined belly to her broken leg. "But I don't do anything for free, Kenzi Brooks. I expect you to help me too."

Pain meds. It had to be all the pain meds. She was hallucinating or dreaming. *Yes, dreaming again. Likely.* All she needed to do was quiet her mind and let the metronomic sounds of her own heartbeat lull her back to sleep.

"I just want to see my friend Gloria, I want to make sure she's OK without having to deal with the fucking cops," she murmured.

"Why is this woman so important to you?" the nurse who probably wasn't a nurse demanded.

Lily's jade eyes bore into Kenzi's bicolored ones. It was as if the woman already knew the answers, but Kenzi found her mouth opening and giving Lily whatever she wanted.

"My mom, she always had some issues with depression. I mean, even when I was little, she would spend days locked in her room. My brother took care of me, made us cereal and cheese sandwiches. We called them her bad days. My dad, he was—I guess he still is probably—a trucker, so he was gone a lot. I mean he would be home on weekends and stuff, but he liked to watch TV, so we had to stay out of his hair."

Lily was back to canvasing the room, as if she had heard all this before. Kenzi continued but kept the woman in her peripheral vision.

"When I was seven, my brother and I were on our way to a store, and he got hit by a car and killed."

"And you? You were not injured?" Lily interrupted.

"Oh, well, no. I, I thought I saw something and I stopped on the curb."

"What did you see? What stopped you?" Lily rushed back to her side—intensity to her stare, hands resting on Kenzi's scarred arm.

"I had this, oh, I guess he was an imaginary friend, it was the first time I saw him, it was like an hallucination or something, and it made me stop. He was so different…I don't know, it was fate I guess."

"Fate," Lily echoed. "I need you to tell me exactly what he looked like. What happened after your brother got hit."

Kenzi sighed. They had taken a tangent in the conversation. Lily was no longer interested in Kenzi's love for her friend Gloria or how the woman had become a surrogate mother. The Scribble Man was an even more uncomfortable topic than her devotion to her stand-in mom. It had been a long time since she'd tried to discuss him with anyone. Lily was the first person to take it seriously. Compelled by perhaps that alone, Kenzi described the scars and the black hooded vest. The crisscrossed belt thing that held the hour-glass where he'd put Robbie's silvery ghost. Lily sat down on the bed beside her as Kenzi tried to recall all the details of the childhood friend she'd left behind years ago.

"After all that, my dad sort of faded out of our lives and it was just me and Marilyn—my mom. She did her best—well, there were times where she did—before she got mixed up in drugs. I used to act up at school, got in trouble all the time or whenever I tried to talk about The Scribble Man, I'd end up in the principal's office waiting for my mom to come pick me up because no one wanted to deal with me. But see, that's where Gloria came in. She was always there when Mom wasn't. She would come get me when Mom didn't care... or couldn't." Kenzi shrugged. It was that simple and that complicated.

Lily sat, listening. Kenzi's tongue stuck to the roof of her mouth. Where was that damn tray filled with all sorts of liquids the other nurse had promised? She reached for the cup of ice chips on the bed-side stand.

"Here, let me. You must be thirsty," Lily said. She reached over Kenzi to grab it. The necklace popped free of her cleavage and the hairless foot with its bloodstained claws swung like a pendulum over Kenzi's middle. It was her foot—no doubt about it—and this strange woman had it.

The ice chips sat on the spoon waiting for her to bite. She swallowed. Their angled edges softened as they slid into her stomach. The icy trail warmed and then faded entirely to became one with her body's own temperature. The process slowed her pounding heart and tamped down the adrenaline surge that came with the realization that this woman wore Kenzi's keychain around her neck. Instead of asking about it directly, Kenzi returned to her tale, adding details, and watching the woman intently.

"I know it seems like a petty thing to remember but I had this keychain that was super important to me. I found it the day Robbie died. I used to think that the Scribble Man gave it to me, but now that I know he was just imaginary, I suppose I picked it up from the wreckage. It was old and nasty." No facial change in the woman on the bed.

"It was a rabbit's foot. You know, like a lucky rabbit's foot? Only most of the hair was gone, so it looked like just a scary mummified monster claw instead. I loved it for that, you know? It was freaky like me and it made me feel invincible. I carried it with me all the time, and it felt as if I could use it whenever I wanted to bring the Scribble Man to visit me—I suppose I could in my mind. Until I couldn't, and then I started to use it to hurt myself."

"Hurt yourself?" Lily asked as if she hadn't seen the cuts on Kenzi's arms.

"Yeah." She held her arm out with the scar in a child's scrawl of KENZI starting near her elbow and working down to her wrist. "I remember seeing Robbie's name on the Scribble Man's arm that day, so I guess I thought if I did the same with my own name, it would make him come to me. That started a life-long bad habit."

"Well, finally, your tray came!" The other nurse, Jane, breezed in the room carrying a tray covered in a variety of fluid-filled vessels and interrupting Kenzi's memories.

Lily didn't move, never turned her head to acknowledge the woman and the nurse didn't seem to notice her either. She sat the clear fluids on the bedside tray and moved the ice chips beside the other Styrofoam cups.

"See how you do with these. If you keep it down, we'll try some soft foods for breakfast."

"OK," Kenzi said.

There was nothing else to say. The odd exchange that occurred as if Lily, who was smiling like the Mona Lisa, didn't exist, had robbed her of any words she might say.

Before she could organize her confusion into a question, a siren-type wail rolled out of the space around them. Blue lights in the hallway began flashing and a voice called out over the speaker system.

CODE BLUE, ICU ROOM 402. CODE BLUE, ICU ROOM 402.

The nurse ran out of the room. Lily stood up, still smirking. "I'll be going as well, but I will see you again soon."

She walked out the door and disappeared into the mass chaos ensuing near the nurse's station.

Chapter 19: Book of Kenzi 7

The burn of a branding iron woke Sariel from his slumber in the corner of Gloria's room. Enoch and he had been careful to spend Kenzi's waking hours here watching over the woman until he decided the best way to re-enter Kenzi's life. An alarm rang wildly for only a short time before the room began to fill.

So many mortals, like ants whose pheromone trails had been disturbed, scuttled about haphazardly trying to alter the inevitable. Interested in the battle waging against him, Sariel wove between the chaotic dancers in blue scrubs as they worked their medicine on the fleshy shell of Gloria Paulson. The room was packed and yet more congregated outside the door near the desk that sat in the center of a semi-circular ward. He counted them—a way to occupy a mind filled with indecision and angst. *One, two, three, f…Lilith. Lilith, he was absolutely sure,* slipped out of the room a few doors down and floated unnoticed like a wolf among sheep.

Sariel stepped into the corridor but she was gone—vanished within a mass of flesh and bone. She'd been in with Kenzi, two doors down, there was no doubt. He stepped to Kenzi's room in one movement, unencumbered by the physics of the mortal dimension.

A waif, thin and pale, stood wavering by her bed. She had the same frightened little bunny look in her eyes he'd seen the first day he met her. The electronic blip of her heartbeat kept an up-tempo rhythm.

"Kenzi," he said softly.

If he'd had a heartbeat, he was certain in that moment its pace would have rivaled hers. She looked him in the eyes, seeing him clearly as if he were as mortal as she.

"Kenzi, I—"

Kenzi screamed and stepped out with her braced leg as if to try to run, He rushed to her, put his arms around her and they tumbled.

"Where am I?" Kenzi asked the darkness.

For the moment, it was pure black—a complete absence of light. With it, Kenzi realized, came a complete absence of pain. Her other senses heightened. Damp chills nibbled at her. She hugged herself. The tube was gone, and she was standing, unencumbered by any medical equipment. If she weren't so damn cold, she could think. Vegetal rot mingled with wet earth in her nostrils. Kenzi had never been in the graveyard during a rain storm but she imagined it would smell like this.

"This is my home, my prison. A punishment for disobedience," a voice to her right echoed. It was deep and ethereal like the autotune all the rappers used. The echo gave a sense of vastness to the space they both occupied. The opposite of a shadow formed in her vision. A large male shape gradually focused like a polaroid picture. His pale skin almost glowed.

She opened her mouth to ask his name but screamed instead. Cold, clammy appendages tickled at her body—some gaining purchase on her loose hospital gown.

"Step toward me," her companion said. "They can't reach far."

She inched toward the voice, careful to keep some distance between them as well.

"What the hell is going on here?" she asked. "Who are you? Why am I here? *Where* is here?"

"You know me, Kenzi. You've known me for a long time." He took her hand and gently ran it down the topography of his forearm. Kenzi could almost see it in her mind. Scars of human names carved into the almost pure white flesh. The Scribble Man—she had to be dreaming. He did not exist.

"But you aren't real," she insisted.

"Walk with me and stay close. There is much to clarify and a short time to do it."

He pressed her fingers around his forearm as if he were a gentleman simply walking a lady home. He felt solid enough. Every one of her senses activated, each insisting it wasn't a dream. If he was real, this changed so many things. She wanted to know more—needed to understand how he'd come into her life and why now, years later, he was back.

"I warn you, it will not be an easy tale to hear." He patted her hand paternalistically. "As a mortal, you should never have to be exposed to any of this, yet here you are. It's time I told you the truth about your past, so you can understand the danger in your future."

"This is so fucked up, you know that, right? I mean you're just an imaginary friend." Whatever drugs they were giving her had to be to blame for this. The Scribble Man said nothing in response. *Maybe he doesn't even realize he is imaginary.*

As they walked, the walls and ceiling began to take shape. Gnarled roots of trees reached desperately down into the tunnel. They seemed almost animated, like the claws of giant trolls, grasping blindly for something to eat. Along the sides of the hall they were walking, vaguely human shapes writhed restlessly against the dirt walls. Unlike the roots which only gave the impression of despair, these things grabbed out hopelessly for salvation or perhaps, in hunger. Kenzi shivered and squeezed in closer to the Scribble Man.

"Be careful not to wander too close to the Nods. They are desperate for escape. It won't do either of us any good if you get a rider. It would make our relationship too obvious." He ushered her back toward the center of the tunnel.

"What the fuck are you talking about? No, what am I talking about? I'm insane! Clearly, I'm insane."

He gestured to the human shapes that pushed out of the dirt walls. Covered in a gauzy, shimmering drape-like shroud, they reached out for both of them. "Nods are the souls of non-believers. Those who choose to spend eternity in nothingness. The Creator thought it would be a fun little revenge to put them here, trapped in the realm of Death but with their consciousness intact."

One of the Nods leaned far into the tunnel, arms outstretched like Frankenstein's monster. Sariel shoved him back into the dirt wall with his foot. "Although I don't know who's being punished by that idea—them or me." He sighed. "If they get ahold of you, they'll hang on to your soul like a parasite—a rider—and stay there, feeding on your life force until they can hitch a ride with you into an afterlife, piggyback style."

"Nice," Kenzie said disgusted. Something fell from the ceiling and stuck in her hair. It squirmed.

"Ugh!" Kenzi cried out suddenly, frantically shaking her mop of red hair. "Stuff is dropping from the ceiling on me." She shivered.

"Maggots, beetles, eaters of death and rot," Sariel said nonchalantly.

A bird, enormous and black as the tunnel itself swooped in and snatched a plump, squirming grub from her hair. The sound of its beak gnashing on the larva was almost more than Kenzi could handle but at least it was gone now.

"Thanks," Kenzi said to the bird who settled on her shoulder.

"Enoch has always favored you."

"She's sweet," Kenzi said.

The Scribble Man laughed. "Just like when you were a child. You insisted Enoch was a girl."

"Look, I made her up in my head just like I made you up, which is probably why I know she's a girl bird. Now, you two are drug-induced hallucinations. Right before I was attacked, I'd been thinking about you—the both of you. I even wrote about it in my memoir journal."

"I know, I read it," Sariel said. Kenzi snapped her head to look directly at him.

"You read my journal?" Another bug bounced off her elbow and Kenzi picked up her pace.

The light intensified as they neared the end of the tunnel. It was enough for Kenzi to see more than she wanted. They were walking in what could be called a human-sized ant colony. Tunnels branched off willy-nilly up, down, right, left. It was dizzying to see how large the network was, but it was worse knowing where the bugs were coming from. It was as if these tunnels ran under an endless graveyard.

Neatly arranged, but in advanced states of decay and partially embedded in the ceiling were human bodies. Drawn into a trance by the horror of it, Kenzi could not pull her eyes away until a pustule on the thigh of a male corpse began to pulsate and then it popped like a zit, spilling a mass of larvae down from the sky. She flinched in reflex. Enoch hopped off her shoulder and feasted.

"Just give me back my journal and get me the fuck out of here," she said. "Please."

Sariel continued down the hall, deeper into the underground world. It was as if he couldn't hear her or perhaps he was just ignoring her.

"Hey," she grabbed his arm. His skin was cold and firm like a corpse. *Like Robbie's corpse.* Smooth, ropey scars were scrawled all over his skin. Names on top of names on top of names. "I want to go back now. Take me back. This isn't funny."

"A woman, dark hair, dark skin, walked out of your room when the alarm sounded," Sariel began.

"The pregnant one nobody seems to see but me?"

"She's pregnant?" Sariel asked.

"Oh yeah. Lily. She's pregnant all right. Weird. Asks a lot of questions."

"Kenzi," Sariel's voice grew soft and gentle. "What happened to the talisman—the rabbit's foot—I gave you?"

"I think she has it—Lily—she's my nurse," Kenzi sighed. "I think she might have been at my house and killed this guy and his partner. They were attacking me." She thought back to that day. "Or maybe there was a snake that actually killed him? I don't know, it's all so foggy."

"But how did she get out?" Sariel asked.

"How the hell would I know? The only thing I know for sure, is this…" she swung her arm around in a half circle, "…is all fucked up. I want to go."

"But you are all I have. I need you," he said. He put a hand to her face. His thumb brushed across her skin. She didn't know if it was meant to be fatherly or romantic. He dropped it away suddenly as if he just realized what he'd done. "Lilith could be dangerous. She must be stopped before she gets any stronger."

"So, how am I supposed to help you?" Kenzi yelled. "This is insane! And me? I'm just some dumb-shit white girl. I can't help you. I lost the foot. I am sorry, I am, but you see? I can't be trusted. I just want to get out of here, seriously."

A hand fell on her shoulder and bounced onto the floor with a splat. Maggots wriggled off her after their prize while others who'd managed to hang onto the limb feasted on the bloated necrotic tissue.

"Ahh." She stomped in place. "Get me out of here right now!"

Sariel grabbed her wrist. Without a word he led her through the labyrinth of tunnels. Kenzi thought of a movie she'd seen once with a young Kevin Bacon—*Tremors*. Giant underground worms terrorized a small desert town. In her version, the giant worms here were just a mass of tiny opaque larvae and she was running from them. Nods, riders, uber-worms. *Fuck this shit,* she thought *give me Silvio's goons any day.*

Up ahead the passage widened into a cavern of sorts. In the center of the space, a thick trunk of tree worked its way through the floor and ceiling. Branches swept out to infinity. In the small spaces between intersecting limbs, the dirt was gone. Kenzi could see a star-studded sky stretched like cloth where there was no roof. It was dizzying as if they were in the center of an asteroid floating through space. It wasn't far-away sky she saw. It was the universe pushing in.

A full moon, bigger than any she'd ever seen, shone like daylight through the gnarled limbs. Metallic charms, some gold, copper, silver, some wood, hung from the mass of vegetation on chains, leather straps, and mildewed rope. They threw reflections of the moonlight about the cave like a disco ball. In a different situation it might have been really cool. At least in here, there were no dead bodies, no Nods, and no bugs.

Here it was warm and comfortable. The air was fresh and clean. Kenzi picked up notes of cinnamon, and maybe vanilla. Warm scents, comforting. She sat down and leaned against the tree. Sariel sat beside her. After a moment of silence, he handed Kenzi her journal.

"I read what you wrote. You are a wonderful story teller." He paused when he noticed her holding the book white knuckled. Her face displayed anger and hurt.

"So, you read it and you stole it too? Now, what? You're bribing me with it? Ya know, maybe it's you who can't be trusted."

"I'm sorry for…invading your privacy, but I'd so hoped you'd remembered me, maybe written about me. I knew I would need to speak to you again, I didn't want to frighten you."

Kenzi laughed. "Nope. This place isn't scary at all. I mean a little grub rain is always refreshing when you're in hell."

"This isn't hell, Kenzi. I know what it must seem like to you, but it's safe."

"Safe from what?"

"You can't trust Lilith. She might be dangerous."

"She seems fine. She's pregnant. She's about as dangerous as me."

"You have to get the talisman back and together we must trap her in it again. She will not come to me, but she has an interest in you. I need you." Sariel grimaced, clearly frustrated in this unfamiliar position.

"Kenzi, please. Remember when you were young, and we used to write each other messages? I wrote you the story of Lilith in here. It's just as much my story as well. I want you to understand my concern. I need you to stay safe. I care about you Kenzi."

She opened the journal and shuffled through the pages until she discovered the unfamiliar scrawl.

"Jesus, you wrote your own damn book in here."

"Just read it, Kenzi. Then, you'll understand."

She blinked and the darkness returned. She fell into it like Alice down the rabbit hole.

Chapter 20: Book of Kenzi 8

"Kenzi? Miss Brooks? Can you hear me?"

Kenzi jumped at the touch on her shoulder. *Another fucking grub.* She let out a small squeal betraying her tough-girl exterior, shivered, and smacked at it. It wasn't a bug of any kind though, it was a hand. Soft and warm. A living, human hand. Patel.

She opened her eyes. She was back in her own hospital bed. The sunlight shining in the window was at the level of her upper thighs which, she'd learned, meant morning. A tube was draped across her face and two small prongs shoved themselves up her nostrils. The air was dry. She had a sudden urge to rip it out and shove her fingers up there to de-crust her nasal passages, cute doctor watching or not. A cuff wrapped around her upper arm squeezed hard; just as she was about to rip it off, it began to slowly deflate. The small black screen that hung above her bed and kept time with the rhythm of her heartbeat now sent out a high pitched double beep signaling the end of the blood pressure taking process.

"Hello, Miss Brooks. Are you with me? Awake now?" He smiled.

My god, his teeth are perfect. Why does he have to be so perfect? I'm dreaming, still dreaming. If so, this dream was much better than the last. It was already fading from her memory, except for the feeling of being buried alive. Cold, damp, earthy stink and the Scribble Man was there. He had told her things, but she couldn't remember them now. Dreams. Just a bunch of bad dreams from being stuck in this place. The drugs and death everywhere that made her think of Robbie and her imaginary friend.

"When can I get out of here?" she asked, ignoring his questions.

His brow furrowed, and a shadow crossed his face.

"Miss Brooks, you tried to get out of bed last night without assistance. You were found lying on the floor. You mustn't push it."

"I must be doing well enough to get myself up, so just discharge me. I want to go see Gloria." *And I want to get the hell out of dodge before the cops start asking me questions that I can't answer.*

"Miss Brooks, I'm sorry, but I am not your doctor anymore. I am here right now as… well, as a friend. Call me Henry. I wanted to check in on you and to talk to you a little about your friend Gloria, and your mother."

"My mother's dead. I know that. And I know Gloria has a long road ahead of her, but she'll be OK. She's one tough cookie. Trust me." Kenzi assured him. Then her brain processed all that he'd said. "Wait, why aren't you my doctor anymore?"

The day shift nurse came in then, checked her vital signs on the monitor. She nodded to Dr. Patel and then turned her back to them, stopping at the small supply cart beside the sink, where she decided was as good a place as any to do some paperwork. Dr. Patel paused for a moment to watch her. When it became obvious she planned to stay in the room, he turned back to Kenzi. His words came out slowly, as he evaluated each one.

"Well, I'm just a—" He interrupted his own sentence. "I made a decision about your care. It was fine, I didn't make any mistakes or anything. I mean, look at you…you look… great." He smiled and blushed. "But I made a management decision that I did not first clear with my attending."

"Which could have caused you a setback," the nurse said, coming over to fiddle with Kenzi's IV.

Kenzi yanked her arm away, pulling the line out of the nurse's hand. "Can you just leave us alone for a while? Seriously. Get out or else I'll tell that doctor that I don't want you as my nurse anymore."

The nurse pursed her lips together and put her hands on her hips. She glared at both of them and left the room. Dr. Patel laughed.

"Maybe I should have you with me all the time. Those nurses can be vicious."

Kenzi rolled her eyes. "They're just jealous. They think they know more than you or at least they think they know *better* than you. Anyway, what did you do to me that got you fired?"

This time Patel's laugh was nervous and Kenzi could see that he was fiddling with his hands held behind his back. The gaping white coat revealed well-made, tailored clothing. Resident or not, he was still making some serious cash.

"I extubated you—took the breathing tube out."

"So? Good. Frankly, that was annoying as hell."

"And you didn't need it, but still, I should have asked first. After that, I let you have those ice chips." He shrugged his shoulders. "Anyway, Dr. Altrey took me off your case. So now, here I am, just Henry Patel, Internal Medicine resident on his ICU rotation coming to speak to you about your mum and your friend. That's all I have to offer you today."

He shrugged again. His hands were busy. Fiddling. A nervous habit she could totally relate to.

"Well, damn. I thought you were going to ask me out to lunch." She picked up a small plastic cup from her bedside table. "One can only take so much apple juice."

He laughed nervously, his hands dropped to his side. It was the most relaxed he'd been since he walked into her room.

"I'd be honored to take you to lunch. But, only when you are ready and well enough to be discharged. Don't push it, all right?" His smile dropped away, and he clasped his hands together, tightly in front this time. Even white knuckled, he worked them subtly.

"Seriously, Miss Brooks, your friend Ms. Paulson, as you may or may not know, is barely hanging on. Very early this morning, she coded—her heart stopped, and she stopped breathing. For a moment, she was clinically dead."

Kenzi remembered the alarm that caused both nurses to rush from her room. The image of The Scribble Man here in this room flashed in her mind. She looked at her nightstand. The journal was gone.

"I know," she muttered looking around the room and patting her bed.

The Scribble Man had written in it. She needed to see it. She wanted to read what he'd written.

"What? Who told you?" he asked, his eyes darting toward the door where the nurse had been just a moment before. "If a nurse told you that, and you got up and fell, you have to tell someone. That's not OK."

"You told me she was here. When I heard the code, I knew it was her. I got up to see. And I must have knocked some stuff over, I had my journal. I need it."

Henry pulled the journal out of his white coat pocket. "You have a lot of personal things written in here. Your nurse must have picked it up. It was out at the desk when I was doing rounds. I took it. I don't think it's anybody's business—certainly not that of the police."

He shook his head and pursed his lips. "But please don't do that again. You'll never get out of here if you keep having these setbacks."

Kenzi rolled her eyes. "Dr. Patel, I've survived more shit than you'll see in your entire career. I'm pretty good at taking care of myself."

She grabbed the journal from him. It took all her self-control not to open it and start reading immediately. She needed privacy though; she'd need to ask him to leave. But a big part of her wanted him to stay. She was torn.

He nodded. "I can see that about you, but something tells me your strength came from living through a lot of trauma, which is why I insisted on coming to talk to you. I must be blunt, and I hate to have to tell you this—I just didn't want it coming from anyone else. Your friend is unlikely to survive the shooting. If she does by some miracle, she will not be the same woman you remember."

Kenzi sat silently contemplating what exactly to say next. Why was he being so sweet to her? Why did this doctor care what happened to a hood rat like her?

She laid the journal on the bed beside her. Right now, she just wanted to spend time with him. His curls, dark eyes, warm brown skin, and those nervous hands that made him seem more human than any doctor she'd ever known. It put him on her level and she loved him for that tiny show of imperfection.

"Look, Gloria is like a mother to me. She was always there. If this situation had been the other way around, and Gloria was dead, and my mom was the one vegging out in there, I'd tell you to pull the plug. Marilyn's got nothing left to live for. But Gloria is a fighter. She taught me how to live through everything life throws at you. She'll get through this. She will. I just need to get out of here and be with her. She needs me and then she'll be fine." Her voice cracked, straining against the lump growing in her throat. Hot tears burned the corners of her eyes and she knew if she blinked, they'd go rolling down her cheeks.

"I understand, Miss Brooks."

"What the fuck, Patel? Are you sixty or something? Seriously, my name is Kenzi, can you just cut the doctor crap? You said you were here as my friend, so be my friend. Call me Kenzi." It was best to change the subject. *No more vulnerability.*

He held up his hands in surrender and followed her cue and moved on. This guy was unbelievable. *Don't fall for him. Not now. Not ever. You gotta get him out of this room. You gotta read that journal, and you gotta get the fuck out of here.*

"OK, OK. Kenzi is beautiful name. Is it short for something?"

"Nope. It's just Kenzi." *Or, I guess we could keep talking.* "The original plan was to name me Mackenzie after my dad; his name was Mac. He took off on a run right before I was due, and my mom had me alone. She was so pissed, she dropped the Mac and named me Kenzi. The birth certificate was signed and filed by the time he got back."

"Well, I like it and I understand how you feel. I have a complicated relationship with my parents as well, but they are all we have," Henry Patel said. "Your mother though, how long did she have a drug problem?"

Damn it, if he wasn't so cute with those smoldering dark eyes, she'd tell him to get the fuck out.

"Too long," Kenzi answered.

That's it. That's all the personal information he was getting. He already knew way too much about her. Besides, there was nothing exciting to tell. Marilyn was like any other druggie. The tales were all the same, chronic pain problems that lead to pain pill addiction which lead to money issues and then trading favors for illicit drugs until strange men in the house was nothing new and fending them off became a daily routine. Nah, he didn't need to hear that. What would a rich doctor like him ever understand about her life anyway, even if he seemed to actually care. Time to change the subject again.

"So, what about you, Dr. Patel? Henry. We're friends now, right? How'd a nice guy like you end up in a shithole hospital like this?"

Henry grabbed the visitor's chair beside the wall and dragged it to the bedside. He fell into it and slouched.

"That is a long story too. I was born and raised in India where both of my parents are physicians. Because of their schedules, I spent many summers with my grandfather in the English countryside. He had a lovely cottage and was a beekeeper in his retirement. Prior to that, he'd been a book-binder. I loved the romance of his life and the tales he would tell as we collected the honey together. When we split his colony, he gave me my own and I found my passion. I studied plants and pollens and how they affected the flavor of the honey.

"When I graduated college, my father presented me with a ticket to America. He'd arranged matriculation at Wayne State Medical School and for me to live with a surgeon friend of his he'd met during a mission to Guatemala. The problem was, I hated medicine. I never wanted to do it in the first place, but my father would accept nothing less than his son, 'the surgeon.' When I failed to get a residency, I tried to kill myself, Kenzi." He sighed and took her hand, rubbing it with his thumb. "My life is by no means glamorous. Money can't buy happiness. That's true, and it can't take away misery either. I was miserable. It got so bad once that I tried to hang myself, but I couldn't even do that right. It was all hushed up and my father had to accept defeat. His friend had a friend here who happened to have an open Internal Medicine spot. With a generous donation from my father, I got the spot.

"But all I really want to do is go back to England and take over my grandfather's farm. He sends me honey from time to time and it only makes me miss it more."

For a moment, her hand in his, his thumb caressing her skin, she allowed herself to imagine a life in the country. Writing books by the window of a small cottage, a flower-scented breeze blowing in tousling the papers. Henry walking back to her with a bucket filled with honey. *Shit, was that right? Does the honey just drip out of the hive? Or would he have to cut the hive off the tree and bring it into the house to scrape the honey out? How did any of that work?* The confusion in her fantasy brought her back to the present.

"I'm sorry, Henry. I'm sorry you're so unhappy. But you're wrong about money not helping. Maybe in the middle of the country in a cottage someone gave you, life would be livable, but not where I'm from. Money is life and death. That's why I'm writing about it. A kind of memoir of what it's like living this life. Hopefully, people like you will read it. Then you'd see that you don't have it that bad and you'll tell your rich friends to read it, then I'll become rich and famous and I can get the hell out of Detroit forever."

He rubbed her hand between both of his. "I'm sure you're right. I can't imagine how hard it must be for you. But you aren't like your mother, you know that? You deserve a better life. I bet you could write a book or do anything you want, Kenzi. You're a very smart girl and very determined."

His stare reminded her of the dark caverns in her dream, but instead of chills, his eyes radiated warmth. She pulled away. No sense in imagining anything with this guy—their lives were worlds apart.

Henry picked up the journal from beside her. "You must have been writing in this when you fell. I'd love to read some of your work."

She grabbed it from him. "No!" He looked surprised at her shout. "I mean, yes, I would love for you to read it someday, but it's not ready. This is mostly snippets and notes and it's a mess."

He laughed. "All right, you work on it. But you better remember that I get to be the first reader when it's ready. I bet my dad knows some publishers too." He winked and smiled that gorgeous, perfectly white-toothed grin.

His lips managed to keep their fullness in the smile as if they were formed in that exact position. She smiled back at him.

"PATEL!" a voice called from just beyond the door. Kenzi jumped. Henry stiffened. Dr. Altrey stood in the doorway and the day nurse just behind him, a Cheshire cat grin on her face.

"Fucking snitch," Kenzi growled.

"Give me one more moment, Dr. Altrey, Miss Brooks is still considering her options."

Henry leaned in and spoke quietly. "He wants me to talk you into pulling the plug on Gloria. I'm going to tell him no. Is that all right? That's how you feel, right?"

"What if it were your dad? What would you say?" she asked, stalling.

"Patel! Now!"

"That's not a good question to ask of me just now." He squeezed her hand one more time. "The police will come soon too. He's given the go ahead. Sorry, I thought we'd have more time to talk about this."

Kenzi sat in stunned silence as he walked out of the room leaving the weight of a thousand problems still clinging to her.

Chapter 21: Book of Kenzi 9

The room was quiet again. The sunlight warming her ankles suggested it was almost lunch time. The loud voice of Dr. Altrey faded away with a group of footsteps suggesting Henry had been berated in front of an audience. No wonder he wanted to quit.

She touched the journal. *What if…? What if she really could write a best seller? And what if they fell in love?* He could quit, and she could write, and they would live in the country far from Detroit. He wouldn't need his dickhead dad's money. Maybe Gloria could live with them too.

And what if you open this journal and find chapters you didn't write? What if The Scribble Man is real. How about that?

The book was warm, and it either vibrated in her hands, or she was shaking. She opened it and flipped through to the chapter she'd written about Robbie. To the questions she'd written: *Where did the rabbit's foot come from? Who was The Scribble Man? Was he someone I saw that day? Was there a bird? Talk to Gloria about school drawings, letters to The Scribble Man.* Her handwriting ended there but a new, more elaborate scrawl continued for pages afterward. Kenzi took in a deep breath and blew it out slowly; willing her tremors to stop, she began to read.

My name is Sariel. You call me The Scribble Man and you may continue to do so, but my given name is Sariel. Before the earth was created, my home was with The Creator. There were many others like me, but I was held in high esteem by the Creator. We all watched Him design this world—a world like ours—but filled with a myriad of new colors and shapes. A finite land filled with strange creatures. We'd never seen anything other than the beings we were. Time passed, and they evolved. Plants and animals grew, procreated, and changed. It was like a coloring book; every millennium a new page of backgrounds and colors. We fell in love. We begged Him to let us visit with the exotic beasts He'd created. He laughed and told us to watch. He said we hadn't seen anything yet.

Ha. Maybe he should have stopped while he was ahead. What kind of Creator can't see the future?

The day he created man and woman, we sat in stunned silence. The Creator gathered the soil and clay, forming first a mortal that looked just like us. Only we were not of the flesh, we were merely energy with the idea of a body in His image. Nothing more than sentient possibilities. Our shocked admiration continued when next He created another so like the first yet different than anything we could imagine. This one had curves and hair like a willow tree. She was the most beautiful thing He had created so far. When He breathed life into them, we grew obsessed, observing their behavior, their everyday interactions. We watched ceaselessly as they discovered their new home and each other.

I (and probably the others as well) found myself completely taken with the female. Her name was Lilith; her husband was Adam. Adam was formed as a flesh-covered version of ourselves. He acted and spoke just like us, but Lilith was graceful and had a smile that made me warm inside. She was simply fascinated with the plants and animals around them. Through her eyes, everything was new to me as well. I found myself wishing I were mortal and feeling, for the first time ever, jealousy.

Adam was filled with the power of The Creator's spirit. He knew he'd been conceived first, and he'd been given the authority to name all the plants and animals in the garden. Lilith was given no such duties, only to love and support her husband. I watched with sadness as she wandered about their paradise seeking purpose. At nights, when the stars were the only light, Adam would call to Lilith to come lie beneath him. We'd seen this sort of interaction between other animals over the eons, but never between those so much like ourselves. The Creator encouraged us to give them privacy. Two others beside myself, Malach and Sammael, found we could not look away. Because we did not follow The Creator's instructions, we saw what no one else did.

Lilith was as stubborn as she was beautiful and, in my opinion, more intelligent than her male counterpart. She refused to lie beneath him every time during the act of procreation. She insisted they take turns or else lie on their sides so that no one was submissive to the other. Mind you, she never argued that she was dominant in the relationship. She only asked for equality. To me, this was reasonable. I found myself angered with Adam's insistence that he was to be obeyed.

"She was a total bad-ass. I love it." Kenzi said, underlining the paragraph.

"Who are you talking to in here?" Her nurse entered with a new tray of liquids for her.

"Oh, no one. Sorry. I must have been talking in my sleep."

The nurse—younger than the others she'd had so far—put the tray on the bedside table and left without another word. Kenzi rolled her eyes and went back to her work. There was nothing about the smells arising from her "lunch" that activated her hunger center.

So many emotions I'd never experienced and couldn't understand ran through me as I watched The Creator's masterpieces find faults in each other. I wouldn't dare question The Creator, of course. So, sadly, we watched as they grew further apart.

One day, after weeks of refusing to yield to her husband, Lilith was bathing in the stream. I was the only angel left watching. At this point, the others had grown bored with the constant bickering between the two. Adam rushed in behind her and grabbed her by the hair. He dragged her to the shore and forced her beneath him. My back stiffened. My hands curled into fists. Heat shot through me in a wave of emotion I was unfamiliar with. She fought, kicked, and scratched at him but it did no good; he had his way with her. I could only observe, helpless to stop it although I wanted to.

She was just like me. Poor thing. Trapped.

That's when I decided to confront The Creator. I was going to ask Him to give me access to walk the earth, to become as they were. I would give up my immortality for her. That's how affected I was.

A movement from below caught my eye. Lilith had managed to push him off. She ran toward the Tree of Knowledge, the one place they were forbidden to go.

Her screams brought back Malach and Sammael and we cowered when we heard her. She stood at the base of the forbidden tree, calling out to The Creator—calling to Him by name. When He arrived, He saw her insolence, her disobedience to her husband, her audacity to call out His name. He admonished her and banished her from the Garden. His anger shook the heavens, and we were all afraid.

Fearful of His wrath, she ran far and out of our sight. Somewhere, beyond the lush valley created just for the two of them, existed land neglected by The Creator. It was land that evolved on its own to become the wilds. It was there that she settled.

For a time, peace returned to the Garden, but soon Adam became restless and he called to the Father, begging for the return of his companion, vowing this time to be gentler. Vowing to lead with a soft handed approach rather than the rough force he'd used previously. The Creator heard his pleas and called to Malach, Sammael and me.

I was all too happy to be asked to go down to earth to find Lilith and bring her back to the Garden where once again I could revel in her beauty and dream of mortality. Sammael and Malach also seemed pleased to be asked. We spent some time getting used to our skin, to the earth's gravity, and basic locomotion. Soon, it became second nature. We set off in the direction Lilith had fled.

Why? What kind of selfish asshole would bring her back to that hell? There better be a good explanation for this.

We found her living near the shores of the Red Sea. She had built herself a small lean-to shelter and was hunting quite effectively. She'd fashioned knives and spears out of wood and stones. She defended herself as best she could. My heart broke for her. I wanted to take her into my arms and protect her from this dangerous place.

Initially, she did not see us. She squatted at the water's edge, cleaning the carcass of a small mammal. She'd made a fire near the lean-to. I was impressed. She really was intelligent and strong, just like you, Kenzi. At that time, I experienced a feeling of incomplete peace. As if the only way I could feel whole again was to know her and share my existence with her.

There would be no time for introductions, however. Sammael and Malach immediately approached her, grabbed her by the arms, and pulled her to her feet.

"Please, let me go," she begged.

She fought against them hopelessly. They were supreme beings with other-worldly strength.

"You have been commanded to return to your husband," Sammael said.

He laughed, as if he enjoyed her struggles. Malach, too, seemed energized by the fight. I stood there frozen and useless, saying and doing nothing to stop them or to help her. Her eyes pleaded with me. Finally, I spoke up.

"The Creator has commanded you to return to Adam. Your husband has promised to use a gentler approach with you. He will no longer be so harsh and demanding."

Nice work, Scribble Man. Way to save the day.

"And am I still to lie beneath him? Am I still to submit to him as if we were not made of the same earth? What exactly is it that you promise me?"

I said nothing. I couldn't answer her. Her intuition was right. Nothing would change. I knew that. I hung my head and allowed my brothers to have their way. They grabbed at her in all the areas that differed from their own. Malach, pushed his hand into her secret center.

"This is why you will never be equal." He worked his hand harder into her nethers. "You are missing something right here. You have a hole which needs to be filled. You are incomplete without Adam."

"The Creator will not be happy to hear of this treatment," I finally said. "We should take her back to the Garden and her husband now." I didn't want to do that any more than I wanted to continue watching this strange display of unnecessary aggression.

"No!" she cried. "Please don't make me go back there. I'm not hurting anyone here on my own."

"Perhaps," Sammael interrupted her protests, "There is another way. If she chooses not to return, perhaps we, as her guardians, must see her to safety."

His smirk betrayed the kindness in his voice, but I could not imagine what alternative he had in mind. One thing was obvious: Lilith did not want to return to her previous life. Perhaps we could leave her and approach The Creator to beg forgiveness for her as well as for our failures.

I nodded. We'd take her to safety instead of back to Adam. Malach's false grin matched Sammael's as they held her up by the arms, dragging her along. The tips of her toes left a trail behind her that I followed. I was ashamed. None of this felt right and I was torn. I did not want to force her to return to a life of virtual servitude, but I did not want to disobey my own master.

We reached a cave on the edge of the sea. Its mouth opened wide. A dark abyss lay in wait just beyond the reach of the light. I looked to my brothers.

"What is this?"

"This is a good place for her," Sammael said.

Lilith, as if sensing her fate, screamed and thrashed to no avail. I felt the need to aid my brothers and grasped her feet. Together we carried her into the cave where a horde of demons waited with lust-filled anticipation.

I stopped, refusing to take her any farther and pleaded with them to rethink the plan. "What will The Creator say?"

"Sariel, you fool!" they laughed at me. "We never planned to return to Him."

"Look around you," Malach said. "There is so much to feel and see and taste and touch."

He spread his arms out as if to punctuate his thoughts. The world down here was enormous and so varied in its colors and textures. I would be lying if I said I hadn't considered the ramifications of staying there myself. But this…? This was turning my back on my Lord, my God. I didn't want to be orphaned here.

And what about her? I can't believe this.

And so, like a coward, I stood just inside the cave's threshold. I let them drag her into what was clearly not the safety of an empty cave. For days, I paced outside, trying not to hear the cries coming from within. Pretending I had no idea what might be happening to the poor girl who only ever wanted to be treated as an equal.

After seven days and seven nights, Malach and Sammael emerged. Scratched and bloodied but smiling broadly. They took positions on either side of the opening as if standing watch. The anguished calls for help only got louder as Lilith was taken by demons—dark creatures from the depths of earth untouched by the hand of The Creator.

Malach and Sammael killed many of the demons' spawn. That is not to say that some did not escape. They did. Half-blooded evil things spilled forth from the mouth of the cursed hole even as Lilith's protestations grew in volume and desperation.

For seven years, I waited. For what, I don't know. Perhaps it was in hopes that I would find the courage to put a stop to it. Finally, I could take no more. That night, when my brothers slept, I journeyed back to the Garden. I knew I couldn't stop them alone, but I had every intention of telling The Creator and Adam about the crimes against Lilith.

Wow, a real hero. And I thought you were there to keep me safe as a kid.

I ran the whole way, exhilarated by the feel of breath filling and leaving my lungs, the sound of blood coursing through my veins and the adrenaline supplying the energy I needed to traverse the distance. I arrived winded and flushed. In the evening light, I could see Adam lying motionless on his back and The Creator's hand working at his middle.

I hid behind the Tree of Knowledge and watched The Creator take a bone from Adam. He wrapped it in clay, forming another female body. This one slighter in build than Lilith, but female nonetheless. As I watched, trying to catch my own breath, The Creator breathed life into Adam's companion before awakening him. Her strawberry blonde hair hung in stark contrast to Lilith's black tresses and her milky pale skin differed from her predecessor's olive tones.

Adam awoke and helped her up. He named her Eve. The Creator nodded and declared their coupling was good. With His blessing, the two were off into the Garden. Eve submitted herself to her husband just as he'd wanted from Lilith and with that, Lilith was written out of the history books and out of life in the Garden of Eden.

I left, furious. Furious with the man who professed to love Lilith, who had begged for her return. Adam would not wait for a servant and The Creator, rather than coming to her rescue, replaced her as if she was nothing more than the soil from which she was made. If not me, then who? Who would save her from a fate worse than death? Who would rescue Lilith from her torments. My wrath provided all the courage I needed.

'Bout fucking time, Sariel.

I arrived at the cave just before daybreak. Before my brothers awoke, I killed them both with a rock I found near the shore. My rage unleashed, I smashed it into them until their flesh tore and their bones cracked. A raven, black as the entrance to the cave, flew down out of the heavens and plucked their eyes from their orbits. It dipped its beak deep into their foreheads and returned to me with golden chains. From each hung an amulet with their sigils. I dropped them into my satchel and the raven lit on my shoulder. Together we walked into the cave.

"Yes! That's the way it's done. I knew that bird was bad-ass," Kenzi said aloud to the empty room. There was more to be read, but suddenly she was famished.

Chapter 22: Book of Kenzi 10

"Hey, nice work on the liquid tray." Her nurse, Emily, feigned excitement. The truth was, Kenzi had managed to eat the Jell-O, the sherbet shake, and one spoonful of the flavorless saltwater labeled "Chicken Broth" before dumping the rest down the sink.

"Yep. Can I try some mashed potatoes for supper maybe?" she faked her own expression of interest.

"I'll check the orders. I think so, but I'll let you know." Nurse Emily flashed another prom-queen smile as she sashayed out.

Kenzi pulled the journal out from under the covers and opened it. The light in the room was dimmer now that the sun had crossed over to the west side of the hospital. She switched on the above-bed light, careful not to call Miss Thing, RN back in the room, and settled back into Sariel's tale.

Lilith was sprawled thin and listless on the dirt floor. At first, I thought she was dead. The demons had ravaged her, sucked her dry of her vivacious essence. I approached her cautiously, aware of the darkness surrounding us, ever heedful to subtle changes in the air that would alert me to the presence of a demon. There was no evidence of other beings, yet I knew these creatures were not like those of The Creator's, I could not predict their behavior.

I touched her, and she shrank from me. She was alive at least. I exhaled and realized I'd been holding my breath since I first saw her lying there.

"Lilith," I whispered gently. "It's me, Sariel. I've come to take you away from this."

She opened her eyes. The gloss, the shine, the vibrancy was gone. A dull grey stare met my eyes without recognition. I wanted to pick her up, to hold her against me and promise her she would never be hurt again. Not physically, not emotionally. I respected this woman. I understood her. Now, I was aware of what pure love felt like. Because, yes, Kenzi, I loved her. I wanted to protect her. I wanted to keep her as my own. I wanted her to be my wife.

It took you seven damned years to figure that out?

But I knew The Creator would never allow it. Even in my fury, my nature bade me to obey Him. My mission was to bring her home to her husband. As it was, we'd taken so long, she'd been replaced. If I tried to return without her, my punishment would be severe. With her, I could prove my loyalty and perseverance. Perhaps, Adam would keep two wives and my reward would be a wife of my own. I would ask for one like Lilith.

Oh my god, what an idiot. How could you believe your own shit like that?

Lilith said nothing. Her wide, frightened eyes watched my every move. The bird cawed, and it echoed in the stone-walled prison. I jumped, Lilith screamed and began to fight. She bit and scratched at me. Her nails were like claws, drawing blood and pain—

sensations that were shocking yet more real than anything I had ever felt in The Creator's kingdom. Ruffling its feathers, my new friend flew away, bothered by the commotion.

"Lilith!" I said more forcefully this time and grabbed her wrists. "Come with me. Let us get you out of here."

She seemed to finally recognize me and stopped struggling. She let me pick her up. She was no more than a dried-up husk of the soft, curvaceous creation she'd once been. As I carried her toward the light, the bird returned to my shoulder once more. Like this, we three walked away from all the evil she'd endured and back to what I still foolishly believed was the love of her Lord and her husband.

But you saw what they did in the garden. You knew she'd been replaced like nothing. Why would you do this to her? That's not love, that's just a different form of control.

It hurt Kenzi to read this. She'd romanticized The Scribble Man—Sariel—all her life. He was her hero, her protector. He loved her and yet, he was nothing more than a brainwashed coward, refusing to accept the truth because the truth wasn't easy.

I did not tell her about what I'd seen in the garden. In my naivety, I simply believed that as a man, Adam had needs that would have to be met until Lilith returned. I assumed that once they saw what she'd gone through to prove her equality, they would reconsider their stance. Adam would want his first wife back. Perhaps The Creator would make a new man for the new woman and together the couples would populate the earth. All these things I told myself as I carried Lilith back to the origin of her oppression.

We stopped for the night not far from the garden paradise. There I fed her and cleaned her in the crystal waters of a moonlit pool. With sustenance and her wounds seen to—and there were so many—she perked up a bit. A fiery hatred danced in her eyes as she told me of her days in the wilds and the horrors she'd succumbed to in the cave.

I should have told her what I saw when I went back to the garden for help. I should have given her the choice, but like every other being she'd known, I used her. For company, for fireside warmth and for a reward from my Creator. Kenzi, I failed her. I thought I loved her, but it was a selfish love that ruined her. I ruled her with silence, I offered her no options. She had no idea of what she was walking into the next day.

That night she slept next to me. I touched her, and she did not flinch away. She curled herself into me. We fit as if made for each other. I told myself this was not true. I reminded myself that she belonged to another, but then I felt her lips brush against my chest. Something in my loins stirred. I felt the rush of vital fluids leave my brain and settle in my middle. Suddenly, I could no longer think. My earth-body took over. My lips found hers in the darkness as if they were a part of my own body. Her hands, roughened from fighting for so long, slid across my skin and pushed me back. She straddled me, and I could feel the heat from her core bearing down on my manhood before it swallowed me inside.

No time in The Creator's kingdom nor in the garden of paradise prepared me for the pleasures of the flesh. It intensified my love for her. As she rode my hips, the feeling grew fervent until I cried out, not in pain, but in a satisfaction I had never before known.

Everything I felt in that moment exploded out of me and into her. She felt it too. Her head dropped back, and she closed her eyes. In that one moment, we made our own paradise, and we were all the other needed.

Please tell me you realized it was a horrible idea to take her back to Adam. Please. You didn't, did you? I mean we learn about Adam and Eve, not Lilith. You took her away, didn't you?

At dawn, I announced that we were returning to the garden. I can still see the look in her eyes. Her confusion turned to shock, which slowly turned to anger. She was so strong and stubborn, but beneath it all there was heartbreak and betrayal. She would never show it. Instead, she stood, head up, and walked on her own back into the garden. She walked back into the bonds of her previous life.

Motherfucker.

I saw Eve, the second wife, standing near the Tree of Knowledge. I should have said something, instead we kept walking. I watched as she and Lilith made eye contact, both refusing to break it until their heads could turn no further. Lilith did not stop. Eve followed us into the camp site where Lilith and Adam had once made a home.

Adam was skinning a fur-bearing mammal—a capybara, I believe—and he looked up. When he saw Lilith, he stood, the carcass falling to the ground with a thud.

"I was told you were dead."

That was it. Not 'welcome home, love.' No 'I've missed you. Let's try to work through our differences.' Lilith said nothing, she simply glared at him. She did not want to come back any more than he wanted her back. What had I done?

"Adam," Eve said, coming around from behind us. "Who is she? What is happening?"

Her soft-spoken, clearly subservient voice and mannerisms told me all I needed to know. She was indeed a replacement for Lilith, not as I erroneously thought, a temporary place-filler. Adam was pleased with her. The appearance of Lilith suddenly made his situation complicated and so he called to The Creator.

When The Creator came down and saw us, He became angry. He was furious with me as well as Lilith.

"Sariel," His voice boomed. "Where are your brothers Malach and Sammael?"

I retrieved their talismans from my bag and held them up.

"I killed them, Father. They did not try to retrieve Lilith as commanded. They attacked her and threw her to the demons."

The Creator responded, "She is nothing but a demon herself. She is a whore, and it was on my command that she be handed over to the filth of her own kind."

Pain flashed across Lilith's face for an instant. Then a look of indignation settled in and sat like stone.

"She chose her fate when she refused to accept her place," The Creator said. "Look upon Eve, Lilith. See that I have made another, a true servant and partner for Adam. You are no longer welcome here. Go back to the cave where you belong. You are banished from all the land that I have created."

She was gone, just like that. Her cries faded into nothing as The Creator sent her back to the realm of demons and all things dark and evil.

This is all such bullshit. No wonder she is super pissed. I'm pissed for her.

I was dumbfounded. Why had He sent us to collect her? So He could punish her? Did He command Malach and Sammael to punish her in that way? I looked up at Him.

"You killed your brothers," He announced as if I hadn't just said that.

Suddenly I felt a searing pain deep in the flesh of my arm. Their names appeared in bright red blood across my forearm. I winced with the burn.

"Sariel, you have taken two lives and thus have been marked with the death of your own kind. You shall be cast out of my kingdom and shall stay on this earth. You will be known as Death. When I command you to collect a soul, you will know by the name writ in fire upon your flesh. For as long as you exist in this state, you will bear the names of all the souls you've taken."

"But, Father," I interrupted.

"You shall stay upon this earth until you have collected all the demons spewed forth from the harlot's womb."

"But Father," I repeated. "You sent her back to them. There will be endless demons. I—"

"You shall stay upon this earth until every last one of her spawn has been collected. You shall take the mortal soul of anyone I command, and you shall live within the earth with the others who have forsaken me."

Before I could protest again, I was in the damp, darkness of Sheol. I smelled the dank earth around me and mourned the loss of everything I knew and loved. For days I refused to move, I huddled against the cold, firm walls and cried. I would leave only when called upon to collect mortal souls. Days turned to months which turned to years. My skin lost its color and the scars began to cover my body.

When I became listless, I walked the earth with Enoch, my bird. It had eyes with which it could see the demons for what they truly were, even when they masqueraded as humans. It seemed I'd been granted the power to force their souls—although you must understand they do not have souls like mortals; theirs are more like black holes—into talismans where they are trapped. As long as I keep the talismans here, in Sheol, safe, they cannot be released back into the world.

Together, we collected many of Lilith's children. With each, I thought of her lying near death in the cave. One day, when I could no longer take the pain of knowing that somewhere she was being tortured continuously, Enoch and I traveled back to the place from which I once rescued her. I was going to save her again, but this time she would not have to worry about ever returning to her hell.

Enoch and I found her, chained to the center of the cavern, arms and legs spread wide. Her body was a labyrinth of bruises and scars and fresh claw marks. My heart ached for her but when she lifted her head, her eyes were dark abysses. There was no humanity left. I had no idea if I could take her life without the commandment of The Creator, but I couldn't let her go like this. Besides, like it or not, she was the mother of demons. She was now responsible for prolonging my earthly punishment.

I touched her head. Enoch dipped his beak into the hole my touch left behind, and he drew out her soul. It was the most brilliant piece of silver filigree I'd ever seen, and I couldn't bear to part with it. A rabbit's foot hung between her breasts and I picked it up. I pulled it gently over her head and used the claw to draw a drop of her blood. With her mortal essence on it, her soul was drawn to it as if it were magnetic. The two became one and suddenly I had her with me again. This was the way I collected the demons' souls. It did not occur to me that Lilith was mortal. Her soul should not have been able to be drawn into a talisman. It did not occur to me at the time, that her years of abuse had changed her. She was no longer a victim of the demons. She had become a demoness herself.

There was nothing left of her. Without her soul, her body slumped lifeless in the chains. I left it there. I wish I could say that I hadn't; that out of respect for her, I carried her back and buried her in Sheol, my home. But I didn't. I left it for the demons to desecrate.

With her soul trapped in its talisman, I carried her with me all this time. I do not know if I will ever be accepted back into the kingdom again, as I am ashamed to say that since that time, I have acted independent of The Creator in similar ways. It is likely I will have to again.

The day your brother died, you were so fearless when you looked right at me. I thought of Lilith in that moment—Enoch did, too. You were a survivor, much like her. We gifted her talisman to you and you have escaped death many times since then. I believe you gained your strength from her. And I believe that is why you are in danger now. I don't know what black magic she used to return but I suspect she needs her talisman back to retrieve the soul I managed to keep. Only with that, will she be truly powerful.

She will not know how to release it from the talisman. Because you carried it, she will think you do. She will need your help, Kenzi, but you mustn't. Remember, she has lost all humanity. She is a demoness. She will lie to you, trick you, do whatever she can to get you to help her.

Get the talisman back, Kenzi and I will protect you. I will not fail you as I did Lilith. You must help me. When you have the talisman, come to me. If you need safety, you are welcome in Sheol. You will be protected.

Chapter 23: Book of Kenzi 11

Kenzi closed the book in stunned silence. If Sariel thought this would help her to understand, he was dead wrong. She felt more confused than ever. Maybe Lilith was mad, maybe she was here for revenge, but could she be blamed? And Sariel—every decision he'd ever made was for his own selfish reasons. Could he really be trusted?

She kind of wished Henry were here so she could talk to him. She really liked him, even more now that she knew he was kind of a fuck up like her. He'd probably never come back though, not since he'd gotten in trouble because of her. Henry, even with all his faults and insecurities, was a better man than Sariel. She needed a friend she could trust. Although what would he say if she told him this story? He'd probably have her put in a straightjacket and she'd for sure never see him again. Nope. She was on her own with this one.

A thousand red ants crawled beneath her skin spreading all her anxiety out with them. They would stay there, tormenting her, driving her insane until she could find a way to release them in a sanguine tide.

There was nothing in this room Kenzi could cut herself with. The straw from her cup did little but cause a sort of burn like the kind she'd get as a kid when Robbie would force her to do the "Sissy Test" and rub an eraser back and forth across her skin until it turned red and blistered. Looking around, she saw nothing that would adequately substitute for the rabbit's foot. She wondered if Lilith, who was definitely not a nurse, would come back again tonight. Even if she did and even if Kenzi managed to get the talisman from her, then what? Would she turn Lilith over to Sariel again? Let him fuck her over once more? Shouldn't sisters stick together? But what if Sariel wasn't lying. What if Lilith was a demoness now? Maybe she wanted to possess Kenzi, steal her body or something. It was all so confusing.

In the meantime, two other things were of the utmost importance; first she had to deal with cops who, if Patel was right, would be coming anytime and secondly, she had to take care of this itch. She felt like a junky in withdrawal. Never had she not been able to make a cut when she needed to. The pink sponges on plastic sticks were gone now that she was on "clears." But no solid food yet, so, even a plastic knife was out of the question.

Nothing. There was nothing in this goddamned room to make the crawling stop. The IV had been inserted into her left hand—an erroneous assumption that she was right-handed she guessed. Her nails were short and dirty, there was no way she was getting an infection by trying to do anything with them. The IV, though—wasn't there a needle permanently buried in her skin right now? Wasn't that how they worked?

Desperate times called for desperate measures. She worked the tape away wincing at the pull on her skin. She took a deep breath and pulled the needle out.

It wasn't a needle. She turned it around with her fingers as it continued to drip saline onto the bed. It was just this soft, rubbery thing that looked like a needle.

"Fuck!" she cried and threw the worthless piece of tubing to the side of the bed.

The tears were hot and unwelcome; proof of her weakness. The angrier she became, the harder the tears fell making the bugs beneath her skin more agitated.

"Fuck! Fuck this shit, fuck this place." She shoved the blankets off exposing the colostomy bag filled with a yellowish sludge. She tore it off too, stifling the scream by biting through her bottom lip. "And fuck this."

The sobs were not coming from her mouth now; they were ripping through her chest like claws. She couldn't get out of bed because of the metal contraption stuck to her leg. A metal contraption with long, metal screws that were obviously sharp enough to burrow through her skin.

Kenzi studied the silver rods embedded deep within her bones. Surely removing one wouldn't affect the healing process. She grabbed and pulled, wiggled, and turned. The pain seared up and down her leg in bolts of lightning, but the thing wouldn't budge.

"Come on," she pleaded. "Just work with me."

Blood covered her left hand and fingers making them sticky and slippery at the same time. She switched hands trying the weaker right one and thought she felt the screw give.

"Oh, Oh!" She worked harder. The pain was replaced by single-minded determination as she yanked at it, pulling, and twisting, and wriggling.

"Oh my God! What are you doing? Oh no." The nurse rushed into the room, depositing a tray onto the bedside table.

"Honey, stop! What is going on here?"

She grabbed at the IV tubing which had left a puddle on the floor. The colostomy bag's contents leaked down the side of the bed, while the deflated bag hung off the side like one of Dali's clocks.

She hit the call button on the bike seat-sized remote. *"Can I help you?"* a disembodied voice asked.

"I need help and have someone call Dr. Altrey," the nurse called out.

She had grabbed Kenzi's bloodied hands in her own and held them together. Kenzi didn't fight her. She knew it was a losing battle, but the ants had not surrendered—in fact, the chaos in the room seemed to drive them into a frenzy.

Kenzi gave in to the madness and began to scream. Amid the flurry of needles and tape, she lost herself in the darkness.

Chapter 24: Book of Conquest 4

"Which one's yours?" the man asked.

Lilith stared through the bank of windows that provided hospital visitors views of the healthiest babies in the Neonatal ICU. Above them, near the ceiling, in brightly colored bubble letters, the nurses had hung a banner reading "Feeders and Growers." Sunflowers in pots flanked the words and happy-faced bumblebees flitted about the letters.

"All of them," she answered, turning to face the faux father.

The man was perfection. Ageless blue eyes so crisp and demarcated they looked more like a computer-generated image of human eyes than actual flesh and blood. His dark, almost black hair was cut in the Caesar style that George Clooney made famous in the 90s and yet, it was as if this man's head was formed specifically for this look.

"You know, some of us give them a little time to grow up and declare allegiance before we try to claim them."

"I said, they are all mine, Lucifer. What do you want?" She had no time for distractions.

"Aw, come on, Lil. You know I had nothing to do with what happened in that cave. Sometimes I wish I had, I'm not going to lie. I mean, we would have made some gorgeous babies, right?"

"What do you want?"

"I want to help you, actually. I want to make amends for all that was done to you. And, if I'm being completely honest, I'd be happy to help you get revenge as well. I'm intrigued by what you've been doing. And I must say, I'm digging the whole gravid look. Who knew pregnant women could be so sexy?"

Lilith had lost interest, her attention turned back to the babies once more. Exhausted mothers rocked them in chairs, fathers shifted weight back and forth from foot to foot not really understanding what their role was in this strange situation. The restless souls inside her womb shifted and pushed against their prison walls. She rubbed her bloated belly.

"Lil, look, you know I'm a proud being. I don't like to do this sort of thing. But I got a lot of respect for you. I've been fighting The Man for my entire existence and I've had so much help. It's only fair to offer you—"

Lilith spun to face him. "Fair? Since when does fair have anything to do with our existence? I do not need, nor do I want your help, demon."

A flash of anger colored Lucifer's brilliant cobalt eyes black. He stepped into her space, as close as her protruding stomach would allow. She did not flinch, she did not step back, instead, she stood her ground. She had suffered thousands of years for refusing to submit, she had been demonized and vilified for daring to expect to be treated as an equal.

"Lilith." He softened his tone and a smile returned to his face although his eyes remained stormy. "You have grown so strong and I look forward to seeing what you will do. You may or may not know but there are few demons left on this earth. Your boyfriend has been busy in your absence."

"Why are you still here?" she asked.

"Because, I admire you. I always have. And because I think you can do something I have never managed to accomplish. I'm here to offer my demons as your servants. It's my reparation for what they did to you."

Without turning away from the babies, without a twitch of a muscle to change her face, Lilith answered, "And they are mine to do as I wish?"

A smile flashed across his face before he responded, "You have my word."

"Your word? Your word, and the paltry number of demons left after Sariel's work, are no good to me."

"And the girl, Sariel's girl." He continued as if he hadn't heard her. "I can deliver her to you. She has been to Sheol, I can smell it on her. She can walk between the worlds. Take her to Sheol and gather all the demons you need. She has the power to release them as she did you."

"The girl will be mine. She is the fourth and final in my quartet." She turned to Lucifer. His black eyes sparkled with anticipation. This time, the smiled stayed on his face. Lilith touched his cheek. "The Creator gave me the mark of the snake, to remind me that I am as low as you. We are one in the same, Lucifer." She kissed him, hard and long. "I'll take your demons and use them as I see fit. What do you want in return?"

He kept his arm around her shoulders and squeezed. From behind, they would appear a loving couple watching their newborn sleep. "I'd like to increase that paltry number you mentioned. Some of those demons trapped in Sheol are your own children. They would serve you as well. Use your girl to release them and I will do whatever I can to see you succeed."

"Asmodeus and Beelzebub to start." Lilith answered.

"Done."

"I will gather what I can from Sheol. I'll need you to keep Sariel out of my way while I do this." Her countenance softened. The child-like look of innocence and fragility was hypnotic. "You never hurt me. I know that. What you did to Eve...I'm sorry, Lucifer. I do trust you, and I do need you." She smiled and nestled closer to him.

"I'm all yours, doll." He grinned.

"Oh, my goodness, what a sweet couple." An older couple approached the window. The woman, short and white-haired, reached her hands out to touch Lilith's belly. "You must be expecting twins. Well don't you worry, our grandson Levi has done wonderful here. These nurses are just amazing."

"My babies are in there now," Lilith said.

"Oh? I apologize, you looked so...well—"

"All right, Maggie, I think you've said quite enough," her husband admonished. He turned to Lilith and Lucifer. "So which ones are yours?"

Lucifer gave Lilith's shoulder a squeeze, turning her around to leave. "All of them," he said and winked.

Chapter 25: Book of Conquest 5

The club was set back behind a non-descript black door at the far end of a well-known bar. Neon purple lighting and red velvet booths worked together with the body-throbbing music to induce a state of hypnotic indulgence. The ambiance itself was a lotus bud meant to abolish time and memories, allowing tourists to abandon inhibitions and experience pure debauchery. At the obsidian bar, back-lit by a glassed-in electric fire that ran the length of the liquor shelves above it, absinthe flowed over sugar cubes while pills marked with E's were passed as casually as the tab.

Lilith, clad in a crimson bra, with her very pregnant belly pushed out above a black leather skirt so short it revealed the belts of her black lace garter, waltzed past the half-dressed wait staff and some of the more unabashed female (and male for that matter) club patrons. She stopped at the bar, stilettoed heel hooked on the foot stand, and took a shot of Everclear followed by hot cinnamon whiskey.

Without paying for the shots, she continued to the back door and let herself in. The music muted significantly behind it and the dim light of the old stone hallway lacked the colorful hues of commercial sex from the room she'd just left.

Her heels echoed dully against the walls of the squat hall. The gate in front of her stood beneath an arch of stone with the words Club D'Libidine scrawled curvilinearly above it. The gate itself was iron, charred with years of flame. If one looked closely, they would observe the thirteen vertical spikes rising to points in a bell-shaped curve mirroring the arch above. Patina-green copper vines wove around them such that they became nothing more than supports for the wild metals of the entrance to the club.

The gate opened inward upon Lilith's approach and without slowing her pace, she continued inside. Here, her shiny red bra stood out among the mass of naked flesh. Bodies covered only by small trinkets pierced through the skin or angry, red welts intersecting across backs and buttocks traipsed drunkenly about the dimly lit studio room. Hands reached out wantonly to caress her swollen abdomen. They pulled her breasts free of the bra, ripped her garter belts, skirt, and shoes so that by the time she approached the man lying on a large silken bed at the head of the oval room, she was as naked as the rest. Fingers traced the line of the snake that coiled in wait around her ample frame.

"Well, well, well, where have you been all my life, sweetheart?" the man asked.

His lower half was covered by a sheet but the shape beneath was in no way human. Two lower extremities of some sort formed unnatural mounds beneath the cover, but one was much larger than the other and the small one's foot seemed to spread out in a flipper shape. His chest was broad and hairy, his face inhumanly wide and full boned. Had Kenzi been with Lilith, she would instantly have thought of the giant from The Princess Bride which was her most favorite movie. But Kenzi was not here and Lilith saw the familiar form of one of her former tormentors, the demon Asmodeus, and swallowed her hatred back down until it roiled in a bilious ball inside her stomach.

"You've certainly found a good place for yourself, all fat and happy, sitting in the back room of some classless dump fucking all these drugged-up mortals." She sniffed. "Mortal sex leaves the stink of death that doesn't suit a demon such as yourself."

"Hey, it's sin city, where else would I find so many willing followers, wanting to worship the god of lust?"

"Oh, you're a god now, is that it? I thought you were nothing more than a mortal-created demon, the sin of lust hidden in the dark of the closet, an embarrassment even to his own worshipers." She smiled. "Who needs Hell, right?"

"You know this is my home, these women are my mothers, the men are my fathers. We live symbiotically here and with each perversion, I grow that much stronger. It's more than you ever did for me." He spat on the floor that lay between them. Lilith watched it smoke and burn through the stone.

"But that is all in the past, isn't it?" he said. "Come to me, love. I've been expecting you." He held out a hand which she took and climbed onto the bed. The ball of acid in her stomach burned in protest.

"Used to be a time when demons could wreak havoc among the mortals. Now you're all living with them like pets." She stroked his unruly hair as if he were a dog. He stiffened. She'd won a point. She continued. "I don't see any women tied up and spread out in the middle of a cave, not that I hold a grudge."

She dropped her hand.

"We were told you'd been taken by Sariel. Of course, over the years, many rumors and tales of your powers abounded. No one knew where you'd gone or what you'd become. None of us felt like asking Sariel, you understand?" He laughed.

He was fishing, she knew it. Fishing for information. What *had* she become? Humanity's mythologies declared her a demon, sometimes a witch, or something else entirely. They'd soon find out the truth. Lilith was a Goddess. No. She was The Goddess. That's what she knew." That's what she knew. Where she'd been or how she'd gotten back here, she was slowly figuring out with the help of her new little friend, her fourth whore, the one who would take Sariel's place—when she was ready of course. Until then, the other whores needed her help. They needed more than Kenzi would and that was her purpose today.

Asmodeus's hand slipped down her back, toying with her buttocks. A young girl was escorted out of the crowd and to the foot of the bed. Her eyes were cast down, her pert little breasts betrayed her age and innocence. Beautiful brown ringlets framed her face.

"My, my, isn't this a pretty little one?" Lilith declared, sliding off the bed to walk around the girl, pushing away the ugly hell-beast who'd brought her as sacrifice to Asmodeus.

"These young ones are tough to tame, Asmo, or have you forgotten?" She could feel the heat of his anger pulsating.

"I haven't." He laughed. "Those were the days, huh, baby?"

Lilith held her anger, eyes closed tight, willing the revulsion to stay beneath the skin. She spun around to face her rapist but kept her arm around the young girl. "I expected more from the great Demon of Lust than an adults' version of Disney World. All this neon gives the flesh a sickly hue, don't you agree?"

Asmodeus sneered. Snot flew from his nostrils in hot droplets as he snorted in disagreement.

She was not ready to let him speak yet, she needed him to know that she was stronger now.

She patted the girl on her puberty-rounded bottom. "Go on, get out of here. Why don't you run along home to your loved ones before this whole world falls apart?"

The girl darted like a mouse, the crowd parted, and the sound of the gate punctuated the end of the child's part in the scene.

"What do you want, Lilith? You want some kind of apology? Revenge? For all the wrongs done to you?" The joking lilt was gone from his voice now. There was nothing in it now but the deep, gravel of a common demon.

"No, you insult me with such trivialities. It seems I have over-estimated you, Asmo," she said. "I came here because Lucifer seemed to think you would be interested in causing a little trouble with me, but perhaps you are too set in your ways, too happy with the *as is.*"

She was walking back to the gate when his voice boomed.

"Go on, you have my attention."

"Well, what a lucky girl I am."

"Lilith, as you can see, I'm a very busy man. I don't have time for your silly childish games."

"I wasn't sure you were right for the job. Lucifer, of course, gives you much credit. This is going to be much more involved than a back-alley blow job." She opened the gate and let herself out.

The girl sat in the hallway, a tattered backpack on the floor beside her. She'd put on a pair of shorts and a faded leopard-print tank top. A cheap pair of flip-flops cut into her feet.

"I thought I told you to go?" Lilith said

"Ain't got nowhere to go."

"If I were you, I'd find somewhere quick. Is this how you want to die? In this stone prison? The world's about to end. You better pick a side."

The girl looked up at Lilith. In the lighted hallway, her cherubic cheeks showed her true age. Lilith touched her cheek, and pain—both the girl's and Lilith's—exploded between the two in a jolt of electricity. Lilith let go.

"Against me."

She kissed the girl on the lips, gently, avoiding any other touch.

"Or with me."

The girl stared in astonishment like a deer hypnotized by the headlights of an oncoming car. She grabbed her backpack, but Lilith had her hand on it. The girl pulled, curling her lip up like a stray cur.

"I like your spunk. With me, it is."

Yanking on the pack, Lilith pulled the girl back into her arms. This time, the kiss was not gentle, but forceful. Lilith's tongue parted the girl's lips, prying her mouth open. The snake tattoo was now coiled tightly around the girl, squeezing the breath out of her. Lilith inhaled deeply. When the girl's soul joined the others deep within Lilith's womb, the demoness dropped the emptied skin to the ground and kicked it and the backpack to the edge of the hall. She shivered and smiled, satiated. Sassy female souls made her feel invincible.

The hinges of the gate screeched behind her. Lilith swung around. Standing in the center of the room, his asymmetry ugly even in the dark sex-filled club, Asmodeus called out to her.

"Lil, come on back, would ya? I'm sorry. Really. I already promised Lucifer I would help you. Tell me what you're thinking."

She grinned, her nipples grew firm and her sex throbbed. The flush of triumph warmed her body. She brought the tears then, weak, and womanly, and ran to him. Forcing her arms around him, she furthered her play.

"Thank you, Asmo. I don't know what I'd do without you."

Chapter 26: Book of War 3

The green room of the Christian Broadcasting Network reminded Melanie Pryor of a funeral home. A lot of mauves, blues, and golds accented the furniture beneath a soft lighting. The art prints decorating the room were on the level of the stuff her mother had tried selling at home parties back when every middle-class woman worth her salt used wall sconces and silk flowers in her décor.

"I guess Jesus approves," Melanie mumbled to herself, still taking in all the room had to offer.

There was of course the obligatory coffee urn and donuts, bagels, fruit, and orange juice on a table pushed against the wall opposite the maroon couch she was sitting on. Glamor shots of all the show's stars and some frequent guests hung above the food. In the center of these framed idols was a large wooden cross with a horrifyingly life-like Jesus impaled upon it.

"Ugh, get me out of here," she said.

The door swung open and a middle-aged blonde in an ankle-length denim skirt with a very pregnant belly came in. She carried a clip board and wireless headphones with mic attached.

"Did you need somethin', Miss Pryor?" she asked in an Alabaman drawl. "I coulda swore I heard you say somethin'," *Ask and ye shall receive.*

Blondie grinned and put her free hand on her belly. Melanie stood and ignored her question.

"How far along are you?" She approached with her hand out. "May I?"

Without hesitation the woman grabbed Melanie's hand and pressed it firmly against her protuberant abdomen. Melanie could feel the child rolling around inside the woman's womb. The woman gushed at the single survivor of the "Attack on Life" as it was now being referred to by the political right.

"Thirty-six weeks. Almost there! This is baby number five—our first boy—Adam. Each one is a miracle."

Melanie put her other hand on the woman's belly and without asking permission kissed it. The baby inside stopped rolling. She looked up and smiled.

"God is always in control, isn't he?" Melanie said, dropping her hands away.

They shared a moment of raptured bliss before the blonde grabbed Melanie by the shoulders and hugged her.

"And that is why He saved you! So, you could come here and preach His word. We're so very honored to have you."

She squeezed one more time before letting go.

"Well, it's just about time to get you out there. My job is to make sure you're presentable."

She held Melanie out at arm's length. "You look good to me."

The woman, who had never bothered to introduce herself, escorted Melanie to the edge of the stage where she was told to wait until introduced. Standing in the darkness, the power of the goddess surged through her. She was not Cynthia Parris any more than she was Melanie Pryor. She was the third whore—bringer of war.

"…Miss Melanie Pryor," she heard the name called, followed by applause.

The nameless pregnant woman ushered her out where she was received by the elderly man who hosted the show and his middle-aged female sidekick—not cohost. As the man, he ran the show.

After the customary small talk, the host got down to business.

"Now, Miss Pryor, we need to ask you about that terrible day last month when someone, and we stress that we do not know who yet, killed twenty adults and seven children, all of them doing God's work. You, by some divine intervention, had walked a block away to a convenience store when the bombs went off, is that right?"

"Yes." She nodded.

"And what were you all doing there on that particular day?"

"We were peacefully protesting the abortion clinic across the street. We try to protest as often as we can."

"So, this wasn't new. You'd been doing it for some time."

Melanie opened her mouth to answer when the sidekick interrupted her.

"As we must, all of us. We have to continue to speak out until Roe v. Wade has been overturned and murder in any form is illegal."

She smiled to herself as the audience applauded. The man gave her a warning look that wasn't missed by Melanie.

"But this was your very first protest with the church, is that right, Miss Pryor?" he asked.

"Yes, I just moved here from Boston and joined the church. I finally found people who shared my beliefs and I wanted to be a part of it." She felt as if she was being interrogated by the police rather than celebrated for surviving a bombing.

"Who do you think did that to your friends? To the church family who took you in?" He asked but took her hand in his paternalistically.

There was an answer he expected from her and the hand-holding was his unspoken way of telling her not to fuck this up.

"I would say, and I hate to make accusations against anyone," she answered slowly, watching his face for approval. "I would guess it was someone who has no respect for human life."

The audience erupted in applause, many standing. The sidekick was in tears, the host nodding in agreement.

"I don't think we need to say any more than that, do we?" And then, "We'd like you to be our guest of honor at the Rally for Life next month, Miss Pryor. I think you have become an important symbol of our fight for life."

"I'm afraid it does seem to be turning into a war," she said, suppressing a satisfied smile. "Aristotle once said 'we make war that we may live in peace.' And I tell myself every day that sometimes we must fight for those who cannot, so that they may live, period."

The cries of A-men and Hallelujah and the thunderous applause did little to drown out the pain-filled screams from just beyond the stage. Those watching from home saw a commercial, while those in the studio fell into their seats. A blonde haired pregnant woman stumbled onto the stage, clutching her belly. Blood flowed down her legs like a river and bloomed across the back of her denim skirt.

"My baby!" The blonde screamed, as the crew and hosts ran to her. Melanie stayed in her seat.

"Is dead," she said. No one heard her.

Chapter 27: Book of Kenzi 12

The light in the room was grey, she'd been out for some time then. The IV was now in her right hand, which, like its partner was tied to the bed. A device was pushed into her nose and the air flow through it was much more forceful than the little tubes that had been there previously. Her leg ached. She had a feeling the screw had been replaced and tightened. Her mouth was dry which she suspected was due to a combo of the air being forced through her respiratory system and whatever drugs they'd used to knock her out.

"I gotta get out of this place," she muttered. Looking around the room for inspiration, Kenzi saw a new addition to the furnishings.

A figure sat in a chair against the wall. It was nothing more than an outline in the dusk of the lightless room. Male or female, she couldn't tell, but either way, her visitor appeared to be sleeping.

A sitter? It was ridiculous—she certainly didn't need anyone watching her. Maybe it was a cop waiting for her to wake up, afraid that if they put off the questioning any longer, they may never get any answers. Kenzi leaned over, trying to see any details. Besides a long, thin frame, all she could make out were the legs sprawled out straight in front of the chair and the head thrown back as if deep in sleep. This wasn't the semi-conscious sleep of a bus ride or air plane; this person was dead to the world. Great job they were doing.

All this and her skin still itched, still begged to be opened, to let the anxiety spill out and leave her. On her side table, which had been pushed into the far corner of the room was a dinner tray and, on the tray, a plate. A plate meant solid food and solid food meant silverware.

She worked at her restraints, twisting her wrists first clockwise then counterclockwise but only managed to cause that same sissy-test burn the straw had caused.

"Ugh," Kenzi huffed. It was useless.

"Were you a cutter before he gave you this?"

Lily was holding the rabbit's foot up by its chain. Her baby bump was impossibly larger than the day before. She was standing beside the snoozing sitter somehow reading Kenzi's mind.

"No. Can you undo these restraints?"

"I can do better than that. I want to get you out of here. I'm here to save you." She stepped closer to the bed.

"What are you, Lilith?" Kenzi asked irritated. "Yes, I know who you are, I know all about you, but what are you here for? Sariel said you're trying to get to me, that you need my help releasing your soul or something. But if that's true, what does that make you: a demon or a ghost or what? And what makes you think I can help you?"

The restraints rubbed deep into her wrists as she rolled back and forth pulling at them. Her teeth clenched, and her lower jaw jutted out in frustration. "And can you please just get these fucking things off me!"

She yanked on the right one to punctuate her demand, but it was no longer there. The surprise came too fast to abort the momentum and Kenzi tumbled out of the bed and onto the floor.

"Oof." The air coughed out of her.

The person in the chair never stirred.

Kenzi stayed on the cool laminate floor of her room assessing the physical damage and pain before trying to get up. There was no pain. None. She wiggled her toes—nothing— and not just that but the backs of both feet touched the floor which meant there was no metal halo around her right leg. She patted herself down the left side and felt no bag bulging from her middle, no pain, no hole in the skin.

"Get up and come with me. There is nothing wrong with you," Lilith said.

Legs, one of which was coiled with a snake tattoo that continued up under the thigh-high skirt, stood next to her. A hand descended into Kenzi's view.

Kenzi worked herself up onto her knees and held up a hand up in the "stop" gesture.

"I'm not going anywhere with you until I get some answers." She stood up and brushed off her hands and torso.

The man in the chair was wearing a security guard's uniform and he was dead. Even in the dark, she could see that. You didn't grow up in the ghetto and not know what a dead man looked like, and Kenzi knew death better than any of her neighbors. His head was tilted back because his neck had been crushed and his jaw hung open as if unhinged. There were dark stains around his mouth that Kenzi guessed would be red with the light on. His short-sleeved, white button down was wrinkled and twisted; the right side had pulled out of its tuck into the pants. He looked as if he'd been wrung out like a wet washcloth.

"What the fuck did you do?"

"You see we cannot talk here. It's far too dangerous." She held up the foot again like a carrot on a stick. "Come."

"First, give me my keychain back. You obviously don't need it anymore. You're here. I just want it back."

She had no idea if Lilith needed it or why. If Sariel was right, Lilith might never give it back, but it was worth a try. After all, Lilith had been abused her entire life and hadn't everyone turned their back on her? So, maybe she understood Kenzi better than anyone else. She'd freed Kenzi and healed her. Lilith wasn't as bad as Sariel feared. If she just talked to her, treated her like a friend, maybe Lilith would reciprocate.

Lilith put it back over her head. "I'm sorry, but not yet. Sariel has controlled you with this for the last time. For now, I will hold it and I promise you: when the time is right, it will be yours again."

Kenzi nodded. *Play the game, don't let on how much you need it, don't focus on the itch.*

"How far along are you? I mean, how are you even pregnant if you've been trapped for so long?" It was a reasonable question to change the subject but also, really, she wanted to know, that and how that baby was growing so damn fast.

Lilith said nothing. Instead she reached out and pushed the hair away from Kenzi's face, exposing her colorless eye. She kept going. *Keep talking, tell her about you so she knows she can trust you.*

"It's called hetero-something-or-other. My doctor—one of my doctors—told me that some cultures believe that people like me can see *both sides.* Like life and death or the afterlife." She hoped it would trigger something from Lilith.

"And so, the day your brother died, you were saved because you saw Death and stopped. Your brother ran on and the car hit him, only him." Lilith nodded as if in complete understanding.

"Yes."

"And what, do you think, would have happened had you not been able to see Sariel?"

"I guess I would be dead too."

"Did Sariel do anything to try to catch your attention? Wave to you, shout at you to stop?"

It was like being interrogated on one of those crime shows. Lilith was leading Kenzi to an uncomfortable conclusion.

"No. I mean, I don't know really. I thought for the longest time he was my imaginary friend. I thought maybe I made him up *after* Robbie died to give my brain something to think about instead of the images of my dead brother. But when I really think about it, I don't know what made me look up—I just did and he was standing there."

"And when did he give you this?" She held up the foot. The itch intensified.

"Well, I remember crying and asking him if Robbie was going to be OK and did he have to take him away. He showed me Robbie's name on his arm, which I think maybe he told me or maybe I just figured it out that it meant he had to take him. And I think I asked him if he had to take me too."

"What did he say?" Lilith asked.

"Well, obviously, he said no," Kenzi answered irritably. She wanted that foot. She took a deep breath and steadied her nerves. "And I think that was when his bird brought me the keychain—well, it was a necklace, but my dad put it on a keychain not long before he took off. Sariel said I could keep it, that it would keep me safe because it belonged to a strong girl like me…so I guess it's nice to meet you finally."

Kenzi smiled reassuringly at Lilith remembering the horrors that this woman went through, some of which were at the hands of Kenzi's very own otherworldly guardian.

"You once gave Death himself a chance, you trusted him. And we share a bond, Kenzi, can you not abide me the same?" Lilith took her hand and when she did, the itching, crawling sensation stopped. The urge to cut was gone. Her heart rate slowed and the tornado in her mind slowed to a light breeze.

"Kenzi, this," she touched the foot resting against her chest, "has been used to control the both of us. All this time. He tricked you into carrying my burden and with it, he cursed you to a life of pain and suffering. I'm sure Sariel has told you many things; some truths, some falsehoods. Do I not warrant the same chance to tell my tale?"

Kenzi could still vividly recall the kindness in Sariel's eyes the day he gave her the rabbit's foot. Besides it wasn't even his idea, it was the bird's—Enoch—the bird was the one who gave it to her. He just let her keep it. And he needed her help. He'd made some stupid mistakes with Lilith, yes, but there was something about her that was off. She could hear her out, she supposed. Besides, going with Lilith and hearing her tale was ultimately helping Sariel, wasn't it? Anyway, she had an idea. If she could get information from Lilith for him, she could use it to bargain for Gloria's life. That seemed fair.

Lilith squeezed Kenzi's hand hard, bringing her back from her interior deliberations.

"Listen to me; I have much to tell you, but we cannot stay here. The police will be here first thing in the morning and your nurse will be doing her rounds shortly. There is a dead man in your room, you no longer have a broken leg, no colostomy, no bruises. How will you explain all this?"

"I don't know," she answered honestly. "I can't explain any of it."

"Then let's get out of here, find someplace safe to talk." Lilith pulled at her hand.

Lilith might be able to just walk out the door and disappear, but Kenzi couldn't. Not out those doors.

But maybe they *could* disappear.

"I think I know where we can go," she said and grabbed the talisman around Lilith's neck. She closed her eyes but not before she saw Lilith grin.

Chapter 28: Book of Plague 3

Daisy had never been in first class, had never even been on a plane for that matter. Even with her limited knowledge, she imagined that in anywhere less than first class, the guy accompanying her would have had to buy two tickets. He was a brute. Big like a football player. But he wasn't a football player or a professional athlete of any kind or else he certainly wouldn't be sitting here with her.

The thing was, he was too big to be a pimp, at least in her experience. This guy was the muscle, the bouncer; the one who beat up unruly johns, the one who collected the girls when they tried to run. These guys never hit the girls though. The small-dick pipsqueaks always did that. The pimps who otherwise hid behind guys like this one, Asmo, he called himself. Dumbass name, probably made up or maybe it was foreign. Russian maybe? What did she know? Anyway, it didn't matter, it was not for her to question.

She'd been chosen because the goddess saw something in her. Something special—the ability to kill, to feel no fear, or just her general distaste for most men. Lilith had given her a special gift—a weapon that spread like a plague.

The behemoth beside her pushed the call light. Besides his size, he wasn't bad looking. Horse-brown hair which was a bit shaggier than one would expect from a guy his size. His arms were tattoo free and he was well dressed in a shirt that left little to the imagination about his level of fitness. She wanted to reach out and put her hand on it, feel the firm muscle beneath the skin and cotton but she feared he might break her wrist. She had nothing on which to base that fear since he'd been nothing but respectful from the moment he showed up at her door telling her to pack up her sexiest outfits, they were going on a trip.

She didn't question anything. The goddess provided and in exchange, she obeyed without hesitation. If the goddess had sent this man to take her to Thailand, then so be it. She'd even left her killing heels behind; she didn't need them anymore. She had the Deathly Vines.

"Hi there, what can I do for you?" the redheaded, over-friendly flight attendant asked.

Asmo took her hand and brought it immediately to his mouth to kiss it.

"You're gonna have to give me a second to think about that." He leaned forward to read her name tag. "Tammy. Since you arrived, I can't imagine wanting anything else."

She blushed like a schoolgirl. Daisy didn't think either one of them noticed her eyeroll. Was he smelling the woman now? His nostrils flared as he inhaled a lungful of scent from her hand. Then, he turned it over palm up and there in the center between her love line and her life line, were the vines. The flight attendant curled her fingers and pulled back. Daisy stifled her gasp of surprise but Asmo acted as if nothing was there at all. He held tight and kissed her.

The visual chill that went through Tammy was a familiar one to Daisy. She could see all the signs of arousal in the young woman. Whatever Asmo was doing had her all worked up. The redhead's nipples pushed hard against her shirt and tiny beads of sweat condensed on her upper lip. Heat radiated from her middle, so much so that Daisy could feel the change in temperature from the other side of the giant.

"Sir, you're just so sweet, but if there's nothing I can get for you, I really should go check on the other passengers." Her bright white teeth gleamed.

"How about you bring me a Sapphire and tonic, and a glass of champagne for my companion."

Without another word, Tammy sashayed to the front of the plane to fulfill his request. Daisy knew the discomfort of the walk with a swollen, wet pussy and felt a stab of sympathy for the girl who she guessed was an experiment in what could happen with both of them working together to spread Lilith's plague. Daisy could see the lust come over the woman, which would conceivably help to spread the vines faster—assuming the effects of his kiss lasted until they landed, and Tammy could find an outlet or two.

She was back with the drinks and her flushed face. Daisy sat her champagne on the tray. Asmo drank his gin and tonic down and, again, grabbed Tammy's hand. She giggled and half-heartedly protested.

"Now, now, don't argue. I won't kiss you again, I just want to read your palm."

She relaxed, opening the palm, showing the vines. He traced the creases beneath them.

"This right here says you are at the beginning of something great." He winked at her. "You are the alpha. I am the omega and together, my dear, we shall do amazing things."

She shook her head and laughed. Daisy watched Tammy sway back to the front of the plane like a little girl in puppy love.

"You have quite the impact on the ladies," Daisy laughed.

"Oh, yes, I think you'll find I do indeed."

He put his meaty hand on her thigh, sending a wave of warmth into her groin. Daisy could feel every line of her STD crawling all around her nethers. She felt for Tammy, knowing the fire burning in her own loins and all she could to do was sit and wait.

Asmo snaked his arm around her shoulders and rubbed the far one.

"Rest now. We'll be in Bangkok in no time, then there will be no sleep for you…well, for either of us." He raised his eyebrows at her suggestively.

She sipped her champagne until her eyes grew heavy and she slept.

"Hello Folks, we're beginning our descent into Suvarnabhumi airport. If you would all kindly take your seats and prepare for landing."

The airport was a pandemonium of strange sights and smells. There was nothing familiar with which to ground herself. Daisy felt her heart rate increase and threaten to burst through her chest when Asmo directed her to a limo awaiting them just outside.

On the ride to the Grace Hotel, she found calm in a couple of glasses of vodka on the rocks.

"Here, put this on. No panties." Asmo handed her a tiny pink sequined dress that managed to cover only what was absolute necessary to avoid a public nudity citation. Did they even have those things here? Watching through the window, Daisy wondered what exactly was off limits in Bangkok.

She was buckling the heels of her stilettoes when the limo stopped in front of a large building that looked like a couple of giant Connect Four games. Asmo crawled out his side of the car. Apparently, manners were off limits here or else he was going out of his way to treat her like trash. Dressing her like a hooker and treating her like one made it obvious to every other man in the area that she was up for grabs. Fine. That was fine now. In the past, he might have gotten a heel to the temple but that was before the goddess changed everything.

Her door was opened by an average sized middle eastern man in a turban and a white suit. He offered a hand to help her out of the car. With his touch, the familiar zing of heat traveled straight to her groin. She furrowed her brow.

"Come on, we don't have all night to speak of hows and whys." This was not some fancy-costumed stranger—it was Asmo, the giant she'd sat beside the entire flight. He had changed his entire anatomical make up right down to his height and weight. Daisy took the arm he offered.

The inside of the hotel reminded her of the cheap, old, off-the-Vegas-strip hotels where the alcoholics and gambling addicts always stayed. Perhaps it had once been opulent, but the avocado green carpet and the gilded trim left a strong impression of Saturday nights at the disco, John Travolta, and bell bottoms. The fashions worn by the hotel's guests were not much different than what she and Asmo wore. Most men were well-dressed Arabs in turbans and beards accompanied by short-skirted, high-heeled young Asian women who appeared to have no interest in the men attached to their side.

The room was no better, but no worse, than the cheap motels in Vegas. Daisy had a feeling she wouldn't be spending much time in this place anyway. The sex trade here was more impressive than what she'd seen anywhere in America.

"Well." Asmo plopped himself down in an uncomfortable looking chair facing the bed. "Show me what you got, girl. I need to know what I'm working with here."

She'd like to know what exactly his job was in the first place. It might be nice if they were both in on this new plague plan. But she reminded herself, she was an agent of the goddess and must trust in her plan.

She began to gyrate her hips to a silent music only she could hear. With each rotation she brought herself closer to him. He grabbed her shoulders and stopped her just as she was about to climb onto his lap.

"Sweetheart, I hate to be the one to break it to ya, but you're not in Vegas anymore. You ain't gettin' anywhere with this standard whore routine. Although I've heard you aren't exactly interested in repeat customers, so perhaps you've never felt the need to up your game."

She was pissed. She could rock his world if she wanted to, but this didn't feel like serving the goddess, it felt like she was being conned for a freebie.

"Climb on up here and make me cum with nothing more than your body. No fingers, no mouth, no pussy."

Daisy closed her eyes before rolling them. Oh, how she wished for her sharpened stiletto. The goddess would forgive her. After all she, Daisy Fields, was the second whore of Lilith's apocalypse. She was needed. She was Plague.

The thought of the importance of the vines growing up and out from her mons, brought back the throbbing heat she'd felt on the plane. She rocked her hips involuntarily. Sliding onto his lap, she wriggled and writhed. He was the charmer and she was the snake. His hands were all over her now. The rules were not reciprocal. Rubbing his thumb across her lips, she parted them, taking him in. At the same time, his other hand had found her secret spot. She felt the moisture and his fingers slid effortlessly into her. She sucked harder and he pushed deeper with both hands until his fist was inside her vagina and four fingers were pushed far into her mouth.

"Hmm," she moaned, hoping to get him off soon before he shoved himself so far inside that he did damage.

He thrust deeper with both hands as if he was trying to wear her like a muff.

"Sorry, honey. This ain't your turf, it's mine. I need to borrow all this for a bit."

And then, there was no air with which to moan. His entire arm was down her throat, blocking off all respiration. The other arm was elbow deep inside her pussy. Edges of her vision began to grey and then blacken just before the searing pain ripped through her. He was splitting her open like a book—no, not like a book, like a pair of footie pajamas.

Daisy or at least her essence, curled up in the fetal position inside her brain. There was no pain now, but there was also no control of her arms, legs, or even her face anymore. She was a helpless passenger and Asmo was the driver. He'd stepped into her and put her on like a skin suit.

The goddess's will. This is her will.

They looked in the mirror. The body they shared was perfect, as if it had never been bisected by some shape-shifting monster man. And it was her body, no doubt. The deathly vines receded back to her lower belly like they'd been when Lilith gave them to her.

Daisy watched from her mental cubby hole as her own hands pushed and prodded at her face, stretching features, pinching lips together until the woman in the mirror was not Daisy from Vegas but a Taiwanese model-level escort.

"Don't worry, I'll give it back to you when we're done—in its original package." Asmo brought her hands up to the breasts they shared and ran them down her belly to the black lines branching out from her pelvis. They stuck to the fingers like tentacles only releasing when Asmo pulled her hand beyond their reach. "Yes, it will be all yours soon enough, I don't want an STD," he laughed. "Not like this one."

He brought her new baby doll lips into a seductive grin.

"Now, let's go have us a good time."

Chapter 29: Book of Plague 4

Bangkok was certainly different from anything Daisy had experienced in the US. There was so much frenzied sex in the clubs that her skin became sore. Not from chaffing, thanks to Asmo her body's lust and therefore natural lubricants were relentless, but from the strange pinch of the sticky transfer of branches each time another's skin touched hers. It didn't matter though; the pain had become like a Pavlovian response. When someone else touched her, even brushed against her, a piece of her disease stuck to their skin and began to grow as did their libido.

Daisy knew whoever it was, male, female, old, young, would turn around and sexual chaos would ensue. And she was sure to be a part of it. Her body, driven by the demon, couldn't get enough. Already, she'd slept with rich Arabs and poor white boys. She'd fucked old Japanese executives, and teenage Scandinavian girls who'd been lured into the sex trade.

She lay on the bed in the Grace Hotel, Asmo snoozing inside her, leaving her back in control. She wondered if the black vines would stay with this body or if they would be back on hers when they split up and she got herself back…if she got herself back.

Mindlessly, she trailed her finger down her naked skin to where the branches crawled up toward her belly button. She tapped the edge of one and watched it cling to her like a kiss. She watched as her skin transferred the brand of the goddess from her belly to her finger. Like a tiny snake, it elongated to wrap around her digit. She made a fist, stood up, stretched, and padded to the bathroom to pee.

It burned a little but that was from overuse and not an infection she assured herself. She felt fine otherwise. Besides the marks themselves, there were no other physical signs of disease.

She looked at the girl she was pretending to be in the mirror. The beautiful almond eyes smiled, and she felt herself lose control of her muscles as Asmo stepped into the driver's seat.

"I have a surprise for us tonight. We're working the fishbowl at the Soapy Kisses Massage Parlor," her voice said. She felt tingling in her groin that signified her lust was awakening fully. "And then, when you've finished your shift, you will be given your body back and we can go. Our work will be completed."

Her hands ran to her pert breasts, smaller but firmer than her own, and tweaked the nipples. Continuing down, she watched herself caressing the skin of her belly, her mons. It was odd to be able to feel all the sensations but at the same time have no control of them. The vines began to crawl up and around her hands as her fingers disappeared inside of her. Daisy watched in helpless fascination as she masturbated in front of the hotel's mirror, each thrust pulled more of the vines inside her. She felt her muscles tense and knew the orgasm was near, but with Asmo in control, she could do nothing but wait for it. He would claim the climax. As the spasms of pleasure raked through her body, she watched all signs of the branches leave her skin and like the legs of a hermit crab, withdraw deep into her womb.

Asmo brought her fingers to her lips and pushed them inside. She suckled them or rather he, controlling her body, did.

"Such a perfect little dish…sweet and sour, my favorite," Asmo spoke from her mouth. "Let's go, my little fortune cookie, time waits for no whore."

Chapter 30: Book of War 4

The invitation to dine privately with Senator Allan Weyer, the Republican from Louisiana, was unexpected. Thus far, inner voices from the darkness Lilith had placed inside her instructed not so much with words as with instinct and knowledge. She simply had to follow what she already knew to be the "right thing to do."

She'd dined with a variety of Republican senators and representatives after the initial meeting at the White House. Senator Weyer had been strangely absent from the congratulatory meetings and festivities. His request for a private dinner at his personal residence came without explanation or option to decline. It included details of when she would be picked up and where she was to wait for the car. As she was not inclined to do otherwise and with still a week before the Right to Life Rally, she accepted.

Dr. Cynthia Parris wore her long hair in braided rows that she often gathered in the back in a knot. Melanie Pryor took on a more Caucasian look with shoulder-length straightened waves and blond highlights. The Michelle Obama 'do worked well with the brick red conservative belted dress she chose for the special occasion.

"Welcome, Ms. Pryor," the senator said, smiling broadly. His salt and pepper hair was cut close to his head in a relaxed military style which made her feel safe. "Won't you come in and sit down?"

The suite was modest, not what she'd expected from a Senator, but she'd recently discovered that many who were not from or near D.C. actually slept in their offices and did not even have apartments. This was a condo though and had likely cost a fortune. The foyer was sparsely decorated in shades of cream and sand. On the center of a single table sat a deep-red vase of yellow-edged tulips. She followed him through a hallway; on the right, a closed door did little to stifle the fragrance of garlic and rosemary or the sounds of pots clinking. Staff was hard at work preparing a delicious smelling meal. The hallway walls were a dark bronze color and just as stark as the foyer.

Two large mahogany doors loomed at the end of the hall. Senator Weyer pulled them open with a flourish and stepped through, turned, held his hand out to Melanie. She took it and he drew her into a completely different world.

The rectangular and impossibly long dining room was filled with baroque style pieces, ornately carved in golds and bronzes. The walls were a deep merlot, the table, which, like the door, was mahogany, ran the length of the room and displayed a two-pronged golden candle holder every yard of its length. Every other square inch of surface was covered in foods presented in an artistry fit for the likes of King Henry VIII.

A crackling fire framed by a large black marble and gold trimmed fireplace along the far wall warmed the room. Above it, Goya's menacing Saturn stared out at his fellow diners as he devoured his son.

Melanie took the center seat directly facing the flames while the Senator chose a throne-like chair at the head.

"How many more are you expecting?" Melanie asked taking in the myriad of dishes presented on the table.

Behind her, a buffet of sumptuous desserts centered by an enormous chocolate fountain seduced her senses with sugared aromas.

"Just us. I prefer to do my business in private." He rang a small bell and without hesitation, a parade of servants arrived to pick up and present the dishes to them in a merry-go-round fashion until waved away by the senator.

She nodded. Dr. Cynthia Parris would have laughed, perhaps even chastised him for being so wasteful, but Dr. Parris no longer existed. Melanie belonged to the Goddess and meant only to do Her bidding. Everything that had happened, everything about to happen was planned precisely and it was not her place to question the Divine One.

"Do you mind," the senator asked, "blessing this food before we partake?"

"Bless it?" *Did Christians typically ask anyone other than God to bless the food?* "Oh, yes, sure," she said.

She held her hands up over the dinner table. "Blessed be that this food shall fuel us in our pursuits." She looked at the senator, who was grinning.

"Perfect," he said.

She picked at her food during the long lulls in conversation as her host gorged himself on both food and wine which never seemed to diminish.

"I find it most interesting that the direct descendant of a confessed witch would end up the face of an anti-choice movement," Senator Weyer said, pausing for an answer although he had not asked a question.

Sipping her wine, Melanie chose her response slowly and carefully. He was testing her; she was sure of it. She did not yet know why, though. When it was clear that she would receive no instruction from within, she spoke.

"I believe it is a woman's choice to stand up and defend her opinion. I wouldn't call that 'anti-choice' senator."

"Please, call me Allan. But you stand against abortion, a woman's right to choose what happens to her body. Your ancestor performed them, and if I am not mistaken, you did as well before you changed your name to Melanie Pryor. Isn't that so, Dr. Parris?"

He was pushing her harder. She could almost feel his own dark, yet unseen mental fingers probing her brain for information. She was stronger than he was and even without the aid of the Goddess, she inherently knew this man, like all men, was placed in her path to be manipulated into helping in some way. She'd just need to tread lightly until she could determine in what way that was.

"I admit, I was once a murderess like my ancestor, but I was saved by a very special patient. That day, I left my practice and my heathen identity behind. Please respect my choice, senator—I mean Allan—I am on your side, I truly am."

"Oh, I believe that." He shoved a piece of shrimp on toast into his mouth and chewed, nodding the entire time. Washing it down with a large, unmannerly gulp of wine, he wiped his mouth. "That is why I brought you here. I want to help you in this endeavor which I dare say will be much more dangerous and involved than your little trick with the coolers."

A fly buzzed Cynthia's head and disappeared into the vastness of the room.

"Senator?" She cleared her throat. "I'm not sure what you mean. I was protesting with the group of people who died. I only survived by chance."

He really did know everything. Certainly, if he meant to disrupt the Goddess's plans, she would appear and stop him. Her lack of presence and instruction of any kind signified to Melanie/Cynthia a consent to this strange—but now that she thought about it— necessary partnership. If she was going to start a war, really get the fires of hate going, she needed help to take down an entire city.

The senator said nothing, he simply continued to shovel food into his maw while never taking his eyes off Melanie as she mulled over her options.

"Dessert," he declared. "We'll discuss your plans over dessert and I, as a favor to your family lineage, will help in whatever way I can."

This time, no servants were called, instead, they stood and served themselves. The dessert plates were larger than the abnormally generous dinner plates had been. They were practically the size of a serving tray. As she waited for the senator to finish coating all his chosen pastries and tarts in melted chocolate from the fountain, she admired the décor above the buffet.

"Is that Doré?" She pointed to the framed etching centered between two black-glass mirrors. The drawing showed a figure—presumably Satan—presiding on an altar in the center of a ring of dancers that seemed to be made up of both demons and witches alike. A snake slithered toward the dancers in the foreground of the print. It was this snake that had caught her eye. It resembled the one tattooed on Lilith's body.

"*La Danse Du Sabbat*. It may be Doré but could have been one of his apprentices. No one knows." He shrugged.

Chocolate dripped down his fingers, wrist, and forearm, but he seemed oblivious. The once pretty, pastel macaron in his hand had been soiled thoroughly with the stuff and when he'd finished with it, his mouth, too was smeared with chocolate.

Seated, satiated, and clean for the moment, the senator folded his hands together beneath his pointed chin.

"I trust you enjoyed our meal together?" There was a vibrato to his voice that she hadn't noticed before.

The room was so hot, and her stomach was full. Melanie's head swam in a sea of wine.

The senator's eyes grew blacker until there was nothing left in them but darkness.

"Yes, of course. It was—" she searched for the right word, "limitless."

An odd choice but appropriate. He smiled, rubbing his hands together.

"Loaves and Fishes."

"I'm sorry?" she slurred.

The wine and full belly worked at her eyelids and she struggled to maintain focus. He waved it off and picked up a dinner roll from a full basket on the table.

"Did you know there is a theory that the witch hysteria of Salem was brought about by a wheat mold—ergot—which caused hallucinations and mass hysteria?" He broke the bread in two and took a bite. He held the other half up to Melanie's mouth. She leaned forward as if accepting communion.

"And Jesus said *I have compassion for the crowd.*" He took another bite. "*I do not want to see them hungry.*"

He came even closer toward her until their heads were almost touching. His tongue, stained brown, shot out and licked the air between them. She tried to pull away from his fetid breath, but he grabbed her by the back of the head and forced the rest of the roll into her mouth.

"Are you in there Tituba?" he asked, watching her work on the bolus of bread. Her head swooned.

"My name is Melanie Pryor," she said.

His eyes changed again—this time growing so big they bulged from his head.

"Your name is Cynthia Parris, you are the daughter of Tituba, a powerful witch. I, Beelzebub, was once her master. She promised herself to me. Thus, I was drawn to you by her magic and by Lucifer's command, I am now *your* servant. Together, we will return her to this earth. She will once more bring chaos and paranoia down upon The Creator's mortals. The dark times will come again, and we will reign once more."

Senator Allan Weyer's chin split and lengthened, his nose thinned, pushing itself down between the halves of his lower face. The air turned rank as the food on the table rotted in liquefied gurgles and gaseous pops, burping out putrefaction.

Cynthia watched in disgust as Weyer's bloated body blackened and burst forth through his clothing. Buttons whizzed and bounced off walls. One fell with a plop into a gelatinous heap of grey mold that was once a perfectly seasoned rack of lamb. Cellophane wings erupted like botfly larvae out of the skin of the senator's back.

Just as the demon Beelzebub's full transformation completed, a massive horde of flies spewed forth from the muck-covered table and swarmed to envelope Cynthia in a living cocoon.

You will stay with me until the war has begun, and then, you will help me bring her back.

The words were not spoken as much as vibrated from all around her, buzzing into her ears and embedding themselves in her bones. Yes, yes, of course. Bring back, bring back her Goddess, the Divine Female, Lilith. This was right, it was where she was supposed to be.

She fell into unconsciousness amongst the slurping sounds of a gluttonous swarm.

Chapter 31: Book of War 5

Cynthia walked the strangely empty streets of Washington D.C. at dusk, just an orange hue in the sky to light her way. All the street lights were out.

"Hello? Is anybody here?" she called out.

A siren answered. Its high pitched wail caught her by surprise and she jumped. Explosions and gunfire erupted around her as if she'd just been transported into the middle of a war zone. Black smoke filled the streets and out of the smoke, thousands of people appeared. Some clawing at each other, screaming profanities and ethnic slurs while others threw themselves out windows or down the steps of the Lincoln Memorial. Their arms waved frantically, and their eyes were wide with disbelief. She was watching a war taking place right in the middle of the nation's capital.

The panicked runners veered around her but gave no impression that they even saw her standing there. Buildings that were not already reduced to rubble or on fire were suddenly crawling with oily black barbed vines—like the roots of some giant fungus—*ergot?*—that ate concrete and steel as if it were nothing more than soft, rotted flesh. Tendrils spread out over the sidewalks and benches with the same effect. The only things unaffected by the destruction were the teal green food trucks scattered about the city. Painted on their sides in stencil were the words "Loaves and Fishes" and beneath that, a large dinner roll and a fish leaping from unseen water to eat a fly buzzing in the air.

The people, an infinite number it seemed, filled the street crying out and screaming. Some prayed, others fought. One man shot a woman and the child she carried in her arms while only a few feet from them a couple fucked joyfully without a care in the world. A small circle of men and women gathered around a fire where it appeared they were roasting a dog. It was like a scene from Bosch's *Last Judgement.*

The death-colored smog ebbed and flowed like a curtain in a play revealing scenes of repulsion, redemption, and reaction. Then suddenly, it closed and engulfed her until she was in the eye of it. Just before she began to panic, the smoke parted in the way the Red Sea parted for Moses, and a woman, naked and blemished only by the mark of a snake wrapped around Her entire body, walked toward her.

"Lilith. Please tell me you've come to take me from this madness," Cynthia said, holding out her arms.

"My love, I have come to show you what is to be. This—" She turned a full circle, "is the Apocalypse that we shall bring to this land."

"I can't do all this alone." Cynthia admitted.

"No, of course you cannot. I have gathered two others, and each with a purpose. This is what we four will accomplish together. The seals have been opened. The four whores of the apocalypse are riding out into the world."

The black smog dropped away as if succumbing to gravity. The landscape changed. A tropical forest stood where there was once a concrete cityscape but the people who were there before remained, still fucking, and crying and praying and killing. The smoke formed into the torso of a female, winged arms outstretched. She wore a gown of rolling inky mist. The woman flew up just high enough to cover the human bodies spread out before them and as her blanket of soot draped over them, they fell dead.

When Cynthia was a child, she'd dreamt of a similar biblical vapor coming to kill her as the first born in the family. It was then that she began to question a god who would heartlessly kill children to make a point. She'd never understood the plagues of Egypt and lost her faith that night when she woke, heart pounding and sweaty, fearing that her life was about to be extinguished by an angry storm cloud.

Now she was in another dream and watching others fall victim to the same fate. This time, she was not afraid, because this was a revolt against that god and death itself. Finally, they were going to get their just deserts. The Goddess saw that she, Cynthia Parris, was the perfect woman to aid in the defeat of an unjust deity. She should not be afraid.

"All I ask is that you begin the process here, accept the help that is offered to you, and then come to me. I will take care of you."

The smog lifted. They stood in front of the reflecting pool facing the Washington Monument. The once white marble surface had taken on a bloated and bruised look. It crumbled at its base, tipped, and fell forward into the pool. The wave it created was tsunamic in size. When it reached them, the woman reflected in the liquid mirror in front of her was not Cynthia but resembled her in the way an ancient ancestor might.

"…Tituba."

Cynthia jumped awake. "What?"

The senator, in his handsome, middle-aged form stood over her. He took her hand and helped her up off the chaise lounge she'd fallen asleep in and led her to the large picture window overlooking the city. Blue-green food trucks dotted the landscape.

"I said I hope you are ready, daughter of Tituba."

"Oh yes." She yawned and smiled back at him. "And I hope the same for you."

Chapter 32: Book of Sariel 5

Sariel looked over the devastation. His body stung with the names of the dead to be collected. A bus lay on its side, fluids dripping from broken pipes, errant limbs poked through broken windows at odd angles. Smoke and flames gave the whole scene a dream-like quality. The wreckage of the tractor-trailer that hit the bus was a Picasso version of itself. Bloodied and fractured bodies were strewn across the field below the road. Some still hung half-in and half-out the bus. The cab of the 18-wheeler was on fire. Sariel knew there was a body inside. It could wait though. Earth time stopped for death, and there were plenty of names searing his flesh.

Enoch's shadow swept over the meadow, the only thing moving besides himself. He supposed he could get started gathering souls or he could stand here by the bus and wait for Enoch to collect and deliver them to him. He didn't want to do anything. *Can Death get depressed?*

He used to revel in high mortality tragedies like this, but right now, he wanted to be curled up in Gloria's hospital room as close to Kenzi as he could be. Had she read his story yet? He wasn't sure what he hoped for. If she had, she'd not come to him which likely meant he'd lost her forever. If she hadn't, then Lilith still had the opportunity to twist her mind against him and still he'd lose her forever.

"Enoch." The bird seemed to be having the same issues as he. It hadn't come down from the sky for a single soul either. His flesh stung with the list of names. They would get this finished and get back to Kenzi.

"Performance anxiety, eh?" a voice beside him said. He jumped and then relaxed. He knew the voice. As of late it haunted his dreams—if he had any.

"Lucifer. To what do I owe the pleasure this afternoon? Is one of your demons among the dead? You want me to leave him be? Give him back? What is it today?"

"Oh, geez, no. I mean, clearly this is just a bunch of dead mortals. You know me, though, I like to come and admire my work once in a while. This one in particular I'm quite happy with."

"Happy because you managed to tear open the flesh of both my arms with this one?" Sariel asked, brushing past him, and stooping for the first soul. Enoch landed beside the head and cawed.

"What is it? Are you going to help me or stand there looking foolish all day?"

"Oh, it probably just noticed the surprise I left you in the big rig over there," Lucifer smiled and winked.

Enoch cawed again.

"Damn it all to Hell, Lucifer! I've spent an eternity cleaning up for you and The Creator. Would it be too much to ask to be left in peace to do it?"

Lucifer laughed. He bent over, holding his stomach, tears dripping from his eyes. Enoch took off and landed on the roof of the truck. Sariel continued collecting souls from the bus as if neither of the other two were there.

Stifling his laughter, Lucifer followed him. "Look, all I'm saying is how many parents would be OK with their little princess dating Death?"

"What are you talking about?" Sariel asked.

It was easier at this point to keep working and try to tolerate Lucifer's presence than to stop and humor his nonsense. He found the more souls he gathered and wounds healed, the more he could handle the demon.

"I killed her dad. That's what I'm saying. I mean, there were some innocent casualties." He swept his arm across the tipped bus scene in front of them. "But Mac Brooks took a light nap and well, the bus was just in the wrong place at the wrong time, I guess."

Sariel looked down at his arms, turning them around every which way until he saw it. Cut in diagonally beneath another name. Enoch cawed out from the truck.

"Lucifer," Sariel growled. "Why? Why would you do such a thing? The girl has no one as it is."

"I don't know. I guess I'm bored. I mean, I'm out here all alone, so few like me to talk to. And you, I've tried so hard to be friends with you but you're always so busy. I guess I just needed attention, good or bad." He did his best to keep a straight face, but a smile flirted at the corner of his mouth.

Sariel walked to the cab of the truck. Flames licked out at him. Enoch hopped off onto Sariel's shoulder. Its claws warmed by the hot metal it had perched upon. The body inside the truck was charred and lacked any identifying characteristics. On the dash, a piece of pink construction paper with a child's drawing of the big rig and two rudimentary people—one big, one small—waving in front of it, was signed, "Love, Kenzi". The edge was smoldering. He picked it out of the truck, folded it, and slipped it beneath his belt. Enoch pecked at the dead man's head and dropped Kenzi's father's soul into Sariel's awaiting hand.

"Thank you, bird."

"Look, I'm sorry, Sar. Really. I just don't understand why you won't listen to me. Do you love this girl? Because you need to take my word for it when I say that she is in danger. Lilith is much stronger than you think. You need help, more than that bird—sorry sweetie—but you're going to have to let me help you. Release my demons before it's too late."

"Enoch is a male. Don't call him sweetie. Why does everyone think he's a girl?" Sariel pushed past Lucifer and continued his work. "I have seen nothing that makes me believe I need more help. Kenzi is a strong girl, she will be fine. She barely knows her father. This isn't the worst thing she'll go through."

There were at least twenty more souls to gather. The bus had been filled with a high school band returning home from a competition in which they'd come in second place.

The broken trophy lay among the rubble. Enoch was back at it and together they collected most before the bus too caught on fire.

"I wonder what Lilith is telling Kenzi right now. I wonder if she read that sweet little bedtime story you wrote to Kenzi. Imagine if she had, would she agree with your memory? Would it make her happy to read what you wrote? I think you should be considering—"

"Lucifer! I demand you go. There is no woman, demoness or mortal, that could cause me near the difficulties you have. Do you understand? I will never release your demons. I do not want nor do I need their help. I do not want to spend any longer on this earth with the likes of you. Do you understand? Now, go and leave me in peace."

Lucifer looked at the watch on his wrist, nodded, and turned around to walk away. Sariel watched with furrowed brow. The demon was up to something and it was more than his usual "release the others" campaign.

"Let's get this shit taken care of, Enoch, and get back to Kenzi. Something's up."

Enoch cawed in agreement.

Chapter 33: Book of Conquest 6

The graveyard-scented chill enveloped her and Kenzi knew she'd pulled them into Sheol. This time, the darkness wasn't as frightening. She'd been here before and survived. Lilith was beside her still, Kenzi could sense more than see her.

"So, this is his prison?" Lilith said. "More room than he gave me, but reminiscent of the cave where I learned just how painful it is to be created a woman."

"Yeah, we sure got the shitty end of the stick," Kenzi agreed. "There's a room in here though, where it's warmer and lighter. I think I can find it." She began to walk, remembering to stay toward the center. "Watch out and stay close to me, there are…uh… things in the walls that will try to grab you."

But nothing reached out at them. It was as if those sad creatures had retreated into the dirt walls; as if the Nods were more afraid of them than they were of the Nods. The maggots and death beetles did not shy away, and the ceiling sprinkled its creatures upon the pair like holy water. Lilith showed no bother or even acknowledgment of their existence so Kenzi tried hard to be nonchalant as well, suppressing the shivers while brushing them out of her hair. The gooseflesh, however, had a mind of its own.

The light grew from pitch to storm to dusk to grey as they traversed the main passageway. Neither was interested in following the trails branching off back into the darkness. Kenzi wished Enoch were with them. The bird left no doubt in her mind where she stood. *Or what gender she is, poor thing.* What would Enoch think of her bringing Lilith here though? But Sariel needed more information. He said he needed help. He couldn't ask for help, offer Sheol as a safe place and then get mad at her for using it.

Up ahead, golden lights danced like fireflies beckoning them to the cavern filled with the enormous tree decorated with millions of trinkets, many of which were gold.

"That's where we're going." Kenzi pointed.

There was a slight curve in the tunnel obscuring the entrance. They picked up their pace. For Kenzi, it was simply a matter of getting out of the insect rain, but Lilith had a look of determination on her face as if she were about to engage in a duel.

When the tree with its pageantry of talismans came into view, Lilith froze. She took in the enormous lifeform, all its branches and décor. She shivered and stepped through the threshold into the honey-glow of the cavern. Kenzi followed her. Lilith touched the trunk of the tree. She rubbed her hand up the trunk and the snake, which just seconds before had been a two-dimensional tattoo, slithered up her body, across her arm and encircled the tree.

"Did you know this is the Tree of Knowledge, Kenzi?" Lilith asked.

Now free of the snake, she walked beneath the branches, allowing her fingertips to gently brush the lowest hanging baubles.

"No." Kenzi didn't know if there was an expected reaction for this particular revelation, so she left it at that.

"You know the story of Adam and Eve, the Garden of Eden, the forbidden fruit and all that, do you not?"

"Sure, yeah. She picked an apple and gave it to Adam and then they got kicked out of the garden for it. Right?"

"Yes, they did. Because this tree's fruit bore the knowledge of good and evil, it was the motherboard, if you will, of the entire creation. Like the computer in *The Matrix*, do you follow?"

"I think so."

"And so, The Creator's secrets were within this tree. He did not want His creations to ever reach the same level of enlightenment as He because they would then be His equals and He would no longer have any sway over them. He plays the dominant role, always." The snake slithered around the tree, finding a limb from which it could anchor itself.

"I suppose eventually, I too would have eaten the fruit of the tree, but my stay in the garden was short. Eve would never have dared had it not been for the serpent who told her the secret. Do you want to know my secrets, Kenzi?"

"Yeah, honestly, I would. That's why I brought you here. I mean what do you want Lilith?"

Lilith plucked a shining medallion off a low hanging branch. She studied it for a moment before looping it onto her wrist, where it fell to her bent elbow. She then took another and did the same.

"Hey, you can't—" Kenzi began but the snake whispered in her ear. She quieted. It told her an ancient story. One of betrayal and suffering.

"Look upon Eve, Lilith. See that I have made another, a true servant and partner for Adam. You are no longer welcome here. You are banished from this paradise I have created."

The booming voice of The Creator came from all around. There was a blink of darkness. The hue of light that appeared was orange rather than green.

A clay-colored sea spread out to the horizon where it curved, seemingly falling off the face of the earth. The rocky shoreline was stippled with caverns and crevices. The sun shone hot, baking the peaks so that they shimmered like a mirage. Dark shadows at the mouths of caves promised cool air and respite from the insufferable heat.

Inhuman cries of pain and torment echoed from the dark abysses. Moans of eternal misery slithered onto the scrub grass just outside the entrance. Lilith flinched and gave those caves a wide berth. Lilith's fear chilled her veins even as her skin burned red beneath the unforgiving sun.

A cold breeze blew out of a broad, but low-mouthed cave set back among the tall mountains. Drawn by the comforting music of the wind singing over hollows of various depths, Lilith entered the respite of natural shelter.

For many nights she lay curled around herself aching for acceptance, for love, for company, and sobbing into the dirt. Days were spent foraging for what few edible plants and shore creatures could be found. It seemed that no matter how long she went without food, she did not die. She grew painfully thin, her lips cracked, and skin sloughed from sun exposure.

"There were days, Kenzi," Lilith's voice whispered from the snake's mouth, "when I imagined returning to the demons who raped and tortured me just to break the isolation and hunger I suffered under The Creator's banishment. I was weak, and I had come to the realization that I was meant to suffer upon this earth for centuries as punishment. For what, I did not know? Asking for equality? To be treated the same as His other creations? What had I done to deserve this misery?"

"You didn't go back to them!" Kenzi shouted. It was more of an exclamation than a question.

"I couldn't stay there anymore. I'd lost count of the years I suffered in isolation and I couldn't take the chance of going back to the demons in that cave. I chose emotional pain and starvation over physical and sexual torment. My hatred for The Creator and all his biased power fed me and kept me alive. If I were to suffer, it would be in my own way and of my own doing, but I wasn't going to rot away in the dark, unseen. I set out to wreak as much havoc upon His earth as I could."

The serpent's narration began again. The abrasive sand and brittle shrubs wore away at her skin as she made her journey. Hunger evolved from a minor annoyance to racking pains to finally numbing relief. The days were suffocating, the nights were long and cold. The Garden of Eden shimmered on every horizon and faded away with each step she took toward it.

When she arrived at the forest that bordered the Garden of Eden, the opaque shimmer like a veil of spider webs billowing just in front of the trees mimicked every false vision she'd had so far. Crestfallen, believing this too was just a mirage, she continued forward awaiting the fade away, but it did not. Instead, the veil held her back. It would not give. Turning but trailing a hand along this strange new addition to the oasis, she walked on attempting to circumnavigate it and enter the garden at its far end.

"But I found it surrounding the entire garden. I'd been locked out. There was no admittance. I was going to die here, just outside the home that by all rights should have been mine. I did not think I had the strength to go on, but I could not allow any of them the satisfaction of watching me die such a pathetic death.

"On my knees, I sat watching through the milky screen for the two humans who were living a life without a thought to the evil that their creator did to me. Yet, I saw nothing. No signs of life within. Was it possible they too had been banished? Was The Creator busy making new creatures, ones that never erred or questioned his motives?

"It was this curiosity, this vague satisfaction of something I couldn't explain but I now recognize as revenge, that built in my middle. A surge of energy drove me on. I would find them and revel in their misery, for they deserved their punishment."

Here in the more tropical inland, the journey was easier. The rain wet her lips and provided much-needed moisture to her broken, peeling skin. Lilith came upon a valley where the scent of animals and smoke drifted out to greet her, the sounds of life, both human and livestock, followed. Rounding a bend, there sat a small hut made of mud and grasses, roofed by large palm fronds.

A field stretched out behind the hut where tall green stalks of grain waved in the scented breeze.

"In that neatly grown garden, I crouched, watching the family go about their work; tilling the soil, caring for many beasts both large and small. I watched as a woman carried woven baskets filled with water from a stream somewhere beyond the shelter and a man with his back turned to me tended a fire. He controlled its flames. I was astonished. I saw no signs of The Creator.

"And then the man stood and turned to look out at the very field where I sat watching. It was Adam, my husband. He'd aged, and his skin had darkened from his time under the sun. So, he had been driven from the garden. It was not hard then, for me to see the familiar features of the woman who'd replaced me in the water bearer beside him. Her body which had once been thin and healthy now sagged with loose skin and her hips had spread so that her curves were greater than my own."

"Who are you?" a voice surprised Lilith and she fell over. "Hey, you're crushing my wheat, get up."

She dared looking up at him, a face that resembled Adam's, but was thinner with a well-cut jaw and stunning dark eyes, was staring down at her. His brows furrowed in both confusion and anger.

"I apologized for ruining his vegetation and kept my back to Adam and Eve as I walked away. He stopped me and asked who I was. I lied and said I didn't know, I said I'd been living on the edge of the sea for so long, I couldn't remember. Surely everyone had heard of my failures by now. He walked me to the stream and I did not stop him from watching me as I washed. I could see that he was aroused, and a plan began to unfold in my head. I would seduce him, perhaps even bare a child, gain as much information as I could about his parents, take what food I could, and burn them all down.

"That's not fair, Lilith. He was helping you. Not all guys are evil, you know." Kenzi said.

She'd become so mesmerized by the serpent's storytelling that she felt as if she were seeing rather than hearing. The tree, the talismans, and Lilith herself were gone. Kenzi sat in a field of wheat watching the tale unfold.

"But something happened." Lilith's voice continued as if Kenzi had not spoken. "Cain built me a shelter in the woods just beyond the stream. He brought me food and nursed me back to health. I grew stronger. He was all the good things I remembered about Adam.

Some days, when he'd finished with his farming, he would spend hours telling me about his mother and father who were often so unhappy they'd go for days without speaking. In fact, he told me they had not attempted to procreate in sixteen years, since the birth of his brother Abel.

"Karma," Kenzi added.

"Perhaps I should have pitied them in their misery, perhaps I should have blamed The Creator solely for all of our mortal pain, but I could not let go of what Adam did to me and I hated Eve for being weak. I wanted to love Cain but there was no room for love in my heart. All that I could offer him was focusing my hatred on his parents and his younger brother, who was favored by Adam and clung-to by Eve who, I'd discovered had such pain in his delivery, she feared ever having more children. She knew he was her last.

Abel was a herder. He would often drive his flock of sheep through Cain's fields, letting them trample and destroy his brother's crops. He was all the things I hated in Adam. He felt privileged, he was selfish and greedy. He kept other animals too. He would set traps and keep anything he caught alive. Rabbits, minks, goats, foxes, wolves, even cats ended up fenced in small areas under the care of Abel."

Kenzi could almost hear the animal cries, Cain's angry rages against his brother, and Abel's mocking laughter. She could smell the acrid smoke on Cain's clothing and in his hair. She imagined the taste of bland and tough meat on her tongue, as she listened to Lilith's tale of living the dichotomous life of a kept woman and at the same time one plotting revenge and independence.

One day, Lilith discovered Cain pacing angrily in his field.

"How can He choose Abel over me? I offered the best of what little of my crops survived Abel's flock. I checked each individual blade of wheat, each bundle of millet, every ball of cotton. Every one was the best I had. I made the offering, I asked for His blessing and He forsakes me!"

Rage boiled inside Lilith. It was in empathy, a flashback to the unfair and confusing treatment by The Creator during her own time in the garden as Adam's wife. Cain pumped his fists, kicked at stones and trees. He stormed off further into the woods without another word to her.

Picking up the largest of the abused rocks, Lilith walked through the field toward the alter that sat near the hut on a piece of land bordered by Cain's garden and Abel's fence. There Abel sat, kneeling at the altar. A golden glow surrounded the ashy remains of his animal sacrifices. A ram's horn jutted out above a bulging white eyeball, a gnarled, clawed foot of a rabbit, and a small chain of bones that was once a tail were the only parts that could still be easily identified.

Cain's crops smoked in a heap of black and grey ashes, all color drained. No holy light of The Creator's blessing shone on them.

"Bile, thick and bitter, rose into my throat and pure hatred warmed my blood. It rushed through my body like a wild jaguar trapped in a cage. It needed to be released. The rock I'd carried was suddenly weightless and it were as if it floated up above my head on its own accord."

Abel turned just as gravity found the escaped rock and yanked it back down. There was a wet cracking sound as it struck Abel's head. The rock came up and dropped repeatedly in perpetual motion. Copper scented the area covering up the scent of charred remains. Blood sizzled on the dying embers of the boys' offerings and the cracking sounds gave into a wet sucking. Until the red swamp that was once Abel's head sucked so hard on the rock, it slipped from Lilith's hand.

"It felt good: better than sex, Kenzi. The release that rolled through my body was like nothing I'd ever felt."

Kenzi felt it too. The tale had become so real, she could feel the adrenaline pushing her heart to pump faster, her lungs to breathe deeper, and her endorphins to surge through her. It was exhilarating. The only thing close to this feeling was cutting. But this was better. It was scary to feel that way, but it was. She kept that to herself though. No way did Lilith need to know how her story was affecting Kenzi.

"What have you done?" Cain said. He held in his hand a heavy looking wooden club. There was no question that he'd come for the same purpose and she'd simply beat him to it. Lilith turned to face him. Her eyelids stuck open. Her face felt tight with drying blood.

"What have you done?" he asked again, staring at his mutilated brother in disbelief.

"What you were about to do, Cain," Lilith answered.

Cain's wide eyes jittered about frantically, taking in the scene. He dropped to his knees and pulled a dagger from his brother's belt. He grabbed the unburnt foot of the hare that hung off the side of the altar and cut it free from the charred body. He pulled the leather thongs from his brother's sandals and tied them to the foot.

Draping the makeshift necklace over her head, he took her face in his hands and kissed her lips.

"This foot has been blessed by The Creator. I do not know if it will be enough to keep you safe, but it is all I have to offer you as protection," he said and then pointed north. "Run until you find a village. There is one, I have seen it. I do not know where the people come from, but I have seen and watched them. They will accept you and take you in. If I can, I will find you there, but I must take care of this first."

He pulled a leather satchel from his belt and gave it to her.

"Some water. Now go!"

She ran. Hard and as fast as her healed and fed body could carry her. When she came to a stream, she cleaned herself and washed the leather scraps Cain had given her to cover her breasts and loin when she'd first arrived.

"It was days before I found the village Cain had described. Entering, I was shocked. It was populated by some of the very children—grown now, of course—that I had conceived during my time with the demons. Those that were not my children bore a striking resemblance to Adam. Perhaps Cain was not the only one to stumble upon this village.

Most were half-breeds, that was easy enough to see. Some appeared to be like me and Adam. Had The Creator made and thusly abandoned even more than us? It appeared so.

"Cain was right; they took me in, fed me, gave me a home. My children knew nothing of me and did not recognize me. I let it be of course.

"Several weeks passed, then Cain finally arrived. By then I knew I was carrying his child. He told me that The Creator had banished him and showed me the mark he'd been branded with. It was, he'd been told, to protect him from murder, but I knew it well. It was the sigil assigned to me when I was given to the demons. It was The Creator's way of letting me know that he knew the truth, it is the only reason He chose to let Cain live. He banished him to the Land of Nod, where he knew I would see it.

"It seemed The Creator would never allow me peace. He enjoyed my suffering. He had created and discarded me, but would not let me die, would not release me. I knew that as long as I lived on this earth, I would suffer."

"I feel like that too," Kenzi muttered.

"The people of Nod knew of no Creator because most were not his creations. I suspected that He might have created some which He immediately deemed unworthy and abandoned here in Nod. It was His wastebasket and were I not living among them, He would forget their existence. I hated them all for that. Even Cain."

When the time came, Lilith labored in a small, windowless hut. It was dark, and the heat was stifling. The mat of straw beneath her was itchy and damp. An invisible knife plunged into her womb and twisted every few minutes. This was Eve's curse, not hers, but she was made to bear it as well. Sweat stung her eyes.

The rug that hung from the entrance moved and grey light rushed in bringing a cool breath of fresh wind with it.

"Get out!" Lilith screamed, and the rug dropped, plunging them again into the stagnant dark.

Pressure built up until the urge to push overcame the fear of pain and she pushed. Throughout the long night, she pushed, losing consciousness between the efforts, and waking again when the pain returned.

It was in the deepest of night, that the serpent entered, sliding beneath the hanging rug. In the blackness of the hut, she did not see him, but she felt his presence enter the space. It slithered onto her leg and writhed its way up to her sex, swollen and spread open by the head of the infant about to be delivered. It flicked its tongue, tasting and smelling, before continuing its journey to her ear.

"It is a son. His father shall name him Enoch and he shall rule this land under his own name. But he will forsake you. He will call you a whore and claim Adam and Eve his grandparents. He will seek to bring The Creator, the god of his grandfather to this land, to bless his people and you shall be the sacrifice of atonement," it whispered.

"No," Lilith moaned, pushing the head further out of her body.

"Kill him. Kill him now and then kill his father while he mourns. You will never be accepted even as your children will. Kill them all, Lilith, and every child to come in this village. You can stop this; you can keep The Creator from ever populating this earth with his foolish followers. You will never be their equal. You will never have the things He will give them. You will never—"

Her scream interrupted him, and the child delivered in a wave of blood and agony. It was, indeed, a boy. The light of dawn shone beneath the covered entrance. Lilith stared at her baby while the serpent coiled himself around her body, resting his head on her shoulder.

"Are you the serpent in this story?" Kenzi asked, unnerved suddenly. The snake ignored her interruption. It had reached the climax of Lilith's saga and would not be halted.

"Kill him now, before he cries out," it hissed.

Her hands, shaking and damp, reached down for the child. She touched his head, his perfect little body, and ran her fingers down his chubby arms. The babe brought his fists up and scrunched his face. He was about to take his first breath and cry. The hands—her hands—wrapped themselves around his tiny neck and squeezed.

"I felt the bones inside my baby's neck buckle like a bent straw. But I could not release it, I could not stop what had to be done. This was the only way. I gave full control over to my rage. It was clear the baby was dead and yet my hands held, white knuckled around the child that had just been delivered from my own womb."

"Lilith, what have you done?" It was a familiar voice in the hut. There'd been no movement of the rug, no increased light streaming in behind an intruder and yet, there was another inside.

Sariel stood, the raven perched upon his shoulder, above them. His skin was much smoother in this, his early days as Death, but otherwise he looked the same as he does today.

"What are you doing here? How did you find me?" she asked.

"This is my punishment for our sins. I have been cast out of The Creator's kingdom to this earth and below it. Until His bidding is done, I will walk this world collecting the souls of the dead and removing all demons and half-breeds. If I do as He asks, I will one day be welcome again in His kingdom."

"Even the murderer who refuses to follow The Creator's plan receives mercy," the serpent whispered to Lilith.

"There are no souls here to collect. We here are the abandoned ones, those who The Creator has turned His face from. You have no business here," Lilith spat.

The raven hopped off Sariel's shoulder, fluttered slowly to the ground, and waddled over to the dead infant. It appeared as if it was going to eat it. It plunged its beak deep into the center of the baby's frontal soft spot and pulled a silver thread from the cavity. It curled and wriggled slowly in the bird's beak like a worm before the bird gobbled it down.

"Come on, now. Why'd you do that, bird? You know that's not how this works," Sariel admonished.

"He is my son, Enoch. My son. He has no soul. Take your damned bird and get out of here."

Sariel held his arm out, showing her his newest cut. Enoch was scrawled in bloody letters across his arm.

"Wow, that sicko started calling his bird Enoch because it swallowed your son's soul? The bird's not even a guy, she's a girl. She was probably trying to protect your baby," Kenzi said.

Lilith was laden with the metal chains of many talismans.

"My son was the chosen one," Lilith answered. "I did the right thing by killing him. Sariel was and will always be a servant of The Creator. He wasn't just there for my son. He was there for me—to collect me and destroy me."

"But he didn't destroy you," Kenzi said. "I mean, he saved you, sort of, in that rabbit's foot. If The Creator wanted you dead, then he broke the rules for you."

"He did not make that choice. The choice was made for him."

Lilith continued her shopping. Her snake, still wrapped around the tree, began again. The whispered ending of the tale worked its magic on Kenzi, bringing her back to the scene in the hut.

"You have what you came for. Now go," Lilith said to Sariel.

"You know there is one more thing I have to do. I'm sorry, but…" Sariel said.

"You're sorry? Sorry? For what? You only mourn for yourself. You have always bowed to The Creator's wishes, always doing what He wanted even if it went against your very nature. You've been poisoned by Him, and now, you know nothing of love and kindness, only selfishness and death! You've come to take me back to Hell and I swear if you try to take me back there, I will take you with me."

She tore the foot from her neck and used it quickly to slash deep into her wrist, blood arched out in spurts like the pain of contractions. Sariel grabbed the undamaged wrist and held it easily. Her body was weak with childbirth and blood loss. But the bloody wrist, which had cramped up into a claw, swung at his eyes and face, making shallow contact several times.

The bird entered the fray and its big black wings flapped rapidly causing a strobe-like effect so that all motion seemed slowed. Sariel pried the foot away from her and bore the beating from the bloodied claw. He set the foot on Lilith's forehead and the bird landed on her mass of matted, black hair—digging its claws into her scalp.

In the present, Lilith interrupted the ending with a scream. Kenzi snapped out of her hallucination to see an image closely resembling the scene that was just described. Enoch was attacking Lilith. Dust piles covered the floor around the sparsely decorated tree and the serpent who, just moments ago, was telling Kenzi of the downfall of Lilith, was now slithering through the piles of crushed demonic souls to rejoin his mistress.

"Enoch! No, leave her be. It's all my fault. I brought her here," Kenzi shouted, waving her arms at the angry raven.

Enoch let go of Lilith and flew at Kenzi. She brought her hands up to cover her face just as the bird's talons grasped both wrists. Enoch continued forward and Kenzi felt herself fly backwards, landing with a thud on the floor of Gloria's hospital room.

Chapter 34: Book of Plague 5

The bleacher style seating behind the wall of glass made Daisy think of prison executions on TV crime shows. Twenty beautiful girls dressed in the same black skin-tight miniskirts and tanks sat with her. The similarities ended at the tags pinned to the tank straps, each sporting a number and one of three colors—yellow, orange, or green. Sharing a body with Asmo meant she also shared his knowledge. She knew the colors corresponded to different prices and those prices were based on perceived beauty. She also knew that her color—green—was the costliest and most sought-after. Perhaps a death-row prisoner wasn't far from the truth of it.

Asmo smiled for her and blinked her eyes in that cartoony flirtatious way she hated. But since she was nothing more than a passenger, with no control over her own body, she could only observe. She was in the fishbowl of Soapy Kisses Massage Parlor. Men and an occasional woman came in, window shopped—some even used binoculars to get a closer look—then paid for the girl they chose by her number. *Should call this thing the lobster tank instead of a fishbowl* she thought and Asmo snorted. The other girls looked at her, disgusted with the unlady-like noise, as if what they were doing was more demure.

A man showed up, hands in pockets, head hung sheepishly. He stole short glances at them through the window. His glasses were oversized, the kind everyone wore in the eighties. Daisy had an embarrassing picture of her mother wearing them and a "church dress" in a family portrait that was done before Daisy was born. She liked to look at it when the ghost of her mother's hate-filled words haunted her. Jezebel, harlot, slut—her mother, the poor Christian woman who gave birth to a murdering whore.

The shy man went to the counter, handed over a large sum of money and Daisy was called forth. Asmo held onto control of their body, but let Daisy to do the talking. Apparently, he trusted her to know the right things to say to a man. With the demon of lust inside her though, her vagina throbbed and swelled with moisture at the thought of what was to come. This reaction was not typical for her business dealings.

She led him to her assigned room which was spatially divided into two portions: the wet side and the dry side. The wet side contained a large jacuzzi tub surrounded by potted orchids and seafoam colored tiles with painted koi swimming about. On the far side of the tub lay a vinyl air mattress and a fancy tea service cart stocked with lush white towels and a variety of lotions, soaps, and a dish of chocolate covered strawberries. On the wall separating the room halves sat a shelf occupied by champagne flutes and an ice bucket. Two scantily clad women dressed in teal green nurse uniforms awaited on either side of the shelf.

After the drink girl took their order and the bath attendant let him choose the soap, they were left alone.

"My name is Daisy, what's yours?" she asked, leading him to the tub, where she began the water.

"Jack. I. Don't. Want. To. Talk," he said. Each word was clipped as if it stood alone in the sentence.

"You don't have to talk, I will."

"No. No. Talking."

You're doing just fine, doll. Give him a bath and a nice blow job. I'll take it from there. Asmo's thoughts filled her head and she had control of their body again.

She nodded and undressed the man. She'd had men like him before. Shy and uneasy. They liked to be led as if they were not in any way responsible for what happened. She didn't mind. They made the easiest customers and often paid tips. He had his bath, letting her wash him and kept his eyes glued to her breasts as she washed herself in front of him. She took his hand and pulled him from the tub. She dried his legs and he did not stop her when she took his erection in her mouth. He finished quickly and followed her to the air mattress without incident.

The foam and oil body massage portion of the night was so silent that the wet noises made her glad that Asmo took back over. She would have lost her groove, but with Asmo, Jack was obviously enjoying it. After rinsing him off and drying him again, they walked together to the bed. A large bowl of condoms sat on a nearby stand. She was supposed to insist that the customer put one on prior to relations. Asmo was certain the man would refuse under the influence of lust. Her hand couldn't even reach for one before Jack grabbed her wrist.

"No. Condom," he said.

For the first time in the "date" he took control. He pushed her over onto hands and knees and shoved himself inside her. Keeping an arm wrapped around her stomach he pumped hard and fast. It took her by surprise but Asmo didn't seem concerned, so she kept quiet. Jack did as well. No grunts, no huffs, no satisfied sighs when he came inside her.

"No. Shower," he said. "And. Don't. Look. At. Me. Anymore. Stay. There."

She did. He left without a word.

There was no tip, nothing left behind but a mess for her to clean up. Daisy used the shower head as a douche and took a little extra time to get off using the powerful spray of water on her clit. Asmo didn't fight her for control, instead he seemed happy to enjoy taking a voyeuristic break. Within minutes she was dressed and back in the tank with the other lobsters.

The rest of the night's customers were pleasant and talkative enough to make up for the first freak. With Asmo at the helm most of the time, her body entertained an entire bachelor party. Each regaled her with tales of drunken debauchery in their celebration of freedom before the wedding. They tipped well and were all so drunk that not a single one noticed a lack of prophylactics. Their focus was on trying to reach climax in their intoxicated, half-flaccid states.

Her favorite customer was Wayne, the pilot from America who had moved to Bangkok after his wife divorced him.

"It was fine by me. I never really treated it much like a marriage, more like a hotel with benefits, you know. A place to keep my stuff with someone around to watch it for me."

He liked the Suvarnabhumi airport as his home-base because it serviced so many other countries.

"I've got women like you in London, Paris, Dubai, and Cairo."

He had his hand wrapped tight in her hair, shoving himself so far down her throat Daisy thought she might vomit.

"For a bachelor like me, sex is a hobby. Some people travel to exotic places to try their cuisine, me I go for the pussy."

Her eyes watered from the hair pulling and the choking, but his seed went down easy and left a sweet aftertaste. Daisy hadn't played the submissive role in a long time. She liked him, which was unusual for her, but he reminded her a lot of herself. He was matter-of-fact about sex and his "don't give a fuck" attitude was a refreshing change from the jumpy, nervous suburban johns she tolerated. Because she was so into this one, Asmo had let her take over while he napped away in the back of her head.

She could feel Asmo stir in her consciousness while she rubbed her body all over Wayne's. Wayne was a talker. From what he said, Bangkok was the perfect choice for STD central. With men like Wayne, spreading the disease all over the non-American continents would be a piece of cake.

"Ladies always want to meet the pilot and I have a good crew looking out for me. If they see a gal who's my type, they'll offer her a tour of the cockpit once we land." He laughed and turned over for the front half of the body massage. "Lots of women have earned their wings in my cockpit."

He wagged his dick up and down as if it was some fancy trick. Daisy couldn't help it—this guy was charming with his ever-loving ego.

She rubbed herself up and down his shaft.

"Now, I usually insist on protection, sweet-tits." He smirked and winked at her. "I didn't get to be a world-class Casanova by being reckless. But for you, I'm gonna make an exception. You get the full monty."

Daisy smiled and tried to look grateful. She had an idea that Wayne said that to all the girls. Penetration or no, the branching vines had already noted the foreign skin against her own. They tickled in a good way as they creeped out of her and wrapped themselves around his shaft. For a moment, Daisy was connected to Wayne before the tendrils broke apart and buried themselves among the pubic hair around his balls.

"You ever been to Copenhagen?" he asked as she rinsed and dried him off.

"No, I've never really been anywhere outside the country besides here."

That was the truth. She found it easy to be honest with him.

"Well, you ought to see it. One of my favorite places in the world. Gorgeous. That's where I'm flying next. I could get you a ticket if you wanted to accompany me. Wouldn't mind the perks." He winked down at her.

She dried his feet. Without thinking, she kissed them. After all, here was a man offering to take her to see the world even if it was about to end.

You're getting too sentimental with this one. Asmo, fully back from his nap, said in her head. *So much for letting a woman do a man's job. Let's finish this. I'm tired of driving you around.*

She watched the rest of the date from the nook inside her consciousness while Asmo finished him off one last time. Somehow, he'd managed to get her up on Wayne's face for a bit and Daisy wondered if Wayne could feel the vines wrapping around his tongue.

When it was over, Wayne handed her his card with an American hundred-dollar bill folded around it.

"You look me up over at the Suv if you ever feel like getting out of the fish bowl," he said holding her hand longer than necessary to pass the bill. "You really should, Daisy, before it's too late."

It's already too late, she thought.

Asmo used her mouth to thank him and kiss him goodbye. She watched him walk out of her life while the demon tucked the money-wrapped card between her breast and the tight dress.

"Let's get out of here—I want my cock back. I need to dip into this city a little more. You got the rest of the night off. I think Wayne will help us out immensely in fulfilling our task, don't you?"

Chapter 35: Book of Plague 6

Asmo let Daisy do the walking. They would split up at the hotel so as not to arouse any suspicions. He fell back asleep quickly once she took over, apparently spent. The streets were still packed in the early morning hours so that as much as she wanted, she could not remove her heels and walk home barefoot.

She bounced through the crowd like a pinball, not in any hurry at all. The Grace hotel was two blocks up and two to the left, but there was a large park in the diagonal space between. It was lined with street vendors. If she took the shortcut, she could get a drink and get out of her shoes. Only one small area on that route was poorly lit, but it didn't bother Daisy—she could hold her own.

She stopped for a Thai iced tea and let the sweet, thick milk cool her overused throat. Standing in the dark sipping it, she rested.

"Don't. Scream," a voice said as an arm wrapped around her throat.

A blade—cold and sharp—pressed against her throat. The cadence of the command gave him away as the shy man who'd been her first customer of the evening. Jack. He must have waited outside all night and followed her until he felt safe making a move. She dropped her tea and tried to relax, knowing that a struggle would get her killed while giving in would get his guard down.

He dragged her to a bench behind an SUV limo. A shrub on the other side of the bench created the perfect privacy. She wasn't afraid, in fact she was energized and hoped that Asmo would stay asleep. She missed handling men like this. But if the demon did wake up, she thought, with a murderous rush of adrenaline, she might just be strong enough to hold him off, show Asmo what happens when a man interrupts a woman doing *her* job.

Jack pulled her shoes off. *Go ahead and throw them. Just make sure you toss one this way.* He did, dropping them beside the bench, before tearing her dress and shoving her legs up. She was expecting him to push himself into her as he had in the room but instead he sniffed at her.

"How. Many. Men. Have. You. Had. In. Here Tonight? I. Can. Smell. Them. On. You. You. Didn't. Wash. Up. Did. You, You. Little. Whore?"

Without another perfectly enunciated word, he buried his face into her. He sucked and nuzzled like a piglet at its mother's teat. She dropped her arm off the bench and stretched her fingers out toward the strap of a shoe. The tip of his knife poked into her stomach. She realized he had it in his hand pointed into her gut so that she couldn't attempt to sit up.

She was never good at math or physics so she had no idea what would happen next but there was little time to think. Without Asmo's influence, there was certainly no physical pleasure to muddle her thought process. She bent sideways, careful not to push her torso up into the knife and managed to hook a shoe with her middle finger. She dropped it in surprise when he bit into her clit. The pain was sure to wake Asmo up. If she was going to put a stop to this, she needed to do something now. Besides, if she didn't, Jack would destroy her.

An electric shock shot through her when she tried to move. A whimper escaped her lips. "Shut. Up. Or. I. Will. Use. The. Knife," Jack warned. "And. I. Prefer. To. Eat. My. Prey. Alive."

His teeth were a vise grip on her clit. Her flesh ripped, and the warm rush of blood heralded fiery pain. Suddenly, a knife to the gut didn't seem too bad a risk. Her clit was gone, he'd swallowed it. He gnashed at her labia.

She sat halfway up impaling herself, hoping there was some extra fat to protect her intestines. She'd seen enough knife wounds to know what happened when the bowels got involved.

The shoe, mercifully, was still within reach. She managed to get it up and over her head as he tore off another chunk of tissue. The agony pushed itself ahead of the clean heat of the knife in her belly. The knife slid out of her as she arched further back with the shoe and knew if she didn't get the heel in his skull now, she never would.

The blood loss was making her weak. Asmo stirred, the cacophony inside her mind too much for anyone to sleep through. But Daisy didn't want him to intervene, not just yet. She'd rather die than need his help and she might.

The stiletto slid through Jack's skull like a lawn jart into mud. His body went rigid and his teeth relaxed on the piece of tissue he'd bitten into. She pulled her right knee up and into his flank. He fell off of her, the knife tinkling like a dainty bell on the cement. The pain in her groin was gone now, replaced by adrenaline-fueled rage. She got on top of him and buried the heel into his eyes one by one. The pop of each orb transferred easily through the solid spike and quelled her anger.

What the fuck is going on? Asmo demanded inside her head. She ignored him and went on putting holes in Jack's body. *This ain't my gig sweetheart, you're on your own. Have fun.*

He ripped himself out of her body but she paid no mind—she was already torn into pieces. Jack was dead, and her crotch was on fire. There was a cool, wet spot on the front of her ruined dress and she touched it remembering the knife wound. She needed to get back to the hotel and clean herself up before anyone saw her or found Jack. She stood up gingerly, focused on the blood spilling out of his body and ignored the hot pain seeping from her own.

A movement from Jack's head caught her attention just as she was turning to leave. She stopped and watched as the blood no longer passively drained from his wounds but instead crawled out in black tendrils that reached the steel of the bench leg and wrapped themselves around it. Other vines spread out faster, up over the bench, covering it in some organic mesh as still more worked their way out of his penis and mouth. They extended to the SUV parked beside them and began to coat it in a similar fashion. By the time the vehicle was covered, the bench was gone, dissolved, or maybe eaten away by the very same organism that currently resided in her own ruined sex.

She backed away. When it was clear everything the vines covered would soon be gone, she ran. The bloody shoe still in her hand, she ran to the Hotel Grace and straight to her room. The key was gone. She no longer had it. Daisy Fields crumpled in front of the door, hands in her face, and cried.

Chapter 36: Book of War 6

Melanie Pryor stood on the stage at the northernmost speaking point of the rally. Thousands of men, women and children gathered in the center of the Mall. Almost every one of them picked at the free food distributed by Senator Weyer's donated Loaves and Fishes trucks. Even counter protestors enjoyed the spoils offered them in a show of peace and good faith.

There were other important speakers scattered throughout the area with major stages set at the four compass points around the mall. Sound techs checked microphones and amplifiers unaware of the bombs hidden inside the podiums. She wasn't worried about her own safety; she knew that the Goddess had more work for her to do. Melanie Pryor would escape unscathed. The senator was about to introduce her. After that, there would be only a short time to incite as much animosity between the two opposing groups as possible. She approached the lectern, chaos on her breath.

"Hello everyone. I suppose most of you know me. My name is Melanie Pryor and I survived the Attack on Life bombing."

The crowd broke out in applause. She smiled but did not pause for long.

"I'm here today because I will not be silenced. My life is worth risking for the lives of so many innocent unborn children. While I would normally never advocate violence or murder because it is the very thing I stand here against today, I also understand that these people who choose to kill their own children and these doctors who kill many babies each and every day only understand violence as a means to communicate. They will not hear reason, they cannot see that it is human life they are destroying." She pointed to the protesters.

Cheers and applause bloomed from the seeds she'd just planted. Those poor souls in front of her wouldn't have the chance to follow through with the violence she was inciting, but the ones who heard her words from the safety of their homes would use them to honor her and the other victims.

"The Lord says an eye for an eye and I say we must keep fighting in the way He commands. We can rally, we can protest but I fear it has come to war and we must fight for what we believe in."

Shouts of agreement came from the crowd that gathered closer to the stage, wanting to hear her inspiring words.

"Are you ready to stand beside me?"

The crowd responded favorably.

"Are you ready to fight for our future?"

"YES!" Fists in the air, signs hoisted, banners held high.

"Are you ready to meet violence with violence? Murder with murder if necessary?"

The screams and frenzy that broke out in front of her told her the answer to that question. She smiled down at them with the serenity of the Virgin Mary.

Gunshots rang out from behind them and then the first of the food trucks—laden with hallucinogenic fungal spores—exploded.

When the tangled mass of hysterical bodies slammed against the podium, threatening to bring Cynthia into the fray, the senator's arm caught her and pulled her into silent darkness.

Chapter 37: Book of War 7

"Oh my gawd, Annika. I can't believe we're doing this." Jessica said.

Giggling and shushing, the girls stumbled through the woods. Their unspoken leader stomped ahead carrying the Ouija board.

"What if we, like, start a forest fire or something?" Lauryn asked.

She'd been designated to carry the bags from the New Age store where they'd purchased the black candles, the crystals, the chalice, and the long matches that Annika insisted they would need to make the experience more witchy.

Annika stopped and stared at them. "OK, anyone who is too much of a pussy can go right on back to town and participate in Beth's parents' haunted ghost walk tonight."

Beth winced. She'd invited them along as a fun outing and to save herself from being dragged along on her parents' historical tour of Salem. Having parents who wrote historical nonfiction for a living provided Beth all sorts of boring travel opportunities. This year, her sixteenth, they'd allowed her to bring friends. She'd known Annika, Lauryn, and Jess since elementary school and the trip to Salem started up some crazy talk of witchcraft and covens—*American Horror Story* type stuff.

It seemed like a great idea back home in Minneapolis but here in the woods—maybe the very woods real witches used to practice real witchcraft—Beth wasn't sure dabbling in the dark arts was such a great idea anymore.

"Come on. Right up here." Annika said.

The book, stolen from her mother's current stack of research material, was sweaty beneath Beth's hands. If her mother noticed it was gone, this would be the first and last time she brought anyone along on these "vacations." It contained her mother's margin notes on the diary of Abigail Williams, one of the girls whose accusations fueled the madness of the Salem Witch Trials. She'd let Annika read it. Her friend had been fascinated, especially about the midnight rituals Abigail participated in with the servant Tituba. It had inspired this crazy scheme: the four of them would escape into the woods and perform a séance.

"Let's call on Tituba and find out if she really was a witch!" Annika said and they'd all agreed.

It was getting dark and as they neared the clearing Beth was having second thoughts. She looked back at Jess and Lauryn. They both wore grins, but their eyes were wide and paranoid.

"Here it is!" Annika said.

It was strange to see in real life a place where people had gathered for the same thing over four hundred years ago. It was especially dark in the clearing, as if the trees were purposefully holding back all the light. No wonder witches were drawn here. A breeze coaxed goosebumps up her arms. Beth shivered.

Annika took the lead, setting up a circle of candles with the chalice at the northern-most point. Beth had read the diary; the chalice was for the blood of a sacrifice. She supposed for Annika it was just part of the show, but that didn't stop the hairs rising on the back of her neck every time she looked at it. Annika was taking it all so seriously, Beth wouldn't have been surprised if she had carried a knife along with the compass in her pocket.

Lauryn was given the honor of lighting the candles and reciting the words Annika had written on a set of notecards in order to call upon the influence of the elements. Jessica carefully placed crystals and gems strategically around them as well.

Jessica, who practically worshipped Annika, plopped down in the center, and put the Ouija board on her lap.

"Come on you guys," she laughed. "We're really going to do this."

Beth and Lauryn sat inside the circle on their knees—Annika had insisted that they could not cross their legs—while Annika took her seat on the far side of the board.

"Beth, read the opening, please," Annika said.

"With the power of the elements, we are protected from all evil spirits, entities, and influences."

"Let's begin," Annika said. She and Jessica circled the planchette around the board before stopping in the center. "We call out to the spirit of Tituba, servant of Samuel Parris, true witch of Salem. Tituba are you here with us?"

The girls leaned in solemnly, watching in the flickering light of the candles for some slight movement when the planchette began spinning wildly across the board.

"Oh my god!" Jessica screamed and pulled her hands off the game. Lauryn cracked up giggling and Annika hit her in the arm.

"Knock it off. If you can't be serious, you can leave."

Lauryn's laughter stopped abruptly.

Hands returned to the planchette and Annika repeated the call out to Tituba. "Are you with us?"

This time, the planchette moved steadily but slowly up to the NO in the upper right corner of the board.

"Who is—" but before Annika could finish, it whipped their hands down to the letters on the board.

"S-O-O-N, soon?" Jessica read aloud.

"So, you are not Tituba, but you will get her for us? Can you do that?" Annika asked.

"YES," Jessica spoke for the board.

"What is your name?"

"L-I-L-I-T-H, Lilith?"

"We can read, Jess," Annika said

"Sorry."

"Wasn't Lilith a demon?" Beth asked, recalling something she'd read in her parents' library.

Before anyone could answer, the planchette ripped out of the girls' hands and slid directly to NO. Beth let out a little scream but it was drowned out by the others' gasps and squeals. The planchette moved again on its own, spelling out GODDESS.

"Vain much?" Annika said.

The candles blew out, the girls screamed, and for each, the world went black.

Chapter 38: Book of Sariel 6

Sariel folded the scorched remains of Kenzi's childhood drawing and slipped it beneath his belt. He had to tell Kenzi that she was officially an orphan. Sariel and Enoch would be there for her as they always had for as long as she would let them. Lilith certainly made the situation challenging. But Kenzi belonged to him, with him. She'd have to see that too.

He could have appeared in her room beside her, but he chose instead to gently knock and receive permission to enter. He brushed past the guard scrolling through Facebook.

"Kenzi?" he said quietly, poking his head through a crack in the door.

He didn't wait for a response when he saw the room.

The bird flew ahead and cawed madly. There was no sense to be had within. A dead mortal slumped in a chair like a stuffed Halloween dummy on a porch. He was soulless yet lacked the tell-tale sign left by Enoch. His smooth forehead and desiccated body left no doubts about his demise. Sariel stepped over the legs to the unmade and empty bed. The metal cage that once held Kenzi's leg bones together lay empty, nothing more than a hollow exoskeleton itself. There were various other medical devices left behind on and around the bed. It was as if the patient simply disappeared, taking nothing with her.

"What is going on here, Enoch?" It was a rhetorical question.

The bird flitted from place to place just as confused. It landed on the corner of Kenzi's writing journal that lay open, pages folded haphazardly beneath it. Its cry was mournful. Sariel knew then what it must feel like to have the bird plunge its beak into your soul because the call shot deep into him.

Sariel picked up the book and straightened its pages, peeking to note anything recently written by its owner. Nothing. He sighed and placed the folded drawing inside it before closing it and slipping it into his belt where the paper had just been.

"Well, Enoch, I—" The sound of a scream and breaking glass interrupted him.

Enoch squawked in surprise. Sariel turned to see a nurse frozen in shock at the doorway, broken plate and scattered fruit on the floor at her feet. For a moment, he thought she could see him; that Death frightened the woman. But it was death slumped in the corner and an empty patient bed that surprised her. Nothing more.

"This is not good," Sariel said, again rhetorically. "There is the stink of Demoness in this room. We must find Kenzi. When we do, I will tell her the entire truth, and then, we together, will destroy Lilith. There is no other option. I'm done with this damnation."

"Code Blue, ICU room 402. Code Blue, ICU room 402"

The nurse was gone already, likely off to call for help. This room was 406, not 402 and Sariel had been in enough ICUs to know what a code blue meant. He knew this code blue was for Gloria even without looking at the still-smoldering pain on his arm.

The cacophony in the room coupled with the number of bodies scuttling about made it difficult to see the maneuvers in the battle of life and death. It didn't matter though, the spoiler alert searing into his flesh was all he needed. This time, Gloria was dead.

"So, did anyone find a next of kin or get that other one to sign an emergency POA?" a doctor at the head of the bed asked.

Group mumbles hummed like white noise punctuated only by popping glass ampules, Tourettic shouts for meds, and crumpled plastic wrappers. With no definitive answer, work continued.

"236 is missing. Gone. The sitter in her room is dead. Cops are everywhere. I don't know what the fuck just happened." A nurse, Kenzi's nurse that dropped the plate, spoke from the door.

Her bun fell off to the side of her head and mascara raccooned beneath her eyes. The hospital sound system came to life again calling out *Code M* for missing patient with a vague description of Kenzi.

"I can't take this one now. I can't take her without Kenzi here to say goodbye, Enoch. She's lost everything." But he had to take this soul. There was no way he could even chance disobedience now. As it was, The Creator must have noticed something amiss by now. Lilith's little war was turning into an apocalypse and if he didn't get control of it, there would be literal Hell to pay.

"What the fuck is going on around here?" the doctor yelled. "I thought there were cops outside her room. 1 more amp of epi…Now! Where's the fucking MDA? I can't get this fucking tube down her fat fucking throat!"

The pulseless line and continual beep that had been the background music for the entire resuscitation crescendoed to center stage. In an unusual beat of silence, it screamed.

"Fuck it. I'm calling it," the doctor said.

"Sheol," Sariel said. "I told her Sheol was safe. But, she did not go alone."

"Time of death 17:43." The doctor threw the laryngoscope on the floor. It bounced once then slid to Sariel's foot.

"Stop," Sariel commanded. The room froze. "Enoch," he began, but the bird was already gone.

Chapter 39: Book of War 8

Thumping pressure behind her eyes coupled with an ache in her shoulders brought Beth back to consciousness. She knew immediately that she was upside down. Her arms were stretched out in a T. The ropes were scratchy at her wrist and just above her elbow. She tried twisting her arms, judging their tautness by the maximum movement they allowed. They allowed none and even the attempt elicited a prickly burn.

She took inventory of the rest of her body. Feet were tied together at the ankles and thighs. She felt no pain elsewhere and she was still clothed, although not in the jeans and sweater she'd worn into the woods. Even in mid-April, New England winter fought to remain. It had to be night yet, because she was freezing and there was no light shining through her eyelids. She was wearing a sort of thin sheet like a toga.

"Oh my god," someone whispered. It sounded like Lauryn, but she couldn't be sure.

Beth opened her eyes. At first there was nothing—pure darkness—no light whatsoever. But slowly, her brain adjusted to the upside-down view and the limited light from the candles they'd lit earlier. On a large post directly across from her, Lauryn was wrapped and presented in the same way as Beth. Ninety degrees to Lauryn's right and left were other poles. Jess and Annika were tied to those. Their inverted crucifixes positioned in the same directional locations as they'd placed the candles—north, south, east, and west. Everyone's eyes reflected the light of the candles which accentuated the terror on their faces.

"I'm so glad you four want to speak to Tituba," a voice echoed. "But I know a much easier way."

"Who are you?" Beth tried to sound calm.

"Only she who you have called upon," the voice answered.

"We wanted to talk to Tituba, not you," Annika said.

"Silence," the voice ordered.

The girls watched as a figure obscured by the darkness entered the circle made by their crosses. She was pregnant. Very much so. Beth sighed. This had to be a joke. Which one of the girls had set this up? Probably Annika, she was certainly acting tough right now and didn't seem scared at all. The whole hanging upside down thing was pushing it way too far. Plus, they all must have been drugged or something. And shit, what were her parents going to say about them being out so late. None of this was funny at all.

"OK, I don't know who did all this, but enough is enough. Do you guys know how much trouble we're in? Seriously, get us down right now and maybe I can make my parents believe it was all a bad joke," Beth said.

"I asked for silence," the pregnant woman said again. "You will stay where you are until I give word that you can be taken down. You four have committed to bringing back the witch Tituba therefore, you will help me do so."

"Please, please let us down. We thought it was a joke, we thought it was a game," Lauryn sobbed.

"That is the problem with women like you. You think you have no authority; you think it's a show, a game to be played. This world has not evolved in favor of women's minds and influence and that is why I must destroy it. You four will learn the potency of your bodies soon enough. That is my gift to you—you will live long enough to know that your life holds power." The pregnant woman rubbed her swollen belly.

Beth screamed, and the others followed. It hurt her head, her eyes burned, and the tears flowed. How could it not be a joke? A *pregnant woman* was talking about killing them. It was insane. She closed her eyes. Maybe this was some sort of hallucination. One of the girls must have drugged them as a prank—LSD or something like that. She sobbed and could hear the others doing the same.

Just go to sleep again, go to sleep and when you wake up, this will all have been a nightmare Beth promised herself and tried to send the same reassurance to the others telepathically.

The ground shook with a thundering boom and a smell of charred meat filled the clearing. The air warmed and scorched Beth's face. There would be no sleep because this was not a dream.

"Where are we?" An unfamiliar woman's voice shouted. Someone else had just joined the party.

"Shh," the pregnant woman this time—Beth was sure of it. "Quiet, daughter of Tituba, you are safe here. You have done well."

Beth kept her eyes shut tight wishing it all away.

"Beelzebub, thank you for bringing her to me."

Beth knew Beelzebub as a number of possible incarnations. The Devil himself, Prince of the Demons, Lord of the Flies. He was also considered the demon associated with gluttony in the seven deadly sins. This realization as well as the association with the name Lilith blew into her mind like a typhoon. Images from her parents' books on demonology swam in and out of her mind's eye. As a child, she had loved to look at them even though they frightened her. The reality in front of her though, made those books seem like Mother Goose characters.

Lilith—first wife of Adam, demon baby killer, succubus. If they'd conjured demons of this caliber with the Ouija board, they were undoubtedly about to die.

Chapter 40: Book of Plague 7

Asmodeus, demon of lust, wrecker of marriages, rapist and sadist walked into the bacchanal buffet of flesh that was Bangkok's sex district. Taking on the image he'd started the evening with, the rich Arab gained many glances from both women and men. Tonight, he would test the waters of this country. Perhaps it was time to relocate.

He was done with Lilith and that whore of hers. Let them do whatever it was they thought they could do without him. Why he'd ever agreed to help that silly little girl, he didn't know. Humanity may have bestowed the demon moniker on her, but she would never have the strength or will of a true demon. What was Lucifer so worried about? Women were meant to be used until broken and that was what he'd done to both her and her stupid human. It was time to move on. That mortal cunt was trouble anyway.

"Hi there, handsome."

A hooker—a young one at that—rubbed his bicep. He looked at her tiny body and small but perky tits. He'd split her wide open before he was done with her. Yes, that was exactly the kind of release he needed.

"You have a room somewhere?" he asked her.

Without a word, she took his hand and led him through the bustling bodies farther down the street. The sun was just beginning to lighten the sky and it was almost as if the crescendo of sirens—a constant background noise in Bangkok—were heralding its arrival rather than cleaning up the previous night's debauchery.

The little whore stopped along the side of a grime-covered building just as the sun peeked over the horizon. She led him down into a basement. Smoky, opium scented air and dim lighting were just his style. He followed her to a corner enclosed by red curtains. Once inside the hideout, she pushed him back onto a pile of pillows. She lit two lanterns that hung above them and plucked an opium pipe off the wall.

He shooed it away and gestured for her to undress. She did, dancing a little for him. Her movements were awkward, and her adolescent clumsiness remained. She hadn't gotten used to the curves of a woman's body yet. Perhaps it was the uneven surface she was dancing on, but he preferred to think she was only thirteen or fourteen. He snapped his fingers and the lights in the lanterns flared. He wanted to see her better.

She had a nice little patch of pubic hair which was a welcome change from all the bald, stubbly ones he'd been seeing in Vegas. She bent over and began to undress him. With each button she worked with her tongue, he felt himself get bigger. Oh, how he'd missed his dick. Being a girl was no fun. He liked being the aggressor, the one to always, ALWAYS get off. That required a cock and he was quite pleased with his.

Her little head looked so pretty bent down working on his pants. He shoved it into his crotch. She took him into her mouth and he could feel her throat straining against its bulk. She pulled back after only a few strokes and grabbed it with her hand. A classic move for buying time. Stupid women, they were all the same. Who taught them this stalling tactic?

She smiled, and her rheumy eyes told him she had been trying hard not to gag. This pleased him even more and he flexed her head toward his cock yet again. This time she held back, in fact, she slipped out from under his grasp and scurried away from him like a crab. She spat on the floor and coughed frantically. He looked down at himself.

His cock, his big, thick, beautiful cock was enmeshed in black, barbed vines that had sprouted out of his urethra like the devil's cum and imprisoned him.

No. No. This wasn't right. He was a demon, immune to the ravages of mortal flesh. And certainly, immune to a *woman's* creation. His true form began to emerge, trying to escape the tightening net of disease growing around him. He clawed at it, scraping his nails along it but the lines only bit deeper into his flesh. The girl was gone, having run away in fear. Curtains hung open and a crowd gathered, whispering in their sing-song language.

The more he fought, the further the vines grew, onto his stomach and down his thighs. He growled in fury. His three heads—a bull, a man, and a ram—looked in all directions. The fear-sobered patrons of the opium den screamed and crumpled to the floor as he shoved through them. His feet spread out into their four talons and the scales raced up his legs. He ran like a bird onto the street, his heavy-horned ram's head knocking mortals out of the way,

In this form, he bullied his way through the crowds, past the cordoned off section where a black fungus was spreading over every non-organic surface, strobe lights leaving negatives of the now growing plague on the backs of his retinas. He ignored it all. There was only one thing on his mind—the whores. Lilith and Daisy. Find them, make them take back this wretched disease and then kill them. He would crush their skulls beneath his feet and shove the remains so far into their own wombs, the whole mass would pop out of their necks and form new heads.

The Grace Hotel's flat façade, pock-marked with circular windows, loomed like a slice of Swiss cheese in front of him. Focused only on finding the girls, he didn't see the bodies in the deserted lobby, the festering black growths working their way over man-made surfaces, dissolving them like acid.

The elevator opened directly, no one was one it. It took him to the eighth floor without stopping. The oddity was lost on his vengeful mind. The bell of impending arrival rang, and he shoved himself through the doors.

The whore, Daisy, lay crumpled in a ball in front of their door. Her body was covered with crusted blood. He stomped over to her and picked her up. Her head lolled like a rag doll and he shook her awake.

"What have you done to me?" he roared.

"Wh…what?" she whispered.

She didn't even try to open her eyes. She was light, much lighter than she should be. He ripped her clothes and saw the swollen, bloodied, and chewed up remains of her sex. Her legs were thick with clotted blood. Fuck, she was as good as dead. The black growth snaked out of her, its serpentine branches lifted in his direction as if begging for life.

He stepped into her, possessing her as he had before. This time, from inside her, he tried to scrape his cock off against her pelvic bones, meaning to leave the cursed filth with her where it should have stayed in the first place. Her consciousness put up little fight while he worked on transferring the plague back to her.

"Leave her be, Asmodeus. It is not she who did this to you," Lilith said.

She stood behind them, cloaked in black, bright eyes glowed beneath the darkness the hood provided.

"She is dead anyway, there is nothing you or I can do to affect that," Asmodeus said.

"Even so, remove yourself from her body. She is mine."

He stepped out, true to form. His cock, torso and legs still encased in Lilith's cursed plague.

"And you remove this from me. It was not part of the deal," he demanded.

"You should not trust me to make deals, my love," she smiled. "I wanted nothing more than to see you suffer, but when Lucifer offered you as a hired hand, I realized I could kill two birds with one stone. You have done your job. As we speak my plague spreads across the world. Planes leave Bangkok, traveling all over this continent, Africa, Europe, and Australia. With each touch, it spreads and with each death, more of the mortals' creations will dissolve. Soon this world will be a great garden again—the garden I was expelled from for doing nothing more than existing just as I was made. And you will add to it as you die. This disease has grown from a seed that you and your kind planted within me so long ago. It is harvest time, my love. Time to reap what you sowed."

Chapter 41: Book of Plague 8

Henry Patel yawned as he worked the key into the lock and let himself into his apartment. All he wanted to do was sleep. When was the last time he'd eaten? He didn't know, and frankly, he didn't care. He should probably shower, he'd sleep better, but there was no energy for that. It had been well over thirty-six hours since he'd seen his bed let alone slept in it.

His shirt came off on the way to the fridge where he found a spoiled quart of milk and a single can of red bull.

"Water it is." He unbuckled his pants and let them fall to the floor.

He abandoned his phone and pager on the sink counter, both turned off, and the phone plugged in. Today, he was post-call and as far as he was concerned, sleep was all that absolutely needed to be done. He knew he should read the articles Dr. Altrey had given him on ventilator management, but he also knew that nothing would stick in a brain as fatigued as this.

He shuffled in his stocking feet to the bedroom. There was no light because he had blackened the windows. The white noise machine was on, he must have forgotten to turn it off when he'd left on Friday. The ray of light that streamed in from the door revealed the bedside rug and the otherwise empty room. Other than a bed and nightstand, he kept nothing in there. Bedrooms were for sleep and should contain no distractions.

The bed had been positioned so that no matter how far the door opened, no light would hit him as he slept. Henry had studied much in the way of home design and Feng Shui. He dropped onto the bed with a sigh of relief and felt a body, already lying there, bounce.

"What the hell?"

He jumped up and turned on the light.

The woman on his bed was bruised and bloodied. No doubt she'd been roughed up. The already skimpy dress she wore was in tatters, leading him to a basic assumption. A prostitute had been beaten up by her pimp or a john and somehow managed to get into his apartment to sleep it off. Maybe she'd even turned on the white noise machine. And so there would be no sleeping just yet for him, now he had to deal with this.

"Miss…Miss," he said shaking her by the shoulders.

There were bruises around her neck, and her hands were stained with a black substance the same consistency as blood. A stain spread out in a puddle from between her legs. He was no gynecology resident, but that blood looked too red to be menstrual.

"Oh my god," he said.

This had to be a botched abortion or something. What the hell had happened in his apartment? He ran out to the kitchen for his cell phone to call 911. He wasn't about to get involved in this kind of shady deal.

"There is no need for that Dr. Henry Patel," a female voice said from the doorway of his bedroom.

He spun around to find a pregnant woman, around his own age. She was dressed as if going to some goth prenatal yoga class. Her long black hair accentuated the greenest eyes he'd ever seen. Even at term pregnancy, she was beautiful, and he couldn't turn away.

"I need you, Henry. I need you to help my friend," she said.

"How can I help?" He heard the words, understood they came from his mouth, but did not recall making the mental decision to say them.

"Come, see to her wounds. I tried. Henry, I tried to fix them, I did, but my power doesn't work on wounds caused by my own choices."

"You did this to her?" he asked, confused but obediently following her to the body.

"I put her in the situation. Yes, she was serving me at the time of the attack."

"Was she pregnant too?"

"No," the woman answered curtly.

He approached the dying girl on his bed. When he lifted the remains of her dress, he inhaled sharply, the cool air stinging his teeth.

Her genitals looked like hamburger. Bruised and purple and torn or ripped off entirely, like a botched female circumcision. He was a failed surgery resident. Couldn't even get a categorical spot. He only got the internal medicine residency because his father spent lord knows how much in "donations" to hold him a place. He had no idea how to fix this.

"Let me call the hospital. She needs a surgeon."

"No. That is not an option, you must fix her here. I know you can. Kenzi Brooks believes in you."

The name stirred feelings inside him. Did Kenzi know this woman? Perhaps she had been responsible for Kenzi's injuries as well. If so, the woman was dangerous.

All right, yes, he could do something. He had completed a surgery clerkship in medical school; he knew how to suture. At the very least, he knew how to stop the bleeding until he could get this figured out.

"I will need to do an exam and then I will have to go back to the hospital and obtain supplies. It is not like I have what I need here."

The pregnant woman eyed him warily and then nodded.

He spent precious little time on the exam itself. Henry Patel, a virgin at twenty-five, had never felt comfortable doing pelvic exams. From what he could see her left labia was gone as was her clitoris.

There was a lot of bleeding from the clitoral area—probably an injury to the pudendal artery or vein. If so, she had already lost a lot of blood. There was no way to transfuse her in his apartment. There was a very real chance she'd die here. He ran to the bathroom and grabbed a washcloth silently cursing himself for buying white ones.

"I need you to hold pressure on the bleeding until I get back, can you do that?"

He folded the terrycloth into a small but thick square. Pressing it against the injured woman's vulva, he placed the dubious stranger's hand against the cloth.

Exhausted, he sat at the table struggling to think of everything he would need. He scribbled it on his notepad like a grocery list: suture, lidocaine, dressings, those mesh panties from the OB department—how exactly he'd get them, he didn't know. Antibiotics, pain meds. God, he would have to break into the pharmacy. He'd never done anything so stupid. He couldn't afford to get caught. His father would disown him.

No matter what, this was not going to turn out well, and he knew it. His heart pounded in his chest as he folded up the paper and stuck it in his back pocket. He felt the need to go back to the bedroom one last time.

"Are you going to be all right here alone?" he asked her.

"Yes, of course. But you must hurry. She must be saved. I need her."

He wondered if they were sisters. They looked nothing alike. Maybe they were lovers, he didn't have time to speculate.

"I will try." He turned to leave then stopped. "You say you know Kenzi Brooks? Have you seen her lately? She is missing from the hospital."

"Kenzi is fine. Please, I need you to help Daisy now."

Yes, he would. He would do his best for these two women but only because they knew something about Kenzi and he needed the upper hand.

He grabbed his phone and noticed the Keurig pot. Wondering if he could afford the time it would take to fill a to-go cup, he decided that if he did not, he would never make it through the night. He threw a Dark Magic pod in and pushed the button. Steamy coffee filled his green metallic mug and he breathed in the promise of energy and mental clarity.

Capping the mug, he hurried to the door.

"I'll be back as soon as I can," he yelled and made a mental note to try to snag a bag of IV fluids, tubing, and needle.

He opened the door and stopped. His ID badge. He scurried back to the kitchen. The phone and pager lay beside it. His hand hovered over the mass of responsibility before giving in and scooping them all up. If he was seen without these things, any story about needed supplies would be suspicious.

He was already on academic probation. It wouldn't take much to get him kicked out of residency for good.

Chapter 42: Book of Plague 9

Flights left the Suv airport for London, Hong Kong, Munich, Beijing, and Tel Aviv. The Japanese men who liked to look at the girls in the fishbowl with binoculars flew home to their wives in Tokyo. Arabs who took their escorts to the Grace Hotel traveled back to the oil trade in Dubai. An Aussie named Frank rubbed at the weird spider web-like growth on his upper chest as his plane made its landing in Perth. The sheila who'd given him the soapy massage seemed so clean, it couldn't have come from her. If it was still there next week, he'd see the doc, but for now he was home, and had a gal waiting for him. He intended to give her a good rogering as soon as possible.

The best thing about flying into Copenhagen, Wayne Wilcox decided, was the beautiful women trying to get home. They were typically tall and blonde with porcelain skin and an accent that made their lips pout when they spoke. He loved it. He'd already picked a couple for cockpit tours. It turned out one of the two was a high-priced escort. She was an average fuck, but she blew him without a condom so there was that. Best thing about a hooker—he didn't have to reciprocate, and she earned her wings anyway.

The other one, though, now she was a prize. Assistant to some bigwig businessman who'd been meeting clients all week in Bangkok's red-light district. As pissed as she was talking about it, Wayne was pretty sure there'd been something going on between them before this little trip. But lucky Wayne reaped the benefits of her desire for revenge. She was more than happy to engage in whatever he asked—no request was denied.

Neither one had said anything about the weird black veins that recently showed up around his balls and the base of his cock. Growing old was a bitch, he thought, probably need to start taking an aspirin every day. By the time they arrived in Copenhagen, he'd forgotten about the strange rash and had yet to notice it on his palms as he shook hands with the disembarking passengers.

The boys from the bachelor party had a great time at the Paris wedding. They danced with every one of the bridesmaids and, by the end of the evening, each had a girl only too eager to go home with him. Weddings were great for the libido. Even better were the destination weddings, they agreed. Going back to Canada and leaving all the little French girls in Paris—no strings attached—was the single man's dream.

Sheikh Ahmad Hilaal Al-Qawi reclined his first-class seat, closed his eyes, and covered them with the warm cloth the flight attendant gave him. His member throbbed from the many episodes he'd enjoyed during his stay in Bangkok. The Grace Hotel had been kind to him over the years. They always provided the most beautiful women to accompany him in the evenings after his business meetings. This time, however, was different. He could not get enough of the girls. And, after all that, he was still hard and ready. Even the milk-white attendant looked good to him and he typically despised Caucasian women.

He was trying to keep his libido in check. He'd picked up many diseases from woman before, but his private physician always had them cleared before Ahmad returned to his wife. Was this a new disease—this strange tattoo beneath his skin like branches of a tree? Most rashes itched or burned, but this one felt good, it made him want sex. He hated to have it treated. He wondered if his wife would notice. She would certainly notice the increase in relations, but that was not for her to speak of.

The attendant walked by and, without removing the cloth, he reached a hand out and caught her arm.

"Would you be so kind as to escort me to the first-class restroom," he said.

She did. It was something in his touch, she was happy to oblige him in every way. The sex was over before the seatbelt sign blinked off. He kept an eye on her throughout the rest of the flight. Whatever disease he had had certainly been passed on to her. He could tell by the way she walked, the way she interacted with other passengers and the way the small black lines splintered out from her cleavage to crawl further up onto her collarbone.

Chapter 43: Book of Sariel 7

"What the fuck, E?" Kenzi asked. Standing up and brushing off her hospital gown. "We have to go back, we have to stop her."

"Kenzi!" Sariel shouted. Enoch had found her in time for Kenzi to say her goodbyes.

"Gloria?" she asked, ignoring Sariel and approaching the bed. Motionless mortals stood like chess pieces around the room.

The monitor's flat green line was locked on the screen, and the high-pitched tone of the pulseless rhythm had silenced. The floor was littered with the remains of a resuscitation attempt but even in this strange timeless state, it was obvious that Gloria was dead. She looked swollen, darker than her usual hue, and her eyes were squeezed shut by the abundance of fluid in her body.

"No. No." She looked up at Sariel, finally acknowledging his presence in the room. "She's not dead, right? I mean, you won't let her die. You can't let her die." She turned to Enoch who had perched on the head of the bed, just above Gloria's forehead. "Don't do it, E. Please, don't take her soul."

Sariel moved in behind his ward. He put a hand on her shoulder and squeezed. She turned, and he held out his forearm. Gloria's name was a deep, red chasm cut into his skin. The heat radiating off it made it glow.

"You know I have no choice, Kenzi. I have to." He hung his head.

He would not tell her about her father today, maybe he never would. She fell onto Gloria's chest, sobbing.

"I'm so sorry, Gloria. I'm so sorry I got us all into this. I should be here in this bed, not you. I should be dead. I fucked everything up."

Enoch cooed, soft and gentle. While Kenzi's head lay on her godmother's chest, the bird did its duty. Gloria's soul had a warm, golden aura, and it sparkled like sand in the sun. Sariel paused for a moment. He wanted to show Kenzi how truly beautiful the woman was, but he couldn't bear to cause her even more pain. He slid the soul into the glass on his belt and returned to comforting the girl.

His touch brought her back to the present. She looked at Gloria's edema-distorted face and reached out to touch the hole in the center of the woman's forehead.

"You did that to Rob too and the baby Enoch. Lilith's baby. Why?"

"Mortals can't usually see it, but it is the place where the soul is closest to the surface. It's what humans sometimes call their third eye. It is where they are most in touch with the spiritual world around them. You can see the holes, just as you can see Enoch and I, but mortals cannot see it. It is what I must do when I am called. It is the final step in the process of death."

The full meaning of what she said sunk in then. He had not told her about Lilith's baby.

"Lilith has told you of her past, then. Beyond what I wrote in your book. Kenzi, please, I need to explain to you why I've done the things I have."

Kenzi pushed his hand away, as if reminding herself of what she'd said.

"I don't care anymore. My life is so fucked up and now, I have no one. I'm losing my mind. You're supposed to be some imaginary thing. You're not real. And what the hell *is* Lilith anyway? You hurt her, and now she is pissed. I get it, but also, she's sneaky and that snake of hers probably would have killed me if E hadn't saved me."

"All those times, all the terrible things you've lived through—you were not alone, Kenzi, I was with you. I have loved you from the first day I saw you. The day you looked deep into my eyes without fear or hatred. All I've done, I've done for you."

"Loved me like you loved Lilith? Because I saw how good you loved her and look how that turned out!" She shoved him away. Tears filled her eyes and spilled down her cheeks.

"Kenzi, you have to believe me. I want to help you. I want to be with you always. Your life doesn't have to be this way. I've made a decision."

"How will you keep me safe? Lock me in that cursed rabbit's foot just like you did Lilith? Was that your little way of controlling me? Leaving something so powerful in the hands of a child; now look what's happened. Maybe you just want to trap us both in it forever. Keep us around your neck?"

"That foot was blessed by The Creator. I gave it to you to keep you safe in the world you were growing up in. Kenzi, I have made many mistakes. With Lilith, I was newly mortal. I had so many emotions and feelings that I'd never experienced before. I know I did wrong by her. But it's too late for her, she is too far gone. Now I have to do what I can to make it all right and I have to be honest about my desires. I am serving my punishment but after four thousand years, it is coming to an end. I have gathered all but seven demons and imprisoned them so that they may not influence mankind. When I present them to The Creator, I will be set free.

"For the longest time, I imagined returning to the paradise from whence I came but when I saw you, and you saw me too, I knew I would choose you. I would choose mortality just to be with you, Kenzi. I want you to come with me. But to do that, we have to stop Lilith. We have to end her. Then, together we can collect the final seven strongest demons, so I am freed to be with you. We can go anywhere you want. Let me take you away from here."

She rubbed Gloria's hand so much she peeled off a bit of the tape holding down the useless IV. He could see the turmoil in her eyes. He wanted to take it away. Put the soul back and see if maybe Gloria would get a second chance. But it would only work against him. The Creator would add more time or worse, take notice of Lilith's adventures. Then what?

"Still the romantic fool, Sariel," Lilith said. She stood in the doorway, somehow looking even more pregnant than she'd been with her son. She sauntered over to them as if her protuberant belly was filled with helium instead of…whatever it was that was in there.

"What exactly do you think The Creator will do with this world once He has all of Hell trapped in those little trinkets from your wormhole? You think He'll just let all these mortals go on living their lives here like this? All of them going against His neat and tidy plan." She threw her head back and laughed. "No. He wants this world to himself. He wants to live in this kingdom in the flesh—to experience everything He never has before. But, here's the kicker, my love, He wants it filled only with His followers. His small minded, ignorant, blind-faith followers who can't or won't see Him for the selfish thing He is."

She turned to Kenzi. "Listen to me—if Sariel completes his mission, you and everyone you love will die. I'm here to stop that, Kenzi, to stop The Creator from building earth in His distorted image of perfection. Forcing you to bow down and be subservient to Him as you've been made to do with men all your life. We can stop him. We can make all this pointless pain go away. We can punish Him for his trespasses against us."

"He is immortal, Lilith," Sariel spat. "The Creator is the beginning and the end. You cannot destroy him."

"Oh, I know He is immortal, my love. I know. And when He comes down here, to face me, Kenzi and I will trap Him just as you and He trapped us. And He will know what it means to suffer as He allows his own creations to do." Lilith smiled.

"She cannot be trusted, Kenzi. She is dangerous. She is using you," Sariel warned.

Kenzi looked back and forth at the two of them. She drew a breath. "I want Gloria back. Put her soul back and fix her. It's just… I can't think straight with all of this on my mind." She swept her hand over the black woman's dead body. Then looked at Sariel. "Just, for now, please, put her soul back and keep her safe and alive for me. For now. I need to get out of this place, I need to think, I need to figure out who to trust."

She was lying. Sariel could see it in her eyes. She only wanted to run away without the guilt of leaving Gloria's dead body lying unclaimed for months in the morgue. She was itchy, and she would run. He would lie as well. Tell her what she wanted to hear and let her go. The bird would follow her, keep an eye. Besides, if he played the part well, Lilith would have no choice but to oblige and leave her be, elsewise she would prove herself the villain.

Sariel sighed dramatically. "Because I love you, Kenzi, because I will do anything for you, I will replace her soul and swear to you that it will remain within her until you tell me to do otherwise."

"Ask yourself this: did he love you when he took her from you in the first place?" Lilith said.

"He just said he would put her soul back for me, and go against The Creator. He's taking a huge risk. He might never get his freedom, but he just said he would do that for me"

"How gallant of you, Sariel. Forgive me for asking, hard to trust ex-lovers, you understand but didn't you do something like that for this girl once already?"

"I've never asked him to do anything like this before." Kenzi said, coming to Sariel's defense.

"Oh, I know you didn't ask him, dear heart, you were much too young to understand. Tell me, Sariel, what happens to the name on your arm if a soul is not collected. I'm sure you could even show us an example, couldn't you? Does it fester? Does it stink like betrayal or does it smell of the sulfur and clay of a demon-filled cavern?" The spite and anger on her face dulled her perfection. She knew about Kenzi. And now, Kenzi would know.

"What is she talking about?" Kenzi asked him.

Sariel hesitated. "I will just replace her soul, it doesn't matter what happens to me Kenzi. You should go. If I don't leave soon with the soul, these mortals will return to time and you'll be caught."

"Show her the name," Lilith ordered.

He ignored her as if he hadn't heard and went about retrieving his soul-keeper. "Kenzi, do not listen to her. She lies. I told you, it is too late for her. Her soul is black with hatred and revenge. Do not follow her into that abyss."

He whistled. Enoch hopped off his shoulder and onto his wrist. Dipping its head into the keeper, the bird brought up the glittering amber soul. Sariel nodded his head toward Gloria. Enoch flapped its wings and skipped across the air to land on her godmother's pillow. The room was silent. Kenzi held her breath. The bird dropped the soul into the small hole in the woman's head and cocked its own head as if waiting.

Nothing changed. Lilith crossed the room and had Sariel's arm in her grasp before anyone knew she'd moved.

She turned his arm over as if studying the scars. He tried to pull back, but she tightened her grasp. "Wait a minute, what's this? Ouch, this looks sore. I can't quite…does this say Kenzi Brooks? How long has it been here, right beside this old scar that says Robbie Brooks?"

Kenzi inched closer to see.

"Why is my name on you?"

"So, tell me Sariel," Lilith said. "Since we've seen what happens to you; what happens to a mortal when The Creator demands their soul and you do not deliver? For me, at least, I recall you allowed me my life in defiance of His orders and He abandoned me. I lived in misery for many years."

"Am I supposed to be dead?" Kenzi asked.

She struggled to speak past the gorge in her throat. "Am I just walking around here on earth with no purpose, left to whatever happens?"

Sariel lowered his head.

"You left me here to rot, to be abused over and over. That's not love, that's selfishness. That's why you always came around—you didn't *love* me, you felt guilty for what you did to me." She was shaking. Her voice grew stronger and louder with anger.

"Kenzi, it wasn't like that. I…"

"Lilith was right, you ruined my life. How could you do this to me? I trusted you, you were my friend."

She charged at him, pounding her fists on his chest. She kicked him. The dam broke and every emotion the girl had pent up inside her all her life came flooding out to swallow them both.

CODE BLUE LABOR, DELIVERY AND RECOVERY, CODE BABY BLUE NURSERY, FLOOR 4, RAPID RESPONSE TEAM REQUESTED, ALL AVAILABLE STAFF TO LABOR AND DELIVERY. THIS IS NOT A DRILL. CODE BLUE, CODE BABY BLUE.

Mass chaos outside the room ensued. A nurse yelled something about all the dead babies.

"All the mothers, all the babies. Every patient dead!"

Kenzi looked at Lilith. The woman smiled and rubbed her very pregnant belly.

"My babies," she said.

Sariel lunged for her but missed, she was already at the door.

"I'll see you soon, Kenzi."

She disappeared into the shadows.

"Kenzi, go. I must allow time to start. I've held it back much too long as it is. I will take care of Lilith myself. You need to run and hide. Don't let Lilith find you and—"

Kenzi put a finger up in his face. "Don't you ever, ever tell me what to do again. You did this to me. All of it. My whole life is a lie. It has no meaning. You. Your fault. And now, I don't even have my rabbit's foot. She does. Why wouldn't you tell me there was a soul in there?"

"Because you could never release her from it. Only I know that secret. Someone must have conjured her body back. She thinks you know how to release her essence from the talisman. She may, in time, figure it out, but I will destroy her before that happens." Sariel took a fatherly tone with Kenzi, assuring her that she'd done nothing wrong

"But what if I did release her? Me. She showed up right after I took the foot out and she killed those men in my house. Why don't you know this?"

"How could you release her without a blood sacrifice?" He knew nothing beyond the fact that Lilith had somehow returned.

"Blood? I don't know, there was a lot of blood there. They were beating me up and I slashed at one of the guys with the foot. It was all I had. I guess maybe that was enough blood to bring her back." Kenzi was quiet suddenly, her anger diluted by confusion.

"It must be your own blood, sacrificed by you, followed by blood taken from an enemy," Sariel prodded, hoping to spark something.

Her face contorted back into anger again. "Man, you are a fuck up. I'm a cutter." She pulled the snaps open on the sleeve of her gown, revealing her shoulder and upper arm. "I've been using the foot for that almost since you gave it to me. Guess I wanted to be more like you. I had just finished cutting not long before I walked in on those assholes.

"When I got the chance, I tore one of their faces off with it. I keep the nails sharp. That's when Lilith and her snake showed up. Her snake came right off her and squeezed the guys to death."

"Kenzi, I didn't know, I…So, she is whole then." He sighed. This was the worst possible news.

"Yeah, well it is what it is. And good luck with your punishment because if she knows how to release demons from those things—"

"She doesn't know that. Only I, and now you." Sariel interrupted.

"I hope you're right about that, because Lilith stole hundreds of your demon chains from Sheol."

Sariel's jaw dropped. He let go of Kenzi's arms and she ran out into the amassing crowd.

"Enoch! You should have told me. You should have stopped her."

The bird cawed and clacked its beak.

"Yes, of course Kenzi's safety comes first, but this—this could be the end of us both. Lilith could actually complete her version of Revelation. She could win this war." Sariel paced in circles around Gloria's bedside. His hands held tightly behind his back.

The bird grunted and croaked.

"Well, if Lilith told her that, then Kenzi also knows that you swallowed that baby's soul. So, it makes you a monster too." He gave the bird a stern but expectant look as if daring it to disagree. "Now is not the time for bickering, Enoch."

Enoch waddled about the room in its own circle as if considering their options.

The overhead speakers were still calling for help. Sariel absently waved his hand and the room came to life again. Within moments, the two were alone with the corpse on the bed.

What was he going to do now? What could he do to stop this?

Lilith. Damn her. All his talismans.

"Kenzi is the perfect pawn. She'll never be safe as long as Lilith is free."

Chapter 44: Book of Henry 1

The night nurses were much more laid back than their daylight counterparts. Even at the end of their shift, none of them showed any urgency in finishing their chores. The post op floor especially was a different place at night. Rarely new admissions, most patients sleeping, snowed by the pain meds administered by the day shift, families full of questions gone home for the night. Only vitals to take, IV bags to refill and bathroom calls to attend. The nurses played on their phones or checked out upcoming sales on line. No one looked up when he walked behind the desk to study the large dry erase board with patient initials and important stats recorded.

"You on surgery this month, Patel?" the charge nurse asked.

"Yes. Hey, Dr. Galastor wanted me to check on the wound dehiscence in 216. Can I get some supplies out? I will be unpacking it."

"You can't wait one more hour for day shift?" Carol Thompkins, obviously the patient's nurse, asked.

"No. I've got a lot of patients to see before grand rounds, so I need to get right to it. If you would give me the code to the supply closet, I'll get everything out and take care of it myself. I won't keep you from your sign out."

Carol rolled her eyes and grabbed a scrap of paper. She wrote her password to the locked cabinet and he almost felt bad for using it. She would have to answer some questions at the end of the month when they did an audit, but, by then, she wouldn't remember why *she* took out all the strange supplies.

In the closet, he packed his backpack full of suture, IV bags, antibiotics, gauze pads, and anything that looked remotely helpful. Now, he would need to go fake a visit to the poor man in 216. He grabbed some more gauze and a pink basin to make it appear that he was carrying what he needed to change the man's dressings.

"Thanks," he said as he walked passed the desk. No one responded. He entered the room at the end of the hall. The man, initials B.G., was sleeping soundly. A large crater ran down the center of his belly. It had been filled with once white Curlex gauze which was now crusty yellow, like dried snot under a toddler's nose. The entire wound was covered with a thin, clear tape similar to Saran Wrap. Henry stared in amazement at what the human body could endure and survive.

The man stirred. Henry put the tub with the gauze on his bedside table and checked his watch. The nurses should be busy with sign out now, so they wouldn't see him leave. He walked out and quickly passed the desk, looking at his pager as if he'd been called hastily away.

The whole thing had taken much less time than he'd estimated. He'd hit the cafeteria for something to go with his coffee. Now that sleep was out of the question, his stomach decided to make a formal request.

He made it halfway through the sesame bagel and had yet to touch the coffee when he fell asleep in the cafeteria's booth.

In his dream, he stood on a hill, no, a platform. As the scene grew and cleared, he saw that he was both on a hill and on a wooden stage. It was night, but a full moon gave the false sense of a serene summer's evening while lighting the audience of dead surrounding him.

Most of the corpses were adults but there was a whole wedge of land devoted to bloated babies, plump not with breast milk, but with decay. White noise which Henry, in his dream state, first thought was ocean waves in the distance—perhaps below the hill's horizon line—focused into a buzzing.

At the same time his brain made the connection of the buzzing to honey bees, he saw them. Only these were like no bees he had ever seen. Large rounded bugs the size of terriers with bulbous eyes and long proboscises flitted about as if weightless. Henry watched in horror as the mutant bees plunged their needle-thin snouts into the tumescent bodies and sucked. With every insectile puncture, thick, grey-brown pus popped and oozed out around the living straw.

"Death surrounds you." The pregnant woman appeared beside him. He opened his mouth to ask what she was doing there, but smaller insects, normal house flies in appearance, buzzed his head and threatened to enter his open cavities.

"You have no business holding their lives in your hands. Your place is not in medicine Henry Patel and you know this. Look upon the dead you are responsible for."

He shook his head. It wasn't true. He'd made a lot of mistakes, but no one had ever died—that he knew of anyway.

"You want to farm honey, to take care of a little cottage and some clover fields. But look at your legacy, look at what your bees feed on, taste the honey that is made from the foundations you have built." The woman held a dull, silver chalice filled with a milky, curry-colored fluid that could not possibly be honey. He shook his head again, a clear no. He refused to open his mouth.

"Then you will hang," she said. The stage he was on clarified more in the dream, it was a gallows, and the noose was already around his neck.

"All right. I'll drink it," he said holding his hands up in surrender. She approached and when the cup touched his lips he parted them. The viscous fluid tasted sour and metallic. Behind that was a rotted fungal essence that triggered his gag reflex. "No, I can't, I'll vomit."

"Then you'll die," she said, and the floor dropped out beneath him. The shocked jump of his body brought him awake. His pager beeped wildly on his hip and his phone vibrated its way across the table. Overhead, the frantic desk clerk called for manpower to the neonatal ICU for multiple code blues. The cafeteria was deserted, no one there to see that his lag in response time was due to sleep and not just coming from home post-call.

Normally, he would not be expected to respond to any hospital codes when he was off, but this was some sort of hospital emergency and all able bodies were needed. The dream was already gone from his memory when he slid out of the booth and ran to the stairwell.

Most of the staff must have either taken the elevator or else his pager had been going off for a long time and he was way too late to the party. The stairwell was just as empty as the cafeteria. Rounding the stairs on the second floor, he was almost knocked backwards when the door flew open and a body in a patient gown burst though. Her arms and palms still up in a shove position, she ran directly into Henry.

"Kenzi?" he said, shocked.

"Oh my god, Dr. Patel, I…I," she stammered.

"What are you doing out of bed. How are you even out of bed? What's going on?"

"Shhh, shhh," she warned. "I gotta get out of here, can I stay at your place for a couple days, just until I get my bearings?"

"What? No, Kenzi, I—there are probably police looking for you…I cannot have this discussion now, I have to go to the OB floor, I have to help with this code. You need to go back to your room right now while no one is looking. I have to go, something bad has happened. Maybe a gas leak or something big—"

"Henry," she shook him by the shoulders. "They're dead. They're all dead. There's nothing you can do. Just help me get out of here and I'll tell you what I can."

Henry felt his eyes bulging in surprise, his mouth hung open and an image of a large bug with big eyes like tennis balls hovered in his memory and he snapped his jaw shut.

"All right, all right. Come with me and do not say a word to anyone."

He grabbed her hand. It was as cold as death. A chill went up his spine that had nothing to do with temperature.

Chapter 45: Book of Henry 2

The resident call room was on the second floor near the entrance to the ICU. It was the only place he could think of that would offer assured privacy. The halls were bereft of witnesses, but he rushed her in anyway, only fumbling the numeric lock on the door once before getting it right.

The room was small and sparse. A hospital bed, night stand with broken lamp, a desk with an ancient desktop computer and a bookshelf filled with books that were at least ten years senior to the computer. The bathroom was large enough for a walk-in shower and a set of four lockers. A recessed wall opposite the toilet contained a closet filled with teal colored scrubs. Henry stopped and took a long look at Kenzi. Sizing her for a pair of scrubs, he let his eyes graze over as much of her body that he could make out beneath the gown. She crossed her arms self-consciously and he realized how it must seem to her.

"I was just trying to figure out what size you wear…for uh, a pair of scrubs."

Now he was fumbling his words. Why did she make him so nervous? *Because you like her, because you have always liked her and now you have her alone in your call room in nothing but a hospital gown.*

His penis agreed with his brain. It was standing at attention, ready for duty.

"You could have asked me my size," she said and turned to the rack of monochromatic hospital wear. "Where are the sizes on these things?"

He grabbed a pair of smalls with the yellow draw strings and trim and held them strategically in front of his Benedict Arnold crotch. "It goes by color. Yellow is small. I am sure it is the right size for you. I'll just step out and give you some privacy."

He made sure he was turned at least ninety degrees away from her before handing over the hangers. He rushed out, accidentally slamming the door behind him.

"So, is it OK to wear these without underwear, cause uh, I'm au natural under this fancy gown," she yelled through the door.

This did nothing to ease the state of alert in his pants.

"It is fine, I am sure that um, some people do that," he answered through the door. Willing his brain to think of anything else but the thin material separating him from her naked body.

"Yeah, no bra either and my nips say it's pretty chilly in this place. Do you have a hoodie or anything I can put over this?" Before he could answer, she stepped out.

Don't look at her nipples, don't look at her nipples.

He looked at her nipples.

She smiled. He swept past her into the bathroom to grab his black sweatshirt out of the locker. An old Detroit Tigers surgical cap lay crumpled in a ball on the top shelf. Disappointment in himself, his failure as a surgical resident, and the need to have his father intervene just to get a spot in Internal Medicine worked wonders on his libido. When he returned to Kenzi with the jacket and hat, there was no worry about what she might notice.

"Thanks," she said, putting on the sweatshirt and zipping it up far enough to cover her breasts. "What do I do with this?" She held out the hat.

"Oh, yes, can you uh…well…"

He reached up and smoothed her hair back from her head with both hands, pulling it into a pony tail behind her. He was so close he could smell her. She smelled oddly of dirt, soil, and the ground after it rains. Not an unpleasant smell but also not what he expected. He twisted the hair into a loose bun and then with his left hand he worked the hat on her head, around the hair. He tied the back to hold it in place and stepped back to look at her.

Damn it, she's even cuter with the hat and hoodie on.

Before his groin could mutiny again, he decided now would be a great time to ask the million-dollar question.

"Kenzi, where have you been? How did you even get out of your room? There were police officers everywhere."

She started toward the door and he managed to move quicker, ducking around her, and blocking it.

"It's such a long, crazy story. I'll tell you, I promise. But I just need somewhere to crash." She didn't look like she needed rest. She looked all better.

"This," he gestured to her, "is nuts. How are you walking? Where is your halo? How can you be healed?"

"Later Henry. We need to get out of here. For real. It's dangerous for me. It's not that far to your place, if you give me the keys, I can hoof it."

"How…I mean, you know where I live?"

He wanted answers, but mostly he was stalling, trying to figure out how he was going to get himself out of this current situation. He wanted to let her stay, of course he did, but he couldn't explain any of the madness that was currently happening at his apartment. He couldn't have her just go barging in on it.

"Really? That one time, you told my mom and I that you could walk to the hospital from your apartment. I looked you up online and then mapped out your address. Easy as that." She shrugged. "Henry, please. I'm sorry if I invaded your privacy or whatever, I just need your help. You said you were my friend. I feel like I'm going crazy. Like nothing in this world makes sense anymore. I don't know what's real and what isn't."

She put her hands on his arms. "But what I know for sure is that if I get caught here, I'll be expected to know all the answers or else I'll end up in jail."

Henry sighed. Her hands on his arms felt nice. "I want to help you, I do. But I cannot let you stay right now. I—I have to get back to work. I was paged, if I don't respond, I'll be in trouble."

"I asked my nurse to call you this morning. She said you were off today. That's all I need, Henry. Just a day or two," she pleaded.

Her eyes, one blue, the other a domino with a single dot of black at its center glistened up at him. For the first time, he noticed the freckles sprinkled over her face.

"OK, how about this, what if I get you a hotel room for a few days. I will even bring you home-cooked food. You just cannot stay with me. I cannot risk them finding out I helped you."

That was good. It made sense. She could not question that. My god, her lips. Had they always been that full or was she pouting?

"I thought you were different Henry, but you're just like everyone else. No thanks, I got this. I can take care of myself." She tried to shove him out of the way to leave but he stepped toward her and grabbed her wrists.

"Wait. Just wait OK? The truth is; something really strange has happened, and I don't want you involved. I'm trying to keep you safe." Without thinking, he dropped her wrist and touched her face. She leaned closer and for a moment, he thought she was going to kiss him.

She caught him off balance and elbowed him to the side. Pushing through the door, she stopped.

"How the fuck do I get out of here?"

"All right, all right. You win. Just let me scan the hallway and then I will take you to my place. I'll tell you everything on the way."

"A pregnant woman," Kenzi asked when he'd finished his story. "You're sure? I mean maybe she's just fat."

"She is not fat. Give me credit, Kenzi. I know a pregnant woman when I see one."

"And the other one with her is tall, blonde and all fucked up?"

"Yes," he repeated Kenzi's summation. "Very fucked up."

"But how did they find you? I mean how did they know you were a doctor?" Kenzi was asking questions but not the kinds he'd expected nor was she acting all that shocked at the general situation.

"Funny you ask. She mentioned you." He stopped at his front door.

Chapter 46: Book of War 9

"Please don't hurt us," Beth said. She knew she shouldn't, Lilith had warned her twice to be quiet but now there was another woman here, maybe she would be more sympathetic.

"Oh, but we will, we have to," the man who Lilith had called Beelzebub said with a laugh.

She wasn't eliciting any pity points here. Beth decided to follow her friends' examples and stay quiet. Instead, she'd watch, observe, and think. She knew a lot of demonology. Perhaps she'd have a chance of stopping them if she could calm down and concentrate.

"Have you prepared the altar?" Beelzebub asked.

"All but the fire, my darling," Lilith answered.

Altar was bad. Altar meant sacrifice.

"Cynthia, beneath this ground lay the bones of your ancestor. She is needed in order to continue my conquest. Her blood flows through your veins, you must draw her spirit from its resting place," Lilith explained.

Beth peeked to see if the woman was willing to participate in this "conquest" or if she could be counted on as an ally in their escape.

She couldn't make out if Cynthia was nodding or if she'd said anything. Beth hazarded a look at the others, but in the little bit of firelight, she couldn't tell if they were looking or not. Maybe they'd passed out in shock. Just as well. There was no way to communicate so if each girl was trying to work out a plan on her own it could get chaotic.

"We must start the fires; the blood should be warmed," Beelzebub said.

It made sense that he would lead the ritual, he was the demon, he knew dark magic better than anyone. What could she possibly do to distract the devil?

"I will prepare Cynthia while you begin," Lilith answered.

Lilith, if Beth recalled her facts correctly, was also considered a demoness, so, the two might be running this thing together. She wished she'd have read more about this stuff. Was she planning to put Tituba's soul into her baby? This was just too crazy to even think about. God, her head hurt.

Beelzebub started a fire beneath Lauryn's head. It was small but the distance between the two was probably at most three feet. Being directly above it had to be hot. Lauryn squirmed as much as her ties would let her and then she screamed.

"Hush," the demon said. "Let the fire warm your blood."

"No. Nooo. Nooo." Lauryn cried. The heat was too much. If Lauryn had longer hair, it would already be on fire. She couldn't be expected to silence her terror.

Beelzebub turned back to Lilith and a now-naked Cynthia. "I need to spill her blood quickly, I cannot tolerate the screams."

Beth could see the whites of the other girls' eyes because, just like her own, they were wide with fear. The remaining three managed to stifle their cries. Screaming did not appear to be working out well for Lauryn.

I'm so sorry, Lauryn. Beth thought, but it had to be every girl for herself.

Cynthia approached Beelzebub with a chalice. He kissed it and then handed something to her. Beth worked out it was a knife when the light of the fire glinted off it just before Cynthia slit Lauryn's throat. Lauryn tried to scream, but it sounded like someone blowing bubbles in chocolate milk.

Her blood splashed and ran into the cup while Beelzebub fell to his knees and began to suckle from Cynthia's breast. She could see their shadows in front of the fire. It didn't take a pervert to imagine what was happening. The other girls were grunting and gagging, Lauryn, thankfully, had stopped struggling, and Cynthia moaned wildly.

Beelzebub pulled himself off her breast and wiped his chin with his arm. His face glistened with blood. Lilith came to them with a small cup and held it up to Cynthia's chest. She was collecting something, and Beth guessed it was blood as well. When a witch lets the devil suckle, he often bites and takes her blood. It made sense. Lilith mixed Cynthia's blood with Lauryn's.

Blood was common in rituals and they had plenty now, didn't they? Maybe she and the others would just be tortured a little. She could be strong enough to survive anything if it meant getting out of this alive.

Beelzebub chanted something in Latin—maybe—and poured the blood onto the ground in lines connecting one post to another. He stopped at Annika and sniffed up at her. Annika squealed. He laughed and continued. By the time the circle was made, the fire had started to crawl up Lauryn's post. The scent of burnt hair permeated the clearing. The other girls coughed and choked but no one cried or screamed, not after what happened to their friend.

Lilith took Cynthia by the hair and paraded her around the circle. She brought her to each girl so that Cynthia could see their faces. When she looked at Beth, Beth kept her eyes focused on Cynthia's torn and mangled breast.

"I like this one best," Cynthia said in a slurry voice that made Beth think of sex symbols like Marilyn Monroe who tried to sound sexy but typically sounded drunk.

"Very good," Lilith said. "Beelzebub, the other two will take communion now as I make the final arrangements with Cynthia."

"No, please," Jess whined. A buzzing like cicadas on a midsummer's night grew. From the fire where Lauryn's charred body hung, arose a tornado of flies. They enveloped Beelzebub and lifted in a mass, presumably taking him with them. The swarm migrated to the midpoint between Jess and Annika. There, it seemed to pulsate; condensing and expanding over and over. Out of the mass a figure arose, the color and texture of Lauryn's charred body. Horns curled out of its forehead, eyes the size of apples bulged, wings unfurled behind the monster, and a tubular tongue protruded from its mouth like a syringe.

It rubbed its hands rapidly together and approached Jess.

"Oh god. Please don't touch me, don't touch me. No." Her voice rose in pitch. The creature was so tall, he could look her directly in the face instead of up as he had when he was in human form. Jess shook her head back and forth, but he grabbed her and held it still.

"Take communion from me, and allow the madness to consume you," it said. Its voice buzzed in vibrato.

Jess screamed.

It was a mistake. With her mouth open, he thrust his tongue far back into her throat. Beth felt a gorge rise as the creature, too, began to heave. His tongue swelled in Jess's mouth forcing her jaws wide. Her screams turned to moans turned to gurgling and gagging as he pumped his demon bile into her.

When he was done, he slashed at her ties and Jess fell to the ground. Beth didn't know if she was dead or not. She turned away from the grisly scene to see two naked women, writhing about on the grass on her side of the center of the circle.

Beelzebub turned his attentions to Annika who also screamed, but abruptly stopped when his face was in front of hers. Even in the dull light of the fires, she could see Annika biting her lips, trying to keep her mouth closed. She was always the toughest of the four, the no-fear, nothing can touch her type.

"I read the journal," she said to him trying to stall or maybe bargain. "You're the devil that Tituba made a pact with. I can do that. I'll pledge myself to you. I'll never tell anyone." Her frantic chatter left her mouth open and she received her communion in the way Jess had, ending on the ground.

He returned to the women who had by now whipped themselves into a sexual frenzy. Beth didn't want to see anymore but she couldn't look away.

"Take your communion and seal your pact with the devil," Beelzebub roared.

Lilith had Cynthia by the hair again and forced the woman to her knees. An impossibly massive cock rose from the shadow of his dark, bloated, fly-like body. Lilith pushed Cynthia's face onto it and the woman struggled against it. Lilith drove her head back and forth. Beth could see Cynthia gagging. Drool fell from her overly extended jaw.

Movement in the periphery caught Beth's attention. Jess and Annika were getting up, but something was wrong. Their joints bent in the wrong way, they stood asymmetrically and stumbled about like zombies.

"Witch! Witch!" they screamed, pointing at Cynthia.

The girls fell into seizures, growling and frothing at the mouth.

Beelzebub roared with them as he came, the force of his ejaculation knocked Cynthia back into Lilith. Cynthia coughed and spat, but Lilith held her mouth shut.

"Swallow it, take your communion, you belong to him now, witch."

The girls tore their clothes off. They clawed at their own faces and ripped out chunks of hair.

"The witch is pricking us, oh how it burns," they cried.

Beth could do nothing but watch in horror as her blood-covered friends destroyed themselves. The girls screamed in lunacy until their three captors approached and fell into the frenzy. Jess and Annika died in a bloody, satanic orgy. Beth was the only one left and she feared her fate would be the worst of all.

Chapter 47: Book of War 10

The early morning chill slapped at Beth's cheeks, bringing her back to consciousness. Spring's yellow-green light added a cartoonish quality to the shredded, broken bodies of her friends lying akimbo on the ground. She was glad that her brain was as numb as her body. She felt nothing. She'd used up her supply of adrenaline. All she could do now was pray for her own life. Pray to every god her parents had introduced her to and hope that one just might listen. Beyond the carnage in the foreground, Cynthia lay on her back, her naked body covered in symbols drawn in blood. Lilith stood at the woman's head, holding it steady. Her pregnant belly forced her to bend forward slightly so that her breasts hung just over Cynthia's eyes. It was the demon, though that held Beth's attention. He was pissing in a circle around the women. When it hit the ground, it sizzled like acid and seeped into the dirt forming a deep moat. A sour stink steamed up out of the newly formed border. It rose in a cylinder of mist so that Beth could only make out shadows and movements behind the curtain.

Beelzebub's voice boomed from within, deep and gravely, shaking the ground. "We call upon the spirit of Tituba, first and most powerful witch of the colonies. We offer you the body of your own descendant. Your powers of persuasion, chaos, and provocation are needed. I, as your master, the devil to whom you pledged your allegiance with blood, body, and soul, demand you return."

Beth's last semblance of hope faded as she realized she'd never be able to scream louder than his voice. No one was coming to save her, no one would find them.

"Grandmother," Cynthia said, her voice trance-like and void of emotion. "I offer you my body as I give my soul to the Goddess for keeping. I am open to receiving your spirit now."

A low grumbling chant came from the center of the altar. It was not Latin. This sounded even more archaic, more primitive. Light flashed in strobe pulsations giving Beth a strange view of the activity going on within. The pregnant Lilith squatted over Cynthia's face.

Beelzebub mimed several common holy blessings but—unless she was wrong because she was viewing it upside down—he was doing them backwards.

A woman's scream accompanied the last flash of light. Cynthia's body arched up off the ground. Beth remembered a picture she'd seen once of a man in the final stages of tetanus, his body rigid and spasmed in this same way. It looked as if her back was about to snap.

A gust of wind blew up from the ground, putting out the candles and fire. The piss-screen around the altar dissipated on the breeze. Lilith and Beelzebub stood beside the woman who, if the ritual had worked, was Tituba. They helped her up and she surveyed the scene. Her survey stopped at Beth. They made eye contact for what seemed like eternity, before the woman returned her attention to her companions.

Beth focused on her breathing and heartbeat trying desperately to convince herself that everything was fine. It was over, Tituba was here, what did they need her for?

"Welcome witch," Lilith said.

"Thankee."

"And I will take my payment now, Lilith," Beelzebub, still in his demonic form, said.

"Of course, my liege," Lilith responded. "Let us prepare her for you."

Beth squealed in panic.

"Silent," Tituba ordered.

It was as if someone hit a mute button. There was no sound coming out of her anymore. She felt like she was screaming but the witch had taken her voice. She was not getting out of this alive. She knew that now. Best to accept her fate and stop fighting, perhaps death would come quickly.

The women came to her.

"You have been chosen among your peers as the final sacrifice," Lilith said. "You will be given to Beelzebub to thank him for his support."

Beth sobbed silently.

"Do not fret, daughter, for your sacrifice will not be without purpose," Tituba said.

"*I have chosen you for greater things, daughter. You will not die today unless you ask for it.*" Lilith's voice echoed in Beth's head and yet, her mouth never moved.

"Open your mouth and take communion, pledge your soul to me." This time, she did speak aloud.

Beth nodded. She clung to the silent promise—'you will not die today'—so yes, she would pledge her soul to Lilith. It was her only option and it had to be better than what her friends experienced.

"You are a creature of the earth. Like the earth, a woman brings forth and sustains life. Your womb is the universe through which new life evolves. As your Goddess, I ask you to take this communion, the sacrifice of your sisters and my gift to you."

Lilith placed cold, hard bits on her tongue and she closed her mouth around them. At first, she thought they were some kind of pills. She rolled them around with her tongue. There was something familiar about their hard, smooth surface. Teeth. Oh god, they were teeth. Someone had pulled the teeth from one of her friends. Probably Lauryn, burnt and charred as she was, it would have been easy.

"Swallow," Tituba ordered. "Now."

Beth swallowed.

"A woman's voice is her power. She must always speak her mind. Do you see how I took away your vigor by silencing you? Do not let a man control your tongue," Tituba said. "Open your mouth. Take this gift from me and your peers."

Beth opened her mouth and accepted two large chunks of meat from the witch. She knew whatever it was had come from her other two friends and she did not want to think about it. She swallowed them one at a time without chewing. Her eyes watered with the effort.

"Be strong and stay strong, my child," Lilith said and kissed her forehead.

"Blessed be." Tituba kissed her on the lips.

"She is yours," Lilith said to Beelzebub.

"No, please," Beth said, her voiced returned.

"We must take our leave of you both now. There is much chaos and paranoia to spread," Lilith said. "Enjoy your gift, Beelzebub, I think you'll find her to be your equal in sexual tenacity."

Beth was alone with the demon. There were only her dead friends to serve as witnesses to the unholy rape to come.

Beelzebub dropped to the ground on all fours and crawled to her post like the fly he was. He shimmied up the pole. It shook with his weight. He climbed over her body as if it wasn't there. Her legs were released from their ties and they fell forward and apart. She had no feeling in them and could not move. Her arms were still attached to the cross, her body folded over at the waist so that she could only see through the triangular window between her legs. The sulfurous odor of him irritated her already compromised lungs. His ability to crawl up the pole and over her like a bug sent chills through her body.

He turned around on her as if the laws of gravity did not affect him. His huge face and protuberant eyes stared into hers. He'd steadied his arms—if that's what they could be called—on the beam attached to her own. Something bristly slid up her thigh awakening deadened nerves that sent pins and needles across her lower half. A bulge of flesh the size of a baby's head pushed between her legs. Beth tensed in anticipation of the demonic phallus about to plunge into her.

The pain was intense. Her tissues burned and tore against the strain of him. He entered slowly as if savoring the torture she was experiencing. She was dry, so each thrust was like rug burn. Beth held out for as long as she could but when it felt as if he'd torn through the top of her vagina and into her belly, she screamed. It was more than a human should have to endure while conscious.

The scream was a mistake and she realized it just as the proboscis-like tongue shot into her mouth. She was skewered. Every move the demon made pulled on her bowels. She knew when it was over, and he pulled out of her, she would be effectively disemboweled.

Beth had never felt so completely helpless and removed from control of her own body. She was nothing more than a puppet and yet, she was no longer afraid. She was angry. Angry that this hideous creature felt it had any right to her body while she could do nothing. She hated it. She filled her head with images of castration and beheading. She wanted to choke him, to force something far down his throat so he was just as trapped as she.

Please help me, Lilith. Help me kill him. She pleaded inside her head, hoping that method of communication could work both ways.

Something jumped to life in her chest and began to slither up against his rounded tongue. Her own tongue grew as well, pushing into his mouth, curling around his at its base. He tasted like curdled milk and sewage, but she didn't stop. She couldn't speak but she had power again. She would use her tongue to wield it. He pulled back trying to retract himself, but another snake-like muscle inside of Beth had wrapped itself around his tongue's tip and he was stuck. Jess and Annika were inside her and they were helping to fight him.

He squirmed and tugged. Like a lever, his pelvis pushed further into her as he tried to free himself from her mouth. Her vagina tightened around him and something hard like bone held it there. Lauryn's teeth. The ones she had swallowed were biting into his cock. The demon tried to howl but with his tongue pulled taut he could make no sound. A weakened mewl escaped in the space between them. She had him! If she was going to die, she was taking him with her. Beth tightened her bite and felt the warm syrupy blood pooling around her vagina dentata.

The demon was furious. He writhed and hit at her with his sticky hands. He kicked but each impact seemed to cause him more pain. Beth was pleased. While she would have liked nothing more than to keep him suffering, she was tired and ready to finish this.

"It is time, my child," Lilith said. She was back. "I chose well. You've used the powers within you to return the assault this demon began on you. He hurt me once in the same way and many others since. You have taken vengeance for us all and we thank you."

The fire began beneath them as if on cue. The flames, unlike the ones under Lauryn, grew quickly and lapped at Beth's hair. Her jaw, her aching shoulders, a sickly gut, and burning womb welcomed the relief. She tightened her hold on the demon as he fought frantically to remove himself.

"Beelzebub, I will give you the same advice you once gave me: lie down and accept your fate. This is what you were made for, it is what you deserve. Thank you for helping my cause. In time, I will forget all that you once did to me, but I do not forgive."

Flames wrapped around the demon like a blanket and released Beth's arms. She fell free of both the cross and the creature.

"And to you, my darling girl, I keep my promise," Lilith said.

Beth's pain was gone. The cuts, scrapes, bruises, and charred skin were all still there, but she felt nothing except fatigue. She sat on the ground and waited for the strength to return to her legs. Tituba approached her and whispered into her ear.

The world was evil, everyone was out to get her. No one was to be trusted, not even her parents. Men were dirty and lascivious, they preyed on girls like Beth. Even those who professed to be God-loving wanted nothing more than the deaths of those unlike themselves. The world must end, no one deserved to survive it. Beth listened first in horror, then slowly, gradually, her sanity loosened its grip.

Twelve hours after she entered the woods with her three friends, Beth ran out alone and insane. She had secrets to tell, ancient secrets. Secrets that once drove a village mad enough to first accuse and then kill its own members. The world was bigger than Salem, though. There was much work to be done.

Chapter 48: Book of Sariel 8

Sariel looked down at the corpse left on the hospital bed while staff saw to more urgent but equally hopeless pursuits. Gloria could never come back, not after the soul had been disconnected. It was just pooling in the hole in her head. Perhaps it was cruel to lead Kenzi on, but someday—soon he hoped—she'd understand that he did what he had to do to keep her safe from Lilith.

"You realize we need help, don't you, bird?" The bird ruffled its feathers, puffing them up to give the illusion of growth.

"She has our demons. We must get them back," Sariel explained.

Enoch clacked.

"I don't know. Destroy them, use them to ally with Lucifer, or worse, use them to lure The Creator to her. I can't read her, I can't begin to understand her motives or objectives."

No matter what, this meant something awful. Awful for him, for Enoch, for Kenzi. Christ, it was awful for the whole damned world.

More to himself than the bird, Sariel mumbled, "The only creatures ever able to truly hold her were the demons." And that was it. The answer he did not want to admit was staring him in the face.

Enoch tilted its head and looked at its master with one alabaster eye. It snapped its beak together a few times, enough to make its thoughts on the matter clear. What Sariel was considering would affect them both and prolong their time in this strange purgatory.

"We can't do it alone, Enoch. Look at all the souls she has already taken right from under our noses. And now, our demons as well. She is bringing about Armageddon, don't you see. She is taking revenge on every man who hurt her or disgraced her. She wants to destroy The Creator and me as well."

Enoch flew into the air, circling the bed.

"I underestimated her. She is so much stronger than The Creator intended. Perhaps the identity of demoness that mortal mythology has applied to her gives her even greater power. Worse, she has other *women* helping her. If Kenzi sides with her, the Apocalypse will come."

Enoch cooed a throaty but sympathetic noise.

"If she brings about a war, our time on Earth will be infinite. The Creator will realize we failed Him—we deceived Him, and we disobeyed Him more than once. If she somehow wins that war—our end will be infinite. You know what I must do, Enoch. Please understand."

Enoch's flight was becoming more erratic. With each pass, it swept closer to the bed, once swiping Sariel's arm with the tips of its feathers. Sariel closed his eyes tight against his constant companion's frustration. Of course, he didn't want to play games or make deals with the likes of Lucifer and his demons. But if it meant saving Kenzi, then he had to. He'd messed up once and let the woman he loved be abused for his own selfish needs. He couldn't stand by and see it happen again. Maybe Kenzi would never be with him in any other way but he had to do something.

"I'll be careful, Enoch. I've lived among the mortals long enough to know how to bluff." He patted the bird's head reassuringly.

Without opening his eyes, he called out to the prince of demons. "Lucifer, I bid you come to me."

The sounds of Enoch's wings beating the air stopped. Scuttling life outside the room silenced. There was nothing. He opened his eyes to darkness. He was nowhere and everywhere. And then there was light. Lucifer, sparkling and warm, his golden wings beautiful in their elegance but useless all the same, hung heavy behind him. In his true form, his beauty was unsurpassed by any living being or deity Sariel had ever beheld.

"My friend," he said in a resonant mellifluous voice. "You've reconsidered my offer."

"I have."

"And shall I accompany you to Sheol or will you be delivering the *goods* to me?"

"How many would you need to do the job?"

"All of them, of course." Lucifer smiled warmly but the heat never reached his eyes.

"Impossible. That is not even negotiable," Sariel said. It wouldn't have been even if he still had possession of all of them. The problem really came down to not knowing how many he had available to offer.

The light around Lucifer pulsed like a solar flare.

"You've always been a fool, Sariel. You had so much potential and look what you've done with it. You're nothing more than a janitor. You have no idea what you're up against. This is not the broken, young creature with which you once toyed. Her capabilities have grown with her rage."

"If I released them all to you, my time here will be infinite. I'm not that foolish." Sariel tried to maintain his cool, even demeanor.

Lucifer's beautiful face distorted and twisted into hatred personified. Black eyes of obsidian glared at him above the flared nose and spittle-covered teeth gnashing inside a mouth much too large for the skull it resided in.

"That bitch destroyed two of my highest-ranking demons. Two of the deadly seven you had yet to capture. Do you hear me, fool? Your pain will be infinite. You've been cast out as I have. There is no return. You will never capture them all because a woman—a piddly little cunt—has defeated you. You are Death and death is infinite." His voice roared and snarled. His wrath flared around him in flames that charred his body.

"No. That cannot be true. It's impossible. Demons had her once, she couldn't overpower them." It couldn't be. She could not have destroyed a demon. It was impossible. The Creator told him this. They could not be destroyed, only captured.

Lucifer's light seeped through the crevices of roasted flesh, flowing out like lava, rebuilding him back into the beautiful angel he was.

"The apocalypse is upon us, Sariel. I need them all," he said. His voice had returned to its mellifluous tone and his eyes sparkled a brilliant cerulean.

Was he playing a game too? Surely, he was. If The Creator couldn't destroy them, surely Lilith could not. No, Lucifer was simply trying to get his way as he always did.

"I'm sure we can come to some sort of compromise, Lucifer. Perhaps a deal involving your own fate."

"It is not my eternity I am concerned for," the angel said, but he leaned in. He was interested.

"There are other things we could bargain. Souls, mortal lives, whatever you ask. And I will release a reasonable amount of your legion, but I cannot let them all go."

The light grew brighter as Lucifer neared. Every step became blinding until there was no darkness. In its place was light so white and pure it was as if Sariel had gone snow blind. He felt the bird ruffle its feathers and resettle itself on his shoulder. Enoch, too was uncomfortable in this white out.

When their eyes grew accustomed to the brightness—or perhaps Lucifer had turned down his glory—they were back in Gloria's ICU room facing each other with the bed in between.

"So, you refuse my offer?" Sariel asked afraid to hear the answer.

Lucifer was wearing hospital scrubs with a stethoscope around his neck.

"I want your promise that during this rebellion, I can have access to any mortal I want—body and/or soul."

He walked around the bed to stand on the same side as Sariel, trailing his fingers along the silver handrails.

"And I want you and your bird at my disposal. If I need deaths, I will call for them just as your Creator does. But until this little hen party is over, you work only for me. Is that acceptable?"

Enoch squawked again. Sariel patted him quiet.

"You seem hellbent on ensuring my eternal punishment. I will do what I can for you, but I am bound to do The Creator's bidding."

Lucifer laughed. "Are you now, Sariel? Funny, I think Kenzi might disagree; I know Lilith would. I have no doubt you are capable of free will. And you know, I could ask for Kenzi, but I wouldn't. She is a special girl, I'll give you that. If we work together, you may still have a chance at her."

Sariel thought hard about it. Did he have the upper hand in this deal? Had he won the bluff? He pounded on the railing. Damn it. It was not his job to have to consider possibilities. To make complicated decisions. To strategize. Life and Death were just that, not some complicated chess game. For a while, a mortal stands on the white square and then he steps onto the black one. The end.

"Aaaarrrrggghhh," he screamed through clenched teeth.

"Is that a yes?" Lucifer, the perfectly coifed doctor, grinned.

"Yes, yes. But I choose the demons to release and I will deliver them to you. You are forbidden to enter Sheol."

"Of course, of course. Completely reasonable."

Enoch, who had taken flight at the anguished cry of its master began its own frenzied calling. The bird was right to be suspicious. It was uncharacteristic for Lucifer to compromise.

"Enoch, enough! It is what we must do." *We'll just have to be ever vigilant.*

The bird's high-pitched squall pierced his eardrums. Sariel watched in disappointment and frustration as the bird crashed through the window and out into the mortal world.

"Enoch!"

"What was that?" a voice from out in the hall called.

"I need an army of at least three hundred delivered to me by midnight tomorrow. Time is short." Lucifer laughed, "Well, not for you of course." He disappeared into the corridor and headed toward the Neonatal ICU.

Sariel's scream of fury echoed in the death-filled room, but no one heard it.

Chapter 49: Book of Kenzi 13

The apartment was silent when they returned. Kenzi knew exactly who the pregnant woman was, but the other one was a mystery. She said nothing when he told her the woman had mentioned her name, only raised her eyebrows. No more talking, it was time to figure this out.

"I need to check on the girl and the pregnant woman," Henry said. He wasn't going to push her for answers. So, for that, she'd give him some information.

"That pregnant woman isn't here. She's back there, wreaking havoc at the hospital or somewhere else by now."

Henry stopped in the doorway. He turned to Kenzi, looking her up and down.

"If I'm going to be involved in all this, I need you to tell me what's happening."

He flipped the light on. Kenzi was right, Lilith was gone. Daisy, the wounded girl, was breathing but unconscious on the bed. Kenzi stood on the threshold, her eyes wide and unfocused. She couldn't seem to get away from all the madness that Sariel had brought into her life. Now, it was spreading to Henry—the only true friend she had left in the world.

Henry swung his backpack onto the bed.

"Can you help?" he asked. Kenzi nodded. "Go wash your hands," he said, unloading supplies.

She did as she was told. The bathroom was directly across the hall from the bedroom. She was in just as much shock as Daisy, but at least she had all her blood still intact. She didn't want to help the girl, she wanted to get the hell out of there. But she didn't want to go alone. She'd be lying to herself if she said she hadn't imagined a life with Henry somewhere far from here. The doctor's wife. Maybe she could go back to school for nursing or something.

When she returned, Henry had all sorts of medical paraphernalia laid out beside the girl on the bed and straightened out a wire coat hanger. A dry cleaner's tag was thrown haphazardly on the floor and a bright white coat was draped over the post at the foot of the bed.

"Here." He tossed a pair of blue gloves to her. "Put these on."

She did.

"I have to wash my hands too. Meanwhile use these prep pads to wipe her arm clean all around where they draw blood. You know what I mean?"

"Yes."

Kenzi picked up the pale girl's arm. It was like holding a dead fish, damp and cold. She watched the chest for signs of life and only after she could perceive a rise and fall did she tear open the alcohol pads piled on the bed beside her.

Henry returned and busied himself by constructing a make-shift IV pole out of the ruined hanger. Kenzi watched him put the tubing together and hang the bag attached to it. He sat beside his patient on the bed, cradling her arm in his lap like a child.

Heat creeped through Kenzi's pelvis as Henry slipped the IV cannula easily into the girl's vein and the fluid poured into her. She held the flashlight and her breath when he probed the stomach wound in his carefully placed surgeon's gloves. She watched in awe as his fingers gently assessed the damage done. She was a total freak for getting aroused watching him work like that. She knew it, but it couldn't be helped, her body had a mind of its own.

"You have good hands, have you ever considered a career in medicine?"

She blushed as if he'd been aware of her feelings this entire time and was trying to change the subject.

"Um, no, not me," she laughed.

"I'm serious. You should think about it. The fact that you don't shy away from all this blood and guts is a good sign."

"Well, I've lived a life full of it, so…" She pulled the sleeve of her hoodie up and showed her scars.

He stared at them and then into her eyes before looking back down at his work.

"I cannot imagine the things you've been through. I hope you'll share more with me when you are ready," he said, blotting at the fresh blood he'd created by trimming away the ragged tissue that was once Daisy's labia.

He looked up at her again. "And I hope you'll clue me in to what is going on here, because I want to help you, but my head is spinning. I'm so confused."

She let the sleeve fall back down and nodded.

"I'll tell you everything I know but let's get this finished and then you take a nap, you look about to fall over." His blood-shot, shadowed eyes blinked in agreement.

He did what he could on what was left of his patient's skin and then covered the mess with a thick gauzy pad. The gloves came off and he rubbed his eyes, squeezing his nasal bone in an effort to release stress.

"You are right, I am beat. I have to shower and sleep for a bit or I will be of no use to anyone."

"I agree. I'll keep an eye on her. I think she's gonna be OK because of you." Kenzi smiled at him.

"Thank you, I will, uh, be back out in a few."

"Take your time, I got this."

He grabbed some clothes from his closet and headed across the hall. Kenzi watched him go. She was falling for him and it was so damn confusing. For the first time ever, she'd met a good guy, an honest to goodness nice guy with a future. And she had no future to offer him back. Plus, she'd already brought all this to his door. He didn't need a girl like her in his life, that was for sure.

She listened to the water running and imagined it cascading down his body. She wondered what it looked like, his body. The woman on the bed stirred. Kenzi pulled the covers up around her and realized that Henry would have nowhere to sleep. There was a quilt, homemade by the looks of it, folded at the foot of the bed. She carried it out to the couch and made up a bed just as she'd done a thousand times before when her mom had a "bad day" and was too unsteady to make it to the bedroom.

She pushed the thought of her mom away. She was dead and Gloria—well, she was only still alive by the grace of Death himself. And right now, she had to come up with a plan. But what the hell could she do? She supposed she could try to find her dad. Maybe partner up with him, get away and see the country.

The sound of the shower stopped and five minutes later, Henry came out in gym shorts and a tee shirt. She saw the look of realization fall on his face.

"I know it's not your bed, but I made up a spot on the couch for you. You need to rest."

"Oh, my goodness, thank you. That was so sweet. Do you, uh, need anything?"

"Actually, Daisy seems to be doing OK right now. If you don't mind, I could use a shower and maybe I could borrow a shirt?"

"Oh sure. Make yourself at home." He started to get up and she shooed him back down.

"I will, I'm pretty good at taking care of myself." She winked at him and headed into the bedroom.

After her shower, she went to work raking her fingers through her unruly hair. There was no way his basic comb was ever going to tame the thick mass of tangles. She peeked into the bedroom. Their patient was sleeping soundly. The bag of fluid hanging from the awkwardly bent metal attached to the room's light fixture was still half full. She was good.

Kenzi tiptoed out into the living room intending to curl up on the overstuffed chair but froze when she saw the quilt spread out on the floor. Two throw pillows lay on one end and another blanket she hadn't seen before covered Henry who was propped up on an elbow on the far side of the makeshift bed.

"I can't sleep and leave you with nothing. We both need rest. I will behave, I promise." He patted the space beside him and she got down next to him, snuggling into the covers. "I really could not have done all that in there without you, you know," he said and hesitantly reached out to rub her arm, the scars of which were exposed.

She had no idea how to respond so she just smiled and touched his arm as well.

"I have a confession to make," he said quietly as if it took all his might just to push the words out. "I've had a crush on you for a long time. I used to volunteer to work shifts in the ER hoping you would come in with your mum."

Before she could respond, he leaned in and kissed her. Just a closed mouth almost child-like kiss that surprised her nonetheless. The shock unleashed a flood of emotions and before she could stop herself, she'd pulled him closer and opened her mouth.

They made love, he for the first time ever and she for the first time with feeling, on the floor of his apartment, while in the bedroom one of the three whores chosen to bring about the apocalypse recovered.

Chapter 50: Book of Kenzi 14

Henry's alarm went off way too soon and they both groaned in protest. He turned it off and pulled Kenzi close.

"Will you stay here while I'm at work today?" he asked, nuzzling his face into her hair.

"I've got nowhere else to go," she said and then quickly added, "and honestly, I don't want to go anywhere else."

"Good. I'd like you to stay for as long as you can." He kissed the top of her head and got up.

She rolled over to watch him tiptoe into the bedroom to check on Daisy and grab his work clothes. She smiled and snuggled into the blankets. It felt like a dream, a dream within the nightmare that had become her life.

"I've left you a note on the table with my cell and pager numbers in case you need anything or if Daisy has any issues," he said once dressed.

"Got it, but don't worry. I won't bother you. I'm pretty good at taking care of myself and I've managed my mom's drug problems, I can manage Daisy." She smiled reassuringly and opened the door for him.

"I feel like I should kiss you goodbye," he said.

"Then you should."

He did.

"Hey, when I get home, I would like to sit down together and talk over dinner—do you like Chinese?—I want to know everything about you Kenzi Brooks and I want, no I need to know, how you got mixed up in all this."

There it was. The nail in the coffin. The fantasy had been great while it lasted but he'd kick her ass to the curb as soon as she mentioned Sariel.

"Henry, I—"

He held his hands up defensively. "I don't care, it changes nothing about how I feel, I just need to know how to help you. I want to keep you safe."

She nodded. She couldn't take a chance of saying anything more for fear the tears would expose her completely. He kissed her once more and was gone. Kenzi turned around and faced the apartment. She let her imagination fill her brain with images of a domestic life shared here with Henry. Whoever could have imagined that Kenzi Brooks would have even the remotest chance of one day being a doctor's wife.

In true Disney princess fashion, she pushed all her recent troubles from her mind. She wasn't Kenzi Brooks—drug dealer, prostitute, hood rat. Today, she was Mrs. Kenzi Patel. The real-life Cinderella.

She pretended it was all true as she folded the blankets they'd slept in and stacked them neatly on the couch. Her eyes caught a stereo on the book shelf against the far wall and decided to play some of Henry's music. Kenzi lived by the philosophy that you could tell more about a person by the music they listened to than a whole night of conversation. Henry was just as mellow as he seemed. Several James Taylor CDs were piled beside the player, and Neil Young's *Everyone Knows This is Nowhere* was currently loaded. She pressed play and swayed to "Cinnamon Girl."

The books on the shelf above the stereo told a lot about the man she had fallen in love with too. *The Beekeeper's Bible, Backyard Beekeeper*, and *The Encyclopedia of Country Living* sat beside tomes like *Harrison's Internal Medicine* and *Schwartz's Principles of Surgery*. She thumbed through *Country Living* and decided that she needed to review England's geography and weather.

A shoebox on an eye level shelf just above the books had *Do not throw away* written in sharpie across the lid. Kenzi contemplated the concept of privacy but like Pandora, she just had to know. Opening the box, she was perplexed and somewhat disappointed to see it filled with pens. Pens in all sorts of styles and colors. On the underside of the lid, written in the same elegant hand read *Works Completed*. She ran her hands through the sea of writing implements and struggled to comprehend what it meant. Picking one up, she tried to match his fancy scrawl on her palm, but the pen left no ink, only a groove in the skin. She shook it and then pulled it apart. Empty. She tried another and another. They were all empty. Then it clicked, and she laughed out-loud. He was saving all the pens he'd used up—likely taking notes during school and at work. It was such a sweet motivational tool. She put the lid on and found she was even more in love with this genuinely good man.

Once the—their—apartment was spotless, and Daisy had been checked on twice, she plopped down into the overstuffed but ugly brown chair and turned on the TV. She laughed again when CNN came on. She and Henry were probably the most different individuals on the face of the earth and yet, the attraction between them was so strong it didn't seem to be important. She decided to watch a little news for once in her life. It was time to act like a grown up, like a woman worthy of having a physician boyfriend.

The sound was low but the images on the screen screamed loud enough to be understood. Breaking News scrolled on a red ticker across the bottom.

Suspected terrorist attack in Washington D.C. leaves thousands dead and injured.

Lincoln Memorial suffers major structural damage to its famous statue.

Riots and looting have resulted in at least five more deaths as police struggle to maintain order.

Multiple bombs blow up in nation's capital during Rally for Life.

On the screen, dark smoke billowed and blocked out many landmarks so that if one hadn't read the headlines or heard the newscasters' words, you'd never know it was D.C. A deep gnawing in Kenzi's gut told her this was related not so much to foreign terrorists but otherworldly ones—the same ones terrorizing her own life. A photo appeared to the right of the female talking head. A digital label told the viewers that he was a senator and was among the missing and presumed dead. She turned up the volume when they cut to interviews of real life people on the scene.

"…I said this is the end. I mean it's like Armageddon."

"It ain't terrorists, it's those damn godless pro-choicers, that's what this is."

"This could be ISIS, could be one of them crazy left wingnuts with their rights for everyone but God-loving Christians."

"Oh, please," Kenzi said. She lifted the remote, about to turn the station when they cut back to the fancy-dressed news people at the desk.

"Many religious groups are claiming it is the end times as violence breaks out in major cities and rural areas across the globe. Coming up next we'll talk to Dr. Michael Stravinsky professor of World Religions at Yale University, who is going to talk to us about signs of the apocalypse."

"Yes, Nicole, apparently, Dr. Stravinsky believes there is a connection with the rash of violence and our next top story: a new deadly plague and the WHO statement. After this short break on CNN Headline News. Stay with us."

"Fuck," Kenzi muttered. She left it on and got up to poke around Henry's fridge for breakfast. She piled eggs and cheese on the counter and poured herself some water from a filtered pitcher. She made every effort to forget about the news as she mixed the omelet in a bowl and pre-heated the pan. She was no chef, but she'd taught herself to whip up all the basics over the years.

The volume of the background television noise increased until she could no longer ignore it. She turned her head and put her hand down on the edge of the hot pan.

"Ow, shit! Daisy, what are you doing out here?" She rushed over to the naked woman standing in the living room pointing the remote at the TV. Blood dripped from the site where the girl had ripped out her IV and rolled down her finger to the volume button. The news was back on. A suited and bow-tied talking head in the corner was waxing on as the network flashed clips from some official statement on a deadly plague.

"I did this," Daisy said in an almost whisper. "I started it. See."

She turned and jutted her pelvis toward Kenzi. Spreading out from the woman's blood-clotted pubic hair, a network of dark purple veins trellised over her skin like a time elapse film of a river forming. What the fuck was that? It had definitely not been there earlier. It was as if Daisy had just made it suddenly appear.

"Are you contagious? How did you get it?" Kenzi asked.

She tried to focus on what was being said on the TV. She heard and processed bits and pieces like *highly contagious* and *possibly the deadliest plague in the history of man*—phrases that made it hard to also hear what the victim of this plague was saying to her as well. But she had to listen. This was bad, very bad.

"I am the alpha, patient zero. I do this in honor of the goddess who saved my life and my soul." Daisy sounded like a robot, monotonous and without feeling.

"Lilith? Lilith saved you and then gave you this plague? Why?"

"I was living a life beneath me, and she chose me. She chose me to be the harbinger of her return. I can't remember everything, but there was a demon and he got inside of me. I think maybe he did this to me," she said and gestured to her damaged vulva. "All I know is she freed me from him and brought me here. I only know that my body serves the goddess now, and I must share this gift with the world." This time she traced the branching lines up to the stab wound in her gut and winced.

"You, um, you should go back to bed, I think." Kenzi took Daisy's arm and walked her without resistance back to the bedroom. "I'll get you some Tylenol and then I'm going to call Henry. He needs to know about all this and you need that IV put back in."

Daisy slipped beneath the blankets as if hypnotized. Kenzi jogged across the hall to the bathroom and scoured the medicine cabinet. No Tylenol but there was some Motrin. She read the instructions and poured two pills and then added another into her palm. If two was good, three had to be better—at least that's what her mom always said.

And look where she ended up, Kenzi reminded herself. There was no cup for water in the bathroom, so she pocketed the pills and headed back to the kitchen. She recognized the president's voice on the news and slowed.

"…we've got information that this was a domestic attack. I think if you remember the violent protestors outside my rallies, you'll know that we have some very, very bad people on the left. I don't have to tell you how many ugly protests, and trust me, they were not the peaceful protests the fake news reports, OK? I've seen the footage, OK? I'm talking some evil, satanic stuff here. Baby killers, child molesters, rapists—that kind of people."

"Sir? Sir, are you blaming pro-choice counter protesters for this attack?"

"I'm saying there are a lot of people—bad, very bad people—being paid—and by the way, a lot of the people on the left are atheists and Satanists, OK? And they pay protestors, violent ones, to show up. And now, this, this is a game changer folks. No more Mr. Nice Guy. We have to face violence head on and we're gonna have to do some pretty drastic measures. And by the way, we're not the only ones taking these extreme measures, OK? Many, many other countries are facing this sort of trouble and they are talking about the same thing. I've been on the phone since this attack with a lot of important and prominent leaders and they tell me they hate to do it but it's time for national registries."

A rapping on the door made her jump and she dropped the glass. It shattered, and water splashed up her leg.

"Goddamn it!"

The rapping started again. Strong and fast with urgency. Whoever it was, they weren't going to take no for an answer. She slalomed through the glass shards and stepped lightly to the door. She put the chain lock on as quietly as she could.

"Mr. President, are you suggesting extreme measures such as things like identifying arm bands or tattoos as in Nazi Germany?"

She opened the door slowly and peeked out the three-inch crack.

Gloria stood outside the door, hospital gown floating out around her in the wind. IV tubing dripped dark, almost black blood on the stoop. Her ashen grey color frightened Kenzi.

"I'm suggesting we do whatever it takes to protect ourselves and our loved ones." The president prattled on.

"Gloria! Are you OK?" Kenzi closed the door and quickly removed the chain.

"But you're suggesting we basically register everyone based on their beliefs or political views. Don't you think this sort of action would cause mass hysteria and paranoia?"

When she opened the door, the massive woman fell into her. "Kenzi. Help me." The words came out in a gaseous puff more than purposeful speech.

"Right now, unfortunately even in our own country, it's got to be every man for himself, so we deserve to know who we're fighting."

Kenzi took on Gloria's weight and backed them both into the apartment.

"That's marshal law. Are you declaring marshal law, Mr. President?"

"Take me somewhere safe." The bloated puffer-fish looking version of her god-mother said.

"I'm saying every man for himself. The end times are coming. Mark my words."

"It's safe here, Glo. I promise."

"Nowhere on earth is safe right now." Her speech was gaining strength. It was almost as if she had to learn to speak again at a most primal level. How to get the air past the vocal cords.

"I don't know…" Kenzi began. But she did know. She knew one place they could go. Sariel had promised her that. And Gloria needed help. He'd put her soul back, but something was off about her. She was like an animated corpse. She even smelled like a corpse. Her eyes had no sheen and her body was cold.

"OK, I know a place we can go." Kenzi held tight to Gloria and closed her eyes. This would be Sariel's chance to make things right. To prove to her she could trust him.

Suddenly, the floor beneath them was gone and they were falling down into the darkness.

Chapter 51: Book of Conquest 7

The paper weighed heavy in his hands. He dragged his feet on the sidewalk postponing his return to the apartment. How could he face Kenzi and admit that he was, indeed, a failure? The day had started with such promise. He finally had a future worth fighting for and for a few hours he believed he could actually succeed in medicine. He wanted, for the first time ever, to be a good doctor.

Did his father know already? He certainly had enough cronies at the hospital and word spread fast when a resident got fired. He supposed he'd be disowned as well as jobless. It was actually quite difficult to be fired as a resident and he could probably fight it. After all he was post-call when the emergency page went out. What if he'd had the beeper turned off? The problem stemmed from that damn ICU nurse who saw him walk out of the call room with a girl and wrote him up. He swore that woman had it in for him. Half of the nursing complaints filed against him were from her. His presence wouldn't have made a difference anyway, since everyone on the floor was dead when they were found, even the nurses and a cleaning lady.

Just like the dream—I'm blamed for all the deaths.

He shook the image of the bloated corpses from his head and tried to find the positive. He really liked Kenzi and she was so easygoing. She didn't come from money, she didn't seem like a gold-digger. He thought she would be happy just to get away from Detroit. They could be happy in the country together on a little farm. Even if his father disapproved and forbade his mother to acknowledge him, he knew his grandfather would always welcome him. Besides, unbeknownst to his father, it was Henry who was set to inherit his grandfather's country estate, not the man's son. Who knew, that little shocker might be grounds for his father to disown him even if he did manage to get out of this failure. Ultimately, what was the point of fighting anything? Either way, he had something to offer Kenzi.

As his mood stabilized, he quickened his pace. The door to his apartment was open just a crack but he distinctly remembered locking it that morning as he always did. He pushed the door further. No Kenzi, but the place had been cleaned up which he assumed she'd done. Certainly, no signs of a struggle.

"Kenzi?" He called out. He tossed his backpack on the chair and frisbeed the letter into the kitchen.

"Henry, thank goodness you're here." The very pregnant woman stood in the doorway to the bedroom. She was huge, so much larger than yesterday. It made him uneasy to have a woman so close to delivery in his apartment.

"Where's Kenzi? What's going on?"

Daisy was sitting up in bed. She looked surprisingly good.

"She was kidnapped. The door just kind of exploded open and I heard her say 'you get out of here' and I hid because I was scared and too weak to fight. I had to call Lilith back to help me. I'm sorry Henry, I'm really sorry." Her voice was strong and steady as well.

Lilith put her hands on his shoulders and looked him in the eyes. Her stomach pushed against his and he fought back waves of revulsion as it undulated with activity.

"Listen to me, Henry," she said soothingly. "This is so much bigger than you know. If we're going to save her, there is much I have to tell you."

"Yes. For goodness' sakes, enough of all this mysterious drama. Someone had better tell me just what the hell is going on around here."

"It's not safe just now." She leaned further into him as if trying to look past his shoulder and out the door. "We have to go somewhere else. I know a place. Do you have a car?"

He nodded.

"Let's go. I'll tell you as much as I can on the way."

It was difficult to focus on the road with Daisy in the backseat. They shouldn't have brought her along. She wasn't stable yet. But then, it was clearly no longer safe at the apartment.

Lilith remained silent until they stopped at the first red light. Young students, backs laden with heavy packs, passed in front of the car.

"When Kenzi was seven, she witnessed her brother's death. They were crossing a road when he was hit and killed instantly. Do you believe in God, Henry?"

"I believe in a higher power, yes, but our gods may not be the same."

"Then you must know that other sub-gods also exist. Some call them angels, or demons, or even ghosts. There is a being who was once an angel but as punishment for insubordination, this angel, Sariel, became what mortals call Death or The Reaper."

"The Reaper is a personification of a natural process…"

"Henry, please, listen to me. If you cannot suspend your disbelief, Kenzi surely has no hope. Death first saw Kenzi when he arrived to collect her brother's soul. He became obsessed with her, perhaps even at that early age, he fell in love with her."

"What? Please stop. Seriously? I'm sorry, this is too much like a fairy tale. It's ridiculous. Surely you don't believe it. The Grim Reaper fell in love with Kenzi when she was seven? Why would you make up a story like that?"

"Why would I, Henry? You have to believe us: Kenzi is in danger."

"You need to listen to her," Daisy said. She was lying in the back seat holding her belly, panting.

"Turn right," Lilith said.

"All right, all right. I'm sorry. But can you just tell me where you think she is or who took her?"

Lilith continued without response. "He began to visit her, pretending to be her friend all the while leading her into trouble and then rescuing her. He got off on being the hero instead of the bad guy. The bottom line here, Henry, is that he is deranged. He has spent some four thousand years at this job and, in Kenzi, he's found an outlet, some excitement. He wants her with him always. Can't you see all this death around her? He's using it as a means to trap her."

"But how do you know all this?"

"Because we have both fallen victim to his morbid affections. I thought, or at least I hoped, that by bringing Daisy to you, Kenzi might see the danger I have been trying to warn her about. I fear he has manipulated her again."

"So, the man who took Kenzi is the same one who did this to Daisy?" he asked.

"He's not a man, I told you. He is Death."

Henry hesitated to ask for any more details. Either these two women were simply insane, or someone had tortured them into believing this insanity. He knew enough psychology to understand that after enough abuse, victims will buy into their abductors' stories and lies.

"Lilith, is it his baby you're carrying?" He had to know.

"Most definitely. This is the seed he planted a long time ago. Pull in here. This yellow house with the police tape."

Goosebumps broke out on his arms and legs. The tape said CRIME SCENE in big black letters against a bright fluorescent background. This felt like a trap all of a sudden. He was not in the least bit worried about a pregnant woman or the injured waif in the back seat, but what if there were others waiting inside? But why? What would they want with him? Ransom?

As if reading his thoughts, Lilith said "This is where Daisy was attacked. He raped her, he stabbed her, and he mutilated her. I got her out before he could kill her but there was enough commotion and blood for the cops to be called and to realize something bad had gone down. That's all. Trust me."

"But you say he is Death. Why would he have to do all those things to kill her? Can't he just touch her or something?" Henry stalled. He didn't want to go in that house. Something was off.

"Death does not take the life. He is a collector of souls. Death, the ending of life, I mean, is a natural thing. He is simply called to collect the soul and accompany it to its afterlife. What he is doing with Kenzi is like a cat and a mouse—playing with her for the sheer thrill of it. He did the same to me, once. Took me to the brink of death. I've seen the scars on Kenzi's body, do you think she is mentally strong enough to survive his games?"

She opened the door and heaved herself out. Daisy managed with minimal assistance and together they stood waiting for Henry. Lilith opened the door and leaned in.

"It's safe. He'd never think to come back here on his own."

"But we need to find him, not hide from him. We need to find Kenzi," Henry could barely bring himself to finish the sentence, "before it's too late."

"Trust me, Henry. We're not hiding, we're preparing. They'll come to us. I have a plan." She smiled.

The house was barren except for the rusty stains splattered throughout the room where Lilith led them. A noose hung from one of the barn wood trusses in the high-arched open ceiling. *The dream. Lilith and a noose. I gotta get out of here.* Hanging everywhere else, from the other beams were hundreds of charms on chains, leather cord and even what appeared to be cat gut. They caught the sun streaming in the windows. Reflections danced throughout the room like fairies.

Henry, transfixed by the strange décor, jumped when a black woman, wearing a bright orange turban on her head like some Caribbean voodoo priestess, stepped out of the double door walk-in closet on the opposite side of the room.

Just beyond her, inside the space she'd come from, candles burned, and a cheap TV stand sat covered in an array of things suggesting some kind of ritual. This was not the haphazard set up of a homeless squatter.

"Ah, Tituba, you've done well," Lilith said.

"What is this?" Henry asked. The black woman with the familiar name stood motionless, staring directly into his eyes. She had a dagger in her right hand and a silver goblet in her left.

"This," Lilith stepped forward, arms outstretched. "is your sacrifice so that Kenzi can be saved."

Henry backed up toward the door. His stomach lurched and twisted as if wringing all the water out of his body and leaving his mouth cotton-dry. Daisy leaned against the wall beside the door. He didn't want to hurt her but if she tried to stop him, he'd do whatever it took to escape this snake pit.

Lilith followed, maintaining the distance between them. "Henry, what have you got to live for? You're a failure and a disgrace to your family. You can't help Kenzi. You know it as well as I do."

Lilith fixed her stare on his eyes. He couldn't look away even as he sensed that she was removing her clothes.

"But we can save her. Her sisters will save her from Death, forever. You want that don't you?"

Daisy closed in on his right and Tituba bordered his left. They were going to kill him, he had no doubt.

"But I saved *her*." He pointed to Daisy. "I helped you."

Lilith reached out to Daisy and pulled her close so that her body was a shield between them. A snake tattoo wrapped itself around her body and from the periphery of Henry's vision, it seemed to be breathing or filling up with air into a three-dimensional creature.

"Oh, no, silly boy. You didn't save her, but you did help me by being so very predictable."

He wanted to run, the space behind him was wide open, but he couldn't. He couldn't tear his eyes away from the naked woman's dark, abyss-filled eyes.

"Please, give me a chance. I want to be with Kenzi." He was begging. It was pathetic, but he couldn't help it.

The voodoo priestess moved closer to him and raised the knife as if in offering. His head remained locked toward Lilith but his eyes broke free to see the means of his imminent death.

"Prove it," Lilith said.

The knife was suddenly in his hand. He glanced down at it and back up to Lilith. Daisy struggled against her. A snake wrapped across the woman's forehead and upper arms. Lilith had a handful of Daisy's blonde hair pulled back so that her throat was offered to Henry.

"Prove that you have what it takes to save Kenzi. Show us that you are man enough to do what must be done."

"What are you talking about? No! No way."

Daisy squirmed but the snake used her movements against her and squeezed tighter. Hoarse whimpers vibrated the exposed flesh.

"Kill her. Slit her throat!" Tituba yelled.

Daisy could no longer move, and it was apparent that she could barely breathe. Her mouth opened and closed like a fish. Lilith caressed her face and kissed her ear.

"Shh," she whispered. "You've done well my darling, and you've suffered so much for me. But now your task is complete, and I have no further use for you."

"Now, do it," she ordered Henry.

He did nothing.

"Do it!" she screamed.

"I can't! I saved her!" he cried.

"Then give me the knife, you coward."

Lilith snatched the knife from his weak grasp and sliced Daisy's throat in one quick motion. Blood arched out, spitting in Henry's face. His knees buckled. He hit the floor in time to feel the thud of Daisy's body as it crumpled. Panicked, he searched for the snake that was no longer holding the dead girl. Lilith wore it once again. It was nothing more than a tattoo decorating a nude body.

"Why? Why are you doing this?"

She smiled. Walking around him, she stopped to wipe the knife off on his back.

"Did you know that thirteen women were hung during the Salem Witch Trials and oh so many thousands more were killed world-wide. And why was that, Henry? Because they were forward thinkers, because they believed they were just as smart as men and had just as much to offer. And who found them guilty, Henry? Who hung them, who pressed them, who raped them and then called them whores?" She faced him again, so close he could hear her jaw muscles tensing as she finished her speech through clenched teeth. "Men. Men who feared anything they did not understand. Men who wanted to believe they were more potent than women and that The Creator had bestowed that right to them."

"I'm so sorry. I'm sorry," he sobbed. "Men died too. Men were accused of witchcraft you know?" It was a stupid thing to say, instigating her like that.

"Yes, but who has history vilified? Who do they still call witches?" Tituba asked.

Lilith put her hand on his head, smoothing his hair. "History, religion, men in charge—don't they always vilify us? We're witches and whores and demonesses sent to corrupt men and take away their power. So, isn't it time we lived up to their expectations of us?"

"But that's not me. Not all men are like that. I would never…" Henry blubbered still sitting in Daisy's blood pool.

"Are you certain, Henry? Are you a good man?" Lilith asked.

"Stand up, Henry," Tituba said. She wrapped her arm around to steady him and helped him to his feet. He wanted to believe they were giving him a second chance.

"Kenzi needs you; I need you to be a good man," Lilith said, caressing his face. She was so close he could smell her breath. It was cool and vegetal like his grandfather's root cellar.

The scent brought him home to the cottage. He let her lead him. He could hear his bees buzzing, he could almost make out words. They were whispering to him, chanting. They told him to obey her. Follow the goddess, do as she says, and then, he could go home.

"Be a good man, Henry," Lilith repeated.

"I want to. For Kenzi."

"Then be a man for her."

The bees chanted. He turned to look for them but there was only the priestess Tituba. She carried the silver cup. It was full of honey or maybe it was blood or something far worse, more foul. Something familiar about this. A sense of déjà vu overcame him. He should know what it was, but he couldn't think anymore. It was time to go home. Home to Kenzi and his bees.

"Be a man, Henry," Lilith said and slipped something over his head.

The priestess with the voice of a hundred bees sang and painted him with the contents of the cup. A star perhaps, on his forehead. She sipped from it and handed it to Lilith who did the same.

"Be a man," they sang in unison.

They were beneath him now. Was he on a hill or were the women sinking back into the earth? Tituba held the cup high above her head and he took it in both hands.

The taste was tart and thick but not unpleasant. It made his head spin. He felt drunk and giddy. Tituba saw his unsteadiness and took the cup from him.

"For Kenzi," they said.

"For Kenzi," he whispered

Lilith kicked the chair from beneath him and he dropped. It's like Alice falling down the rabbit hole, he thought.

Chapter 52: Book of Kenzi 15

Kenzi's arms flailed. Her body reeled, still feeling the fall. Her hand brushed the ceiling. Only it wasn't the apartment. It was cold and gritty, some of it packed under her fingernails. She lost balance and stumbled backward, hitting her head on a cold, musty wall. Pebbles or something dropped from above and landed in her hair and on her shoulders. The debris wriggled and creeped like bugs—or worse—worms. She screamed and smacked at herself blindly, making sickly, inhuman noises as the phobic shivers overwhelmed her.

In the chaos, she hadn't realized that she could see once more, though the light was dim. Gloria stood motionless like an anemic wax version of herself.

"I guess we're here, Glo. This is Sheol. It's safe here. It's also super gross but I don't think anything evil can get in."

Gloria grinned, showing her teeth, many more teeth than Kenzi had ever seen. It was an odd grin but then, she'd begun to think that maybe Gloria had some brain damage. This place would be perfect for her godmother to recuperate but Kenzi would have to help her past the Nods. They'd go to the tree room. It was warm and cozy there.

The path to the cavern felt narrower. Walls seemed to be closing in on her. The arms reaching out were so close, she thought they brushed against her a few times. She picked up her pace. Gloria, somehow, kept up. The woman hadn't said a word since they'd arrived and it worried Kenzi. The falling bits of dirt and the nasty little grubs raining down on them no longer bothered her as much as the swampy smell that emanated from her godmother.

They neared the turn in the path just before it widened into the only welcoming space of Sheol and Gloria's breathing changed. Short, grunting puffs came and went almost like a dog on the scent of a rabbit. Suddenly, the woman shoved Kenzi aside and entered the room filled with roots and branches of the Tree of Knowledge. Without all the metallic charms dangling in the light, the room seemed duller, colder, and unwelcoming. The wall she fell into grabbed at her and she had to pry off the hands of a Nod trying to hitch a ride.

"Hey!" she yelled to Gloria. "What gives?"

"Where are they?" Gloria asked. Her voice low and graveled.

"Sariel and Enoch?" Kenzi asked confused.

Gloria cleared up the confusion easily enough when she started plucking down the few remaining charms hanging about the room. When her arms were filled with close to twenty, she turned back to Kenzi.

"What has he done with them all?" Gloria, arms dripping with gold and silver and nickel chains, pendants tinkling together like coins in a collection box, was even more bloated than she'd been at the apartment.

She looked like a tick about to pop and her eyes were pure black. Nostrils flared. Maybe she was dead after all. She sure wasn't acting, looking, or smelling right. Was she a zombie or something? A zombie that ate shiny metal things instead of brains.

"Glo? Gloria?" Kenzi approached her slowly as she would a strange dog.

"I know you brought Lilith here, did she take them?" Gloria growled. "Give the rest of them to me now, bitch!"

"What the actual fuck? If you aren't dead, I'll kill you myself. Who the fuck do you think you are? I saved your life."

Kenzi's godmother grabbed her by the neck and threw her. She landed with a thud against the far wall, the impact knocking the wind out of her. In those breathless seconds, she wondered if it was possible to break your ass because she wasn't sure she could stand.

The avalanche of death-eaters helped her find air and her strength to move quickly enough. Kenzi balled her fists and held them up to her temples. What the hell was going on here? She roared in frustration and paced in circles.

Her skin itched. How long had it been since she cut? A small voice in her head whispered that she hadn't even needed to at Henry's. But now, she wanted that foot. Everything fucked up in her life—the cutting, the sex, the drug addicted mother, and now Gloria with her crazy brain damage—was all Sariel's fault.

"Get out, you stupid little whore. You've done nothing for me. You're no longer needed nor wanted here." Gloria handed Kenzi a scalpel. "Do us all a favor and cut deeper next time."

Kenzi fought against the softball sized lump in her throat. Part of her wanted to take it and do exactly what Gloria had suggested. Just end it all here and now. There was nothing left for her. She looked at the mother figure she'd grown to cherish more than her own true mother. No, that wasn't her. It was not Gloria.

"If you're looking for the demon charms, they're not here. Lilith took most of them and since she didn't return them to you, I guess you are shit out of luck." She laughed and pointed the scalpel toward whatever it was inside her godmother. "I don't know who or what you are, but you are not Gloria. You're a fucking piece of shit."

The thing which was not Gloria lunged for Kenzi. It grew larger as it neared and then impaled itself on the blade. The knife punctured Gloria's bloated belly and a puff of putrid air popped out like a bellows. Kenzi suppressed a gag. It spoke.

"I am the night. I am the end of life, the omega. I am the one who waits in the darkness, and I will devour you." The voice booming from pink lips that had once kissed her forehead was deep and threatening.

Kenzi was so taken aback by this dichotomy, she could only stare, slack-jawed as Gloria's body broke open with a sulfurous stink and a behemoth stepped out. The creature's horns twisted in a mockery of pain, and dug grooves into the ceiling. When a grub or maggot was dislodged and fell onto the monster, it sizzled and popped as if it were in a burning log. The monster's eyes, or lack thereof, were black holes that seemed to draw in all of the light. Kenzi knew instinctively that if she looked directly into them, she too would be pulled into the abyss never to return. It reached out to her with impossibly long fingers tipped with equally impressive claws.

"No! Lucifer, you have violated our contract," Sariel said.

He stood in the entrance of the cavern with Enoch on his shoulder. The ground shook and the walls began to crumble. Enoch lifted off the ground at the same time, talons outstretched toward Lucifer. Swooping away at the last moment, it grasped many of the chains knocking them off the demon's arm.

"Get her out of here!" Sariel called to Enoch. The cacophony of destruction was deafening as the space began to cave in around them. "I'm going to finish him."

Kenzi had never seen Sariel like this. The Scribble Man, her imaginary friend who drew her pictures and wrote notes in her journals, was furious. He, like Lucifer, grew until he filled the cavern and shook its walls. Kenzi backed up until she reached the wall.

The two titans tore into each other. Teeth gnashing, claws tearing at scarred flesh; at the same time, a pale hand wrapped itself around the neck of the demon.

"I'll destroy you or send you back to Hell for good. You're no different than Lilith," Sariel growled.

His fingers wrapped around the demon's windpipe as if there was no skin there to protect it. Only garbled sounds came from the demon, but it bucked its head about wildly slicing off tree branches and ripping the ceiling apart.

Sheol caved in around them. The Nods, hordes of them, were freed from their dirt prisons and they rushed at Kenzi. She screamed as bodies piled around her, dragging her under the sea of rotted flash. Ancient arms and hands touched her everywhere, grabbing at her flesh, her hair, her clothes.

Enoch, also gigantic, beelined to Kenzi and grasped both her shoulders. It lifted her out of the fray and enveloped her within its giant wings. She was propelled forward and fell to her knees. Sobbing and shaking with fear and grief, she could no longer move.

It was quite suddenly, and in an otherwise silent space, that she could hear Enoch's talons clicking on the faux hardwood floor of Henry's apartment. He laid his beak on her thigh. She rubbed her finger down his head.

"What the hell is happening, E?"

Enoch only chattered her avian language.

"I wish I knew exactly what you were saying, my friend. Get inside your head and see the things you've seen. Then maybe I would understand this better."

She inhaled deeply through her nose and exhaled through her mouth. The exhale was a lot shakier than she would've liked. "I gotta pull myself together. Henry will be home soon, and I'd better check on Daisy."

Enoch, as if in understanding, moved her beak off her leg and backed away. She took to Kenzi's shoulder when she stood and together they went to Daisy.

The bedroom was empty as was the rest of the apartment. Confused, Kenzi remembered the note with Henry's numbers she'd left on the kitchen table. Lying on the table, where the note had been, was a letter with the hospital's header. She picked it up.

Dr. Henry Patel,

We regret to inform you that the unanimous decision of the Internal Medicine Residency Board is to dismiss you from the program. During your two years in this program, you have had multiple disciplinary actions for tardiness and poor academic performance on exams.

Your lack of response to the recent call to all physicians to present for the tragic emergency in Labor and Delivery cannot be overlooked, especially in light of the above named offenses….

Kenzi dropped the letter. Henry had been fired? He must be devastated. So, where was he? She scanned the living room for any notes he may have left her, but the room was spotless except for his backpack thrown haphazardly on the comfy chair. Checking the door, she found the chain still in its locked position but dangling from the wall. He must have had to break the door open or someone did. What if he thought something happened to her and he had taken Daisy out with him to find her. She touched the splintered wood as if trying to have a psychic vision of recent events.

The phone rang, and she jumped. Enoch cawed out in surprise. Kenzi ran to the bedroom where the sound seemed to be coming from. The cordless phone glowed blue on the far side nightstand. She belly-flopped onto the bed and grabbed it.

"Henry?"

"Kenzi?" Lilith said on the other end. "I need you to come quick, something's happened to Daisy and Henry."

Chapter 53: Book of Kenzi 16

Enoch sat on the porch of a modern two-story home wrapped in faded and weather-worn crime scene tape. The sun was at the level of the railing on which it sat so that all she could see was the dark form of a bird surrounded by a golden glow. If this were a movie, it would be the scene where the hero shows up at the last minute to save the day. She smiled. Enoch was the only thing she could trust in this fucked up situation.

She was out of breath from running. She'd found enough money in Henry's backpack to pay for a taxi but was afraid to give the exact address, so she picked a 7-11 near the house and ran the rest of the way.

"Hey, E. Let's go get Henry," she said holding her arm out.

Enoch ignored it and chose the shoulder instead. She let out a low, airy squawk. Kenzi leaned her head to the side in a sort of head-hug and Enoch rubbed its beak up Kenzi's face. Right now, this bird was her hero.

Enoch led her up the stairs, which she took two at a time. At the top, they immediately turned left to enter what certainly looked like a crime scene. Henry's lifeless body hung limp and bloated, a swollen black tongue pushed out of his mouth. He looked like a poisonous mushroom ready to spore. All the talismans Lilith had stolen were hanging around him as if he had now been relegated to their ranks. Kenzi screamed at the same time her knees turned to jelly. She managed to stay upright long enough to grab for him. Catching his legs, she lost her balance so that for a moment, she hung with him. Realizing what she'd done, she let go and fell to the floor into a sticky mass of blood.

Lilith stood naked and morbidly gravid beside a black woman in an orange sarong and turban. Beside the snake tattoo encircling her body, Lilith wore only Kenzi's rabbit's foot around her neck, taunting her.

Kenzi couldn't breathe. The air was gone from the room. It had to be a dream. Henry could not be dead. It made no sense. *Get him down, help him, CPR, maybe it's not too late for CPR. Christ, I don't know how to do fucking CPR. Come on, Ken, you've seen it done a million times, it can't be that hard.* Her strength returned, and she filled her lungs with air.

"Get him down from there!" she screamed.

Lilith remained stoic, life swam within her protruding belly in direct opposition to Henry's body hanging beside her.

"What did you do to him?" Kenzi sobbed.

She brushed past Lilith and climbed up onto the chair behind Henry. She worked frantically at the knot embedded deeply into the swollen flesh at the back of Henry's neck.

Enoch flew up to the post acting as the gallows and pecked at the rope until it thinned, frayed, and snapped, dropping Henry's heavy body to the floor with a thud.

"Oh," Kenzi yelped. She fell to the ground beside him.

"Kenzi, we tried to save him, but Death is far too strong to overcome," the black woman said, putting her hand on Kenzi's shoulder.

"Don't you fucking touch me. Who the hell are you anyway and what the fuck are you doing here?"

"I am Tituba, true witch of Salem, I was called by Lilith for my skills in dark magic to try to bring back your beau."

"His name is Henry," Kenzi corrected. "What happened? Did he do this? Did he kill himself because he got fired?" Her throat spasmed and it hurt to talk past it. She looked around the room for signs that might help her put the pieces together. There was fresh blood on the floor hinting at something recent. Henry was not bleeding though.

"Where's Daisy?" she asked, hand on Henry's chest willing him to breathe again. *Just be OK. Be alive. Come back to me.*

"We don't know," Lilith said. "Of course, I thought perhaps Henry had taken her but then I realized he wouldn't know how to get here. So, either Daisy brought him here or someone else did."

"Where is here?" Kenzi asked.

"This is Daisy's home where she was attacked," Lilith said.

"Who else knows about this house?"

"Only one other. Sariel."

"That makes no sense, why would Sariel bring them here?" Kenzi couldn't slow the Tilt-a-Whirl of thoughts and emotions in her head.

"Because you had plans with Henry, because you fell in love with him and he, with you. Henry was standing in Sariel's way and, in the same way he used you and your godmother, he abused his power for personal gain." Lilith shook her head and squatted down to Kenzi's level. She touched Henry's cold, dead arm.

"But what did he do to Daisy? Why would he bother with her?" Kenzi asked.

All she wanted to do was to fall into Lilith's arms and cry. The things Lilith had done before, the evil deeds, escaped Kenzi's mind. Right now, Lilith represented the mother goddess and Kenzi needed a mother.

"Daisy was in the way, I assume. I don't know where she is. Perhaps she got away, but I fear she's suffered a similar fate."

"But how can you be sure? I mean—" She sniffled, sucking in the tears. "I found a paper saying he'd been fired. I know what that had to do to him. What if Henry did this to himself? And maybe Daisy got scared and ran away."

"Then where is Sariel? Why is he not here to comfort you? Why would he not bring you here to say goodbye before collecting the boy's soul. No, my love, he hides away, leaving you, yet again, confused and hurt. Did he not do this before with Gloria?

He did not come for you or try to find you to say goodbye? It was your bird that thought of you."

It made sense, what Lilith said. Where had he been before he suddenly arrived in Sheol just in the nick of time? Enoch had remained quiet during this interaction as if she too was considering the possibility. The only reaction it had was to squeeze its talons on her shoulders several times. She was glad she'd worn a hoodie or else it would have left deep punctures. As it was, its tense responses had surely broken the skin.

Kenzi's eyes fell on the rabbit's foot resting just above Lilith's ample breasts. She reached for it. She needed it, her security blanket, her method of release.

Lilith stopped her hand by placing her own on top of it.

"Soon, but not yet. It will be yours again but first, we must discuss the future."

"What future?" Kenzi asked and the dam broke, tears flowed, sobs shook her body.

Enoch pushed off her shoulder, landing on the floor near Henry's head. Tituba bent down to Kenzi and collected several tears into a dulled and dented silver wine cup.

"What are you doing?" Kenzi asked looking down to the small puddle in the bottom of the cup.

The woman did not answer. Instead she approached Lilith, removed the rabbit's foot necklace, and walked to the closet on the far side of the room. Upon opening the door, the smell of burning wax candles and beneath that, a thick livery smell permeated the room. A pool of blonde hair shone in the candlelight just before Tituba closed the door.

"What is she doing? I think she has Daisy," Kenzi said.

"No, I'm sorry, love, Daisy is gone and though it pains my heart as well, we must move on." Lilith took Kenzi's hands and pulled her up.

She was so lithe and flexible even at that size. Kenzi had never seen a woman at the end of her pregnancy move so quickly and easily.

"So, what is she doing in there?" Kenzi pointed. Lilith's hands on her face were as cold as Henry's body but Kenzi let them turn her back to Lilith.

"She is spell casting. She will use your tears and my talisman to bring Sariel to us."

"And then what?" Kenzi asked, mesmerized by Lilith's eyes.

She could see the whole world in them. Like those pictures the astronauts took of Earth from the moon. Greens and blues swirled round in her irises and in her pupils, a universe filled with stars and galaxies.

"And then we kill him."

"Kill him? Sariel? You can't kill Death," Kenzi said, looking at Henry.

She wondered what would happen if you could. Would recent deaths be reversed? Enoch was still inspecting Henry's body, tilting its head back and forth as if confused.

"Yes. He can be destroyed if his power is removed or transferred."

"Are you going to transfer his power to you? If you do that can you bring Henry back?"

"I have chosen you, Kenzi Brooks, to take his role. And yes, if it is not too late, we may be able to return Henry's soul. But first we must take it back from Sariel and I can't do that

Kenzi. I can only facilitate the transfer of his power to you. Will you stand beside me? Will you take on the injustice of this god-forsaken world?"

"But, I don't understand," Kenzi said.

"The world as you know it is about to end. Armageddon begins with myself and my three chosen ones. You are the fourth and final creature I shall release onto this earth and you will stand beside me when we have conquered it."

So, Lilith was responsible for all the talk of end times on the news? She and Daisy and this Tituba person?

"No, no, I don't want that, I don't want any of this."

Kenzi only wanted to return to her vigil at Henry's side. She needed to feel the weight of Enoch on her shoulder. She felt weak and incomplete without it.

"Kenzi, your whole life people have hurt you, belittled you, taken away your control. The Creator turned His back on you and left you to the wolves. Sariel chose for you and has since held you back both directly and indirectly. That will not be so in my Kingdom. Never again will you live beneath the thumb of a man made in His image."

Lilith was right, even loving Henry had caused her pain. *Whatever killed Henry is responsible for your pain. Henry didn't hurt you.* She ignored the voice in her head and continued her self-pity. Everyone she'd ever trusted had betrayed her or abandoned her. Even her own God, The Creator of all things, turned his back on her. And it really was Sariel's fault. It all started when he abused his power. He chose to take away her only promised right as a mortal—the right to die and find peace. If she were in his place she would never allow her own feelings to interfere with anyone's right to the death and afterlife destined for them. *Except for Henry. You did beg them to bring him back.* She shook her head, imperceptibly and subconsciously at her own thoughts. *That's different. It isn't his time and we'd just found each other, and I could have loved him.*

But isn't that what Sariel did for you, isn't that what you asked him to do for Gloria? Another part of her brain asked. *Is Gloria dead because of Sariel's actions or because you brought drug dealers into her world? Love doesn't disappear when it makes a mistake. We don't know that Henry didn't do this to himself, and maybe Sariel is out there right now trying to find you. Maybe he got held up by that demon or he is trapped in Sheol. You can't make any decisions when you're this emotional. You should at least hear Sariel's side.*

Did it really matter though? Henry was gone, her mother, brother, and godmother were gone, and the world was ending. No matter how many times it had felt that way in the past, for the first time in her life, she was truly alone. Without further thought, she faced Lilith and nodded with conviction.

"OK, yes. I will stand by you, Lilith. And if we can't bring Henry back, then at least I will be able to carry Henry's soul into the afterlife. He deserves peace."

Lilith smiled.

"When She opened the fourth seal, I heard the voice of the fourth living female saying, 'Come and see.' I looked, and beheld, a pale whore. And the name of her was Death, and

Enoch followed with her. And the power was given to them over a fourth of the earth, to kill with blood-letting, with wanting, with death, and by the beasts of the earth."

While Lilith spoke, Tituba approached them. She carried a dagger in both open palms presenting it to Kenzi who took it hesitantly. Tituba bent in a low bow to Lilith who slipped the rabbit's foot off the witch's neck and put it back on her own.

"Has it begun?" she asked.

"It has, my Goddess," Tituba answered and extended her arm to the window.

Lilith approached it and looked out at whatever was happening outside. Tituba stood, hands clasped in front, waiting for her goddess to give her the next order. Kenzi held the handle of the dagger in her hand where it felt as if it had always been, it had the familiar feel of the foot. She could cut herself with it and it would feel the same. But she had no desire to cut herself anymore, not now that she had made the decision to follow Lilith in her crusade.

"Awck, Awck," Enoch called to her. Oh yes, Enoch. The bird would be Kenzi's now. Her eternal companion. It would never leave its new mistress. The bird hopped about wildly, feathers ruffled and wings flapping.

"Come on, E. I'll take care of you now," she said bending down to offer it her arm.

She couldn't help but look once again at the man who, for such a short time, held promise of something better for her. Henry's face had paled as the effects of gravity pulled his blood away.

"Oh, Henry," her voice creaked. "If I can't bring you back, I promise to see to it that your soul finds eternal peace."

She leaned to kiss him when Enoch pecked hard at Henry's forehead. She pulled back. Enoch pecked at it again and cocked its head, so a single marble-white eye peered directly into Kenzi's colorless one. She reached up and touched her own head and then ran her fingers over the scar of her name on her arm. Once more Enoch poked at Henry. His beak left dimples in the dead flesh but did not break it. She touched the divot, resting her finger in the shallow defect. It did not fall deep inside.

Enoch hopped backwards and flapped its wings silently. It seemed pleased at her discovery. She nodded in understanding.

"Go find him," she whispered.

The bird took off out the door and down the stairs.

"Kenzi, if you have said goodbye to your life as you knew it, come see what my whores have done. See our vengeance on this biased, judgmental world," Lilith said, never turning away from whatever scene played out on the other side of the glass.

The action on the street outside the cozy suburban family home was nothing Kenzi hadn't seen before in Barton-McFarland. Granted, she supposed she'd never seen so much violence all at once but maybe this was a gang fight. If this is what Tituba could do, she was no more powerful than a crack whore who didn't get her five bucks for a blow job.

She jumped when the gunshots began, but again, wasn't shocked. When the first of the victims fell, however, something new and strange occurred. A black lava-like substance rolled out of him and sort of morphed into tentacles that grew impossibly long and thick like Jack's magic beans. They climbed up the house closest to the body. As the number of casualties increased releasing more of the crawling goo, the house began to melt beneath them as if maybe it was releasing some acid onto it. In a matter of minutes, the entire structure was gone, the black vines lost their shape and seeped into the dirt left behind. The image of Daisy's weird disease flashed in her mind. This was the same thing just on a much larger scale.

"There now, see, we are starting over from scratch," Lilith said. "Soon, when we are through here, and Sariel has been destroyed, this house and all the talismans will be swallowed up by my plague. Very good, Tituba, you've done remarkably well. The hysteria is palpable."

Tituba bowed her head in humble acceptance of praise.

"Now kill her, Kenzi," Lilith ordered pointing to the black witch.

"What?" Kenzi asked, shocked. Tituba snapped her head back up, eyes wide. She began to chant beneath her breath. Kenzi couldn't make out any of the words and wasn't even sure they were English.

"She has served her purpose. Kill her. That is your job now, Kenzi. Silence, Tituba! Your spells won't work on me and I have no further use for you. Return to the hell from whence you came."

Tituba's incessant chanting became insects in Kenzi's ears, her head, and vibrated in her jaw bone. She couldn't take much more of it. Like biting on tin foil. She clenched her fists and felt the knife the witch had given her sitting in her hand, waiting to be used.

Kenzi thrust it into the witch's gut and then her chest and once she started, found she could not stop. Tituba crumpled to the floor. Her blood rushed out to kiss her killer's feet. It was suddenly freezing in the room. Kenzi shivered, her teeth clattered together. She opened her hand to drop the knife, but it stuck there, clotted to her palm.

Had she sealed her fate just now? Was she Death? Dead herself? No. No, that is not what was supposed to happen. Death was supposed to come save her or to die by her hand. She could not remember. She closed her eyes and took three deep, cleansing breaths. If eternity felt like this, she'd bury that knife in her own heart.

"Kenzi!" Sariel's voice called.

Opening her eyes, she determined that the voice had not come from inside her head. He was here in this room: The Scribble Man.

Chapter 54: Book of Kenzi 17

Enoch sat on Sariel's shoulder. The bird had done just as Kenzi asked.

"Ah, Sariel. You do know how to make an entrance," Lilith said. "And just in time. Kenzi, I believe, is ready to repay the favor you did for her when she was a child."

"Oh, Kenzi, what have you done?"

"I…" she began but the thing was, she had no idea what she had done or what she was doing. She shook the knife loose from her palm and it skittered across the floor.

"She has pledged herself to me and joins me in my war," Lilith answered for her.

"And how long before your little war catches the attention of the deities? It's been no trouble seducing demons or promising mortals the impossible, but what happens if this goes any further? You must stop, Lilith." He stepped closer to Lilith but turned to face Kenzi. "Forgive me for speaking in your defense, Kenzi." He spun back to his ex-lover. "How can she be sure serving you will not end in the same way as your other—what are you calling them, whores?"

Lilith leaned into him, their silhouettes were that of lovers about to kiss. Kenzi's heart threw itself against her chest trying to escape. There was nothing to do but watch. Now that he stood before her—her childhood friend and sometime hero—she knew she would never kill Sariel. It no longer mattered what he'd done, he'd never meant to hurt her. She also knew that she would never serve Lilith. Perhaps once the woman was an innocent victim of inequality, manipulation, and abuses at the hands of The Creator, men, and demons. She'd let her anger destroy her. She bore as much hate and prejudice as The Creator she wanted to dethrone. At this point, there was nothing else for Kenzi to do but trust in fate and act on intuition—it was how she'd survived her whole life and she excelled at it.

"What have you come here for, Sariel? Have you come back to return this to its rightful owner?" She pulled Kenzi's journal out of Sariel's belt. A scrap of pink paper, singed at the edges, fell to the ground.

"What? What is this?" Kenzi asked, picking it up. She unfolded it and stared. The picture was signed in a child's messy scrawl and showed a stick figure waving in front of a long rectangle with circles for wheels. "I gave this to my dad. A long time ago. How did you get it?"

"Why don't you tell her, Sariel. Tell her how you came upon this picture. Did her father throw it away? Did he burn it? We're dying to know, *Death*." Lilith smiled. Kenzi looked at The Scribble Man with the eyes of her seven-year-old self.

He sighed. "Your father was killed in a car accident. His cab caught fire and I managed to save it for you when I gathered his soul. I was going to tell you, but then Gloria passed, and it was too much for you. Too much all at once."

"Once again, he determines your life, Kenzi. He decides what is best for you, what you can and cannot know. Is this who you would choose to spend eternity with?" Lilith asked.

"I'm sorry, Kenzi. I'm still learning. After four thousand years, I am still trying to understand mortal feelings. Mine are simpler than that. I know that I belong with you and you with me. I know I want to always keep you safe. I will always be your Scribble Man."

"They all talk a good game, don't they, Kenzi. But in the end, they abandon you, they seek to control you. You deserve freedom. You deserve a life that you created. I am the alpha, you, the omega. Together we will recreate this world in our image. You can have that Kenzi."

The book in her hands grew warm. She leafed through it. The Scribble Man glowed on every page it was written. A red, painful glow similar to the scar he bore of her name. Her words had power too. Perhaps she wrote him into this feeling, confused character. This foolish, child-like man. Maybe she controlled him as much as he did her. Was that possible? Were they linked inexplicably the moment they had first made eye contact? Maybe her life did have a purpose, maybe all this was supposed to happen.

"Perhaps it is not Kenzi you came for, but me. Have you come to end me once and for all?" Lilith took the talisman off her neck and held it up to him. "Will I be going back in here or are you over me completely?"

"Lilith, you know this is wrong. I was wrong too—" Sariel began.

"Am I too strong for you?" She sliced her palm open with the rabbit's foot. "Should I play the helpless victim to gain your pity again?" Blood dripped down her wrist and Kenzi felt the familiar itch.

"Please don't Lilith. This isn't worth it, I'm not worth it." Sariel pleaded. He was soft and clueless. Kenzi didn't like it, the way he gave in to Lilith's manipulations. "You know what I came for. This has to end…"

Before he could say more or Kenzi could wrap her brain around her own feelings, Lilith slashed his chest using the whole foot. It left three vertical lines and three horizontal, forming a large letter 'L' on his skin. She put her bloodied palm on top of the cuts.

"Well then you better take all these deaths back," she said.

Sariel's skin began to break and invisible forces began cutting names of all the lives Lilith had taken of her own accord into his flesh. Every exposed inch of him ripped open. Dead tissue hung in strips and pieces. Some fell to the floor where names intersected. Enoch launched off its master's shoulder and hovered above him. Sariel fell into a fetal position as he bore the pain of every life Lilith took before its time.

"Enoch, if you are going to join Kenzi, you must prove your loyalty as well. Remove his talisman."

Enoch hesitated, snapping its beak in protest.

"It's OK, E. Just do it," Kenzi said.

She heard herself give the order but had no idea what she was doing. But it was as if all this was meant to happen this way.

The bird dipped its beak deep into Death, its only companion for the last four thousand years. Out of Sariel's forehead, Enoch returned with a silver coin.

"Give it to your new mistress," Lilith ordered.

Enoch obeyed, dropping the irregularly shaped disc into Kenzi's hand. One side was embossed with a skull and the other, the head of a raven. She turned it around. It was warm. There was an energy within. It hummed in her hand.

"Swallow it," Lilith ordered.

"What?" Kenzi asked.

"Swallow it. By taking his soul into your body, you will gain his abilities, his immortality. Go on," she said.

Kenzi followed orders. It went down easily enough, dissolving as it traveled into her system. Her arm burned like fire. A thousand bees stung her at once, and their stingers were pumping lava instead of poison.

"Oww," she said, turning it to see a red welt raising and then cutting into her flesh, spelling out a single word: Sariel. "Oh no."

"You are Death now, and you must end this poor body's suffering, Kenzi."

"But I already took his soul. That's all that Death does. You said. No murdering."

"*Death's* body does not age, does not die. It can only be ended by Death or The Creator. You are Death now. He is nothing more than an ancient, tired, used-up hull." Lilith touched the angry red script on Kenzi's forearm. "As your Goddess, I have called upon you to end his presence on this earth."

Lilith grinned but there was no joy in her eyes, only rage. She found her pleasure in pain.

Don't ever let me become that kind of person. There was no peace in a life like that. *Not much peace in the life of The Reaper either and that's who you are now.*

"No, it's not," she whispered

Kenzi stared at Sariel's filleted body curled up on the floor only five feet from the dead body of Lilith's third "whore." Kenzi knew now without question that if she opened the doors to the closet, she'd find the second whore's body. Death was a lonely state, for both dying mortals and the shrouded escort they feared. No wonder he'd sought out a vivacious child full of life and too young to have learned to be afraid of Death.

"Here you go, my love. We don't need your gifts or The Creator's blessing," Lilith said.

She tossed the rabbit's foot onto his chest. It rolled over twice before wedging itself into a bone-deep crevice where a nipple once sat. Kenzi bent down and put her palm on top of it. His weak respirations were barely palpable. This man, The Scribble Man, once a giant porcelain-skinned god to the child he had saved, now lay broken and feeble at the feet of the women he'd loved.

It was Kenzi's turn to save him from himself.

"End him, Kenzi. End his suffering if nothing else. We have a world to conquer." Lilith's voice was high with an almost sexual excitement.

She picked up the bloodied knife used to kill Tituba and handed it to Kenzi..

She's no different than my mom—always the victim. A crack whore who uses her body to get what she wants, and then cries about how her body was used and abused. And, to get revenge, she stoops lower than the ones she accused. She'll use and discard anyone. I'm done. I'd rather stand with idiots like Henry and Sariel and die for something than to live life on a hamster wheel of hypocrisy.

"Of course." She bent her head over his ruined body concentrating, listening, laying out the position of everything and everyone in the room. Tucking the bloodied foot in her right palm, she raised both arms up over her head as if planning to plunge the knife into Sariel.

Instead, she leaped. Dropping the knife, she slashed out with the foot and cut deep into Lilith's pregnant belly. With her free hand, she punched through the skin and underlying tissues. The smell of rotted, necrotic flesh coupled with the rice-pudding-like consistency of an infected womb brought an olfactory memory to the surface. A dead thing in the sewer grate beneath a car where she once had hidden from men trying to kill her. The memory was filled with fear yet all she felt was anger.

"I think these souls belong to me now," she said ripping out a fistful of wriggling, silky filaments. The rest oozed out onto the floor in an iridescent puddle. Devoid of souls, Lilith's empty body fell beside them. Kenzi bent over her. "And don't worry, I'll be sure to see that your soul is ended and not trapped in a little girl's plaything ever again. Even you deserve your peace."

Once she and Enoch gathered all the souls and collected them in the hour glass, Kenzi dragged Daisy's body out of the closet. She laid the three women together and put Henry's body beneath the window far removed from his murderers. The candles were still burning in the closet and she put them beside Henry.

"I'll see you soon, babe."

She pulled the foot out of her pocket.

Just like old times. She smiled.

"Hey, E," she said cutting her name into her flesh over the scar she'd made so many years ago. The bird waddled over hesitantly, never taking its eyes off her. "I'm not gonna hurt you, I need you to help me."

Her arm was numb at this point, the sting of Sariel's name had overwhelmed her mortal pain sensors. Numbness was good though. She hoped the anesthesia extended elsewhere on her body as well. The blade she'd used to end Tituba was lying on the floor. She put the foot away and picked up the knife. Enoch hopped backwards and clacked.

"I told you, I would never hurt you," she said and plunged the dagger into her stomach.

The pain was deep and nauseating like a cold ache rather than the searing sting of cutting skin. Before she lost her nerve, she yanked it to the side cutting a wide gap into herself. Heaving, she let her knees give and slowly went down on them.

"Get the coin," she coughed the words out of a mouth that only wanted to vomit.

Enoch wasted no time, flying straight at her, it grabbed her pants with its feet and held onto them. Plunging its head into the gash with wet, sucking sounds, the bird pushed deeper into Kenzi's body.

"Ugh," she heaved again.

The pressure was intense. She needed to stay conscious only a little longer. Every little movement of the bird was magnified by her body. She gulped for air and let the excess saliva fall out her mouth rather than swallow it which might make Enoch's search even more difficult.

Stay awake, stay awake, just a little longer. She repeated the mantra in her head concentrating on it instead of the pain.

Kenzi couldn't imagine anything worse than what she was currently experiencing but then the bird reversed and pulled itself out. Feathers protested being rubbed in the wrong direction and popped up catching the edges of her wound. Screaming hurt worse than the heaving so she whimpered instead. The cold she'd gotten used to dropped at least twenty degrees and she began shivering again.

"T-t-take it over t-t-to Lil-lith's-s-s b-blood," she instructed. She didn't even have the strength to pull her hoodie around her. The bird, as if trained to do all these death tricks did so. It looked like a sick parody of a fantasy tea party. An animal dipping its cracker into tea. It turned back to Kenzi for the next step. There was no way she could muster up the energy to speak again plus she was so cold she could barely move.

She had to, though, all this could not be for nothing. With the last of her reserves, she mimed putting it into her mouth and then pointed to Sariel. The last thing she saw as she closed her eyes on this life, was Enoch pushing its beak into its master's mouth in a life-giving kiss.

Chapter 55: Book of Genesis 2

Warmth rolled over Sariel like waves lapping at his wounds. As each one crashed upon him, his skin healed, scarred, and numbed. He was conscious again but kept his eyes closed. Letting whatever spell was upon him work its magic. He listened. Silence. Clicking of talons on hardwood, clacking of a big black beak, but no breathing of mortal bodies. When most of the pain had subsided and the tide returned to the sea, he opened his eyes and sat up.

Bodies lay neatly arranged on the blood covered floor. Enoch stood an arm's length away from him. The bird's feathers were awry, sticking out in all directions and clumped together in clotted blood. He had only a short time to ponder his familiar's current condition before seeing the body lying behind him. Kenzi.

"Enoch," he said, his voice was strained, his mouth felt dry and ancient. "Did Lilith—" he began and then saw her body with its tell-tale snake tattoo.

A bloody gash tore through the snake just below her belly button. The center of the cut looked as if she'd taken a shotgun blast. The only one who could have done it was also dead.

"She sacrificed herself, didn't she?"

Enoch clacked its beak and cawed softly.

"For me." It was not a question. "Oh, Kenzi. All I can offer you now is peace. Come Enoch, we have a job to finish."

He lifted her body, still warm, blood slowed but seeping, onto his lap. He caressed her hair, tucking it behind her ears. Her eyes were closed but, in his mind, he saw the deep blue one and the white one that matched his bird's. She was ethereal, and his heart ached. He'd never mourned a death before, but it would be hard to let her go. There was something clutched in her right hand. He fished it out. The foot dangled from a leather thong. Even blood-stained and hairless, there was no doubt that it was the one that had started this whole mess. For a moment he considered it, watching it swing to-and-fro in his hand.

Enoch hopped onto his arm, making him drop the foot. The bird gave him no time to make another fatal mistake. It dipped its beak deep into Kenzi's forehead and pulled out an iridescent opal colored ribbon. Rainbows glittered in the flickering lights of the hanging talisman, but the soul seemed to give off its own glow. He held his hand out beneath Enoch's beak. He wanted to hold it, to feel its weight in his palm. Perhaps he would hold onto it the entire way to her afterlife.

Instead the raven tilted its head back and snapped its jaws, swallowing the soul in two quick gulps.

"Enoch NO!" Sariel shouted but it was too late, she was gone. "Why, you stupid bird? Why would you do that to her?"

His familiar used its wings to make the long jump from Sariel's arm to Kenzi's shoulder. The bird nuzzled its face into hers. Clacking its beak quietly against her ear as if whispering its own goodbye.

Enoch pushed Kenzi's head gently with its beak. Her lips parted as her head turned away. The bird, ever ready, dipped its beak into her mouth. Sariel let go of her in surprise as Enoch's belly and throat bulged, regurgitating life back into her. Just like a mother bird. She gasped, sat up, coughed, and retched. The bird steadied itself on her shoulder, talons digging into her flesh. She didn't seem to notice. She stood slowly on wobbly legs like a toddler just learning to walk. Sariel waited quietly for her to get her bearings.

When Kenzi faced him, he jumped back. Her eyes were both colorless white orbs. Gone was the heterochromia, the single white eye, and the beautiful blue one. Stunned and unsure of what had happened he looked up to Enoch for answers. Enoch cawed and clacked as if in explanation that she—*the damn thing had been a female after all*—had given the girl life. They belonged together as a pair now. The bird nuzzled down onto the shoulder of her immortal child.

Epilogue: Genesis 3

Sariel smiled. He reached into his belt and retrieved her journal. Handing it to his newest companion, he whispered. "I think you have some stories to tell."

About the Author

EV Knight is an American author of horror and dark fantasy stories filled with bad-ass females. She has just released her first novel, *The Fourth Whore,* the story of a young woman's fight to find the truth in time to save her world after she accidentally releases an ancient demoness who has a vendetta against God Himself. EV is currently working on her second novel which takes place in her beloved home in Michigan's Upper Peninsula.

Raised on Grimm's Fairy Tales in a country home near the woods, EV inevitably developed a whimsical imagination and lifelong interest in the macabre.

These days, when not writing something spooky, EV spends her time taking long walks through graveyards and visiting haunted houses. She collects skull art and death-related oddities. When she is feeling adventurous, she enjoys road trips to unusual roadside attractions. Yes, she has, in fact, been to see the biggest ball of twine in Minnesota.

EV is inspired by mythology, fairy tales, and history such that there are often kernels of truth in her fiction. No scary thing is off limits. And she doesn't shy away from gore. Like Frankenstein, she likes to experiment and piece things together until her creation breathes on its own. EV hopes you'll love her monsters as much as she loves making them.

CPSIA information can be obtained
at www.ICGtesting.com
Printed in the USA
BVHW081736160821
614506BV00007B/227